SILENT MERMAID: A RETELLING OF THE LITTLE MERMAID

THE CLASSICAL KINGDOMS COLLECTION, BOOK #5

BRITTANY FICHTER

WANT MORE FROM YOUR FAIRY TALES?

Sign up for a free no-spam newsletter and free short stories, exclusive secret chapters, and sneak peeks at books before they're published.

Details at the end of this book.

SILENT MERMAID: A RETELLING OF THE LITTLE MERMAID

Cover Art and Design by Armin Numanovic
Edited by Meredith Tennant

To my grandparents, who fell in love even though you were from different continents and spoke different languages. Your hard work and life of love is the stuff of stories. And Appa? We love and miss you so much. You left behind a legacy of courage, honor, and love.

BORN OF SUN

"*B*ut how did they get all the way to the mansion courtyard?" Giana gripped her husband's arm more tightly with her right hand as she held her protruding belly with her left.

"Last night's storm swell must have pushed them in!" Amadeo said over the Protectors' songs. "The guards say more than usual escaped from the Deeps. It's a wonder these two didn't cause any harm before we found them!"

As the Protectors continued to wrestle the sharks back out of the city with their songs, Giana wondered at the fact that her husband wasn't more disconcerted by the whole ordeal. The storm itself had been especially violent. Even from the seafloor Giana had been able to feel its tenacity while it raged above the water's surface all through the night before. But then, Amadeo had always been particularly fascinated by the creatures that lurked in the Deeps. Giana wondered if all Protectors were so obsessed with danger. Healers surely didn't harbor such feelings.

The closest guard had been successfully luring the smaller of the frill sharks away from the royal mansion when a distant Grower's song floated in on a current. The creature jerked its head toward the sound, and in doing so, made eye contact with Giana. In the split second they held one another's gaze, she saw all of the contempt and darkness of the Deeps in those serpentine eyes. Its red-gray gills flared out, and its long body stiffened.

Giana was off as fast as her fins could push her. Through the courtyard's open roof she fled before continuing to lead the creature above the city. Pink, red, orange, gray, and white coral rooftops sped beneath her as she swam with all her might. It would do no good to try to escape the creature through the city. She would be hindered there by the people and buildings. So up she climbed. She could hear the Protectors' songs behind her, including her husband's, but the creature's pursuit continued.

Every time she glanced behind her, she could see the creature's long, thick body ripple as it gained on her. Giana tried pushing out her own song as she pressed on. Not the Healer song that came so easily to her, but the simple Protector song she'd been taught as a child. Still the creature continued as though she hadn't even made a sound. She could feel the disturbance of the water as it began to snap at her fins with the hundreds of teeth that edged its long jaws.

Help! Giana cried out to the Maker as she struggled to keep up her pace. Her swollen belly slowed her down, and she could feel her muscles straining dangerously as the child within her began to move. *Not now!* she pleaded as her body begin to contract. *The baby has still another month!*

She could hear the shark's jaws snap over and over again as they came closer and closer, but Giana was still tempted to slow. They were too high, too close to the surface, and the sun would be rising any moment. She risked another glance behind her. Where were the guards? Just feet from the surface, however, there were no guards close enough, and a glancing touch of the shark's teeth to her left fin made Giana's mind up for her. Launching herself out of the water, she landed on a sandbar.

Let them come! she begged the Maker. *For my baby's sake, let them come!* Her body was wracked with pain as the contractions began to come faster and closer together, and her head felt fuzzy as she tried to breathe in the air that was far too light, too different from the comfortable, heavy pressure of the seafloor. Rolling over, Giana gasped, trying to see whether or not the beast had been captured. Through the rippling water, she could see that the guards had finally arrived, at least a dozen, and their Protector songs began to rise as they coaxed the creature down.

But their work wasn't swift enough.

The child was born there on the sandbar, coming much faster than either of Giana's other children had come. Giana hugged the little girl close and tried in vain to brush off the sand that stuck to her tiny arms, back, and tail. As the light around them moved from gray to pink to gold, Giana's back began to burn with each new touch of the sun. The tears that couldn't be felt below the surface stung her eyes as she used her body as a shield over the baby, who gasped and choked on the strange air but couldn't seem to gain enough breath to cry.

How long they lay like that, Giana couldn't tell. All she knew was that as the sun's rays began to grow in strength, her own strength slipped away. The world around her faded in and out. Soon she was unable to even hold herself on her side, and to her horror, before the world went completely black, she rolled on her back just in time to see the child engulfed by the sun.

$$\sim$$

Giana wanted to shriek. Jarred from the nightmarish haze by the searing pain on her back, however, she knew better than to interrupt her Healers' songs. That would only make the pain worse. And yet, as she held herself still, she knew she was forgetting something.

The storm.

The shark.

The sun.

The baby.

"Amadeo!" Healers' songs or not, Giana bolted upright from the sponge bed they'd laid her on. "Amadeo! The baby!"

He was there in an instant, but that didn't stop Giana's weeping.

"The sun touched her! It touched her, and I didn't stop it!" Giana was gripped by self-loathing as she clung to her husband. If her child was dead, it was because she hadn't been strong enough. Her daughter's blood was on her head. Giana imagined all the horrible ways her child had suffered. And all of it without her.

"Giana, listen to me!" Her husband grasped her firmly about the arms and pushed her back to look into her eyes. "You're not listening. She's alive! The baby survived!"

Giana stopped writhing and stared at her husband. Still, her daughter's survival only brought on more dread. "The sun . . . did it—"

"Come see for yourself."

Gently, Amadeo lifted his wife and, holding her, swam to the other side of the mansion to the nursery. Or rather, they started in the direction of the nursery. Instead of taking her to the east wing of the mansion, Amadeo took her to the highest tower of the entire structure. To Giana's surprise, he took her to their chamber.

The Nurturers parted at their arrival, leaving an open path to the gemstone-edged infant bed. Giana felt the pain of her burns with every flick of her husband's fins, but she couldn't have cared less. Only when she was gazing into the clear blue eyes of her daughter was she able once more to breathe freely. No burns were visible on the baby's skin. In fact, there was no sign of any deficit other than her unusually small size, which Giana blamed on her early arrival.

"It was a miracle, Lady Giana." One of the Nurturers swam forward and gave her a tentative smile. "She suffered no burns from the sun even though she was directly in it. She wasn't even scratched by the rocks or shells in the sand!"

"She's perfect," Giana breathed, no longer able to resist stroking her baby girl's soft pink cheek.

"There is . . . something . . . that sets her apart," Amadeo said from behind her.

"I'll say." Giana laughed, nearly giddy with relief. "I don't recall the last time a mermaid had blue eyes or," she ran her hand over the child's head, "such pale hair. It's almost white!"

"That's not it," Amadeo said.

As if ordered, the Nurturers began to clear the room, and though she was absorbed with her child Giana didn't miss their exchanged glances. She turned to her husband. "What is it?"

"She's three days old now, so we have had ample time to watch her," Amadeo said slowly, holding his hands out in front of him.

"And?"

"It seems . . ." He took another breath, then frowned. "She has no voice."

CHILD'S PLAY

*A*rianna had nearly given up hope and returned to the water by the time they ventured out. When she heard the little girls' shrieks, however, she stopped fiddling with her necklace and pulled herself back up on the rock. They were late. Usually the prince and his nieces were out playing on the terrace before noon.

"Uncle Michael!" the eldest girl called. "I want to play on the rocks today!"

If Arianna could have groaned, she would have. As of late, Claire had decided that her favorite place to play was on the rocks that lined the terrace and overlooked the ocean. Whenever the girls and the prince played there, Arianna had to dip back under the water where it was harder to see and hear them. To her relief, however, Prince Michael told the girl no.

"Your mum will be very angry with me if I let you play over there again. You're not big enough. Besides," he hefted the baby, who was very nearly too big to be called a baby anymore, on his hip. "Lucy might fall in. She can't walk as well as you."

"Why do we have to take her?"

"Because she's your sister."

"You don't take Lucas everywhere! And he's your little brother!" Claire stuck her bottom lip out.

"Lucas is big enough to take himself places," Michael said. His expression made Arianna smirk. She'd heard the brothers argue enough times to know how Prince Michael felt about his own little brother tagging along.

"There will be none of you out on the rocks or playing anywhere on the terrace today," a familiar, low voice called out from the terrace's door.

Arianna pressed herself down against the rocks again. She could just barely see the head housekeeper make her way out to the children to join them. Not that Prince Michael was really a child, but the housekeeper treated him just the same way she ever had. Now Mistress Bithiah crossed her arms and looked down at Claire. "I have got tables to set and a ball to plan for tonight of all nights, and none of you will be of much assistance to me underfoot."

"A ball?" Claire clapped her hands and squealed, her brown curls bouncing. "Who is it for?"

"The Sea Crown and his family are coming up to meet with your grandfather. And I will not have them thinking your grandfather inhospitable on my account." She shook her head. "Even if they do plan such meetings with less than a day's notice."

"When?" Michael tried in vain to hold a squirming Lucy as he asked.

"Tonight. As I said. Now, be off with you all. There are date cakes in the kitchen, and don't you eat too many, Michael. You don't want another stomachache."

Arianna reluctantly let herself slip beneath the waves as the children went back inside the palace and Bithiah began ordering about her horde of servants. Arianna didn't mind so much today, however, that her observance had been cut short. Not if there was a ball to attend.

Though Arianna was in no rush for her lessons to begin, she

swam steadily back toward her tower. Her aunt would know about the ball. She might even be able to convince Arianna's parents to let her go. Arianna clutched her bag to her side as she pushed herself even faster. She imagined getting her own little charm to wear around her neck. What would it feel like when she emerged from the water and the charm split her fins to make two sturdy legs? Even better, what would the beautiful skirts feel like that the charm would fashion to cover those legs?

Most importantly, she would finally meet Prince Michael face-to-face. He wouldn't know her, of course, but she would know him. She would know those wide, cautious eyes before she even drew near, and the way they crinkled when he smiled.

Would he ask her to dance?

The shiver of delight that ran down Arianna's back was immediately followed, however, by a sensation that was far less enjoyable. She gave her body a shake, but the feeling only persisted. Her fins, arms, stomach, and even her gums tingled as she slowed and searched all around for the feeling's source. The sensation was slight, but even so, it made her feel sick, as though the water had grown thick and hot. Protectors' songs floated in then, and Arianna no longer swam at a steady pace but darted up as high as she could go, stopping to float just below the surface. She'd barely turned to look down again when the scene unfolded in the very place she had been swimming.

The figure of a merman zigzagged below her, so low he was nearly smacking his tail against the seafloor. He swam, if it could be called that, but with each push of his tail, he writhed so hard Arianna was sure his back would snap. The blue-green of his fins was quickly fading into a nameless shade of brown, and the screeching howls he emitted were far from the song they should have been. Instead, they caused the fish to scatter and the plants that could, to withdraw into themselves.

Arianna's breaths came hard and fast as she prayed he didn't see her floating above him. Afraid to swim for fear he would notice her movement, she watched instead as the guards encircled him, five of them, their voices rising up in a reverberating chorus of Protectors' songs.

The man continued to writhe, but the power of their songs pushed him down upon the seafloor until he was pressed flat against the sand. Still, his screams and grunts persisted even as the Protectors huddled over him. When they pulled back, he was bound with ropes, and they began tugging him toward the city. Arianna followed. Her mother would disapprove, and probably her aunt too, but it had been a long time since she'd seen a man touched by Sorthileige. Was it really as horrible a sight as she remembered it being?

She followed along at a safe distance until they came to a stop in the main city circle. She would have liked to get closer, but as usual, her head began to pound and her vision grew blurry when she tried to perch on a lower seat, so she contented herself instead with resting on one of the taller rooftops and nervously fingering her necklace as the merman was moved from the ropes to the stocks. By now, his screeches had become more guttural, like he was choking. And she couldn't be sure, but she believed she saw his eyes roll back into his head at least twice.

"Let it be known," one of the guards, Lorenzo, called out in a loud voice to those who had stopped to watch, "that this is what happens when our sacred laws are broken and one chooses to enter the Deeps!" He gestured at the thrashing merman behind him.

People had begun to gather quickly. There hadn't been a Sorthileige case in over a year.

"There is a reason only the Sea Crown himself is to enter the Deeps, and this is why! The Sorthileige—" Lorenzo directed his glare at a group of small children who had crept in for a closer look —"will take your mind and body and twist them into a monstrous work of darkness." The children pulled back a bit as he held their gazes. When they were finally with their parents again, he continued. "You may think you are too quick to be touched by the dark water. You may have even dabbled in playing on its edges before. But sooner or later, the Deeps will drag you in, and you will find yourself imprisoned by a force far more powerful than you could ever use or want. It will control you—"

Someone screamed as the man's face began to contort. Arianna gripped the rooftop's coral edge tightly as gills began to cut their way into his face; gills that looked much like the ones on the large white sharks. He twisted and bucked against his restraints as the holes continued to grow in his cheeks.

"Arianna!"

Something cool touched her back, and Arianna shot up from where she was resting. Looking down, however, to her relief and immediate embarrassment, she saw only her Aunt Renata. And Renata did not look pleased.

"This is no place for a princess. Come."

For once, Arianna was grateful for her aunt's firm tone. She didn't think she would be able to sleep if anything else had happened to the merman. Still, she knew from the stories exactly the fate of those touched by Sorthileige. She shivered as she swam after her aunt. At least she wouldn't have to watch.

As they swam, she realized that not the entire city had turned out to watch the man's agonizing end after all. Arianna followed her aunt, gliding above the domed city dwellings, and slowly, the sounds of daily work and friendly chatter helped quiet her thundering heart. Growers sang their songs to budding gardens on the seafloor. Other Growers could be heard singing in the baby nurseries, fish farms, and the towering kelp forests farther out of the city. A few were so bold as to swim halfway to the surface and hum at the boxed oyster beds above them. Nurturers did much of the same as they sang to their pods of children, schools of young dolphins, and even homes that just weren't growing fast enough. Brightly colored fish swam lazily in and out of the small and large coral dwellings that the Growers and Nurturers were still building, and larger creatures, such as sea lions, looked on with a lazy interest.

The sound of one Nurturer in particular caught Arianna's ear and made her pause. Renata stopped and came back to float beside her as Arianna tilted her head and listened to the familiar sound.

There were many Nurturers out with their pods of children, for the water was warm and inviting as the early summer sun cut all the way to the seabed from the surface above. There would be no lessons in their coral dwellings today. This particular Nurturer had the children perched on a natural bed of coral instead, higher than most Nurturers took their pupils. Her willingness to bring the children so high was a practice Arianna had always loved about her. For though Arianna had been unable to remain low enough to join a pod of children herself, she had spent many hours from afar listening to this Nurturer teach her little ones.

"Wasn't that Rinaldo's Nurturer?" Renata asked, moving closer to Arianna.

Arianna nodded as she watched the scene intently. The woman began to sway her arms from side to side, and the children began to sing.

Child of sun,
Child of sea,
Destined to silence,
Destined to sing.
One nature to rule,
One nature to fight,

Only when owned can two peoples unite.

"And just what is that face supposed to mean?" Renata was studying Arianna with one eyebrow quirked, but Arianna just rolled her eyes and flipped her tail a little harder as she resumed their swim to the tower. "No," Renata said, keeping pace with her easily. "You can't tell me that you still doubt the prophecy."

Arianna only swam faster, so Renata grabbed her arm and pulled her to a stop. "That prophecy was given to us over five centuries ago," she said.

Just another reason not to pay it heed, Arianna thought, holding her aunt's gaze unflinchingly.

"Just because you can't sing doesn't mean this doesn't involve you." Renata still grasped Arianna's arm. "The holy man who made that prophecy could see the division that was forming between the Sea and Sun Crowns even then. He saw the estrangement of the Sun and Sea Crowns far before his time, and that gap is only growing wider now." She glanced down at the children and their Nurturer, her brown eyes softening. "Don't blame them for hoping."

Then she turned back to Arianna, her gaze narrowing again into one of her best glares. "You may not think it affects you, but a third of what we use here comes from the Sun Crown and his people. If your father cannot find a way to bridge the gap for the time being, I'm not sure how much more trade there will be." Renata pursed her lips. "If you ever paid attention on holy day, you would know this by now."

Arianna listened with painful fortitude as her aunt spoke. Interrupting with a gesture or scribbling a note would do no good when she was receiving such admonishments. It was easier to bear them silently.

What Arianna did not tell her aunt as they continued their

swim, however, was that she *did* listen on holy days. That she always had. For years, she had tried to work out her place in the orderly world the holy man seemed to believe existed for every one of his listeners. But for a mermaid without a voice, those particular speeches about such a prophecy of song could be paid little heed. Pinning her hope on a miracle such as that which had been denied Arianna completely seemed of little reason. If the prophecy were true, it concerned someone else.

The Sun Crown's ball, however, didn't.

Suddenly she grinned, remembering what she had wanted to ask her aunt. She touched her aunt's arm then pointed to an outcropping of ancient volcanic rock that overlooked some of the sponge and the bottom of the floating pearl farms. Her aunt nodded, so they turned and settled upon the shelf's edge. As soon as they were sitting, Arianna pulled the bag from her shoulder and dug through it until she found one of the waxy leaf parchments, the sheet of slate rock, and her pressing knife. Placing the thin leaf up against the rock sheet, Arianna cut her question into the waxy surface and then handed it to her aunt.

Renata took it, but Arianna could immediately see her dissatisfaction with the question. Shaking her head, she handed the leaf back. "Your father will say no. You know that. Now, it's time to practice your sums."

Arianna just stared, refusing to give in to the nagging sensation that her aunt was right. Shaking her head, she wrote again. *No merman will marry me when I am grown. I won't be able to go down to live with him, and he won't be able to come up to stay with me so near the surface. Shouldn't I have a night every now and then to enjoy a celebration of some sort where I can be everyone's equal?*

"Married or not, you are a princess," Renata said firmly. "And a princess needs to know how to manage and organize resources. Your brother and sister have learned such, and you must as well. Now, figures."

Arianna pouted, but did as her aunt instructed and pulled another waxy leaf from the bag. This leaf had lines and columns of numbers already aligned for her, cut in the heavy hand of her father's steward. But the numbers in their neat lines and columns could not occupy her, and it wasn't long before she was cutting words between her numbers.

Why is the ball even taking place? What's the occasion?

Renata only crossed her arms, so Arianna tried again.

Thirteen is only four years from marriageable age. I am old enough to know.

They glared at one another, but after a few long moments Renata sighed and uncrossed her arms. "You are old enough, aren't you?"

Arianna nodded emphatically.

Renata sighed again, then stared out at the fields around them, pulling her fins up to her chest. Her dark hair floated about her face as she thought, and when she spoke, her voice sounded old. "Your father hasn't told me as much himself, but I think it will be a meeting about the pirates. Your father thinks the Sun Crown isn't doing enough to protect us."

That sounds boring. Why is there a ball then?

Renata laughed. "Precisely because such a discussion is boring. Besides, it's more difficult to be uncivil when you're surrounded by your family and everyone is dancing. The wine helps, too, of course."

Then why shouldn't I go?

Renata studied her for a long moment before shaking her head. When she spoke, her voice was gentle. "Very well, then. Finish your sums, and as soon as you're done, I'll make the request to your father."

Arianna hugged her aunt as hard as she could. Then she remembered the gift she'd snatched from the surface. Digging through her bag again, Arianna pulled the red flower out and presented it to her aunt.

"The red poppies are blooming!" Then Renata's smile melted and she leveled a hard look at Arianna. "You're sneaking up to the surface again."

Arianna simply grinned. Her aunt knew exactly where she went every day. Arianna rarely brought proof home, however, to further incriminate herself. She half-expected another lecture about what her father would say if he knew, but instead, Renata only held the flower close. It was somewhat battered from bouncing around in Arianna's bag, but Renata touched each petal with the tenderness of a mother. Arianna's grin faded as Renata bit her trembling lip.

"He would have liked you so much, Ari," Renata whispered. "Your spirit is much like his." She gave a shaky laugh. "Sometimes I don't know what I shall do with you, but I am always aware that I could *never* make do *without* you."

As she wrapped Arianna up in a tight embrace, Arianna decided that she had a good feeling about the ball after all.

3

PREFERENCES

*A*rianna would very much have enjoyed watching the sunset from her favorite rock above the surface, but the discussion she knew her parents would be having that evening was far more tempting than a stolen pink sky from above.

As she settled on her usual spot on their roof, she thanked the Maker that her parents' tower was so much higher than the other mansion chambers. If she was careful, she could remain above their window for just under half an hour before the ocean's weight became too great and she was forced to return to her own tower.

"For once," Giana was saying, "Renata is right. Arianna deserves to *do* something."

"And, pray tell, just how *does* she while her days away, since she apparently does nothing for the rest of the time?" Amadeo retorted.

"She's sneaking to the surface, you know."

"I am well aware of that. Here, come tuck this in, will you? I can never get the abominable thing to lay straight." He paused, and Arianna imagined him frowning at the mirror as he tried to lay his charm flat beneath his ceremonial sash. "Rinaldo!"

Arianna heard a door open. "Yes, Father?"

"Get your charm and Lalia's from the charmer's shop, will you?

And for the love of the triton, hurry your sister! Remind her that this isn't a trip for niceties."

Despite her adoration for her older siblings, Arianna couldn't help the twinge of jealousy at such instructions.

"Don't change the subject," Giana said once the door had been shut again. "Arianna craves the time and attention just as much as Lalia ever did. Just because she can't dwell with us down here doesn't mean she doesn't want to."

"So what do you suggest I do about it? If my own father couldn't awaken her voice or render her able to live with us, what do you expect of *me*?"

"We already know that she can remain above the surface without negative effects, even without a charm *and in the sun*, no less! All of her hours spent above testify to that. Renata says she's no different after surfacing than before. Why not give her a charm and let her have an evening of walking about with us?" Giana's voice fell so near to a whisper that Arianna had to strain to hear it. "Why not be a family for once?"

There was a pause, and Arianna prayed as she had never prayed before. Her mother might not be able to stay with her comfortably for more than a few hours at a time, but tonight she spoke as though she could see into Arianna's heart. Arianna strained to hear her father's answer.

"No."

If Arianna had been above the water, her eyes would have welled up with big tears, and if she had the legs a charm would have afforded her, she would have kicked something.

Giana began to protest, but Amadeo cut her off. "We don't know enough about her form as it is. Who knows if she will even be affected by a charm? What if its powers are ineffective and her hopes are dashed for nothing?"

"Don't you want her with us? Don't you wish to have three children instead of two?" came Giana's cry, nearly a sob.

A long moment passed before he spoke again, and Arianna wondered bitterly if he was consoling her mother or simply fiddling with his charm again. "I would prefer a daughter who is far off, to a daughter who died because of my stupidity and selfishness." He paused before calling out in a louder voice, "You understand that, don't you, Arianna?"

Arianna sighed and swam through the window into her parents' chamber. She peeked up sheepishly at her father. As she did, a writing tablet and waxy leaf caught her eye. Darting over to the desk, she snatched up the writing utensils. *I won't be disappointed if it doesn't work. I promise. Just let me try.*

Amadeo shook his head and returned to trimming his silver beard in the mirror. "It's too dangerous."

Arianna jabbed the words into the waxy leaf. *Why?*

"Because I said so."

You let Rinaldo go when he was five. And Lalia went for the first time when she was four.

"Arianna," her father said. "Let it go."

Why? she wrote again in very large letters.

"I am not keeping you here for my health!" he roared, throwing down his trimming scissors. "I am trying to keep you alive!"

She crossed her arms and set her jaw.

Amadeo rubbed his eyes and spoke in a softer tone. "Suppose that word got out that the youngest princess was out in society. 'A gentle, quiet soul,' people would say to one another in their daily gossip. The pirates would eventually hear about it from someone."

"Amadeo, don't you think you're being a bit dramatic?" Giana asked, but Amadeo only shook his head and continued talking to Arianna.

"I know your aunt hasn't told you this yet, but I'm going to tell you now. Pirates don't just attack our guards. They take merpeople and torture them. They put them through agonizing pain until the merperson shows them where we keep our pearl storehouses. Then they auction the merperson off to the highest bidder to be kept as a pet . . . or worse!"

That won't happen to me, Arianna wrote. *I'll be safe with you.*

"You're not listening! It's not just *tonight* that I'm worried about. Do you know what lengths men would go to get you, once spotted? And worse, when you couldn't sing to show them the treasure they demanded of you, you would be considered a novelty for all sorts of other debauchery. I do not know who will be at this ridiculous gala, and I will not have you gawked at like a speckled crab in winter."

Arianna glared at him, but he continued.

"That you're a princess will only make you more intriguing. No. You are not going." He held up the charm she'd begged out of the Charmer, and Arianna gasped. Where had he found that? She thought she'd hidden it well.

"And if I find you trying to pilfer one of these again, I will lock you in your room myself until this horrid night is over!"

4

STOLEN MOMENTS

"*If* you absolutely must go, then at least wear your black camicett." Renata eyed Arianna from her perch by the tower window. Though Arianna's aunt rarely used her monocle, as she claimed it made her look old, she peeked through it now, her leaf and pressing knife still in hand.

Arianna would have protested on any other occasion, but her guilt was too great this night to argue. That Renata wasn't reporting her disobedience to her father was a gift enough in itself, so she flipped back into her little chamber and changed into the black camicett as requested.

Arianna inwardly groaned at the tight, slick material as she pulled it over her head. Wearing the night apparel felt much like she was wrapping her top half snugly in waxy leaf paper. Her aunt was right, though. Swimming about at night was a trifle to most merpeople. For them, the black camicett was simply a precaution, a preventive measure against being seen by pirates. A mermaid without a voice, however, couldn't be too careful, and the sleek black shirt would make her less visible in the inky waters of the eve.

As she launched herself through her tower window, Arianna felt a shiver of dual fear and excitement run all the way from her shoulders to her tail. Her father would pop a scale if he could see what she was doing now. Darkness had begun to fall, and the sea already felt different. The waters were eerily silent, no longer filled with the working songs the merpeople spun throughout the day. Only the Protector songs of the distant guards were audible as they continued their constant murmurs at the edges of the Deeps.

The water was still warm from the day, but all the pleasure its heat should have brought her was chased away by the guilt that gnawed at her stomach. True enough, Arianna broke the rules daily with her excursions to the surface. Amadeo rarely reprimanded her, though, and even the guards turned their backs whenever she swam by. The absolute warning in her father's voice earlier that evening, however, had been steel and stone. He did not want her going to the ball.

Though she had wavered in her determination as he spoke of the ways she might be tortured, should she be captured by pirates, his threat itself was what had made up Arianna's mind entirely. If her father wasn't going to treat her as a member of the family, then she didn't need to act like one.

Or at least, that was what she had been telling herself all evening. Even now, she nearly turned back as the moon rippled into view above the surface she was fast approaching. By the time she broke the surface, doubt had nearly killed her determination completely, and she had resolved to simply glance at the party and then scurry home to her aunt in their lonely tower. But then she glimpsed the ball.

Taking care as she always did to keep the end of her tail in the water, Arianna pulled herself up onto the lower ledge that jutted out just below the Sun Palace's terrace.

Despite the dark of twilight, the terrace was nearly as light as day. Dozens of torches stood several feet above the heads of even the tallest people, their flames not only yellow, but also blue, green, pink, and even purple. Tables lined the terrace's edges, and from the way the guests hovered around them, Arianna could only guess that those tables held all varieties of food. Lalia swore that human food was nothing special. Most of it was so dry it was inedible, she'd complained once to Arianna after a similar event a few years before. But now Arianna was sure her sister was only feeding her own prejudice. There were too many smiling people standing around the tables for the food to be bland or dry.

The people themselves were stunning. Arianna gawked as men strode around with confident swagger in their steps while the ladies flitted, their fluffy, lacy skirts swishing gracefully from side to side. Arianna stared at the colorful gowns longingly. Merpeople never wore so many clothes. Not only was it unnecessary, cloth hindered swimming significantly. Still, despite the impracticality of the humans' clothes, as Arianna was sure that they could have been covered adequately with less than half as many clothes, their attire was so very pretty.

It didn't take Arianna long to spot her family. Her sister and mother were standing close to her father's elbows, watching the human merriment with cool, collected eyes. Her father's scowl was so deep that Arianna first feared he'd seen her watching them. Before she dove back into the water, however, she realized that he was scowling at everyone and everything. The food, the dancing, the children running about underfoot, and especially the Sun Crown himself. At least, Arianna guessed he was the Sun Crown, judging by the oversized golden diadem on his head and the horde of admirers encircling him.

It took her a moment longer, however, to locate her brother. Rinaldo was chatting animatedly with another young man. When the young man turned, Arianna sucked in a quick breath.

Prince Michael wore black trousers and a brown doublet that made his olive skin look tan even in the dark of the evening. His curly black hair had been cut more neatly than Arianna had seen in a long time. Arianna smiled to herself as he tugged nervously at the bottom of his jacket. The fitted coat did indeed look restricting. But, oh! The effect of the clothing on his shoulders made her chest tight and her breath catch in her throat.

His charms clearly weren't lost on the human girls, either. Arianna's delight in his appearance quickly disappeared as she noticed a number of them eyeing the prince as well. All too soon, the young men finished their conversation, and Prince Michael turned away and bowed to a young woman nearby. They promptly began to dance.

Arianna's annoyance about the forced proximity that human dances required was interrupted by a small splash behind her. She nearly dived back into the water when Rinaldo's head popped up from the waves. Arianna felt the color drain from her face.

"And why am I not surprised?" he asked.

Arianna couldn't meet his eyes. Instead, she stared at his drenched shirt.

"Not to worry," he said, following her gaze. "The charm will dry them as soon as I get out of the water." He paused for a minute, and Arianna finally dared to sneak a peek up at his face.

His brow was furrowed, but his mouth was set in a crooked grin. Arianna dared to swallow. Did that mean he wasn't going to tell their father?

"I shouldn't be doing this, but since you're already here . . ." He bowed his head and removed the fiber string from around his neck. Arianna's heart beat fast as he handed the little shell to her. "Just a few minutes, then I need to get back."

Arianna stared at the charm, still afraid to put it on. It was too good to be true. But her brother only shook his head as he took it back and put it around her neck himself.

"I really do need to get back. So get on with it."

Arianna's mouth fell open as her tail began to quiver. The trembling grew so strong that it itched, but her discomfort was forgotten as a black skirt began to extend down from the bottom of her camicett. And at the bottom of the skirt appeared two little slippered feet.

Rinaldo let out a deep laugh as Arianna turned and bolted up to the edge of the terrace. She wondered at how easily her new legs moved. Bending and turning, they moved in directions Arianna had never even considered human legs moving. And every movement felt as natural as swimming. Kneeling behind a bush, Arianna watched the ball from a position she had only ever dreamed of reaching.

A new dance had begun, and Arianna wished more than ever to give her new legs use. Prince Michael had switched partners. Now he twirled with a girl with hair the color of ebony and skin the color of sand. Keeping perfect time to the music, the prince never once missed a step. Not until he turned and looked out at the ocean, that is. Arianna froze as his eyes swept the horizon. She was sure, if he ever saw her, that those eyes would be able to look inside her soul. At that precise moment, those eyes stopped their sweeping and settled on the bush she hid behind. Was it possible? Did he see her behind the leaves through which she now peered?

They stayed that way, Arianna holding her breath and the prince staring with a crinkled brow, until his partner said something and he returned those dark eyes to the girl instead. Arianna dared to breathe again when her brother's voice came from the water behind her.

"So I see you've found Prince Michelangelo."

Arianna turned to find Rinaldo's face twisted into an amused smile.

"He's highly sought after, for sure, but not unworthily, as many of his station are. The lad's a good one. I think the Sun Crown will be far better when he sits on the throne."

Arianna turned back to look at the dance floor, and a hollow ache filled her chest. If her father had only listened to her mother then she might be the one dancing with the prince now. She would wear the frilly dress the charm had formed on her—though she would have chosen her blue camicett instead of black—and her skirts would swish and sway gracefully in time to the strange but entrancing music.

But then, she sighed to herself, what would she have said to him? Nothing, of course. Even the charm couldn't give her a voice. Her parents had tried that long ago. No, she would have been the silent maiden, laughed at by the human girls and thought dull by all the court boys. The prince himself might even have thought her dimwitted. But no. She shook her head. Prince Michael was too kind for that. And even if he had thought it of her, he would still have asked her to dance. He was good like that, too.

"I'm loathe to do it," Rinaldo's voice had lost its laugh, "but I'm afraid I shall need that back. Father will be missing me soon if I don't return."

Arianna shot one last longing look at the terrace. Her normal view seemed suddenly far away when she returned to her perch at the bottom of the rocks, but at least it was better than being in her tower. As she removed the charm and handed it back to her brother, however, a flash of light off the darkened horizon caught her eye. It glimmered for no more than a second, like a flame extinguished upon the water.

Rinaldo had slipped the charm back over his neck when Arianna patted his shoulder and pointed to the west where the light was flashing again. He turned, and his eyes immediately hardened into an expression so fierce it was nearly frightening on his gentle face. "No human ship should be that close to the Deeps. Unless . . ." he let his words trail off. "Stay here," he muttered, tossing the necklace back at her. Then he plunged beneath the surface.

It occurred to Arianna that she might put the necklace back on and return to the party, but the look of dread on Rinaldo's face haunted her, and Arianna could only clutch the charm to her chest as she prayed for him to resurface and tell her it was only a falling star.

The wait felt like hours, but it could only have been twenty minutes before he was back. She sighed with relief when he rejoined her, but the set of his jaw told Arianna that the flame had certainly not been a star.

"I want you to go as deep as you can," he said as he put the charm back on. "Even lower than the tower. Stay there until you can't possibly stay down any longer." He began to climb the rocks as soon as his legs were returned to him. Before he could leave her, however, Arianna reached out and grasped his foot. When he turned his expression was grim, but upon meeting her eyes, his face grew soft.

"I promise, I'll be careful." He reached back and squeezed her hand. "Leaving you to your own devices would be a terrible thing."

Arianna held on for a moment longer before nodding once and throwing herself down into the waves. He had promised to be careful, she told herself over and over again. That was all she could ask.

5

WHAT STRONG GIRLS DO

*A*rianna tried to obey her brother's wishes. But only minutes after reaching the seafloor, she began to feel as though someone were poking her with urchin needles all over, and her head felt as if a manatee were trying to sit on it. Gasping, she pushed herself back up toward the surface, to the sky that now glowed orange. She began swimming back to her tower. It was built into the side of a sea cliff below the Sun Palace. Surely it would be safe enough if she and her aunt covered all of their algae lanterns.

But she'd only swum a few fathoms before Arianna realized the battle was raging in between her and the tower. The merpeople had been quick, particularly the Protectors. All of them, even her father, had taken off their charms and moved out toward the ship before she had even reached the seafloor. By the time she was on her way back up, their haunting, minor choruses had filled the sea like beams of the sun's light. Arianna could not imagine what kind of ship had risked sailing so close to the Deeps and then straight over her father's city. As she drew nearer to the surface, she could hear the voices of her people straining in their warfare.

The ship above her was neither large nor small, but something had to be wrong. So many merpeople's songs should have splintered it already. Arianna had seen her father's guards practice, and the song of a single Protector could burst a fishing boat in one or two minutes. This ship, despite the strongest songs of her people, however, continued to sail right toward her parents' home and the city that lay below it.

That was when she realized that there was not just one ship. There were ten.

Still, the Protectors continued their fight. She could hear her father's deep baritone voice resonating louder than all of the others, and Rinaldo's alto song was not far behind. And as long as they sang, she felt confident enough to continue her slow swim to her tower.

An explosion so loud that it drowned out all of the voices from above brought Arianna to a halt. A strange red light filled the choppy seas above her. Arianna's stomach nearly heaved as the bodies of mermen and mermaids—their Protectors—began to go limp, drifting with the waves. Arianna wanted to scream.

Rinaldo's orders forgotten, she streaked up to the nearest body she could see, a female Protector who floated on the water's surface, a black contour against the orange-red sky above. Arianna hooked her arm through the woman's and pulled her down until they were deep enough to be free of the continuous barrage of explosions, songs, and human shouts from above. But a moment of listening to her heart confirmed what Arianna had most feared. The woman was dead.

Arianna stared at the body, dropping it immediately. Her hands shook and she fought the sudden urge to swim as far away from the body as she could. Somehow, touching the body suddenly seemed even worse than watching the Sorthileige's transformation of the merman that morning. At least she had never touched him.

Nothing short of another explosion was able to pull Arianna's attention back to the surface. Letting the tides take the body, Arianna raced back to the top for the next body she could see, praying the whole time it wasn't one of her own family. Lalia and Giana were Healers, so they wouldn't even be at the surface, much to Arianna's relief. They couldn't be dead.

And her second body wasn't, either. The merman was breathing in slow, shallow sips, but at least he was still alive. Arianna dragged him as deep as she could go and handed him to the first Healer she could find. For by now, Arianna wasn't the only one darting up to the surface for rescues. Dozens of other merpeople were doing the same, snatching the bodies and dragging them back down to the Healers.

Arianna quickly grew tired, but it was all manageable until one more song stopped. Arianna paused as she began her ascent once more. *No,* she begged the Maker. *Not that one. Anyone but that one.* But as she feverishly pushed herself to the surface, the song did not return.

Without his song, she couldn't find him. If Arianna could have screamed, she would have shouted his name until she lost her voice again.

Some part of her wondered what her father would do to her later if he caught her at the surface during a battle, but she didn't care, for Rinaldo's voice was silent.

She was nearly blinded by another explosion as soon as she broke the surface again, and it took her a moment to find her bearings. Only then did she realize that the first ship wasn't setting the explosions. The ship itself was exploding. That didn't seem to daunt the sailors too much, however. Large rowboats floated all over the choppy water. Some of the boats' occupants were doubled over, their hands covering their ears as they begged for the songs to stop. Some of the men even cried.

Not all were so affected, though. At least half of the men were still rowing. They called out songs of their own as though to drown out the ringing choruses of the Protectors. Rain began to fall, but whatever was on the ship continued to burn. The flames reminded

Arianna of why she had come to the surface in the first place, and she squinted through the rain and smoke.

She was so distracted that she forgot to watch her back.

The roll of cloth that was drawn about her mouth tasted sour, and Arianna choked as it was tightened behind her head. She thrashed about, trying to dive back below the waves, but whatever force had gagged her now grabbed her arms as well, and she was lifted out of the water and tossed backward, landing with a sharp crack at the bottom of a rowboat.

"Quiet now," a man standing at the back of the boat ordered, his dark eyes glinting orange in the light of the burning ship. "We wouldn't want you overusing that voice so soon."

Arianna tried to push herself back against the side of the boat, but she found that she was already as far back as she could go. A dozen men leered down at her from their benches until the man that had spoken to her barked at them to keep rowing. Arianna tried to move her arms up to untie the rag, but whoever had so expertly tied her gag had also bound her wrists tightly. She tried then to flip her body backward over the side, but her tail wasn't long enough or strong enough. Instead, her green-blue scales only glowed orange in the fire's light as she quivered.

"She's tryin' t'scape!" a rower beside her called back as he glared at Arianna. She glared back, particularly at his sand-encrusted beard.

The man who had addressed Arianna before now walked toward her, leaning heavily to stay upright as the boat tossed and turned in the waves. When he was nearly on top of her, he placed a thin hand beneath her chin. "She's young."

Arianna yanked her chin from his grasp. He didn't grab it again, but that didn't make his next words any less horrifying.

"After she talks, she'll go for a good price in the east. Young, but pretty enough. Sovereign Yanni prefers them so."

Arianna heaved her supper all over his boots.

He made a clucking sound and muttered under his breath. Just as he opened his mouth, however, and his beady black eyes fixed on Arianna again, the boat rocked hard to the left. Arianna was knocked forward into him and they nearly toppled over the boat's edge. A second jolt to the boat succeeded in smacking the man's head against its side, much to Arianna's satisfaction, and she almost managed to pull herself over the tilted boat's edge until he grabbed her by the fins and held on so tightly that she wanted to cry out.

"Let her go!"

Arianna turned to see her brother climb into the boat, his charm dripping as he stood tall once again. The movement of the waves didn't seem to affect him or his balance as it did everyone else in the boat. Arianna reached out to him, but before he'd taken a step toward her, the man with the dark eyes pushed himself between them, his red coat slapping Arianna's face as he did. The other men looked back and forth between their leader and the young man who now stood on their boat. Arianna wondered if they could feel his power even when he wasn't singing. Whatever their reason, they looked nervous as their rowing ceased and their hands moved to their weapons.

"She's too young for you," Rinaldo said in a low voice.

"Actually, she's going to make me a good deal of money. I think the pearl farms will be our first stop, wherever those are. Then she'll take us—"

"She can't sing."

The man stared at him.

"She can't even speak," Rinaldo continued. "You would get nothing out of her because she has no voice."

"A mermaid without a voice."

Rinaldo only nodded, but the man laughed.

"I'm hardly a wise man, but you can't expect me to be fool enough to believe that." As he spoke, a particularly rough wave hit the boat, and they all tumbled forward. Before Arianna could right herself, however, she was lifted into the air by strong arms. Blessed, warm water enveloped her as those arms dumped her over the boat's side. For the first time in her life, Arianna swam straight down as fast as her fins could push her. She was nearly ten fathoms deep by the time she realized a familiar song was echoing above her.

Shouts rang out from the boat, and Arianna turned and pushed herself back toward the surface. She knew something was most definitely wrong. Other Protectors should have heard and joined him by then. No merperson was supposed to fight alone. The song her brother was using was his fiercest, and even her ears slightly burned as he pushed it out. Bodies spilled out of the boat and kicked about at the surface, trying to flee the song. The red-coated man did not fall into the water, however. As Arianna looked around to find help, she realized that there were simply too many pirates. Every Protector had risen to the surface, and every one of them was involved in the fight of his or her life.

Another explosion went off above the surface and, finally, a twelfth body appeared in the water. As Arianna began to rejoice, however, she realized that this body didn't wear a red coat.

No speed was fast enough as she darted the rest of the way up. When she finally reached the surface, there was no sign of the little boat anywhere. Just debris and flaming ships everywhere. Tongues of fire danced on the water as pieces of the broken ship floated about and the smaller boats began rowing to shore. But Arianna's only thought was for her brother.

Rinaldo's eyes were closed as he bobbed up and down with the waves. He opened them, though, when Arianna gathered him up in her arms. Hot tears mixed with sea water as they rolled down her face, and hatred for her silence surged as she looked at the wounds on his chest, arms, and face that she should have been able to heal with her voice.

How had this happened? Her brother had one of the strongest

voices in their guard. How did a mere pirate best him? And why were there so many? Where was the Sun Crown's navy? She tightened her grip on her brother as she prepared to pull him down to their Healers, but he shook his head. Confused, she allowed the water to push them back up to the top.

"Tell Father—" Violent coughing choked his words off, and Arianna waited in agony until his fit was over. "Have Father ask the Sun Crown—" More coughing wracked his body, and Arianna held on as tightly as she dared. When he was finally done, his breaths were shallow and his eyelids seemed heavy, but he lifted one shaking hand to touch her cheek.

A sudden boom in the distance made Arianna look up.

"Took them long enough," Rinaldo wheezed.

She frowned at him in confusion.

"The Sun Crown has deigned to send his navy to assist us."

Arianna looked back up to see if any ships were close enough to hail for help, but a flash of red caught her eye instead. Less than ten fathoms away floated a beaten but buoyant boat. In it was the pirate with the red coat. And he was rowing right for her.

"He's coming for you," Rinaldo said, coughing again. Arianna prayed that the red on his lip wasn't what it appeared to be.

"You might as well remain, child," the pirate called out in a silky voice. "Can't leave him to die alone, now, can you?"

"Arianna." Rinaldo pulled her face back down to look into his. "The Maker has made you strong. Don't ever forget that. And don't let anyone else forget it, either."

She glared at him. Why was he making this speech sound so final?

"And do you know what a strong girl knows how to do?" He smiled at her scowl. "She knows when to let go. You need to let me go, Ari."

Arianna shook her head so hard it hurt, but he just gave her a sad smile.

"Let me go."

Why? She mouthed.

Instead of answering, he yanked the charm off his neck. As soon as the string had snapped, his two legs shimmered back into his blue-green tail. In one swoop, he pushed her down into the water with his right arm before using his tail to launch himself at the pirate in the boat. Arianna watched in horror as the boat splintered from the strength of his impact. A fight ensued, but Arianna couldn't tell who was who. She could only hope and pray.

Finally, the tussle subsided. The body in the red coat floated on the surface. The one with the tail cascaded slowly down.

6

DANGEROUS MOURNING

"*T*hank the Maker it's cloudy today," Renata muttered as she packed up a little bag of objects for the mourning ceremony. She darted to the door before pausing and turning back to Arianna, almost as if she'd forgotten her niece was there. "Your father says you may sit with the family for as long as you can remain," she said gently. "I'll be helping your mother finalize the funeral details. You can come, though, whenever you want."

But Arianna couldn't return the smile as her aunt swam away. She knew Renata only meant kindness. She must have begged and pleaded for such an allowance from Arianna's father, particularly with the humans coming down to join them. But what joy could be derived from such a victory? Was she expected to rejoice that she might attend her brother's funeral as part of the family?

But she couldn't be upset with Renata, she reminded herself. None of this was Renata's fault. In fact, Renata was the reason the humans were coming at all.

Undesirous of company, Arianna slowly finished donning her mourning attire alone. She had put on her black camicett and black pearl earrings already, and her hair was as tightly pulled back as ever. Today, however, she was allowed to adorn it with the obsidian pins her aunt had loaned her for the awful occasion.

By the time Arianna was finished with her personal preparations, there was still too much time left before the service started to do anything but sit and stare at the giant coral box that held him. So she set off to watch the humans descend instead.

The irony that the humans were using charms to attend the merprince's funeral just three days after the ball was not lost on Arianna. But now she wished with all her heart that they weren't coming, that her aunt had not won the argument with her father to invite them.

For once, the confrontation had been one Arianna had not meant to listen in on. Rather, she had been waiting to see if her mother might join her for some time in her tower. But as she waited up on the roof of her parents' tower, she had immediately realized her mistake, and would have swum away if she hadn't been so frightened of being noticed. For it was not her mother's voice she'd heard inside the tower, but her aunt's.

"They're asking for charms," Renata had said quietly. "Your steward reports that they've requested again and again to offer their condolences."

"They only wish to ease their singed consciences," Amadeo had snapped. "They know it was their fault the pirates were so bold to begin with."

"So what if it's so? Perhaps this might buy us time! Perhaps their guilt will provide us some provincial peace . . . even if just for now!"

"You would pardon them!"

"You forget that if anyone has a right to be angry with the humans' negligence, it's me, brother! First Angelo. And now my nephew has been stolen from me!" Then she had paused. "But it is tradition to honor such requests. You know it is. Perhaps this can stave off war. At least for a little."

There had been a long silence, so long that Arianna had

wondered if her father was too angry to speak. But when he finally did speak, the longing in his voice surprised Arianna.

"You've changed much in the last fifteen years."

"Not changed," her aunt had replied in a taut voice. "Just wiser."

Now, Arianna placed herself in one of the shallow alcoves where she could watch the humans begin their descent, thanks to her aunt's efforts. The spot was one of her favorites, a little cavern carved out of one of the sea cliffs by the constant pounding of the waves. During high tide it was covered. But during low tides, Arianna could sit and watch the human shore while she fingered her little conch necklace.

This particular line of shore was usually rather quiet, but today it crawled with humans. If she hadn't been mourning the loss of her greatest friend and companion, Arianna would have smiled at how ridiculous the humans looked as they tried to board the dolphin sleighs. It was as though they'd forgotten they were wearing the merpeople's charms at all. Hadn't they seen her own people parading about with charms in their own world a few days before?

But she couldn't smile today, not even at irony. Since she was a small child, and he would sneak up to see her and bring her treats, Arianna had longed to tell her brother how much he meant to her. With her own voice, wherever it was. Someday, she'd promised herself from a young age, she would utter the words herself. She would make him proud.

But now she never would. And to make her pain worse, her chest physically ached with the song of mourning that needed so much to burst forth.

"I want to ride with Uncle Michael!"

Arianna turned when she heard the familiar voice from the other side of the beach, then slid into the water to swim closer for a better look. When she surfaced behind an outcropping of rocks, little Claire was clinging to Prince Michael's leg and jutting her bottom lip out pathetically. Baby Lucy was nowhere to be seen.

"I'm not sure this is a good idea." A young woman pursed her lips and looked at the man beside her.

"No need to worry," Prince Michael said, hoisting Claire up onto his shoulders. "We'll keep our sleigh right next to yours. Rinaldo told me that the merpeople drivers are very accommodating."

Arianna couldn't help the sad smile that came to her face as she watched the prince's face fall while he spoke these words, and she wondered how close he and her brother had actually been. Rinaldo had been to shore several times that Arianna could remember, and several times before even that, as he was five years her senior. But now she would never know.

"You put a lot of trust in these merpeople," the woman said, eyeing their waiting driver as though he couldn't hear them.

"I trusted Rinaldo."

In that moment, Arianna wanted to kiss the prince.

"Very well, then. But hold onto Claire tightly! None of this shoulder business. And Claire, hold onto the sleigh's railing with one hand and your uncle with the other. And don't you dare take that charm off to play with it!" She turned again to the man beside her. "We should have just left her at home with Lucy."

The sleighs began to make their slow descent into the waves, and Arianna decided to swim alongside the prince's chariot, just far enough away to stay hidden behind the coral beds. She could hear several shrieks as the humans first dipped their heads below the water, and she decided that the humans would benefit from venturing into the sea more often.

The shrieking soon stopped, however, as the sleigh drivers hummed their gentle songs to the dolphins, and the dolphins, two per sleigh, cut smoothly through the water. The human panic was soon replaced by squeals of delight. The clear blue of the water, the great varieties and colors of flora that blanketed the shallow seafloor, even the low, constant choruses of Arianna's people were praised. Despite her sorrow, Arianna couldn't help feeling just a bit proud. Rinaldo would have been proud.

Prince Michael pointed everything out to his niece as they went, and the woman watched them throughout it all with a furrowed brow. But Prince Michael didn't seem offended in the least bit.

"See that, Claire? That's called an urchin. See how pointy its spikes are? And that there is called a—" His lesson broke off, however, as a great shadow blocked the weak light that filtered through the water.

Arianna frowned up at the shadow. The day should have held only thin cloud cover. Her father's trackers had sworn there wouldn't be a storm for several days. As she wondered what else the shadow might be, however, a distant flash and explosion from above told Arianna that there was indeed a storm.

"Claire!"

Prince Michael's voice snapped Arianna's attention back to the humans.

He was staring in horror at his niece. "Claire! Talk to me! Claire, what's wrong?"

Claire didn't answer, but it was clear that she was panicking. Her eyes were wild, and she began to thrash as though trying to escape his arms.

"Maura!" Prince Michael yelled over to the other sleigh. "I don't think Claire can—" His own words were cut off as he, too, began to choke. Arianna looked frantically all around her at the other humans in the sleighs, and the sounds of fizzling, dying charms filled the water. The charms that should have lasted another four hours were losing their songs, fast.

Arianna was at their sleigh in seconds. She grabbed Claire in one arm and Michael in the other. But he pushed her outstretched arm away. She tried to gesture that she was going to take him to the surface. She was trying to save him! Why was he fighting her? She reached down and grabbed his arm again. Only when he pushed her hand off and thrust it at Claire, though, did Arianna realize what he was trying to say. For a split second, she stared into his hazel eyes as he continued to choke. But the smaller weight in her arms reminded her of what she had to do.

Their descent had seemed so gradual, and yet the party must have come farther faster than she'd thought. The trip to the surface was agonizing. Claire didn't make it easy, either. She continued to thrash and kick as Arianna dragged them upward.

Hold on! Arianna thought at her. *Almost there!*

They broke the surface only to be tossed hard by a gigantic wave. Arianna had to fight to keep them from being dashed on the very rocks she'd hoped to take shelter on. The child's clear scream was more beautiful to her ears than any merperson's voice had ever been, however, for it meant that she could breathe. Claire was alive.

But they weren't out of danger yet. It took Arianna a good twenty seconds more to push her way through the storm to the other, more sheltered side of the rocks where the surf and stone met sand.

After laying the little girl down on the sand, Arianna motioned for her to stay put before diving back down again.

Please make this stop! she prayed to the Maker. *If you care for us, then you can make this stop!*

But the storm did not stop, and Arianna gasped in dismay as she reached the place that the sleigh had been. Humans everywhere were trying to swim upward, many clutching their charms. But where were the Protectors? Arianna looked around for Michael or the guards, but none were to be found. It was hard to see without the day's light to pierce the violent waves, waves that could be felt even as far below the surface as she was. And the water had grown so cold it made her shiver.

Just as she was about to despair, she caught sight of the prince trying to swim up just a few dozen yards away. She streaked across the gap and grabbed him beneath his shoulders, propelling them up as fast as she could go.

He was heavier than she'd expected, however, and the turbulence of the storm above made her journey even more difficult than the first. She wanted to glance down at him to make sure he was still conscious, but when she attempted such a feat, she nearly lost her grip as they were slammed into the more shallow sand by a crashing wave.

Eventually they reached the surface, but when they did, there was little to rejoice about. Each time she thought she saw the rocks where she'd left Claire, another wall of water smashed into them. Prince Michael choked again and again, and Arianna's arm strength was quickly fading.

Don't you care? she cried silently to the heavens.

There was no miracle in response. No voice from above or helping hand from below. But eventually, after drifting for several minutes as she attempted to keep the prince from swallowing more seawater, Arianna did finally spy the spot of beach she'd left Claire on.

With her tail so stiff it hurt and her back and arms feeling as though they might fall off, she pushed the prince up onto the sand beside his niece, who immediately threw herself upon him. The little girl was soaked and crying, but Arianna was simply grateful that the child was exactly where she'd left her.

Michael, however, was not as fortunate, it seemed. Arianna's stomach twisted as a few drops of blood dripped down his face and onto the sand beneath him. Had he hit his head before she'd pulled him out?

Just as she leaned forward to examine the cut more closely, a wave engulfed all three of them, nearly dragging them all back to sea. She needed to get them further inland.

Without thinking twice, for the first time in her life Arianna pulled her tail out of the water. Not even the tip was touching. She meant to push herself up the beach a few feet before reaching back to drag the prince behind her. But as she tried to push herself forward, her fins prickled with the oddest sensation, which turned quickly into searing hot pain. It was all she could do to not collapse on the sand and let the pain whisk her into unconsciousness.

Trembling with the effort, Arianna forced herself to look back, and when she did, she couldn't help the silent shriek that escaped her. Instead of her blue-green fins, she found two gangly legs sticking out behind her. The only thought that drowned out her shock was a distracted relief that her mourning camicett was long enough to cover her new strange limbs nearly down to her knees.

A strangled cough from Prince Michael, however, brought Arianna out of her trance. Legs or no legs, she needed to get him to higher ground.

Her new legs proved to be far less able than they had been when brought on by Rinaldo's charm. Those legs had been strong and quick, easily following Arianna's every whim. These legs were clumsy, however, and far from helpful. Pulling her own body up the beach was nearly as hard as dragging Prince Michael.

Only when they were hidden behind a little grove of palm trees did Arianna stop. As she arranged him into a more comfortable position, Claire, who had been trying to help pull him up the shore, surprised Arianna by clambering into and huddling in Arianna's lap. And as the little girl clung to her arm, Arianna realized she didn't mind at all.

The trees offered just enough protection from the wind and rain for Arianna to give the prince a more thorough examination. Though her swim had felt unending, her rescue of both Claire and Prince Michael couldn't have taken more than a minute or so altogether. Surely humans weren't so fragile as to die in such a short time underwater.

Were they?

He continued to cough and sputter. Once she was convinced

that he was truly breathing, however, Arianna was more interested in his head. As she lightly ran her fingers alongside the gash above his right brow, his eyes opened, and Arianna found herself held captive by the clearest hazel eyes she had ever seen. Not dark, like she'd originally thought them to be, they were brown with specks of green and yellow exploding out from the center, like rays of the sun moving out into an outer ring of blue.

Even if she could have spoken, Arianna didn't know what she could have said. She knew she should gesture to see if he felt all right or ask if he could move his limbs correctly, but the way he was staring at her made her feel the same way she had back at the ball when he'd looked in her direction. There was no plant to hide behind this time, however, and no other girl to entice him away.

Briefly she tried looking elsewhere, but that was of little help. Her eyes moved from his face to his person. The contours of his chest and arms were visible through his soaked shirt, and she fought the sudden urge to touch him, just to see if they were as hard as they looked. She never got close enough to see mermen her age. He was perhaps a year or so older than she, but close enough. Did young mermen also seem so . . . transitional? His face, though serious, still held some of its boyish roundness, but his body looked as though it belonged to someone else. Lean muscles clung to his bones, but he was still thin enough to look as though a strong wind might blow him away.

Her stomach felt as though minnows were flitting around inside of it, and she sensed her face growing an embarrassing shade of pink.

No, it was better to look at his face instead. But when she returned to studying his face, he was still staring at her as though looking might unlock her soul.

And for a moment, she felt that it just might.

~

Too soon, however, the prince's eyes seemed to grow heavy, and Arianna's wonder was replaced with worry as she tried to awaken him again. She only received brief flutters of his eyelashes, however, before he was back down again. Frightened, Arianna could only watch for signs of life and pray for the storm's abatement as she cuddled Claire, who was so cold her teeth chattered. And as they sat there together, and Arianna stared at the two new legs that had inexplicably replaced her tail, she felt even more helpless than the night Rinaldo had died.

Arianna hadn't known it was possible to be so cold. The ocean changed temperature in the winter, of course, but the gentle rise and fall in the tides' warmth had never come so quickly. Nor did it bite like this wind. Raindrops came so fast and hard that they clawed at her skin as Arianna tried her best to shield Claire from the brunt of the storm.

Why is this happening? Arianna prayed through tears. *Why won't you make it stop?* Did her parents think she was dead? Had any of the other humans made it to the surface? Arianna couldn't imagine that her people had managed to somehow miss all of the humans floating helplessly below the surface when their charms fizzled out, and she took comfort in deciding that they must have been bringing the humans to the surface further up the coast.

As she looked again for signs of life in the prince, a small dark object on his chest caught her eye. Arianna picked it up and examined it, though seeing the object clearly was nearly impossible in the growing dark. When she touched it, however, she realized that it was a charm. From what she could tell using her fingers, this charm was just like her brother's had been. It was a little auger's shell, no larger than her thumbnail, with smooth sides and a sharp point just at the bottom. The song should have leaked out from the shell's point in order to preserve the spell. But instead of the remnants of a song, there was nothing. Arianna held the shell up to her ear, but even after a long minute of listening there was still nothing. The shell was empty.

Arianna threw the charm into her bag, which had somehow survived all of the day's dangers. If Arianna were ever able to get home, she would show the shell to her parents and aunt. But right now, she was needed for another, more important job. She returned to trying to warm the little girl.

How many hours they spent huddled against the large boulder, Arianna couldn't tell. She did know, however, that her newfound legs began to cramp from being bunched up tightly for so long. Claire's cries eventually fell to whispers, and though Prince Michael never opened his eyes again, he fidgeted in his sleep just often enough to assure her that he wasn't dead. Slowly, so slowly the storm began to lift. So slowly it was excruciating.

Arianna had nearly dropped off into her own light slumber against Claire when a sound jerked her awake. When she peered into the darkness, off in the distance a light bobbed in a line that was coming toward them. She panicked for a brief moment as her father's warnings about humans came back to her. But she couldn't just leave the unconscious prince and his little niece there alone, particularly as the niece had fallen asleep curled up against her chest. Her heart slowed a bit, however, when the humans' shouts became audible and she realized that they were calling out with fearful voices for her two charges.

Gently shaking the little girl awake, Arianna pointed to the group. Claire rubbed her eyes and refused to look at first, but as their voices grew louder, her large brown eyes popped open, and she jumped up and ran, shouting out their names as well. As she did, Arianna threw one more glance at the prince before crawling back to the waves.

When she was waist deep, Arianna stopped. *What if you can't turn back?* a mean voice whispered in her head. *Then not even your aunt will be able to pretend you're one of them.* But Arianna paid no heed to it until she saw that the prince had been discovered. Servants she recognized from all her time spying on the castle descended upon him with loud praises for the Maker and cries of dismay at his condition.

With that, Arianna used her weak legs to push herself deeper. She didn't get very far, though. The currents kept sweeping up her body as though she weighed nothing and pushing her back to the surface. There was also the problem of breathing. For the first time in her life, Arianna choked as she plunged into the water's depths. Soon she wanted to scream in frustration as the water rejected her again and again. *Why do you hate me so?* she silently shouted up at the Maker. *Why do you want me to be alone?* But there was no answer, only dark shadows that passed beneath her now and then as she waited at the top.

Only when she had nearly given up and decided to paddle back to the beach did she feel the prickle on her ankles once more. The change was faster this time. Once again, she felt as though someone were slashing her legs and feet with knives and rocks. She welcomed the pain, however, for after two excruciating minutes, Arianna tried to kick both legs only to find that her fins were once more propelling her through the water.

Jubilant, she sliced through the water at top speed. She would skip the tower and go to her parents' room. Though she wouldn't be able to remain there long, she would at least be able to assure her mother that she was safe.

7

CHARMS ARE FLEETING

"*A*rianna!" Giana appeared as soon as Arianna had just begun to make out the shape of the underwater cliff her tower was cut into. Before she could react, her mother's arms were wrapped tightly around her, the algae lantern in her hand pressing hard into Arianna's back. But Arianna hugged her mother just as tightly. An hour before, she hadn't been sure whether she would get a hug again, ever.

So it was surprising when Giana pulled away. In the yellow light of the lantern's glow, Giana's face was pinched and drawn, and her eyes had the darkest circles beneath them Arianna had ever seen. "I've found her!" she called over her shoulder. Then she glared at Arianna. "Where were you?"

Without a word, Renata appeared behind Giana and handed Arianna her pressing stone, a waxy leaf, and her knife. Arianna threw her aunt a look of thanks before writing her answer. Her mother seemed to forget from time to time that she had no voice. This made Arianna's explanations, which somehow always seemed to be complicated, rather difficult.

I saw the charms fail, so I saved two of the humans.

She considered telling them about her legs but decided it was too complex for a moment like this. She herself would need time, she was sure, before she was able to make sense of it.

"You weren't supposed to be near the surface at all! Today of all days, why couldn't you just *listen?*" Giana's voice was nearly shrill, but Arianna couldn't blame her. Not just a few days after losing her son.

Just then, Arianna remembered why she'd been charging back to the city. She carefully pulled the charm from her bag and handed it to her aunt.

"What is that?" Giana asked impatiently.

I found it after the storm, Arianna wrote. *It looks just like the other charms. But there's something—*

"We'll talk about these later." Renata tucked the shell into her camicett before Arianna could finish writing.

"But what is it?" Giana held her hand out.

Renata looked for a moment as though she wouldn't answer. But finally, she let out a little huff and handed it to Giana. "I realized an hour ago that someone tampered with these after I finished making them. I just wish I knew who."

But what happened to all the people? Arianna wrote. *And why was the storm so bad?*

Before they could discuss it more, an urgent song came from below.

"We'll be there," Giana called over her shoulder. She turned back to Renata and Arianna. "It appears the charms will have to wait. But we *will* be discussing this again, and in depth." She gave Renata a scathing look before taking Arianna's hand.

Arianna shivered as the three women swam down to the mansion's main theater. Reluctantly, she let go of her mother's hand to take her usual spot on the open roof. To her relief, however, her mother and aunt sat on each side of her as well. Usually, the sun's strength kept most of her family from joining her on the open roof's high ledge. But it was night now, and the fear that roiled in her stomach made her crave company more than usual. Much of that fear, she realized, hadn't been present until she'd seen her mother's accusatory glances at her aunt. Maybe they would find out now if her father knew something that would make more sense of it all.

Amadeo took the stage. With sad, tired eyes he stared up at the many levels of seats that arched around him. The crowd quieted as Amadeo cleared his throat, and Arianna hoped her father would be quick. She couldn't stay at such a depth for more than a few minutes. But this night, she was determined to stay for her father's whole speech even if it knocked her unconscious.

"Today was a day of confusion and fear," Amadeo began.

That was an understatement.

"What should have been a day of sacred mourning for our twelve souls lost to the pirates . . ." Amadeo's voice broke, ". . . became one of only more tragedy and heartache. And unfortunately," he turned his eyes up to where Giana, Arianna, and Renata were sitting, "now there is mourning multiplied, and it appears that we might be mourning for quite some time."

Arianna leaned forward and frowned, trying to ignore the press of the ocean on her shoulders.

Her father drew in a deep breath. "It seems that many were injured in the storm today, and twenty-three humans have died, including the Sun Crown's granddaughter, Princess Maura, and her husband." He sighed. "The Sun Crown's son-in-law, Queen Drina's husband, is dead as well. We were able to save some, but . . . others are still missing."

Arianna closed her eyes. Little Claire had survived only to lose both parents. Was this Arianna's fault? Could she have saved them, too?

"The Sun Crown also does not believe that this storm was an act of the Maker," Amadeo continued, "despite my insistence. He has declared this storm our response to the attack of the pirates, a petty attempt to heal our injuries."

The death of the Sea Crown's grandson . . . her brother . . . hardly counted as a mere injury. Arianna suddenly had the urge to slap the Sun Crown for his callousness. Until she remembered that he, too, was grieving.

"So what is it that he has said?" one of her father's advisers called out impatiently from the front row.

"He's convinced that we used Sorthileige to conjure the storm on purpose."

Whispers broke out among the crowd.

"He also believes that we purposely spooked the dolphins so they would flee, and we would have an excuse to ignore the humans as they drowned." Amadeo's tail flicked as he paused, his eyes scanning the crowd. Finally, they rested upon Giana once again.

"The Sun Crown has declared war."

In that moment, Arianna knew that despite her aunt's insistence and her brother's unwavering faith, there was no power in the world or beyond that could convince her that the Maker was good.

8

REMAIN

*A*rianna tried to keep her eyes only on the merpeople as they bustled around loading their bags and their children onto the great line of sleighs that had been prepared for them. The mood was almost hopeful, better than she'd seen in years, and the scene brought a smile to her lips. Smiling at her people was far easier than looking at the ruins that had once been her beautiful city of coral and pearl.

She tried not to look at the smashed roofs and broken streets, or the pearl and kelp farms that were overflowing with untended crops. She shut out the crying and songs of sorrow sung constantly by those who were mourning the loss of sons and daughters and fathers and mothers and sisters and brothers and lovers. Instead, she pretended to hum her own song of hope, the one she would have sung if she could have.

"These clouds are a gift of the Maker, Ari!" Giana chimed as she joined Arianna on her tower's edge. "This is going to be a wonderful day!"

Arianna gave her mother a placating smile, but secretly she ignored her mother's praise to the Maker who had sat back and watched five years of war ravage her people.

"Oh, don't look so gloomy!" Giana laughed, brown eyes shining and her curls bobbing gently in the current as she also looked down at the train of sleighs below them. "You'll love the capital city! Gemmaqua has towers all over, and they're just as tall or taller than yours! Your grandfather keeps them there for guards trained to watch the surface. You might even find some new friends!"

Arianna couldn't help silently chuckling at that. She had never made friends before, hidden up in the tower she shared with Renata, but her mother's enthusiasm was contagious. It was hard not to smile back.

"Are you all packed?"

Arianna nodded back at her bag.

"It's small."

Arianna just shrugged. She didn't have many clothes. No merperson did. And there was little in her tower that she wouldn't be able to find again in the capital if it was as wealthy as her relatives all claimed. A pearl-handled hair brush, her few camicetts, a doll from when she was a child, a necklace from Renata, and a pretty shell that Rinaldo had given her the year before he died. Her collection of human items—a mirror and other little baubles—was unnecessary, though. Besides, with the Sea Crown as her grandfather, there was little she could really lack once she arrived.

Most of them lost everything, she wrote. *I shouldn't be the one to weigh the dolphins down. Our people deserve a new start as soon as they can get it.*

Giana pulled Arianna in for an embrace. "You're a good girl, Ari. I—" She stopped as the last sleigh in the line pulled away from the others and began to climb up toward them. "Here's ours!" Arianna looked at her mother in surprise, but Giana only laughed. "At least while it's cloudy. And see the driver? Your father had a Grower create a full body covering for him so he may keep you higher while we go."

Arianna looked back down at the driver to examine such a suit more closely, but for some reason, he'd pulled the dolphins to a stop halfway up.

"Is something wrong?" Giana called down. Without waiting for his reply, she left their ledge and went to meet him. Arianna felt her heart fall, however, when they began to argue. She couldn't hear what they said, but the way he continued to wave his arm up at the surface gave her a bad feeling. She left the ledge as well and floated behind her mother who was glowering at the burly driver.

"Look, Your Highness, I need to know exactly how far she can descend," he was saying.

"And spend any length of time?" Giana looked at Arianna. "Go show him the depth you would be comfortable traveling at."

Her heart pounding fast, Arianna swam down a few more fathoms before looking back up at the sleigh.

But the driver shook his head and scratched his dark beard. "Still too high."

"What do you mean it's too high? You're here now!" Giana gestured at his sleigh.

"Her tower is built into the rocks, Your Highness. We won't be. Any human sailing above would see her for sure."

"You can't be serious! What are you suggesting? That I leave my daughter here by herself for the humans to find?" Giana straightened and pulled her shoulders back into her most regal posture. "Are you refusing to carry the Sea Crown's granddaughter?"

"I am trying to convince you of the danger it would pose to us all. Including Princess Lalia. Do you want her baby to come during a chase with pirates?"

Giana's face went white.

"Your husband may only be an ambassador," the driver rubbed his temples, "but as you said, she is the granddaughter of the Sea Crown. That would fetch a hefty ransom for anyone, voice or no voice. Driving the dolphins so close to the surface would attract the attention of anyone who would look. It would put our entire party in danger."

Arianna wanted to collapse. She wanted to shout and throw things. If the Maker had been so intent on keeping her silent and weak, why hadn't he just let her die? It would have saved their entire city trouble and heartache. But one look at the broken expression on her mother's face and the way her shoulders drooped rid Arianna of all temptations to throw such a childish tantrum. Instead, she drew in a deep breath and took her hand.

I'll stay, she motioned. *You go.*

"Absolutely not. I am not leaving you here alone!"

"What's the delay?" Amadeo called out as he swam toward them. "General Maro says we should be leaving any time."

Arianna watched her father's face closely as the driver explained the situation. It went from its usual shade of bone white to almost gray. After the driver had finished, a long moment passed before anyone spoke.

"So . . ." He stopped. "I . . . I mean, Ari . . ." He looked at Arianna, his graying hair suddenly looking much whiter than it had before.

In that moment, Arianna realized just how much the war had aged her father. She had never seen him at such a loss for words.

"I will stay with her."

Everyone turned to see Renata swimming toward them. Arianna felt a pang of guilt. Her aunt had been so excited about the journey. Her dark hair was pulled up into an ornate hairnet sprinkled with gems and gold, and she wore her nicest camicett. Arianna shook her head, but Renata put her finger to Arianna's lips. "I'm afraid I had wondered how this journey would work, but I had hoped. Still, it will be little different than it ever was before. And Ari and I have always had good fun together, haven't we?"

"May I speak with you? Alone." Giana was not smiling at all as she grabbed her husband's arm and dragged him back up to the tower. Renata and the driver swam a respectful distance away, but Arianna stayed put.

"Having her raise my daughter has been hard enough!" Giana whispered. "But leaving them alone together?"

"Do you think I *want* to leave Ari?" Arianna's father retorted. "But what else do you propose we do? She will be in more danger if she comes with us than if she stays."

"I'm not entirely convinced of that. The war may be over, but pirates aren't attacking Gemmaqua the way they attack us here. And I know you don't want to listen to me, but on the day of the humans' drowning—"

"I told you we're through with this conversation."

Arianna had never heard her father use that tone with her mother, and it heightened her anxiety even more.

"The charms were tampered with. My sister had nothing to do with that," he said firmly.

"Can you really be so blind? After all the nonsense that happened after Angelo died? You really think she couldn't do something like that *again?*"

"Not another word, Giana."

There was a long pause, and Arianna had nearly made up her mind to swim up to the tower when Amadeo said quietly, "I'm sorry. As much as you may not believe me, I miss her, too." Another pause. "Renata loves her. I've never seen Renata love anyone the way she does Ari, except for maybe Angelo. She would protect her with her life. You know that."

Arianna's heart nearly broke in two when Giana began to sob.

"Let's try . . . just once more!" Giana pleaded. "The journey will take less than a week. Let her try!"

Arianna didn't even pretend she hadn't been eavesdropping as her parents swam down from the tower.

"Simone," Amadeo said in a tired voice, "how deep would she need to be in order to travel safely?"

The merman sang a single note to his charge, and the dolphin arced the sleigh down just below the level of the theater's roof.

"What do you think, Ari?"

"She's been practicing," Renata said as she watched the sleigh come to a stop. "Perhaps . . ." She looked at Arianna. "Try, love. See what you can do."

Arianna took a steadying lungful of water before making the descent. Seating herself in the sleigh's back, she closed her eyes and breathed in and out as slowly as she could, a technique she'd been practicing with Renata for remaining deep. Breathe, she told herself. Be calm. She would sleep if she must.

For several long minutes, Arianna sat still and no one said a word. She could feel the dolphin moving about a little as if to protest their stillness, but she did not allow that to deter her. She would go with her family, she thought to distract herself, another technique she'd learned over the last few years. She would go to the capital and meet friends. Perhaps she would find someone—

Her heart hitched, and the palpitation was enough to ruin her forced calm. Immediately, the ocean pressed her against the sleigh's floor. She slipped down silently as the weight of the waves and tides threatened to crush her lungs and ensure she stayed silent forever.

Just as she was about to lose consciousness, she felt her father's strong arms lift her and tuck her tightly against his chest as he darted higher. Her mother's soothing healing song soon began to lift the effects of the ocean's weight. But it could not lift her spirits.

Arianna didn't know how long her family floated in the same place. All she knew was that her father's strong arms encircled her as he sang his deepest song of mourning. Her mother and aunt joined in as well with their wailing harmonies.

"She will learn!" Renata finally said, pulling back and breaking off the song. "She is eighteen years now and stronger than ever!" She gave a strained laugh. "She and I will practice until she can safely make the swim. Then we will go to Gemmaqua together!" Her cheeks were red, and though there were no tears to roll down her face underwater, Arianna knew that her aunt was crying. "The Protectors taught me to tolerate the sun enough to do my job. She will learn how to accept the ocean enough to make the swim." Renata's smile was fierce. "I promise you, Ari! You'll be with your family once again, if it's the last thing I do."

~

Arianna waited until her aunt was sleeping heavily in the next room over. Their tower was even more silent than usual without the ever-echoing Protector songs in the distance.

This frightened Arianna more than she wanted to admit. They were truly alone now. After waving goodbye to her family that afternoon with the biggest smile she could muster, it occurred to her that she and her aunt were all that was left of the sea remnant that had fought the Sun Crown. And lost. Now there was only one voice left to protect them both, and Arianna was leaving that voice behind her tonight. She pulled on her black camicett and slipped out the window.

The Sun Crown hadn't made an attack for a fortnight. According to her father, Queen Drina and Prince Michael had agreed to end the war completely after the old Sun Crown's death. But did they know the merpeople were leaving the coastal city? Or would they continue to harass Arianna and her aunt until their deaths?

Despite her reservations, Arianna knew she needed to go. She wouldn't go far, she promised herself, and it would only be for a few minutes. But the longer she stayed in her room, the more she felt the tower walls closing in on her. She hadn't had a breath of fresh air since the war had begun, and her need for it was sudden and desperate. It was a foolish notion, but she was convinced that she could leave her pain at the bottom of the ocean if she went high enough fast enough. If she could just breathe.

Arianna had forgotten what winter felt like above the surface, and when she finally broke the waves and inhaled hard and fast, the frigid air felt like it would cut her lungs. But it was a beautiful pain, one she welcomed again and again as she drank deeply of the air.

She had purposefully surfaced far from the Sun Palace. Her father's men had often spoken of palace guards watching for merpeople activity day and night. When she happened to turn in the direction of the palace, however, there were no guards that she could see. There were no warships outside of the harbor. Only one light shone out on the palace terrace. Arianna's curiosity got the best of her, and she allowed herself to swim a few fathoms closer. She didn't dare visit the terrace itself. But she needed to see.

A young man stood alone at the balcony overlooking the waves. She wondered what he was looking at. There were no stars tonight, and the waves must have been nearly invisible to his human eyes. When she drew a little nearer, however, she realized with a start that she was looking at the prince.

He was nearly unrecognizable. He'd grown at least a foot taller since she'd seen him five years before, and his body no longer looked as though he were caught between boy and man. Even his dark contour looked intimidating, for his shoulders had widened noticeably, and his legs were much thicker as well.

What was he doing outside by himself? There were no nieces about, and the wind must be chafing his cheeks and hands uncomfortably. And yet he simply stood there, one foot up on the balcony and his elbow resting on his knee. Her curiosity was rewarded, however, when he took a deep breath and began to sing.

The saddest song Arianna had ever heard floated out to her on the breeze. It wasn't anything like a merperson's voice. This voice was slightly off-key and rather weak. But the way it rose and fell was heartbreakingly honest, and Arianna was suddenly filled with the conviction that she was not alone in her mourning. And though she would not for the world have wished sorrow on him, there was a peace she couldn't deny in knowing that one soul, at least, shared her pain tonight. For one small moment in time, she was not alone.

9

WORTHY OF A PRINCE'S GAZE

"*D*id you get these from the kelp farm?" Renata raised her perfectly shaped eyebrows at Arianna, who nodded happily in return. "Well then," her aunt smiled as she began to stretch the sheets of kelp out on the table, "I am more than impressed. See how far you've come in only two months?"

How long do you think until I'm ready to go? Arianna wrote.

"That I can't say for sure, unfortunately. It's a four-day journey." She touched Arianna's cheek. "But don't lose heart. Your strength is coming. You can't demand your body to change faster than it is able. Now, help me cut these."

Arianna smiled and took the corners of the kelp tightly in her hands. Her aunt was right, of course. Even she had surprised herself with her visit to the kelp farm that afternoon.

The days immediately following her people's departure had been difficult. Every time she stopped and listened to the silence of the ocean, a hole had seemed to open in her heart. Of course, Renata always kept up her songs of protection against the creatures that might come too close to the tower, but the ocean was altogether too silent.

Still, in the two months that had passed, Arianna had found a contentment that she'd never known before. Without the servants to prepare their food or mend their clothes or repair the tower, Arianna and Renata were kept busy. Every moment that wasn't spent practicing in the lower depths was used to keep their little life afloat. And that suited Arianna just fine. She didn't mind hard work. Though Renata was the one to sing the songs of growing, healing, nurturing, and protection, there was plenty to help with that did not require a voice. It made Arianna feel useful, something she was less than accustomed to.

When she stretched and cut the kelp with her aunt or used her little knife to harvest clams, she felt just as useful as any merperson. And she dared to wonder if others might view her that way, too, when they arrived at the capital and her family could see what she had become.

How did you and Angelo meet? Arianna wrote when they sat down later to eat their evening meal.

Renata paused, her food halfway to her mouth. She stayed frozen for a long moment before putting the shell back in her bowl and giving Arianna a far-off look. Arianna tried to calm her suddenly racing pulse. Her question touched territory few were brave enough to broach with Renata. Even now, there was pain in her aunt's lovely eyes, and Arianna nearly felt guilty until she saw the warmth there as well.

"He was a Grower," she finally said in a soft voice. Then she smiled at the kelp on the table. "As I was a Protector, I often patrolled the border between our kingdom and the southern merpeople's. I lived in the capitol back then, of course, and my job was to take note of all who crossed between regions to speak with my father. Angelo worked in the kelp fields near my post, so we saw one another often."

She gave a small chuckle. "The job was often tedious, despite its importance, and he loved to tease. Every day I would take my post only to be greeted by songs poking fun at my koros. I was annoyed at first, as I took my duty seriously, but it wasn't long before I was unable to resist sending back a few lines of foolishness myself."

Did Grandfather mind that he wasn't a royal or noble?

Renata shook her head. "Humans care about such matches much more than merpeople. As only one of his children or grandchildren would inherit the Sea Crown, and that would be decided through the triton's contest, we were allowed to do as we pleased. Your parents are a rare couple, actually, both coming from royalty or nobility. Anyhow, I don't know how it really happened, but after months of making fun of one another, we both came to the sudden realization that we didn't want to tease anyone else for the rest of our days."

Arianna put down her food and leaned forward. How many times had she imagined herself conversing and laughing with a young man? What she wouldn't give to have someone to tease. Or have the voice to tease.

"He proposed at sunrise," Renata whispered. Then she let out a strangled laugh. "He wrote the proposal into a song that made fun of the staff I carried. I didn't even realize he'd asked me to marry him until I had thrown that staff at him for his impertinence."

Arianna gave her aunt a wistful smile. How difficult it must be to not know what would have been. And yet, to have had someone love her that much for even a short time must have been bliss.

"Ari," her aunt said, suddenly shifting uncomfortably. "There's something I've been meaning to talk to you about."

Arianna's appetite disappeared. With a small sigh, she took up a camicett that needed mending and focused hard on the little stitches the sewing required. Sewing wasn't her favorite task, but the work seemed immediately more alluring than whatever topic her aunt was now approaching.

"I know you're excited about our move to the capital, as am I. But I couldn't bear it if you got your hopes up and . . ." She sighed, and Arianna refused to look up. "Most mermen are . . . They are not like your brother. I don't know if your mother ever told you, but our koroses are more than our work songs. They're our soulsongs as well. I don't know how true it is, but many merpeople believe each soulsong is half of an unfinished harmony. We have the four koroses, but each soulsong is unique in its own way. Many merpeople find their spouses through groupsings, where people gather and sing their soulsongs to find other songs that harmonize. And . . ." She stopped and sighed.

Arianna's hands shook as she squeezed the whalebone needle.

"Ari?"

Arianna stared down at her sewing. She refused to let Renata see her cry.

"Ari, say something."

Arianna waited until her hands were controlled enough to grasp her pressing knife. In large, blocky words she wrote,

What else?

"What else, what?"

You were going to say that they were looking for something else as well. What else do they want?

"Actually," Renata paused before swimming over to the tower's southern window. Now Arianna got the feeling she wasn't the only one avoiding eye contact. "I want you to know that you are beautiful!" Renata said in a sudden rush. "But I'm afraid . . . Well, you just look so much like a human! And that's not a bad thing! The Maker simply saw fit to make you different—"

Arianna was up out of her clam chair in a second and then inside her room just as fast, slamming the door shut so hard it banged loudly even in the water. She could hear her aunt pleading with her to open the door, begging forgiveness and carrying on about how she must have spoken too hastily, that some merman would surely see Arianna for who she was, but Arianna ignored her. She threw herself down on her sponge bed and folded her arms tightly over her eyes.

So many times she had come close to telling her aunt about her temporary legs, and how she had used them to save the prince. But after war had been declared, she'd dared no such thing. The last thing her family had needed was another source of conflict between them and their people.

And now, when it was just Arianna and her aunt in the only place she'd known as home, she still couldn't share her secret. Such a story would make her into even more of a monstrosity. Her aunt saw in her exactly what everyone else did, apparently. A half-breed that the Maker seemed to enjoy punishing, though what he was punishing her for she could not imagine. The sins of her people, perhaps? Or maybe he had created a half-human, half-mermaid in order to take out his vengeance upon both peoples for their pride and stupidity. It didn't matter, though. All Arianna knew was that it seemed she wasn't worthy enough for either to look upon.

Crying underwater wasn't as comforting as it was at the surface. There were no tears to roll down her cheeks. But it did tire her to cry below as it did above, and it wasn't long before Renata stopped calling out her name and Arianna was ready to fall into the arms of sleep.

Just as she was about to slip into unconsciousness, however, she recalled hazel eyes like the sun as they had gazed back at her without reservation. Even in the storm, Prince Michael must have seen that she was not the typical mermaid beauty who was said to allure sailors with a single glance. He had stared at her too hard to miss her yellow-white hair and pale blue eyes, or the way her skin was just a shade darker than her people's, thanks to the sun she had spent so many hours beneath.

And yet, for one long moment, she had been worthy of a prince's gaze.

Rebellion pushed her eyes open as she decided to prove her aunt wrong. Tomorrow she was going to see him. And she might even let him see her.

10

IN MY BONES

*a*rianna was awake before the sun the next morning. Her anger from the night before had filled her with a resolve to visit the Sun Palace once again. She needed to think. But first, she needed more waxy leaves, and the leaves were kept in a storehouse deeper than Arianna's usual depth. Renata was usually the one to fetch items kept so deep. Arianna was determined to spend the day alone, however, so she was left with no other option but getting them herself.

As she was ready to swim out the window, however, her aunt's muffled voice came through the door. "I know you're angry with me . . ."

Her aunt's penitent tone did nothing to sway Arianna from her plans. She simply removed her conch necklace and placed it on her bed. The last thing she wanted to do was take Renata's voice with her.

" . . . but please be careful. My songs have picked up more than one large creature moving near the western outskirts, most likely from the storm we had two nights ago."

Arianna adjusted her camicett in the mirror. It was probably just another small whale or sea cow, like the last creatures Renata had felt, Arianna wanted to reply. She wasn't in the mood to listen to warning tales.

"They're fast," Renata urged through the door.

But Arianna was gone before her aunt could say another word. Still, as angry as she was with her aunt, Renata's warning put Arianna on edge as she swam over the ruins of her once-beautiful city. The mansion that overlooked the hundreds of homes on the seafloor had been a rainbow of coral colors, shining in even the dim waters with its pearl finishes, sparkling with the gems set on balconies and scattered on the rooftops.

Where the Nurturers had once kept the coral colors aligned, however, and the Healers had fixed the occasional hole or injury to its walls, war and neglect had now taken their toll. Gaping holes and complete collapse had befallen some of the palace's grandest walls and rooflines. In other areas, the coral had far exceeded its original limits and was growing out of control, like tumors on the side of the palace walls. And so it was for the rest of the houses below as well. The boulders dropped by the Sun Crown's navy had made sure of that.

It was tempting to use her newfound ability to dive deeper to revisit the places her parents and siblings spent their days in. Arianna might even find a few useful items here and there for herself and her aunt. But she knew better than that. The mansion and the houses were too closed off. Without the guards weaving their songs of protection around the Deeps to hold the monsters in, there could be any number of vile creatures waiting for her in the buildings' nooks and crannies. Arianna's anger at her aunt pushed her forward, but with Renata's warning still ringing in her ears, Arianna pushed down her rage just enough to move on to her original destination.

The waxy leaves were in a storehouse at the western end of the desolate city. Arianna shivered a bit as the buildings behind the mansion began to thin out. The water grew colder as she moved deeper, and the ocean was suddenly too open. She felt exposed to unseen eyes as she swam down toward the large storehouse.

In order to distract herself from imagining all the horrible beasts that might be lurking in the shadows below, Arianna imagined what it would be like to picnic with the prince. The idea surprised her somewhat. With her impending journey to Gemmaqua, Arianna had done all she could to put Prince Michael out of her head. After her last glimpse of him out on the terrace, she had kept herself below the waves. But her revelation the night before seemed to have awakened a new hunger in her. She had always been lonely. But this kind of yearning was new, and strong.

What would it feel like to have a man choose her? To walk on the beach holding hands? To talk and laugh? To know she was his choice above all other women?

The weight of the sea threatened to crush Arianna as she moved even deeper, but the pressure was not the reason that she stopped seven fathoms from her destination. A song floated in on the water. It was her aunt's song. But this time it was louder and fiercer than ever.

Arianna whipped around and bolted back as fast as her fins would push her. The song lasted only seconds. The return trip, however, took an agonizing length of time. More than ever, Arianna cursed her weak fins as she strained until her skin grew hot and she gasped for the air that suddenly seemed too hard to pull from the water.

Though she knew it couldn't be done, Arianna tried to call her aunt's name. All thoughts of the creatures lurking below disappeared as she fled back to her tower. The rock wall into which their little home was carved grew nearer at a painfully slow pace, but Arianna slowed abruptly when she finally came close.

Something was definitely inside. She could hear its low grunts as it bumped into the furniture. Only then did it occur to her that she had nothing with which to fight. Without even a basic protection koros, all she wore at her side was the little knife she used to cut kelp. Barely longer than her hand, it wasn't even that sharp. And yet, Arianna took a shaking breath and pulled it from her belt.

Sneaking in through her bedroom window, Arianna was thankful that her door was open just a crack. Her aunt must have come in after she'd left, probably to wait for her return. Arianna floated just inches above the stone floor as she peeked through the crack. It was still dark enough that she had to squint to make out even the low table her aunt used for cutting.

A strange scent filled the air, a mixture of sulfur and . . . Was that blood?

The door banged open, hitting Arianna in the face. Her own nose began to bleed, but there wasn't time to staunch it because she was staring into the face of a long creature with salmon-pink frilled gills and diagonal rows of bent, pointed teeth. Its serpentine head seemed to weigh more than the rest of its body. Her heart skipped a beat when she finally met its inky eyes, and she could think only of the merman she'd witnessed from the Deeps. She and the monster stared a moment longer before the frill shark darted forward, its teeth missing her shoulder by inches.

Arianna threw herself through the open door and tried to close it with her fins. As the shark rammed against it again and again, snapping with its teeth as it did, Arianna looked around desperately for her aunt. Their two clamshell chairs were overturned, as was the table. Several of their eating dishes had fallen to the floor. Containers of kelp had spilled everywhere.

The shark made a particularly hard bump against the door that snapped Arianna's attention back to her own fight. With one final push she managed to shut the door, and she was out the window in no time. The shark wasn't long, however, in escaping through Arianna's bedroom window, swimming fast in pursuit.

She went in the only direction she knew how to go, and that was up. Hoping desperately that the sun had risen enough to confine the shark to the lower regions, Arianna continued her ascent. The months below the surface, however, had accustomed her to the medium depths, making her felt a bit lightheaded as she swam. The beast continued behind her. She could hear it crashing through the shallow seaweeds as she tried losing it in the fauna. Higher! She pushed herself. Higher!

Unfortunately, the seabed was growing shallow much faster than she had expected, and the monster was still following her. Only a few more fathoms and she would be dragging along the sand.

Legs! she cried silently to the Maker. *I need legs!* If there were any goodness in him, she reasoned, surely she would see it now. Even if there weren't, and she died, at least he wouldn't get to toy with her life anymore. Surely he would want to get more misery out of her by letting her live.

A sickening crunch sounded behind her. The pain didn't hit, however, until she glanced back to see the serpentine head hanging off her tail. Arianna tried shaking it off so hard that she nearly hit her own head on a rock. Gritting her teeth against the pain, she grabbed a smaller rock and began to beat the shark upon the head. But the shark still hung on. In one last effort to save herself, Arianna gathered all of her remaining strength and raised her knife above the shark's eye nearest her.

Whether the shark knew what she planned to do or simply decided she wasn't worth the struggle, it finally let go, its head raised and its tail swishing back and forth as it slithered back toward the deeper seas.

A new pain racked Arianna's body. This pain, however, was familiar, and she looked down to find not a bleeding fin, but a bleeding ankle.

Crawling far enough on to the sand that the brutal waves wouldn't continually assault her injury was the hardest thing Arianna had ever done. Before she could rest, however, a voice in her head that sounded much like her aunt's told her to look down at herself.

Unfortunately for Arianna, the camicett she had chosen to wear that day was not as long as the mourning garb she'd donned five years before. And though Arianna knew little of human culture or customs, she did know that human females never walked about without clothing their bottom halves. The best that she could do, however, was to pull a pile of seaweed on top of her spent, bleeding body. Then the world began to tilt as she leaned back and tried to slow her breathing. But little assuaged her pain, nor was she able to quiet the truth that for the first time in her life, she was really, truly alone.

UNTIMELY SURPRISES

"*S*o let me get this straight," Michael said, rubbing his face. "Our other creditors are willing to extend the loans, but the Tumenians are not?"

"He says if we cannot repay him by the summer solstice, he will be coming to collect his due," Master Russo said, his graying curls shaking slightly. He was speaking to Michael, but his eyes were trained on Lucas.

"As if we would allow him to waltz in and take the kingdom without question or objection," Lucas muttered, tapping the hilt of his sword with his forefinger.

"If we are so desperate by solstice, that is exactly what we will do," Michael said. Lucas and Master Russo turned to look at him incredulously, but Michael shrugged and stood. "Grandfather made the deal. Do I have any choice left other than to honor his word?"

Lucas blanched. "You cannot seriously suggest we just hand Maricanta over to him on a platter! You have not seen Tumen, brother, but I have traveled enough to know more than I wish to about that country. You have no idea what kind of darkness—"

"I know exactly what kind of evil they harbor!" Michael snapped. Then he bent over, leaning one hand on his desk and

ing the other through his hair. "Look," he said in a calmer tone,
"test the blasted contract more than anyone else in the kingdom. You don't think I loathe the idea of handing the Sun Crown
over to the vilest despot in the western kingdoms? But I cannot
change the law. No allies would come to our aid if we fought. We
have no money and few weapons. Besides," he let out a deep breath,
"we made a deal. And don't give me that look, Lucas. Your men are
well trained, but they cannot defeat the Tumenian forces alone.
There are too few of us, and you know that."

"If we are able to keep them from entering the isthmus, surely
our navy could hold them off in the bay," Lucas said as he stalked
back from the window he'd been staring out. "They're a landlocked
people. Their navy can't be finer than ours."

"I'm sure it's not. I am also sure they have more than enough
funds to hire a mercenary navy twice the size of ours."

"King Everard would come to our aid!" Master Russo's eyes
brightened. "He has a good heart."

"But he is also a just king, and one I have asked far too many
times for an extension on our loans. No, I am afraid we will need to
pull ourselves from this hole. Without," Michael made eye contact
with his younger brother, who was still fiddling with his sword,
"breaking our word or plunging us into a war we can't fight."

"If only we could forge some new trade agreements with—"
Master Russo began, but Michael interrupted him.

"And trade with what?" Michael pinched the bridge of his nose.
"Without the merpeople, we have no pearls, sponges, kelp, or even
shells to keep the merchants interested. And we can barely produce
enough food to feed ourselves, let alone have a surplus to trade."

Lucas began to protest, but a flash of red at the window caught
Michael's eye. He suppressed a smile as his eldest niece motioned
excitedly for him to follow her.

"I'm afraid something has just come up that needs immediate
attention." He pushed his chair beneath the desk.

Lucas and the steward looked at one another and then at Michael as though he'd lost his mind, but Michael only grinned and leaned toward them over his large stone desk. "In the meantime, I suggest that instead of planning a war, you two discuss ways to actually pay the Tumenians back so none of this doomsday talk must come to pass."

Claire couldn't have come at a better time. Perhaps after some little adventure with the girls, Michael's tired mind would stumble upon a miracle strategy to save his people from his grandfather's foolishness. His steps echoed down the pearl floor as he headed for the garden door, and it occurred to him that if he didn't find a way to pay back his grandfather's loans, the Sun Palace with its smooth pearlescent floors, shell mosaic walls, and glass ceilings would be the boasted bounty of the most despised king in the western realm.

Still, he was strangely buoyant as he stepped out of the palace and into the garden. He fully expected two shiny sets of curls to come bouncing toward him. But instead, there was only one.

"Where is your sister?" he asked as he looked around the garden.

"She's waiting with the surprise."

"What surprise?"

"The one I need you to see." Claire grasped his hand and began to drag him behind her, but Michael stopped the girl and turned her to face him.

"Hold on. You know I'm very glad to see you, but you're only supposed to interrupt me if there is something urgent going on that cannot wait. Is this one of those instances?" He raised an eyebrow. Despite his personal relief at leaving the horrid meeting with his brother and steward, Michael did his best to appear at least decently consistent with his nieces.

Claire nodded solemnly, her eyes wide.

"Well, can you tell me what it is then?"

"I think," she paused, suddenly sounding much older than her nine years, "that it might be best if you simply see. It is difficult to explain."

Michael chuckled and shook his head. "Fine then. Lead the way."

What the two girls were up to, Michael had no idea. They had been particularly adventurous since their nurse had been let go two days before, a point he still had not had the courage to inform his mother about. The girls had climbed trees, buried themselves in the sand, and tried on all of their grandmother's clothes . . . an act that had nearly sent their even-tempered housekeeper into fits. As Claire led him from the garden into the trees, however, Michael felt an uneasiness tugging at him. He suddenly wished he'd brought his knife along. Lucas was always scolding him about forgetting it.

"I specifically told you two to stay in the garden," he said, nearly smacking his face on a branch as she hurried him along. "What in the blazes were you doing out here?"

"Lucy saw something in the water," Claire replied, not slowing at all.

Michael considered stopping her then and there to set her straight, but without Lucy, he would only have to give the tirade twice. Besides, his youngest niece being alone and, it seemed, quite close to the beach made him even more nervous.

"You left her alone all the way out here?" he demanded as they approached an opening in the trees.

"Not alone." Claire finally stopped and turned to look at him, her heart-shaped face innocent as she gestured to the beach. "With her."

Just at the edge of the water, a young woman sat in the sand. She wore a strange sort of tightly fitted blouse and was half covered in a pile of seaweed. Their eyes locked.

It was her. Without a doubt, this was the same girl who had stared down at him five years before, not far from where they stood.

No. It couldn't be. And yet, he knew those pale blue eyes.

His face burned crimson, however, as he took in the rest of her and whirled back around to face the forest. He hadn't looked long enough to be sure, but the young woman also appeared to be half-naked.

"What . . . ?" he tried to regain control of his thoughts. "Miss . . . are you hurt?"

When there was no response, he repeated the question, only to be met with silence again. He turned to Claire, who still stood just at his elbow, looking as if the day was as normal as ever.

"I don't think she can talk," Claire said. "Has she said anything, Lucy?"

"No," Lucy piped cheerfully.

"See?" Claire looked back at Michael expectantly.

"Then . . . can you see if she is hurt?"

"It looks like her ankle is bleeding."

Of course it was. Wait. She had an ankle? But she was a mermaid. How did she have legs now? Though the memory of her face was as clear as any painting, his recollection of the rest of her was less so. He thought he somehow remembered her with fins. But now she had ankles? What was she?

"If she has legs, then ask her . . . then ask her if she thinks she can walk."

Claire laughed. "She can hear us just fine." She paused. "She's nodding her head. But I don't think she looks very good, Uncle. I think you'd better help her."

How on earth do I handle this? Michael looked desperately at the skies. *I cannot carry a woman who has no clothes, nor can I leave her here alone to bleed. Help me,* he prayed.

After a moment of thinking, he came up with an idea. Michael unbuttoned his shirt and handed it to Claire. "Have her put this on. It's long enough that it should . . . cover things. You're a tall girl. Do you think you can help her walk?"

"I know I can," was Claire's impertinent response before she bounded away. "I'm almost as tall as your shoulder." That was an overstatement, but Michael wasn't about to argue with the nine-year-old.

He breathed a sigh of relief when Claire called from behind that they were ready. Lucy joined him and took his hand for the walk back to the palace. The walk was mostly silent. Michael had planned to use the walk to give the girls a good stern lecture about obedience and staying put, but the oddity of the day overwhelmed him. An hour before, he had been trying to think of a way to save his kingdom from an evil king intent on taking his future throne. Now he was leading his nieces and an injured, naked woman back through the forest toward his home. It would be a miracle if he could simply make it through the rest of the day without shattering what little was left of his reputation. Leading a half-naked woman out of the bushes while she wore his shirt would certainly lead to more than a little gossip, even among the few servants they still kept.

The going was slow, and Claire complained that the woman was taking too long and that she was growing tired, too.

"We're almost there," he called back several times before she told him to stop making false promises. He stopped walking and leaned against a tree to think.

"All right, here's what we'll do," he said as he scrunched his eyes closed. "The garden is just over that hill. I'll watch Lucy as she runs to the palace and gets Bithiah. Lucy, bring Bithiah back here. Tell her that I say it's more than urgent. And to bring one of your grandmother's old gowns, one she doesn't wear anymore. Have her tell Grandmother that . . . someone needs it."

While he watched Lucy scamper over the hill, it took all of his strength not to turn and study the young woman's face. He wanted so much to see those piercing blue eyes and her oval face framed by ringlets of hair so pale it was nearly white. And though he had been young, only sixteen at the time, and rather in a stupor from his near-death experience, it had been impossible to miss the hunger in those eyes. It was a hunger he had never been able to forget, despite the years of war and loss.

"Why are we all the way out here, Miss Lucy? I thought you said they were close!"

"We're over here, Bithiah!" Michael called in a low voice.

"There is a reason I stay in the palace—" Bithiah puffed. She stopped and stared, however, when Lucy pulled her off the path and over to where Michael's little party was hiding. He could see her surprise double when she took in the girl wearing his shirt.

"I see," she finally said.

Michael could have hugged her. His mother might have fainted on the spot. He never would have heard the end of her lectures. Never mind that he was trying to help a bleeding woman.

But Bithiah said nothing about his indecency, or about the fact that the woman he was helping was a very beautiful woman at that. Instead, she shooed him away to the next hill over while she got the girl properly dressed. Michael played with his ring nervously while he waited, pulling it on and off until his finger hurt.

"Now," Bithiah said as she emerged from the trees and handed him his shirt, "if you do not mind me saying, I think it might be best if you return with Lucy. Claire and I will take her in separately so no one knows she was with you."

"Thank you," Michael said, grinning. And he meant it.

"I have one question before you go, though, Your Highness."

"Yes?" He paused, his hand already wrapped around Lucy's.

"Do you not know how she got here?"

He shook his head.

"Well, thank the Maker *someone* found her at least."

Michael didn't respond as he pulled a protesting Lucy back to the palace. Mermaid or human, right now she was simply another mouth to feed in a house that couldn't afford to feed itself.

WHAT PEOPLE DO

*A*rianna's thoughts were still hazy, but the screaming pain in her right fin woke her before she could protest. Scrunching her eyes shut, she fought to remember. Why did she have the vague notion of leaving the water? And why had the prince looked so different in her dreams? There had been nothing soft or boyish about him in her strange visions. There had also been a strange amount of detail when it came to the forest, which she had never visited before. She'd even walked, and while she'd walked, she had stepped on some sort of squishy brown blob that had smelled deceptively sweet.

Another stab of pain snapped Arianna's eyes wide open.

It wasn't a dream. Or if it was, she was still asleep. She was lying in a small stone room that overlooked the ocean. The room was scantily furnished with one spindly chair in the far corner and a little square table beside the bed. A small round window was cut into the wall above the bed she was laid out upon. Rather, the bed she was bound to. Cloth rags had been tied around her arms and her . . . ankles, securing her to the bed. So now she had legs again?

The previous day returned to Arianna in a flash. Her aunt was missing. The frill shark had caught her. Her fins had turned to legs once more, and she'd fallen asleep under a pile of seaweed.

And now she was tied to a bed.

Pushing herself up, she strained to look out the window. From the height of the window and the shadow that was cast down onto the sea below, she could only be in the Sun Palace.

The ocean looked as peaceful as it ever had. Had it looked that gentle and calming yesterday when her aunt had disappeared and the shark from the Deeps had tried to kill her? Then a shiver ran down her back. Were the humans trying to kill her, too? What did they want with her? Her foot was wrapped, but what if they simply wanted her healed in order to kill her publicly as the enemy? Her aunt had told her stories of hangings and all other sorts of human justice.

No. No, she needed to find a way out now.

Arianna began to tug at her bonds, cautiously at first, but as the ties held, her breath began to come in and out too fast. She jerked and pulled harder and harder until the cloth strips cut into her wrists and legs. As she yanked at the knots, her father's warnings of all the things the humans would do to her flooded her mind. At that moment, however, voices sounded outside the room, and three humans walked in.

Arianna froze, as did the men and the woman.

It was the older man who moved first. After a few rapid blinks at Arianna, he grabbed the skinny chair, pulled it over to her bed, and set a bag down beside him. Arianna twisted as far away from him as she could while tied to the bedposts, but he simply scooted closer still.

"It would be wise to hold still," the young man said.

For the first time, Arianna looked directly at his face, and was so surprised that she nearly stopped fighting. Her visions hadn't been dreams! Prince Michael had really been the one to find her on the beach! But how different he looked up close!

"If you don't stop fighting us," he continued, "we'll have to put you to sleep again."

Again? How many times had they put her to sleep? And what sort of dark magic did one use to do that? A little ripple of fear put some tension back into her arms, and she twisted away from the man in the chair again. He huffed and turned back to look imploringly at the woman.

Was she the one who would put Arianna to sleep?

"Your Highness," the woman said to Prince Michael. "You'll do no good with such threats! And, you." The woman turned back to Arianna.

In an instant, Arianna knew exactly who she was. Though she had never seen the head housekeeper up close, for she had only ever caught glimpses of her on the terrace, Arianna knew the authoritative voice well.

"If you do not let our healer see you, you will lose that foot. Would you like that?"

Arianna wasn't sure, as she had just acquired it.

Bithiah's voice was firm, but there was a lilt to it that Arianna liked. It was calming, almost musical. With a sigh, Arianna let herself go limp, cringing when the older man's cold hands unwrapped the bloodied bandage from her ankle.

To distract herself from the pain, Arianna glanced up at Prince Michael. He met her eyes but didn't smile.

"I'll need salt water," the old man said as he laid her foot down again and scratched at his gray mustache. "It's not as deep as it looked at first. Still," he turned back to the others, "you'll need to keep her off her feet for at least three weeks. Maybe more. I've got just enough of the Guaarote powder left to make her a salve. Mix it with aloe every day and apply it to the wound. She should be able to hobble in a few days, but it would be best to wait the whole three weeks before letting her stand." His shoulders drooped. "This is the last of the powder I have left. Take care that it is used properly."

Bithiah nodded, but the prince only frowned harder, as though the healer's lack of powder was her fault.

Perhaps it was, but Arianna certainly hadn't asked for it.

Soon enough, Bithiah had fetched a bowl of cloudy water and handed it to the healer. Arianna wondered with trepidation and exhilaration if the water might bring back her fins. Then they would have to let her go!

The only change that the water brought, however, was a renewal of the pain, and Arianna screamed silently as he dipped her foot in the bowl again and again. A cool rag was placed on her head, but nothing could take away the stabbing.

Only when she thought she would pass out did the pain begin to ebb. She finally looked down through tearstained eyes at the man, who was gently rubbing a purple and green salve on her ankle. Arianna let herself fall limply back onto the bed. The sweat on her skin suddenly made her feel cold, but she didn't care.

"I am finished for today," the man finally said, putting away the cloth he had used to apply the salve. "I will be back in a week to see her."

"How is she to get about, then?" Prince Michael asked.

Arianna stared at him. He wanted her to *walk?* Where exactly did he want her to go? Unless it was to the ocean, she was not interested in the slightest.

"*After* several weeks," the healer said, fussing with his instruments, "she should be able to use a crutch of sorts. I'm sure you can piece one together or find a suitable branch in the forest."

"Then that's what we will have to do."

"Michael!" Bithiah said, briefly forgetting his title, it seemed. "That is enough." She stood and beckoned to him. "Come with me."

Without arguing, the prince stood and followed her. The healer paused his packing and looked confused, but Bithiah promised him she would see to his payment in the entryway. Then she led the prince into the hall.

Their whispers were low. Humans probably wouldn't have been able to hear their words through the thick wooden door, but her ears were quite sensitive enough.

"She is not what you think she is," the prince said in a hard voice.

"Pardon me, but I know exactly *what* she is, Your Highness."

Bithiah knew, too? How many mermaids did they keep around the palace?

"I do not know how the girl got legs," Bithiah continued, "but it is ridiculous to expect her to use a crutch so soon."

"What am I supposed to do?" Prince Michael asked in a tired voice. "We don't have the coin for this. The price of the healer alone will cost us another week's horse feed. I don't understand why crutches are so objectionable. Surely they'll be easy to—"

"That girl will not be able to walk on crutches properly because she hardly knows how to walk! Michael, you are always saying the Maker sees and knows all. Perhaps now is the time to actually believe it. Besides," she said more softly, "Rolf fashioned a contraption for the sailors during the war, a little chair on wheels that can be pushed about. I will have him make one for her."

"I don't have the time to push her around. Nor does anyone else around here."

"Mermaid or no, confining her to that room for weeks on end is unfair."

After a long moment, the prince sighed. "Fine then. Have him make one. And . . ." he paused, "invite her to supper tonight. If she's here, she might as well eat with the rest of us."

As the servant bid the prince a good evening, Arianna laid her head back on the strange, flat pillow and frowned. How many times had she imagined him inviting her up to supper? But in her mind, he had always done it with a shy smile and an extended hand, his curly brown hair trying to fall in his eyes. Nothing like the reluctant sigh he'd just given the servant.

Nor in her dreams had he ever given her the cold stare he wore now as he walked back into the room. As the healer excused himself, the little room suddenly felt much smaller. The prince pulled the chair back a few feet and sat in it. He said nothing, only continued to study her.

Arianna swallowed. She wanted so much to study him back, to see those eyes of many colors. But she couldn't raise her eyes, for just stronger than her desire to see him up close was a very real fear of what he was thinking.

"I know who you are," he finally said.

She met his eyes then.

"Your brother told me about you," he said in a slightly softer voice.

Arianna's throat tightened.

"I also know that you saved my life on the day of the Great Drowning. And for that I will be ever grateful. But to be honest, thanks to your people, my kingdom is in shambles. The people are starving. We have no trade, and the Sun Crown is in more debt than you can fathom."

She was sure she could fathom more than he knew, but he didn't seem to notice her offense at his statement.

"As I said, I am grateful for the sacrifice you made to save myself and Claire. I know you were quite young, and what you did couldn't have been easy." He took a deep breath. "But I cannot ignore our times or situation. We have no extra resources to spare here, even at the palace. I will do my best to provide for you while you recover, but the moment you are well enough to walk, I expect you to earn your keep." Then, without another word, he stood and was gone.

Arianna gawked at the open door. Did he really expect her to stay there? At any other time in her life, Arianna would have jumped at the chance to see the Sun Palace for herself. And to get to know him. But that was before her aunt had gone missing.

And for being grateful, he was rather rude.

No sooner had he gone, however, than Bithiah walked in. Without hesitating, as Arianna was sure many humans would have done when confronted with a mermaid, she drew the chair close to Arianna's bed. She reached for the nearest tie that held Arianna's wrist to the bedpost, but paused with her fingers on the knots.

"I am sorry for these." She nodded at the knots. "But every time you would nearly awaken, you would thrash, and it was making your injury worse. I will let you loose now if you promise to be still."

Arianna held Bithiah's gaze for a long time. She knew the value of a promise, and she was convinced that Bithiah had no intention of hurting her. She would make it up to the servant somehow, she swore to herself. Even now, the lie she was about to utter made her mouth taste bitter. But she needed to find Renata. Finally, Arianna nodded.

"You do not have much use for words, do you?" Bithiah smiled a little as she began to untie Arianna's wrists.

If Arianna had all the words she wished for, she would be having a long talk with the world as a whole.

"Nothing is wrong with quiet, child. Sometimes it is more persuasive than words. There will be much talk, more than enough tonight for you and others if Prince Lucas is at supper on time." She stood and put her hands on her hips. "I will have my husband draw and bring you a bath, and I will send Noemi back to help you dress before supper."

As soon as Bithiah was far enough gone that her footsteps disappeared, Arianna ripped the blanket off her legs and began to fumble with the knots on her new ankles. Shark bite or no shark bite, Arianna needed to get back to the ocean. She ignored the annoying questions that kept sounding in her head, like the one asking whether or not her legs would return to fins, or whether the shark would be waiting in the shadows to finish her off.

She would find Renata and then they would go, Arianna decided as she pulled the binding from her left ankle. They would make the swim even if it killed her, and she would never look back at this palace again.

As soon as she even touched the tie on her right ankle, however, Arianna let out a gasp. Her ankle hadn't hurt so much after the healer had applied the salve, but touching it even a little sent bolts of pain up her leg and down into her foot. Grinding her teeth, she managed to pull out half of the knot. Before it was done, however, she was forced to lie back, panting and catching her breath. She glowered down at her new body.

Why had the Maker decided to make human bodies so frail? Her fins would have been healed up in just a few days with the proper healing songs. And why, she wondered as she studied her new legs, was she shaped differently than the last time she'd had legs? Those legs had been skinny and knobby. These legs had shape at the hips and below the knees.

So many oddities that Arianna had never even imagined. What on earth was a bath? Was it a punishment of sorts? Torture? Surely the prince didn't hate her that much, not after he had paid the healer to save her life.

Once again, she looked around desperately for a way to escape, but there seemed none to be found. Her window, though over-looking the ocean, was not close enough to it that she might jump out and land in the water. And after the failed attempt to untie her leg, she knew without a doubt that walking would be quite impossible.

A knock sounded at the door, and Arianna threw the blanket over her legs again. When no one came in, however, she realized that they were probably waiting for a signal to enter. It was another five minutes and three more rounds of knocking before the door cracked open. An older man peeked in, and Arianna did her best to give him a smile as she gestured him in. He stared for a moment, before nodding as though suddenly remembering his task. Arianna gasped as an oblong bucket large enough to fit a human, or even a mermaid, was carried in by the old man and another younger man. Once the giant bucket was in the middle of the room, the two men brought in smaller buckets of more reasonable sizes. Each bucket was filled with what appeared to be water. Again and again they came and left until the giant bucket was halfway full.

No sooner had they left than another knock came at the door. There was no wait for a response this time, however. Two little girls simply walked in as though it were the most natural thing to walk into a stranger's room. They closed the door behind them and turned to study her.

"I don't see why he wants us to stay away," the younger one finally said to the older. "She can't even walk."

"I'm Claire," the older girl said. "And this is Lucy."

Arianna could have hugged them both. At last, here were two faces that were neither angry nor afraid. Just curious.

"I am nine years old," Claire continued, smoothing her wrinkled gown delicately. "Lucy is seven."

"Noemi won't be coming to help you." Lucy grinned, her little freckled nose crinkling. "We're going to help you instead."

Arianna looked at Claire in confusion, and Claire just rolled her eyes.

"What she means to say is that Bithiah told us to tell a servant to help you, but we thought we would do a better job. And," she held up a bag, "we brought you a better dress." She made a face. "That dress you're wearing is horrid."

For the first time, Arianna looked down to see what she was wearing. Someone had dressed her in a gown, but the gown itself was misshapen and possibly the reddest color of brown that

Arianna had ever seen. It was large enough to hang off her shoulders like a bag, nothing like the slick, practical camicetts she was used to. And Arianna knew it was ridiculous, but her heart broke a little when she realized just how unlike it was to the dresses Prince Michael's admirers had worn to the ball all those years ago.

But if the girls had brought her a nicer one, she was more than willing to try it.

Arianna watched in amazement as the girls set to bustling around the room. Claire produced a tear-shaped red glass jar. She shook the bottle several times into her hand, and out fell some little pink crystals that were smaller than the girl's fingernails. With ceremonial solemnity, she dropped each crystal into the water, where it fizzled for a few moments until it disappeared completely. Lucy drew a little sponge from her bag, something Arianna was relieved to recognize.

"You need to take off your dress now," the little girl said.

Arianna stared at her. Why would she ever do such a thing in front of children?

"Oh, come now." Claire rolled her eyes. "It isn't anything we haven't seen before. We helped Bithiah bathe when she hurt her back."

Arianna just frowned. But *why* was she taking off her clothes? How she wished suddenly that she had her waxy leaves and writing utensils.

"How else do you expect to get clean without getting in the water?" Lucy huffed.

So that was how the humans stay clean. The large bucket must be the bath Bithiah had spoken of. But why didn't they just get clean in the ocean instead? It was right outside their palace.

Before Arianna could finish her thought, however, Claire had walked behind her and given the gown a few yanks. To Arianna's horror, the dress began to fall off.

"I think she's shy, Lucy," Claire said as though Arianna weren't there. "Let's give her a moment to get into the water." She glanced back at Arianna. "That bandage should make it interesting. I don't think you're supposed to get that wet."

Arianna realized afterward that she should have taken the girls up on their offer to help her get in. But the puddle on the floor had been small and nearly invisible, and she hadn't expected to fall so fast or so hard. With a splash that sent water flying far enough to hit the window and the door, Arianna landed in the giant bucket. As her bottom sank, her arms and legs shot out, hitting the sides of the tub and sending a pang up her leg from her throbbing ankle. Claire, widening her eyes at Lucy, took Arianna by an arm and began to haul her back up into a sitting position.

"Well," Claire said with a smile that was a little too amused for Arianna's taste, "at least you managed to keep your foot out of the water. Now the room gets a bath, too!"

"Bithiah's going to be mad at you!" Lucy said, her green eyes wide. Then she brought her voice down to a whisper. "Want to know a secret? I hate baths, too."

"That's not a secret," Claire said as she helped Arianna stay sitting up, which was hard with her foot sticking up out of the water. "Everyone in the palace can hear you howling whenever you take a bath. Now, hold on to the sides of the tub. I'm going to scrub your neck, but you have to stay upright."

But Arianna needed to know something first. She plunged her head underwater and sucked in. Instead of regrowing her fins, however, or breathing below the surface as she'd hoped to do, Arianna found herself choking on mouthfuls of bitter-tasting water. Panic took her as she tried to spit it out, to swallow it down, but she couldn't. Nothing she tried could clear her airway.

So this was how she was going to die. After surviving pirates and sea monsters, the youngest Atlantician princess would perish in a giant bucket. In water.

Something slammed down hard on her back. Once. Twice. On

the third whack, the water dislodged itself from her throat and flew back down into the giant bucket in a most unladylike fashion. Arianna continued coughing and sputtering, but found to her immense relief that she could breathe.

"Are you well?" Claire looked on in concern, her hand poised for another strike, the sponge still in her other hand.

"What did you do that for?" Lucy gawked as though Arianna had lost her mind.

But Arianna only coughed harder as tears filled her eyes. Where had her true form gone? Had the Maker seen fit to take her fins from her as well? Had she lost even the little part of her that had been mermaid to begin with? And if she had, how was she ever to find her aunt?

The girls stared at her a moment longer before Claire finally shook her head. "We saw you when you crawled up out of the water. But you're not a mermaid anymore. You need to do what people do now."

Arianna tried to breathe normally as she looked at Claire in disbelief. Did *everyone* know she was a mermaid?

"You're a person here," Lucy finished for her sister. "And do you know what people do?"

She leaned forward as though to tell a secret, so Arianna leaned forward, too.

"They wash behind their ears."

WHO SHE IS

"*A* mermaid?" Drina clutched at her chair's back. "Get her out! I'll not have the enemy in my home!"

"Well, this one is staying." Michael folded his arms.

"Have you lost your mind? They might have fled to their king, but that doesn't mean they're not looking for an opportunity—"

"This mermaid saved my life. And Claire's."

"How so?"

"On the day Father died . . . when the charms failed, she simply appeared. First she took Claire to the surface and left her on the beach. Then she came back for me." When his mother rolled her eyes, he added, "She even stayed with us until the servants discovered us there."

Michael's mother blinked rapidly for a moment before she turned back to her vanity and tucked pieces of stray hair into her crown in dramatic sweeps. "It seems rather convenient that you should only remember to tell me about this now."

"It was the day Maura and Father died," Michael said softly. "I had other things on my mind. Besides," he walked over to the ceiling-high window and stared at the city below, "the mermaid was young, only a girl when it happened."

"That still doesn't explain what she's doing with legs or how you even know it's her." His mother stood and went over to her wardrobe, tilting her head and muttering to herself as she perused the mass of gowns.

"I cannot explain the legs. But, from what I can tell, neither does she. The poor thing hardly knows how to walk." He pointed to one of the two gowns his mother held up. She immediately put it back in the wardrobe and laid the other out on her bed, so he spoke quickly. She would stop listening to him the moment she chose her shoes. "And I know it's her because I remember her face. And . . . because her brother told me she has no voice."

"Her brother?"

"Rinaldo Atlantician."

She turned from her vanity and gave him a stare that rattled his nerve. "You mean to say that I have the daughter of Amadeo—the granddaughter of the Sea Crown—in my house?" Her voice was suddenly far too quiet.

"Rinaldo told me about her the night before he died."

"Well, I would hardly trust the enemy's son to speak honorably!"

"That is enough!" Michael put his hands on his mother's to stop her from trying on another ring.

"You forget, son, that you are not the king yet! I hold the interim crown until you are married," she hissed. "And since you see no reason to follow duty's call when it comes to matrimony—"

"Do not speak to me of duty," Michael said, holding her glare, "until you have spent at least an hour hearing the complaints of our people, or selling a few of those baubles to pay for our guards' bread." At this, he let go of her hand and stepped back, trying to ignore the disgust roiling in his stomach. "And Rinaldo was a good man, much better than his father. Do not profane the name of the dead. Especially that one."

"How can you defend them? They killed your sister! And your father!"

Michael sighed and drew his mother into a hug. He mentally chided himself as she sobbed into his shirt. He knew better than to let her get him riled up like that.

"Arianna—"

"I hate that name!"

"—is no more to blame for the war than I was. Besides, as I said, Rinaldo said she can't sing. That means she can't do us any harm."

"That doesn't mean I have to like it."

Me neither, he thought glumly.

"I hope," she said as she pushed him off and returned to her wardrobe, "that you're not doing this simply because you feel you owe that boy something."

"She saved my life and Claire's. I think that merits help enough. But if you really must know, yes, I do believe we owe his memory some sort of boon. After all, it was our fault he died."

"How so, pray tell?"

He was losing her fast. "If we had honored our agreement with the Sea Crown, the pirates would not have been bold enough to attack our allies right off our own coast!"

"And so after all this, do you suggest she stays here? On our coin?"

"About that . . . I had to send the girls' nurse away a few days ago."

That got her attention. "And just what are we to do with them?" She dropped the gown she'd pulled out to examine and then let out an oath about its wrinkles.

He briefly considered asking her why she needed a new gown for supper when she was already wearing one that was perfectly fine. But he knew better. "I was thinking that she could watch them," he said instead. "They already like her."

"No. I draw the line there! We will not have some mermaid playing all day with the girls. She's likely to drown them."

"Well," he shrugged, "in that case I'm sure you would like to spend all day every day with your granddaughters."

"You and your scruples," she muttered.

"Well," he said again as he turned to leave, "we might be in a better place now if Grandfather had kept any."

"If we are done, then go away." She waved a hand dismissively. "You're giving me a headache. Now, where is my pink brocade?"

A MEAGER NIGHT

"*R*olf said he had one left over from the war," Claire announced as she came in, this time pushing another one of the spindly chairs. But this one was on wheels. "Is she ready for supper, Lucy?"

"Almost." Lucy shook a few wild locks of red hair from her face and stepped back to study Arianna. "Something's still missing, though."

"She can't wear shoes, if that's what you're thinking." Claire joined her sister in staring at Arianna. She tilted her head for another moment, then her face lit up. "I know!" She darted out the door once more and was back a few minutes later, this time carrying something shiny in her hand. Once they had somehow maneuvered Arianna into the chair with wheels, Claire draped the shiny thing around Arianna's neck and stepped back to admire her work. "Yes," she said, placing her arm around her little sister. "I think we've done it."

Arianna looked down and gasped when she saw a pink jewel shaped like a teardrop dangling from a thin but elaborate gold chain. It matched the pink gown perfectly. The dress's material was the softest Arianna had ever touched. If one could pick up the ocean's foam and sew it into a gown, it might have felt half as nice as this. Arianna wished again that she could walk, for even though she would have escaped to find her aunt, she might have paused to twirl a few times. It was exactly the kind of dress Arianna had imagined herself wearing. But where had the girls gotten such a fine gown?

Still, there was little she could do about it now, so she gave the girls her biggest smile. They really had been quite kind, fussing over her as though she were a doll. *Thank you,* she mouthed. They beamed back and then declared it time to bring her to supper.

As they pushed her down the halls, Arianna felt her mouth fall open at the ornate beauty of the Sun Palace, and she immediately saw why the building itself was such a topic of conversation underneath the sea. In the few bits of gossip she had managed to glean over the years before the war, she had never heard a bitter or salty word about the palace itself. The merpeople had never been on easy terms with the humans, at least as long as she had been alive, but to see the Sun Palace had been a privilege of the highest sort.

And now she was being pushed steadily, albeit not in a straight line, toward the great windowed dining hall that could be seen from miles out at sea. The halls alone were magnificent. Millions of pieces of mother-of-pearl had been laid down side-by-side and polished to perfection on the floors. The walls were not smooth or flat but made up of countless seashells, pearls, and other seafloor treasures that had been pressed and stuck into the surfaces in daring spirals and designs. Even areas of the ceiling were made of a blue etched glass that let in some of the sun's dying rays.

The dining hall sat on the northwest corner of the palace. Two of its walls were made completely of windows that looked out to the ocean. Arianna had never been able to see past the windows' reflections into the room itself, but she had spent hours imagining it. And as she finally entered, all of her fantasies fell far short of the truth.

The floor was made of a clear blue glass, and beneath the glass was sand covered in shells and sea treasures of every sort. Tables and chairs were lined up and about two dozen people were seated at them already. The tables and chairs were made of wood but had been carved and painted to look like green, purple, and orange seaweed and coral rising up from the blue glass below. Life-size likenesses of large fish and sea creatures hung from the distant ceiling above.

A slight hush came over the group of humans as the girls pushed Arianna's wheeled chair over to a spot three seats down from where Prince Michael already sat. Arianna quickly lowered her head. Everyone was staring at her as though she'd grown a third arm. She had expected some curiosity, being new to the palace staff, but even the prince was looking at her with an expression of . . . well, she didn't know what his expression was, but it certainly contained *some* emotion he hadn't worn that afternoon.

As soon as her chair was set snugly in front of her place setting, the girls turned and began to walk away. Arianna caught Claire's wrist and gave her an imploring look. But Claire just patted her arm and shook her head. "We have to sit at the end of the table. Grandmother's rules."

Arianna risked another glance around as the girls took their seats. Bithiah was there and the older man who had brought up her bath earlier sat beside her. Three or four other men and women of various ages wore what looked like servants' garb. An older portly man with graying hair and a red face sat across from the prince. His clothes were of higher quality than the servants' clothes, although even his coat had a few patches on the sleeves. Then, of course, there was Prince Michael in the center with his back to the windows. And they were all staring at her.

If they looked any harder, their eyes would fall out of their heads.

"Why, who is this new beauty?"

Arianna turned to see a young man enter from the hall. He was just slightly shorter than Prince Michael, and his hair was lighter, the color of sand. But his twinkling hazel eyes might as well have belonged to Prince Michael had Prince Michael looked less miserable all the time. The young man bounded over to Arianna's chair and took her hand in both of his. He kissed it gently before looking back up at her with soft wonderment.

"Lucas," the prince finally spoke, his voice more composed than he looked, "this is Arianna."

Arianna jerked back to look at the prince. Would he betray her secret by giving her full name? But to her relief, he added nothing else except, "Arianna, this is my brother, Prince Lucas."

"What beautiful tide has brought such a gem to our door?" Prince Lucas asked, still staring into her eyes. "For your eyes sparkle like the very waters of the Sea Crown."

"Sit down, Lucas," Prince Michael said with a frown. "She doesn't want to hear your incessant flirting."

On the contrary, Arianna would not have minded at all. But the younger prince gave his brother a dramatic bow and seated himself on Prince Michael's other side, cutting off Arianna's view of him.

Which was probably for the best. Now if only her cheeks would return to their usual color. Arianna hated blushing. And yet, how could she not? It was the first time anyone had ever called her beautiful. Well, anyone besides her mother or aunt.

Though she couldn't see him, Arianna could still hear Prince Lucas's voice. "Mother will be late again. She says she can't find the gown she had wanted to wear. She has two servants tearing the room apart."

"As if they don't have better things—" But then Prince Michael stopped and turned to stare at Arianna, his jaw going slack. Before he could say anything, however, a shriek sounded from the hall door.

"You little thief!"

Arianna turned to see an elegant woman around her mother's age standing at the entrance of the room. And the woman was pointing directly at her. Arianna blinked a few times and glanced at those around her. Surely the woman didn't mean her. But the woman's glare didn't soften as she stalked forward, her hands balled up into fists at her sides.

"You come into my home against my wishes, and then you have the audacity to steal my gown and jewelry?"

Oh. This must be Queen Drina.

Arianna swallowed hard. She had heard stories of the queen's extravagance. And her temper. Arianna dared a glimpse at the little girls, who sat at the end of the long table. They had both ducked as low as the bench would allow them. Hoping the queen hadn't seen her glance, Arianna immediately straightened and tried holding the queen's gaze.

"Mother, I am sure there is an explanation for this," Prince Michael said. "There is no way she could have stolen your gown. She can't walk. Now please, come and eat."

The people around them were silent, suddenly finding their empty plates quite interesting, and Arianna got the feeling that this kind of outburst wasn't unusual. That didn't make it any less unpleasant for her, however.

"Then how did she get here?" Queen Drina whirled around to face her son.

"The . . . She was pushed here." He paused. "In one of Rolf's contraptions."

Though Arianna could not decide what she thought of this new adult Prince Michael, she was suddenly grateful to him for keeping the girls' whereabouts hidden. Unfortunately, he didn't seem to fool the queen.

"Where are my granddaughters?"

No one moved.

"Girls!"

Finally, Claire stood, but she wouldn't raise her eyes from the floor. "Here, Grandmother."

"Did you take that dress from my wardrobe?"

Slowly, the little girl nodded, suddenly seeming much younger and smaller than she had earlier.

Arianna's throat tightened. Her grandparents had visited her several times, and though they were stern, they had never spoken to her in such a way. She suddenly wished for a voice for an entirely new reason. Yelling at the queen might get one banished from the palace, but she would have felt vastly better, at least.

"What have I told you about touching my things?"

"Mother," Michael said, but the queen ignored him.

"I have specifically forbidden you from entering my chambers when I am not there!"

"But you gave her the ugliest dress in the kingdom!" Claire finally lifted her eyes and met her grandmother's baleful glare. "You could have given her that blue one in the back of your wardrobe. You're too plump for it now!"

Arianna thought she might die of embarrassment.

"Mother!"

Finally, the queen turned, her dark eyes burning.

Prince Michael was now standing, and his voice cut like a shard of glass. "I think it is time for supper. We can discuss such things at another time."

"If that wench damages my gown—"

"We will talk about it later. Please sit down."

The queen and her son glowered at one another for a short eternity before she finally turned with a sniff and glided to sit beside Prince Lucas, her face taut.

The prince stayed standing, however. "Before we say our thanks, I wish to introduce you all to Arianna." He sounded bored, but he did gesture toward where she was sitting, at least. "She was found injured on the shore yesterday. It appears that the fright of the incident has stolen her voice. She will be staying with us until she is able to join her family again. Please treat her with kindness."

When he turned to look at her, Arianna dared to send him a smile. How wonderful it felt to hear him say her name! The way he said it was smooth and clear. But instead of smiling back, he only looked at her for a moment longer, his face devoid of any warmth. Then after he said a prayer of thanks, he sat back down and began speaking with the portly gentleman across the table.

After that, Arianna didn't dare try to look at either of the princes. Thankfully, though, she had little need to as the meal was finally served.

As the servant girl placed the food in front of her, Arianna decided that it looked filling. But it was definitely not as elaborate as Arianna had expected after seeing the Sun Palace and all its grandeur. She thought back to the preparations that had been made for the ball five years before, but the hordes of servants were nowhere to be seen, and neither were the tables of delicacies that had stood out on the terrace.

Instead, the plate in front of her held a slice of simple brown bread and several kinds of plump plant-looking items she was rather sure they called fruit. The fruit was easy, and Arianna found herself wishing for more as the thin fruit skins popped off and the tangy, sweet juices burst in her mouth. As for the bread, Arianna had never eaten it before, but once she learned to swallow the dry, coarse, spongy food, she realized it wasn't that hard.

The wine, however, was another story. Arianna stared at her goblet with a frown, then at everyone else around her. It seemed she had only to lift the cup to her lips and then let it run down her throat. Drinking out of a cup seemed simple enough.

Her attempt to do so proved otherwise, however. As soon as the bittersweet liquid rolled down her throat, Arianna dropped her goblet on the table, choking and sputtering. Her scene drew the attention of most of those around her, including Prince Michael. Unlike the others, however, he didn't look confused. Actually, much to her annoyance, he looked as though he were trying to suppress a smile.

When she met his eyes, he glanced pointedly down at her lap. Arianna gasped as she realized she'd spilled red wine all over the queen's pink gown. Her face heated as she tried desperately to mop it up with the little square of cloth that had been placed beside her plate. She looked up at the prince, pleading silently. If Drina wasn't going to have Arianna's head before, she surely would now.

The prince looked back at the queen before gesturing to someone at the far end of the table. Arianna followed his gaze to see Bithiah.

The servant gave him a slight nod, then stood and walked casually over to Arianna, bending over as though to refill her drink. As she did, she dropped another of the cloth squares in Arianna's lap, covering the stain completely. Arianna gave her a grateful look, but the servant wouldn't meet her eyes.

In just one evening, the only people she hadn't offended were Prince Lucas and the girls, Arianna thought with a sigh. She couldn't imagine what grief the servant would suffer if she couldn't get the red splatters out of the pink material.

A course of thin clam soup followed. Arianna watched her neighbors for a longer period this time before attempting to eat with her spoon as they did. Though the result wasn't pretty, it was far less disastrous than the drink incident had been.

But who could blame her, though. Arianna crossed her arms petulantly. One hardly had the chance to drink underwater.

Aside from the queen's outburst, supper was a rather quiet affair, and once Arianna realized no one else had seen her ruin the queen's gown, she found an unexpected sort of enjoyment as the meal progressed. From the clinking of eating utensils to the other guests' murmurs and the occasional guffaw, there was something happy about being in the middle of many people. It was the first time, as far as Arianna could recall, that she had ever enjoyed a meal with those other than her immediate family. Taking a deep breath, she nearly thanked the Maker for such contentment. Of course, it would probably all end tomorrow—or even sooner, she thought as she looked down at the dress.

The guests began to excuse themselves before Arianna had eaten her fill. Bithiah was soon at her side, taking her chair by its thin handles and turning to wheel her out of the room. Before they got ten steps, however, the queen stood up, knocking her chair backward.

"What have you done to my gown?" Her voice was nearly inaudible, like the quiet before a violent squall.

Arianna looked down in horror to realize that one of the cloth squares had fallen off her lap, and the great red stain was peeking out from beneath.

"Claire!" the queen shrieked. "Claire, get over here!"

Claire did as her grandmother bid. Her eyes became nearly the size of sand dollars when she saw the mess in Arianna's lap.

"This is your fault! Now, you and your sister can go to your room without dessert for the next week!"

"We haven't had dessert in months," Claire muttered as she turned back.

"I meant it! Go! And you!" The queen turned her bright eyes back on Arianna. "Get out of my sight! I don't want to see you for the rest of your stay here! You'll not be staying a single day longer the moment you can hobble!"

Bithiah had Arianna out of the room before the queen could scream another word. Only when they reached a friendlier room with food scattered about and piles of strange empty dishes, did Arianna realize that she was shaking. She could still hear arguing from down the hall as Prince Michael tried to reason with his mother. Bithiah shut the door and pulled down the window coverings before holding up the ugly gown Arianna had been wearing before.

"I think it would be best if you give that dress to me, and I will see what I can do with it. For now, you would be wise to wear this."

Arianna nodded and let the servant help her change clothes, not even minding that someone else was there to see her strange new legs unclothed. At least she was getting out of the gown that had caused the nightmare. Immediately, Bithiah set it in a tall hollow dish of sudsy water, then she helped Arianna change into the ugly brown dress.

As they were heading back toward Arianna's room, voices echoed from the hall they were about to turn into. Bithiah stopped and waited, presumably, Arianna guessed, so that they wouldn't intrude. For it seemed as though the voices belonged to none other than Queen Drina and Prince Michael.

"This was why I didn't want her here!"

Arianna frowned. A ruined dress seemed hardly a reason to cry.

"Every time I look at her face," the queen said, choking with sobs, "I see them. I know she looks human. But I still see *them!*"

"I know." Prince Michael's voice was strained. "But we can't just dump her back on the beach alone. Father never would have approved."

"Your father is *dead* because of her people! And your sister!"

"A fact that has haunted me since I first laid eyes on her." Michael's voice broke at the end. "But she saved my life. I owe her at least a recovery." The queen continued crying as Michael added softly, "It's not as though I want her here, either."

Bithiah put a warm hand on Arianna's shoulder and gently squeezed, but that didn't stop the tears. Ferociously, Arianna tried to wipe them away. The last thing she wanted was for the prince or his mother to see her cry. Crying would look weak, and she couldn't afford to look any weaker than she already did.

But inside, she was breaking.

15

ONE SUN'S TIME

*A*rianna let the sand slide between her fingers and blow away in the wind. After four weeks in the palace, the grandeur had begun to close in on her. The healer had finally declared her ready to use a crutch that morning, a full week later than he had originally predicted, and the girls had immediately decided they should have a day on the beach.

Navigating the sand with her crutch had been more than a slight ordeal, as Arianna was still unsteady on her feet. The girls had been forced to help her most of the way, as the wheeled chair couldn't navigate the sand. She just knew she had to get back to the sea, even if only to survey it. But as her first hour passed, then the second, nothing changed. No monsters surfaced. No aunt. The blue-green waves only continued to roll and crash like glass breaking into foam upon the sand.

As always, though, the girls managed to make her smile. Their giggles and screams were comforting sounds against the roar of the waves. When she was out here, she could pretend that the prince didn't ignore her every time they were in the same room. She could ignore the dozens of stupid, girlish fantasies she had spun during those lonely hours in the sea, imaginings where he had drawn her into warm embraces and smiled down at her with easy familiarity. In those scenes, he had chosen her.

If she touched the water again now, would she change back into a mermaid? Arianna fingered a shell as she stared thoughtfully out at the waves. It would be the easiest way to break free. She would no longer be a burden to Prince Michael, and she could search for Renata.

As soon as she'd thought it, however, Arianna banished the notion. Even if she turned back into a mermaid, she couldn't leave immediately. The children were her responsibility now. No, it would be best if she stayed out of the water just a few hours longer, at least until someone else came down to look for the girls.

A particularly loud squeal pulled Arianna from her brooding, and she opened her eyes to see Lucy splash through the waves up to her knees. She pulled herself up on the crutch and had started toward the girls, who were still chasing one another, when something dark slipped up to the surface of the water and then back down again.

Arianna gritted her teeth against the pain in her ankle as she broke into a clumsy run, tripping over herself again and again. Just when she reached the girls, Lucy stumbled and fell to her knees. Arianna dropped at her side and was trying to pull her to her feet when something began to splash in a frenzied state. One second before the pointed black barb flew up from the water, Arianna threw all her strength into dragging the child from the water and falling back onto the beach. When she turned and looked once more at the water, she found herself staring into the inky eyes of a very large stingray as it hovered just inches from where the waves lapped at the sand.

Its colorless eyes confirmed what Arianna had already guessed. This creature had been to the Deeps. Without the guards to hedge the boundary, it had found its way into the Deeps and come out changed. Just like the shark that bit her.

Lucy started crying, and Arianna let her head fall back in relief. When she opened her eyes again, the queen was staring at them from the top of the beach near the palace's steps. Arianna immediately felt a flash of guilt. She, of all people, knew the dangers of the ocean. She never should have allowed them to take her to the beach while she was still so injured. It was selfish and had almost cost Lucy her life.

Queen Drina began to make her way down to them with her slow, stately walk. Today she wore a blue gown with several layers, despite the warmth of the day. She really was a handsome woman, with her strong angled features and her silken brown hair, and would have been more so, had her countenance not been so proud.

"Claire, Lucy," she said when she finally stopped a few yards from their little huddled group. "I would like to speak with Arianna alone. Go back inside and change your clothes. Bithiah has lunch ready for you."

Claire nodded and began to walk back up the hill, but Lucy still clung to Arianna, shaking. The queen's eyes narrowed as Arianna did her best to pry the girl off and send her after her sister. Only when the girls were halfway up the hill did Drina speak again.

"It seems," she said with resignation, "that you are in fact capable of watching the girls, though I hope you choose more prudent places to play in the future."

Arianna tilted her head. The future?

"I won't mince words. My son had to dismiss the girls' nurse just days before you arrived. It appears," she pursed her lips, "that we no longer have the funds to employ a qualified instructor, so for the time being we will just have to make do with you . . . should you accept."

Arianna looked at her incredulously. After the month of hateful looks the queen had sent her way, and all the ways her son had worked to ignore Arianna completely, were they truly offering Arianna employment?

"We couldn't afford to pay you in coin, of course," Renata continued, fussing with one of her sleeve cuffs, "but you would keep your bed and continue to dine with us each day. That is more than you will be offered anywhere else in the kingdom at this time. I suggest you take it."

Despite her surprise at this turn of events, for Arianna had been sure they would turn her out any day, she couldn't help wondering at the grandmother's lack of desire to spend time with her grandchildren. For a woman who spent all day examining her wardrobe, Queen Drina had precious little time for the girls.

"Well?"

Arianna looked back out at the sea. Though she had no desire to face more monsters like the one she'd just saved Lucy from, she couldn't simply leave Renata. She hadn't been strong enough to walk down the beach without help. But she was still a human, and humans needed to eat. Arianna held up one finger, then pointed to the sun.

"You'll do it for one day?" Drina crossed her arms.

Arianna shook her head and repeated the motions until understanding lit the queen's eyes.

"Absolutely not. Those girls need a nurse sooner than later. I fully expect you to begin your duties immediately if you choose to stay with us!"

"If she needs just one day to prepare, then I think that is reasonable."

Arianna turned to see Prince Michael walking up behind her.

"But the girls—"

"Can spend one day with their grandmother."

As the prince and his mother argued, Arianna looked out at the waves once more. *I'm coming,* she promised her aunt quietly. *Just hold on a little longer.*

16

MORE THAN BELONGINGS

*A*rianna waited until it was dark outside before hobbling back to the beach. By the time she reached the ocean's edge, she had nearly given up for the pain in her ankle. Its throbbing was so great that she wondered if she had undone all of the healing that had taken place in the last four weeks.

Still, she thought as she watched the dark waves, she couldn't give up now. She was too close. So in the cover of the night, she hid her ankle bandage in the crevice of a boulder before shuffling into the water.

Her fear was as cold as the water that splashed her ankles. What if she couldn't change back? Her initial encounter with the bathtub had shaken her confidence in her ability to return to her mermaid form. She had also touched the ocean that morning when pulling Lucy to safety, and nothing had happened. But, she had convinced herself, the tub had held fresh water, not from the ocean. And she had only briefly touched the ocean. This time, she would be immersed.

Her ankle burned as the saltwater touched it, but along with the burn was the sensation of healing. Walking became easier as she moved further out into the gentle waves. When she was deep enough, she let herself float, keeping only her face above the surface as she let the ocean cradle her.

She couldn't tell how long she lay like that, fear and longing battling within her. Long enough that for the first time since the Great Drowning, she spoke to the Maker. *If you give me this one thing, I'll never ask for another again. Let me have my aunt back so that we can join my family, and I promise to never wish for a voice again. I'll be content. Just let me find my aunt.*

There was no audible answer, only the lapping of the waves. She waited so long that she began to shiver without her scales to protect her from the ocean's cold. But just when she was about to give up and swim back to the beach, she felt the now familiar prickling in her legs.

In one swift motion she was below the water, splitting the currents as she dove down in a burst of speed. How wonderful it felt to breathe below once again! And though the descent made her a bit dizzy, she ignored it, not stopping until her tower's cliff face was in sight.

She did slow, however, when she realized that there was no algae lantern bobbing from the tower's roof. Her hands threatened to tremble, but Arianna just clenched her fists and moved on. Renata would never light the lantern only for herself. She was too smart to waste resources like that.

The panic threatened to return, however, when Arianna found the door ajar. Slipping in, she fumbled about in the dark for an algae lamp, which she found covered by some overturned furniture. With enough light to see, she discovered that none of the windows had been closed. None of the furniture had been put to rights. Her sponge bed was still a mess from her fight with the frill shark, as was the little room in the front of the house.

Not forgetting her prayer, Arianna took a deep breath before opening the door to the last room. Perhaps her aunt had been sick or hurt and had been unable to clean the front area without her.

With a sudden confidence that this must be the case, Arianna burst into her aunt's chamber, forgetting even to knock.

Her lapse of manners went unnoticed, because that room was empty as well. Arianna tried to swallow the lump in her throat but she couldn't quell the rebellious sobs that threatened to rack her body. Renata hadn't been here in a long time.

She had been right all along. The Maker did want her lonely.

Arianna had the desire to lie down on her aunt's bed and weep and never move again, but the groan of some unknown creature in the distance pulled her to her senses. The Maker might want her lonely, but she was determined to find love, even if it was in the arms of the two little girls who had wanted her when no one else did. And he was going to have to pry them from her cold, dead hands.

Determined, Arianna set to packing a little bundle to take back to the palace with her. More moans and grunts sounded from outside the tower, closer this time. She gathered what was left of her waxy leaf pile, her writing slate, her pressing knife, and the conch necklace Renata had given her for her third birthday. Then she bolted up toward the surface before any more creatures could discover her.

Her change took place more quickly this time. She had only waited for a few moments at the edges of the waves before she felt her toes and knees scrape the sand once again. Once her aunt's necklace was securely around her neck and she had put her bandage back on, she hobbled up toward the palace.

The seawater must have done something for her, for her ankle hurt just a little less as she used the crutch to climb the slate steps up to the palace doors. She had made it halfway to her room when a sweet, haunting melody beckoned to her from farther down the hall.

The source of the sound was not at the end of the hall as she'd first thought, nor was it at the end of the next hall. Arianna limped along, the halls twisting and turning until she found herself at the great dining hall once more. And outside the glass on the terrace were Prince Michael, Claire, and Lucy.

The girls were curled up against him on the low stone wall where he sat, a short distance from the rocks that had once been Arianna's perch. Prince Michael was singing again.

By this time, her ankle was quite sore from all the walking, so Arianna moved to the far corner of the dining hall and snuck out through a second door there. Once out on the terrace, she sat in a corner that was hidden from the moonlight, and listened.

After a few moments, however, the song stopped.

"The girls sometimes have nightmares."

Arianna jumped, and only then realized she'd nearly fallen asleep. Rubbing her eyes, she tried to look calm and collected. Her traitorous heart thumped wildly, though. For the first time since arriving, the prince sounded neither distant nor angry. And when he wasn't distant or angry, he actually had a nice voice. It was smooth, like winding through the waves on the back of a dolphin.

"My mother says I'm coddling them," he continued, running a hand affectionately over Lucy's wild curls. "Not that that bothers me. They deserve to be coddled sometimes, after what happened."

Was he even speaking to her anymore? Or himself?

He answered her question by looking straight at her. "You went back for more than belongings, didn't you?"

Keeping her eyes on the ground, she nodded, once again fighting the tears that threatened to come.

"I see."

There was a long pause, and Arianna's ankle began to ache again, despite the fact that she was sitting. But just as she was about to stand and gesture that she needed to get to her room, he spoke again.

"I am sorry for your loss." The statement wasn't exactly spoken with familiarity or a great deal of warmth, but it at least seemed sincere.

Without answering him, Arianna turned and began to limp to her room, but he stopped her once more.

"Does this mean you'll be staying with us?"

A single tear fought its way down her face.

Yes. Yes, it did.

17

ANGRY PRINCESS

*M*ichael was straightening another setting of silverware when his brother walked in.

"I'm rather convinced the angle of the silverware will be the least of the pirate lord's worries tonight." Lucas nudged him. Then he looked around. "I don't think we've eaten like this since before Grandfather died."

"We haven't, and I've made sure of that." Michael stood back and surveyed the room as well.

Lucas whistled. "Must have cost a few coins."

"More than we should be spending, but I need to make a point, and it won't do to have our lords or Bras know just how dire our finances are. Now, hand me that vase."

Lucas smirked as he gave Michael the vase. "You know it would be much simpler just to buy my men weapons."

"We can't afford to buy weapons. But we can scrounge up the money for one fine supper. Fine enough, I hope, to keep our enemies from realizing that we cannot afford to buy new weapons." He nodded at the cutlass at Lucas's side. "I'll most likely be needing those flashy skills of yours tonight as well. I get the feeling this meeting will not end diplomatically."

"So you're planning to insult him to his face?" Lucas let out a hearty laugh. "That's bold." He punched his brother in the arm. "I like it!" He paused and ran a hand through his sand-colored hair. "But why now?"

"I've found something in Grandfather's papers." Michael held up the parchment and tossed it to his brother in disgust.

As Lucas unrolled and read it, his face lost all its merriment. "This is low, even for Grandfather."

"Just another gift he left behind for us to enjoy." Michael took the parchment back and stuffed it in his coat. "Anyhow, I need to make it very clear to both our lords and Bras that we will no longer be honoring such a contract." Lucas quirked an eyebrow, but Michael shot him a dark look. "Not a word. Please just make sure this gets done. I need to speak with Russo."

Lucas gave him a long look before finally shrugging and nodding, then he called a servant to fetch several of his sailors from the shipyard. Satisfied, Michael turned and headed toward his study. When a glance inside the room showed his steward wasn't there, he decided to look for him in the stables.

It was warm outside, as spring had been short. He had just paused to roll up his sleeves when he heard giggles coming from the hill beside the stables. Arianna and his nieces crested the hill. The girls were laughing and chasing one another, but the mermaid walked behind a little more slowly. The smile on her face was gentle as she watched the girls, and guilt niggled at him.

If he was completely honest with himself, a battle raged within his heart every time he saw her. He knew he should be grateful and gracious to the girl. She had not only saved his life, but his precious niece's life as well. The war, as he had often reminded his mother, was no more her fault than it had been his. But every time he looked into her eyes, he remembered the hellish day that he had survived only to learn that he had lost his father, sister, and brother-in-law, and Claire and Lucy had lost both their parents.

Their absence no longer felt like a blade in his stomach, but the hole in his heart was just as big.

Still, when he'd run into Arianna the day before, the way she had looked down, as though he'd physically slapped her, had opened his eyes to the reality of the way he'd been treating her. Not well, to say the least. Of course, he'd had his suspicions when she'd first showed up alone. But eight weeks with her had convinced him she was really at the Sun Palace because she had nowhere else to turn. The merpeople had left and for some reason, left her behind as well. Was it because she had legs? Was the merman ambassador so heartless as to leave his daughter behind because she was different?

"Uncle Michael!"

Michael laughed as Lucy leapt into his arms and Claire grabbed his waist. "One day you're going to knock me over and kill me. Then what will you do?"

"Easy. I'll be king." Claire stuck her hands on her hips.

"Kings have to eat all their greens."

"Ew." Claire held her nose. "Never mind. You can be king."

Arianna stood a few yards away, her hands behind her back and her face tilted down to the ground. Michael swallowed and prayed that she might find his tone more civil than she had in the past.

"I hope you're well," he said, trying to catch her eye.

She nodded once and refused to meet his gaze.

He deserved that. He tried again. "I don't suppose you've heard of our guests tonight?"

She raised her head enough to make eye contact.

"I've asked Bithiah to find you a . . . newer dress in honor of the night," he said. Actually, that wasn't completely true. He had argued with his mother for an hour until she had conceded, quite loudly, to give the girl one of her castoffs that was about ten years out of fashion. Bithiah was merely taking the gown in.

This earned him a polite smile that disappeared as quickly as it came.

"Girls," he looked down, "I need to speak with Miss Arianna alone for a moment. How about you get us some strawberries from the garden?" As soon as the girls were gone, he turned back to Arianna and took a step toward her. She stiffened, but stood her ground.

"Our main guest tonight will be a bit . . . different than those I would usually host at the palace. He is of some importance, but there will most likely be . . . tension. At best."

For the first time, curiosity flicked across her face.

Encouraged, he briefly considered telling her who their guest really was. Given that her brother had been murdered by pirates, however, he decided it might be best to leave that little detail out. The last few months had been terrifying enough. Surely, he decided, it would be best to keep her in the dark.

Also, it was difficult to talk to a person who couldn't talk back.

"So, I'll see you at supper?" he finally finished. Why did he feel like an awkward youth again? She was just a girl. It wasn't as though he'd never talked to one before.

She bit her cheek for a moment before looking pointedly in the direction the girls had gone and then giving him a questioning look.

"Oh, the girls are eating in their room tonight. But you're part of the household now, and it wouldn't be fair to keep you away, too. Bithiah will see that the girls are fed and put to bed on time. She told me specifically that she would like for you to enjoy yourself tonight." He paused. "Tonight will be no ball, but this supper will be the closest to one we've had in a long time." Complete with political intrigue and animosity.

At this, Arianna finally cracked a tentative smile. And when her sea-blue eyes lingered on his, it wasn't at all difficult to smile back.

After that, he turned to go, not remembering at all why he had come outside to begin with. A glance at the sun, however, told him that it was high time he returned to the dining hall.

~

"Russo says the northern lords have arrived," Drina said as she wafted into the dining hall. She stopped to pick a piece of fuzz from Michael's shoulder. "I still don't understand why you insist on greeting them yourself. That is what a herald is for."

"And I would use a herald if we had the funds to keep one. But tradition says that without a herald—"

"Spare me the lecture, son. I've heard it before. It's your marriage to tradition that I don't understand." She sighed.

Before Michael could respond, three lords entered the dining hall, accompanied by their wives and a few children. Michael didn't miss the curious glances they cast around the large room. He pretended not to notice the missing tapestries, vases, paintings, or the shortage of servants as he gave his guests a wide smile and extended his left fist. The first lord placed his own right fist beneath it before bowing.

"What an honor it is to be greeted by the prince himself," Lord Fierro said upon straightening up.

"As we have not hosted a feast in a long while, I thought it only appropriate to make my welcome personally."

"Very chivalrous indeed," said Lady Fierro as she fanned herself. "It is refreshing to see the old ways dawn every now and then."

As the couple was escorted to the refreshment table by old Rolf, Michael gave his mother a big grin.

The guests continued to trickle in as the late afternoon became evening, and Michael found himself cautiously optimistic about the night. Although his focus was thwarted somewhat when Arianna walked in.

For once, she wasn't wearing that awful brown sack. Instead, she wore a simple turquoise gown with long sleeves and a little flare at her feet. Once again, his mother had found the least desirable dress in her entire wardrobe. But at least this color made her eyes sparkle.

"Arianna," he said with a small bow. *You look lovely tonight* was on his lips when he remembered where he was and whom he was with. "I hope you enjoy this evening, even if it isn't a ball," he said instead with a smile. Then he bowed forward once more, whispering into her ear as he did, "Remember, there will be some tension tonight. Don't let it alarm you."

She paused, her eyes wide.

How easy it was to get lost in their blue depths. Not just for their beauty, but for all that remained unspoken within them. If only he had the time to read what was there. Her expression wasn't quizzical, nor was it flustered. Rather, she tilted her head to the side and studied him as a scholar might study a specimen of nature.

A cough from his brother brought his attention back to the present, and he nearly elbowed Lucas, who was trying unsuccessfully not to look very smug. There was also a line of four people behind the girl, so Michael let her move on.

His brother was far less ashamed of his obvious flirting with the mermaid, but there was little Michael could do about that. Lucas flirted with everyone. Once, when they were young, Michael had caught him practicing in the mirror with himself.

After the second-to-last guest arrived, Michael quietly instructed his servants to have everyone seated and served.

"We're still missing our guest of honor," Lucas whispered.

"I would like to prepare them for the unpleasantness they're about to witness," Michael whispered back. "Bras shouldn't be here for another hour."

Soon everyone was seated and the food was nearly served. Before thanking the Maker, however, Michael stood and walked toward the door, where his guests could see him well. *Let them see that I mean to act with justice,* he prayed silently. *And please don't let this night end in bloodshed.*

"My friends," he began. "I have called you all here tonight to celebrate what makes us strong. Our unity in the Maker and his gift of the Sun Crown. Though the crown isn't worn by a reigning king right now, it is still the cornerstone of our kingdom, a symbol and sign that reminds us we were gifted with the strength and responsibility to—"

"What is this?"

Everyone turned to see one more guest stride through the hall doors. As soon as he heard the voice, Michael wanted very badly to curse.

"I come early and find that you've begun without me? Bad form, my prince! And just when I thought our peoples had come to terms of harmony!"

Michael opened his mouth to answer, but a movement from the table caught his eye. Arianna had stood and, before anyone could react, charged at the pirate and punched him soundly in the nose.

"You little vixen!" The pirate lord held the back of his hand to his face as blood trickled down and dripped onto his red coat.

Arianna pulled her fist back for another punch. Before she could loose it, however, Michael grabbed her from behind and pinned her to his chest, dragging her back several steps. Bras had half-drawn his own weapon when he suddenly found Lucas's cutlass held snugly against his throat.

A few shrieks and many gasps sounded from his other guests, but Michael was more interested in keeping the pirate from murdering the mermaid than he was making his guests feel at home. Blast it all! This was not how he had planned the evening to go. But the only thing he could do to keep up the facade was to pick up the pieces and go on.

"This is how you treat your guests then?" Bras growled from beneath Lucas's blade. "Allow whorish wenches to—"

"You will hold your tongue!" Michael roared.

The room went silent. Even Arianna stopped squirming in his arms and turned to stare up at him.

"You are here not because you are my guest, but because I found this!" As he reached into his coat, he bent to hiss into the girl's ear. "Return to your chambers now and remain there until I come to deal with *you* later." Perhaps he had been a little too friendly with her earlier for her to think she could take such liberties in his court.

As he spoke, ice formed in her blue eyes, and she shrugged his arms off. After straightening herself, she marched to the doors with her head held high.

Michael turned back to Bras.

"We had a contract!" Bras shouted. His hand moved to his pocket, but Lucas was quicker. In a flash, he had the pirate lord on his knees.

"If you mean this one," Michael pulled the parchment from his coat and held it up for all to see, "then yes, you made an agreement with my grandfather. But my grandfather forgot that all contracts made in defiance of the Sun Crown's oath are null and void." Turning, Michael strode over to the large fireplace and threw the parchment into the fire. The room was deathly silent behind him as the parchment blackened and curled.

"You and your men will leave Maricanta's waters and never return. You will avoid any sort of contact with the merpeople as well. And if you feel the need to defy such orders, my brother and his men will make sure you rue the day."

Bras glared at him through dark eyes, then choked as Lucas's arm holding the cutlass tightened visibly.

"Your navy is weak!" the pirate gasped, a bead of sweat running down from his neat, slicked-back hair. "You wouldn't have the weapons or men to overturn even one of my fishing boats!"

"We're strong enough," Lucas said, turning the cutlass so that a few drops of blood were drawn from the man's clean-shaven neck.

"Get rid of him," Michael told his brother. "Then see to my guests. I have someone I need to attend to." As Michael stalked away from his guests, he could hear more gasps and whispers as Lucas and his men dragged the pirate king away. Michael had planned an entire lecture on the evil of fraternizing with pirates, but he had another priority that needed tending to immediately.

Namely, an unruly mermaid.

18

THUMB TUCKED OUT

"*A*rianna!" Michael bellowed at her door. "You and I need to have a serious talk about propriety and what you will *not* be doing in my court!"

His fury wavered a bit, however, when Arianna emerged from her room, her face red and blotchy and her eyes brimming with tears. But he had to remain strong. So he crossed his arms and looked down at her with his most ferocious glare. "Do you care to explain yourself?"

She only watched him warily. Where she might have cowered earlier that afternoon at a sharp word, there was now defiance in her eyes.

"They may not know who you are," he leaned down, "but I do. And a granddaughter of the Sea Crown should know better than to interfere in the political exchanges of any foreign dignitary, pirate or not!"

At this, her eyes turned icy again, and the girl balled up her fists and began to pace. Several times, she opened her mouth only to shut it again. A ridiculous part of him began to pity her. What torture constant silence must be. Her fair skin turned a deep red and she shook her head again and again. Then her eyes widened as she turned back and ran into her room.

Unable to stop his curiosity, Michael peered through the door to see her bent over at the little table. On the table was a thin flat rock covered by a green, fan-shaped leaf the size of a small serving platter. Arianna had pulled out a small knife and was rapidly carving lines into the leaf.

She was writing! In spite of his anger, Michael couldn't help wondering how quickly she carved the words into the leaf. But why hadn't she written before? She had been at the palace for two whole months. Then he looked down at her feet. A stack of similar green leaves sat beneath the desk. And each one was cracked and torn. As he realized this, Arianna let out a heavy breath and threw her knife against the wall before covering her face and leaning heavily on the table. Michael strained to see the leaf she stood over. It had cracked, too.

"Arianna," he said, this time more gently.

In slow, shuffling steps, she gathered herself and went back out to stand before him. Her blue eyes were no longer brilliant in their shine, but tired and gray, like the sky after a storm.

"What did he do to you?" he whispered.

At this, the girl gave him an accusing look as if to say, *What do you care?* before turning and walking to the window at the end of the hall. This time, she made no attempt to use words. She only stared out at the sea.

Michael took a deep breath and blew it out slowly before rubbing his eyes. *Can nothing go simply these days?* he asked the Maker. Then, walking over to where she stood, he turned her so that she was looking at him again.

"You would have had no way of knowing this," he said, "but I called the pirate lord here to tell him that I had discovered my grandfather's contract with him. And that I was breaking it."

Arianna couldn't have looked more surprised. *Of course she's shocked, you moron,* he chastised himself. *Your people made war on hers for five years.*

"Just . . . in the future," he shook his head, "please leave the court dealings to me. At least until you're back in your own court. And when you get the inclination to hit someone again," he took her hand gently and curled her fingers into a fist, "do it with your thumb tucked *out.*"

19

FIGURES

*T*hough there was none of the spark or romance Arianna had once dreamed of, she did find that she and Michael came to some sort of truce following the pirate incident. He no longer sent her cold looks down the table, and she no longer went out of her way to avoid him completely.

Likewise, her life settled into a somewhat enjoyable routine. She certainly still missed her family, and she never went to bed without trying to glimpse some sign of her aunt through her window, but even so, Arianna found herself eager to awaken in the mornings, excited to spend her days with the girls. Once she was truly convinced that the prince did not mean to humiliate or torture her or even order her from the palace, she found a quiet peace in knowing what each day would bring and expecting the same from it the next.

Suppers were a particular delight. The enjoyment she had found that first night in being surrounded by others did not dwindle. On the contrary, she found that they thrilled her, filling her with energy in a way she hadn't known before but had somehow always longed for.

The servants were far more accepting of her than she would

have ever expected. Unlike her parents' servants, who went out of their way to avoid talking to her, the castle servants were kind, even if they were still a bit cautious. The maids would dare a smile whenever they came to change her bed clothes. Cook and his daughter would often slip Arianna and the girls little bites of supper long before it was done, if they visited the kitchen at the right time. The palace footman was a gentleman always, bowing to every woman even if she wasn't royal, not that he could have known Arianna was. Even Master Russo, the nervous palace steward, would acknowledge her whenever they crossed paths.

There was one part of her life, however, that still irked Arianna more than she could express, and that was her inability to write to the others. When she'd first brought her waxy leaves up to the surface, Arianna had been so thrilled to communicate that she began to write an entire letter to the prince, telling him of all that had taken place so he would know she meant his family no harm. The letter had been so long, however, that she was unable to finish it that first night. She had awakened the next morning keen to finish, only to find that her waxy leaves had dried and cracked overnight.

She had thought of using parchment, of course. Merpeople and Maricantian written language was the same, so communicating with her hosts should have been simple. But the week she had arrived, Arianna had come across Bithiah scolding Claire and Lucy for using their uncle's writing parchments to sketch on.

"Do you think this parchment is without cost?" she had sternly asked the girls. "Your uncle cannot run the kingdom without parchments, and parchment is very hard to find these days. No, you had best run along and be glad it was me who caught you instead of your grandmother."

So parchment was out of the question. She had continued on in silence, staying busy with the girls as she demonstrated figures for Claire and numbers for Lucy. Then Lucy would read to Claire, and

Claire would correct her when she needed it, with Arianna looking on. After lessons came the midday meal, for which Prince Michael often joined them. During the meals, he and Arianna would exchange polite smiles as he teased his nieces. Then she and the girls would play in the afternoon and get ready together for supper in the evenings.

One evening, three weeks after the pirate incident and nearly three months after she had arrived, Arianna had just put the girls to bed and was walking past the prince's study when she heard voices coming from inside. The door was open, and Arianna could see several figures gathered around a desk near the window. Never one to miss a group gathering, Arianna slipped in through the open door and crept silently to a large, red plush chair hidden in the far corner. She'd discovered the spot a few weeks before and decided that it would be a good place from which to observe the humans, unnoticed. But until tonight she hadn't had the chance to watch anything interesting.

Prince Michael was leaning against the wall with his head tilted back and his eyes closed. Prince Lucas was pacing, and Master Russo was wringing his hands.

"I'm not daft, Lucas," Prince Michael said. "I know your men need the money. But I can't give it to you until the Council votes upon it first."

"For the first time in three years, we come upon some money. Michael, my men are floating in rusty buckets!"

Arianna retreated further into her chair so he wouldn't see her. Obviously, this was not a social gathering. But leaving now would draw their attention and interrupt whatever argument they were having. Arianna was stuck.

"Your Highness," Russo twisted his long mustache so hard Arianna wondered if it might not break off, "it is not such a large sum as to turn heads. Surely we can notify the Council of Lords after the ships have had their repairs made."

"No, we're doing this the right way. You may have the money once I've notified the lords. It's how we've done it for generations. We're not—"

"Hang the law, Michael!" Lucas roared, whirling to face his brother. "If you truly want us to pose any sort of threat to the pirates, now that you've ensured Blas's hostility, you need to make sure my men don't sink!"

"Master Russo," Prince Michael's voice was suddenly quiet and sent a shiver down Arianna's back, "please excuse us."

The steward bowed and gave Prince Lucas a long look as he left the room. As soon as he thought they were alone, Michael turned to his younger brother.

"Don't ever talk to me in that way in front of our staff again." Michael's voice stayed deadly. "You know I value your opinion, but they will not respect me if you don't."

"But for once, will you simply do something not because it's dictated to you but because it is right?"

"I am trying to uphold the law! That *is* right!"

"The law was meant to aid us in keeping the peace! We weren't meant to serve the law so completely as to abandon common sense! There are always exceptions."

"Look around you!" Prince Michael made a wild gesture with his arm. "If I could, I would sell the rest of our belongings! I would sell Mother's dresses and jewels, and I would give it all to your men with gladness. But as it is, I have hardly enough coin to keep us and your men fed for the next two weeks, and announcing our distress to others by bypassing the proper channels will only make our need public knowledge."

"That's just the thing! You have the money now. And as soon as our creditors find out we have even this little amount, they'll be banging down the door to demand it. By the time we ask the lords for permission, the Tumenian king and the like will have caught wind already!" Prince Lucas held his hands out, palms-up.

"Without weapons, my men can do nothing to protect our people."

The silence following this speech was a long one. Prince Michael went to the window and stared out, his shoulders set as he folded his arms. Prince Lucas rubbed his eyes as he leaned his elbows on the large stone desk.

"The law is all we have that separates this government from falling into disrepair," Prince Michael finally said. "Without it, we have nothing left!" With that, he stormed out.

Arianna looked back at Prince Lucas to make sure he was still leaning over as she stood and took a few steps toward the door.

"Don't judge him too harshly."

She stopped and looked back at him in surprise. How long had he known she was there?

"He was handed a war-torn kingdom far too young with far too little help." Prince Lucas stood, suddenly looking tired.

Arianna really wasn't sure how to respond. Though Prince Lucas had been one of the few palace inhabitants kind enough to address her directly since the day she'd arrived, it was only ever to do a little flirting or ask her some silly question that couldn't be answered, the same as he did to everyone else he met. But now his eyes had deep circles under them, and his shoulders drooped. His hair was mussed badly, and his clothes looked bedraggled. And though she had thought him imposing the first time they'd met, despite his being slightly shorter than his brother, Prince Lucas suddenly looked older and more tired than any other man of twenty-one years Arianna had ever seen.

"My mother might be the interim queen, but she despises the responsibilities," he continued, leaning over to straighten the ink jar he had upset earlier in his outburst. "All my brother has ever done is try to pick up the pieces and fit them back together the best he knows how. Even when he is a fool about it."

And as quickly as he had begun talking to her, he was out the door and Arianna was alone. She turned to leave as well, but a stack of parchments on the desk caught her eye. Curious, Arianna stepped closer to examine them.

The stack of parchments was full of numbers in red ink. Treasure numbers, she realized as she examined the rows and columns. It wasn't hard, thanks to her aunt's training, to make out which figures were for what. As the columns went down, however, the writing became sloppy and the ink blurred across the page.

As though the writer had fallen asleep while subtracting. This thought nearly made Arianna giggle until she realized that many of the figures were wrong.

Before she had considered its wisdom, Arianna took the quill in hand and helped herself to one of the ink jars. She hesitated, however, before touching the quill to the parchment. She had never written with a quill pen. Claire and Lucy practiced their numbers and letters with their fingers in the sand. Even if she fixed the mistake, would it be legible?

Two broken quills and many red splotches later, Arianna found that she could hold the quill just well enough to drag thin red lines across the page without her numbers being completely unreadable, and it wasn't long before she was too engrossed in correcting the page's errors that she didn't hear the footsteps behind her.

"I don't think my son has been polite enough to share with you the punishment for divulging royal information, so I will do so now."

Arianna turned so fast that she slipped and fell back against the desk. Queen Drina and Prince Michael were standing less than an arm's length away. And though the prince hadn't been the one to speak, his hazel eyes were colder than Arianna had ever seen them.

"I bring you into my house," the queen continued. "I give you employment when I cannot afford to do so, and this is how you repay me!"

It wasn't a question she was asking. It was a sentence of guilt,

Arianna realized. She looked at Prince Michael for reprieve, but there was none.

As Arianna righted herself, however, and straightened her dress, something hot began to burn in her belly. It was barely there at first as she tried to understand why the guilt was threatening to crash down on her. But the longer the prince looked at her with those unfeeling hazel eyes and let his mother shout on, the hotter the sensation grew until Arianna could no longer contain it.

The stupid man could have his privacy for all she cared, and suffer his own mistakes. And his mother's. She had committed no ill. She was no criminal. And she was done.

Pulling herself up to her full height, which wasn't very impressive, Arianna grabbed the parchment from the desk and shoved it at him before stomping out of the room.

Arrogant man. Impudent, presumptuous, self-centered, self-righteous man! Arianna fumed as she stormed along the halls toward her room. Too long she'd been held captive by his pathetic gaze. Well, she would be duped by his personal allure no longer! From now on she was finished helping him. She would help the girls and no one else.

Arianna turned a corner so fast she nearly stumbled, but she didn't slow as she continued to her room. Why had she ever made excuses for him? His life wasn't the only one that was difficult, and if such hardships were revealing the true nature of his heart, then she, for one, was thankful that she was never the recipient of the attention of such a—

Running footsteps in the hall behind her interrupted her personal vent. She refused to turn and give him the impression that she might want his attention. So she continued striding until a hand grasped her arm and spun her back around.

She glared up defiantly at the prince. She would have nothing to say to him, even if she could.

He did not apologize, as she expected, however. He only held up the parchment she had fixed and held it in the air. His mouth opened, but it was a long moment before anything came out. Finally, he said,

"Meet me tomorrow morning at the stables. There's something you need to see."

20

AN OUTING

*A*s he saddled the horses, Michael was still cursing himself for his assumptions the night before. Not only had she saved the crown a bag of gold with her figures, but the incident had proved once and for all what a cold, distant churl he was becoming. He hadn't been the one to verbally assault her, he tried to argue with his conscience. His mother had. But he had stood by and said nothing. And the way Arianna marched into the stables confirmed that.

Her little glance up at the horse, however, confirmed that she was also terrified.

Michael, you are a dolt. Mermaids don't ride horses. Why for the love of all that's holy would you suggest this?

"I'm . . . sorry. I didn't think—"

But she only shook her head and placed one foot awkwardly in the horse's stirrup. Without thinking, Michael extended his hand to help her up, but she swatted it away and continued trying to haul herself up onto the horse. After two minutes without success, however, she let out a huff and held out her hand, still not looking at him.

Although still as angry as he was with himself, Michael

suppressed a grin as he hoisted her up into the saddle. It was like watching a stubborn little bird trying to fly while her wings were still wet. She squeezed the saddle horn until her knuckles went white, and all thoughts of helping her learn to sit sidesaddle vanished from his mind. That she was on the horse was enough.

He didn't try to talk with her again until they were both seated and he had started their animals down to the path toward the city.

"I would offer an apology for the way I've behaved lately," he began, sure he would lose his nerve if he waited any longer to speak. "Since you've gotten here, really. But I'm afraid no single apology would do. I have been detached, suspicious, unhelpful, temperamental at best, and a spineless louse at worst." He turned just enough to sneak a glance back at her.

She was glaring down at her mount.

I know she's listening, but let her hear *me,* he prayed to the Maker. "I . . . I can't blame you for distrusting or being angry with me. I mean, my mother is technically queen, but it is not as though she actually takes . . ." He let the words trail off, however, when her mouth tightened slightly. This wasn't going the way he had hoped. Perhaps he should have left her at home that morning after all.

"My mother is technically queen," he hurried on before his courage left him again, though he couldn't really say why he was nervous at all. "She holds all the legal power of the land until I am married. But as she has no desire to fulfill such duties, and I am next in line, most of those responsibilities have fallen to me. This would be agreeable, except that she likes to take the power back whenever it suits her. Of course, she likes to remind me that it would be easier for all if I just . . ."

He sighed and shook his head to himself. What was he doing? She wasn't even listening to him. " . . . if I just got married," he finished to himself.

When he turned to check on her horse, however, he found that she was staring at him with wide sky-blue eyes, her head slightly tilted to the side. When he met her stare, she made a rolling motion with her hand.

"What?"

She held up her hand and pretended to slip a ring on her finger then pointed to him.

"Oh, you mean about me getting married?"

She nodded and Michael smiled a little at the intensity of her stare. "Nothing you would want to hear about. Here, relax your grip a little. Your fingers will fall off if you squeeze the saddle that tightly the whole ride."

They slowly made their way down the gentle slope of the Sun Palace's great hill to where the path opened up. Michael used the opportunity to draw her horse up beside his and study her discreetly. Even without his mother's gown or jewels, she was uncommonly pretty. Of course, he had thought she was lovely all those years before when she'd saved him, but in a moment of peril, one might think an old salty sailor beautiful for saving one's life. Now that she was here in the weak light of the cloudy morning, though, he was surprised that he hadn't really seen the depth of her beauty before. Not that he had time to be admiring women at the moment . . . but still . . . he wondered what her hair would look like if she let it down. Then it dawned on him that he had never seen her hair in anything other than a practical knot at the back of her head. Curls so pale they were nearly white spilled down in a few places, framing an oval face with eyes the color of the sky. Michael racked his memory to find another merperson with features so fair, but he couldn't remember even if his life had depended upon it. Every merperson he'd ever met had had shockingly white skin, even whiter than hers, and hair and eyes just a little browner than ebony. Her skin, though very light, looked as if she had actually seen the sun once or twice in her life.

They came to the bluffs that overlooked the city and bay. It was one of Michael's favorite spots on the royal grounds. Close enough to the palace that his mother hadn't been able to nag him about wandering, and far enough away not to hear her voice. The only sounds this morning were gulls harmonizing with the wind and the waves. Often he craved such quiet, but now there was one voice he suddenly wished very much to hear.

"I'm afraid I will apologize again and again for my behavior until I feel it is completely pardonable, but I think you might find my actions easier to forgive if you knew what a predicament I'm in."

He didn't miss the spark in her eyes at his mention of his behavior. Good. She was listening, if nothing else. Emboldened, Michael went on. "Unfortunately, it seems that my grandfather was not only involved with the pirates, but he was also frivolous. After growing up in a time of plenty, he had never learned to want. As a result, my mother never learned to want. Everything they wanted they simply had." His throat was suddenly thick.

"My father was different, though. I don't know if you're aware of it or not, but he wasn't like them at all." He felt bitterness sprouting up within him all over again. "He wasn't the direct heir, so he would only have been the interim king after my grandfather passed, had he made it that far." He was very close to choking on his words now. How had this wound reopened so quickly after nearly six years?

Another glance at his companion revealed a much softer look on her face than he'd seen all morning. Her blue eyes were wide, and her lips were slightly parted. Something told him that even in his deepest pain, he was in good company. *What sorrows have you seen?* he wanted to ask her. But instead, he turned back to the path as it wound down the side of the bluff and to the bay.

The city was mostly hidden from view of the castle by the thin line of tropical forest that ran the length of the peninsula. Michael had always wished that he could see the city better from the palace towers, for he had always thought it a pretty scene with buildings bleached white by the sun. The way Arianna's mouth fell open would have been highly gratifying now, had the city been as splendorous as it was six years before.

But now Michael kept his head high and his eyes trained on the royal port as they came to the bottom of the hill and began to move into the streets through the horses, carts, and the throng of people who no longer could afford to keep their own animals. A few of the passersby dropped bows or curtsies, but many only stared as their prince passed by. He nodded vaguely at the ones who showed homage, but the others he ignored, or tried to, anyway. He didn't look at their worn, tattered clothes, nor did he see their thin, hungry faces. He didn't have to. He had them memorized already.

After moving past the first few clusters of homes, Michael turned back to Arianna and mumbled, "the market," without even stopping. If it could even be called that anymore. He'd planned to say nothing more about the pathetic line of stalls, but her eyes implored him so greatly when he glanced back at her that he pulled her horse up beside his again.

"Before the war," he said in a low voice, "this was a thriving center of trade. See how its length is the same as the four streets that meet it? Merchants and traders came from not only the western realm, but even from the east, south, and the far north to gain our treasures from the deep." He gestured to a cart that was selling a load of mottled, skinny carrots and a few bushels of dry corn. "But now we have nothing to trade. Your people were our source of sea goods. And now that they're gone, the fishermen can't fish outside the bay for fear of the sea monsters that lurk even in shallow waters. Like the one that got you."

She turned and looked up at the peninsula's hills, covered in trees.

Michael shook his head. "Our soil is too sandy to grow much more than a few kinds of food, and without trade, we have no money to purchase grain, cotton, and timber from anyone else." He gave a dark chuckle. "Cook doesn't make soup every night because we like it."

He watched her carefully as she frowned in thought. After a moment, her eyes widened and horror washed over her features. She whipped her head around again and began to study the people anew.

Michael felt his heart thump unevenly. "Please do not think I'm blaming you," he said quickly. "You saved my life. Without you, I would have been dead like my father." His throat tightened. "My mother would be interim queen for my brother, who, don't tell him I said this, is a genius with the sword but a dunce when it comes to monetary matters."

She tore her gaze away from the people and watched him with wide, unreadable eyes.

He took a deep breath, suddenly feeling like a fool. "I suppose I just wanted you to know why I've been a slave to my duty. I wasn't always like this . . ." He looked back at the throng they were leaving behind. "I'm just trying to save them the best way I know how." His voice cracked in an annoying way, and he looked back at her, suddenly wishing greatly for her to understand. "Wouldn't you?"

With a sad smile, she hesitated before reaching out and squeezing his hand. She let go immediately, but her message was clear.

Yes. Yes, she would.

They didn't speak again until they reached the naval port. As they rode toward their destination, however, Michael realized that the quiet solitude he so often sought on his horse was not what he wanted now at all.

Emotions flitted across her face faster than he could decipher them, and her silence was charged with tension. She was like a butterfly trying to burst forth from its encasement. What would her voice sound like, he wondered.

"You made it! I was about to send Gilly after you!" Lucas hopped down from the ship onto the dock and held his arms out dramatically.

"Arianna has never ridden a horse before. I didn't want to rush her. All things considered, though, I think she did quite well." Michael dismounted then turned to help Arianna. He had quite forgotten, however, how difficult riding is in the beginning. The look of shock on Arianna's face brought him another round of self-scorn when her legs buckled. Michael caught her just before she hit the ground. A few of the men on the ship chuckled, but one look from Lucas silenced them immediately.

"You had her ride all the way here on her first try?" Lucas leaned over and whispered as he took her other arm. "Are you daft?"

"Apparently." Michael wanted to kick himself. "I am so sorry," he said to Arianna. "You were doing so well that I completely forgot it was your first ride. Will you be all right?"

Arianna's fair face turned pink as she gritted her teeth and let them lead her to an empty barrel. Her strides were wide and bowed, and she continued to clench her teeth. Michael felt relief, however, when she sat and looked as though she might actually laugh.

"So, what was it that you wanted to see me about today?" Michael straightened and looked at his brother.

"Do you recognize her?" Lucas bounded back to the ship and slapped her side.

Michael squinted, then had to suppress a gasp. "Is that our flagship?"

"*Lady Elisabet*? Yes, she is. And she had a run-in with a few of Bras's little shag boats."

Michael let out a whistle as he walked down the dock to see more of the holes that had been blown into the sides of the once-whitewashed ship. Her name was unreadable for the chunks of wood missing from the massive hull, and her sides had been stained black and brown from the explosions of casum ball dust. He felt even more disappointed, silly as it was, when he realized the elegant, shiny red railings had all been either damaged beyond repair or were gone completely.

"How many were injured?"

"By the Maker's mercy, just three. And none of them were mortal wounds. But as you can see, the ship's going nowhere fast. Unless . . ." Lucas gave him a meaningful look, but Michael was already shaking his head.

"I told you. The Council of Lords must approve it first. I've sent missives to them telling them to come to the palace tomorrow. We'll—" Before he could finish, a ruckus to his right turned both their heads.

"What kind of evil have you brought upon us?" An old sailor hollered at Arianna. He had grabbed her arm and was trying to yank her off the barrel.

Michael had his knife out and at the man's throat in an instant, pressing him into the ground. Lucas took Arianna. The old man struggled, but Michael kept his knife steady.

"Since when is it acceptable to assault maidens in the streets?" he growled.

"'Twouldn't be if she was human!" The old man spat in Arianna's direction. "But I seen this one when I was fishing! She'd perch up and stare at the palace for hours!" He glared at Arianna and hissed at her when they made eye contact. "Sure as day, this one's a mermaid." He looked around at the small crowd that was beginning to gather. "Must've used black magic of sorts. Look at her legs!" He leered. "Not bad ones, though."

Michael jerked the old man back and pressed his knife even harder against his throat. And though he didn't have a violent nature, Michael suddenly had the urge to teach the old sailor some manners he wouldn't forget.

"You would insult your future king this way?" Lucas snapped, his hazel eyes boring into the old man's round, leathered face.

"He'll never be king at this rate." The old man sneered. "Have to be married before becoming king! Besides, can't put me in the stocks. I've it on very good authority that you hadn't enough coin to keep your stocks master."

Michael kept his knife pressed hard as he yanked a key from his shirt pocket. "I know perfectly well how to operate the stocks myself. I also hold the key." He shook the long gnarled brass key in the man's face. "So do not for a moment think I have any qualms about locking you up and leaving you to the birds myself."

At this, the old man's eyes glazed over, and Michael stared him down for a moment longer, daring him to say anything else. When he didn't, Michael handed his brother the key and took Arianna protectively in his arms. She turned her face into his chest and pressed herself against him. The way she shook beneath his arms, which he had instinctively wrapped around her, made him burn inside. Michael looked at his brother.

"Have him locked up until his mind is clear of ale. And if he starts on again, return him to me and I *will* do it myself."

When the man had been hauled away, Michael turned back to Arianna. Her face had lost what little color it had, and her eyes were the size of teacup saucers.

"Did he hurt you?" Without waiting for an answer, Michael took her arms and began to look for bruises. As he did, she continued to stare after the man with a look of horror on her face. Why was she so afraid of the old man? She had, after all, struck a pirate lord without hesitation. And Bras was far more dangerous than an old drunk. Then it hit him.

The pirate lord hadn't known her secret.

"Lucas!" But when Michael looked up, Lucas was already gone. So Michael called over to one of the sailors. "Go find Prince Lucas. Tell him instead to take the old man to the palace dungeon. I don't want the lout anywhere near the public!"

As soon as the sailor was gone, Michael led Arianna to a low wall that looked out over the pier. She was still shaking, and Michael felt a new kind of helplessness overtake him.

"What can I do?" he asked. His hands felt awkward and useless hanging at his sides as she wrapped her arms around herself and shivered. It was a position he'd seen Claire take often after her parents had died. And he hated it. What had he done on those horrible days when he'd very nearly lost her? Would his little tricks help Arianna, too?

"Would you like to go out on the water?" he asked.

She looked at him as though he'd lost his mind.

"I mean," he stumbled to clarify, "out on a boat. It's pretty out on the bay, and the sea monsters haven't made it there as of yet."

She studied him for a long moment, a little pucker forming above her eyes. Then, after a long moment, she took a deep breath and nodded.

21

SHIMMERS

*M*ichael smiled wryly to himself as he rowed them out to the center of the bay. How many times had his mother begged and pleaded and cajoled him to woo some girl out in this very boat . . . or anywhere for that matter? And now he was out with the one girl in the world that his mother couldn't stand.

But he wasn't wooing. He was only helping her recover from a scare. It was the chivalrous thing to do.

"I used to bring Claire out here often," he said as he rowed. "After her parents died she had nightmares. Sometimes we would come out here in the middle of the night just so she could fall asleep in the boat."

Arianna watched him, and Michael couldn't help fancying that he saw some warmth in her eyes.

Not that it mattered if he did. Because he wasn't wooing.

She had stopped shaking at least, but the sorrow still hadn't left her face. She reached down and trailed a hand in the water as they went, her fingers moving over its surface like a caress.

He almost asked if she missed the ocean, but checked himself first. They'd come out here to make her feel better, not to remind her of all she'd left behind. "This half of the bay technically belongs to Destin, but King Everard has been kind enough to give us full use of it, as there are no Destinian villages nearby. Its fish are the only reason we've survived this long without trade," he said instead, bringing the boat to rest beneath a hanging tree.

Arianna looked up at the tree and frowned slightly before turning and squinting back at the peninsula across the bay.

Michael chuckled. "We can't understand it, either. Destin is full of evergreen forests, and our little piece of land is as tropical as they come. All we can surmise is that the Maker wanted it that way for a reason. But that's not what we're here to talk about." He laid his oars inside the boat and placed a hand beneath his chin. "We're here to talk about you."

Arianna blinked at him a few times before raising an eyebrow.

"It's a game I play with Claire and Lucy. Just . . . indulge me."

She shrugged, but a little smile surfaced.

"Here's how it works. I ask questions, and you answer me either a yes or a no, and I have to guess what you mean."

At this, her blue eyes lit up, and she sat up straighter.

Her eyes shimmered, Michael realized, like the sun glinting off ocean waves. For some reason this made him happy, and suddenly he was aware of a truth that he probably would have seen long ago, had he not been so wrapped up in his own problems.

Arianna wanted desperately to be heard.

"I know you had a brother. I believe you had a sister as well?"

She nodded so emphatically that a curl escaped her hair's tight knot.

Michael laughed. "Very good then. I will proceed now to guess her name." In actuality, he had met her sister several times, and he was fairly sure her name was Layla or Lilly or something similar, but the look on Arianna's face now was brighter than he'd ever seen it, so he continued on with his silly game. "Is it Mildred?"

She made a face.

"Daphne?"

She wagged her finger at him.

"Audra?"

A roll of the eyes.

"Well, if I'm doomed to get it wrong, then perhaps you can at least tell me what she's like."

Arianna pulled her hand from the water and stared at it thoughtfully for a long moment. Then she placed her hands delicately on her cheeks and gracefully pulled her hands off.

"She's often embarrassed."

Arianna leaned forward and slapped his arm.

Michael laughed again. "Ah, you're saying she was lovely."

Another emphatic nod.

"Was she as lovely as you?"

Her smile disappeared, and she turned to stare out over the bay, fingering her shell necklace as she did.

"Arianna," Michael whispered, "was she as lovely as you?" He reached out and tugged on her shoulder until she was facing him again.

In just a few flustered motions, Arianna confirmed what Michael had feared.

"There's something I should have told you months ago," he said, readjusting his position since it seemed they were going to be in the boat for a while. His silly game seemed to have opened up a wound that, had he pulled his head from the dirt earlier, he should have seen long before.

"The night your brother died," he began, "I had one last conversation with him." She sat up straighter, so Michael continued. "He pulled me aside and told me about you. 'My father doesn't want the Sun Crown to know,' he said, 'but I get the strange feeling tonight that someone *ought* to know.'"

As Michael recalled the moment now, he felt a chill run down his neck. Rinaldo couldn't have known just how important that premonition had been. Michael swallowed hard before continuing.

"'My youngest sister is different from the rest of us,' he told me. 'She can't sing or even talk, and her health grows more frail the deeper she gets in the ocean. But she's special. She sees and hears things no one else notices. And she's determined to live!'" Michael paused.

Arianna's eyes were closed, and tears were streaming down her face.

Michael scooted forward in the boat and took her hand before whispering, "He told me that he was convinced you might one day be the Sea Crown."

Arianna's eyes shot open, and she stared at him as though he'd lost his mind. Then, pulling her hand free, she looked up into the hanging branches above them and opened and closed her mouth before shrugging and shaking her head, tears falling even faster. Her shoulders slumped forward like a little old woman's, and she placed her face in her hands.

Michael leaned forward. "I didn't know him as well as you did, but I got to know your brother well enough over the years to know he was a man of honor. I didn't understand what he meant that day, but I knew that if nothing else, he had faith in what the Maker could do with you." Michael paused, unsure of how to finish his awkward speech. "He was a good man," he finally said. "And he didn't deserve to die so young."

So much for making her feel better. Or himself. And yet, Michael wasn't sorry for what he had said. This connection should have been made long ago, if not for any other reason than out of respect for Rinaldo. He deserved to be remembered with dignity.

"I think I liked him so much because in a lot of ways, he reminded me of my sister, Maura. She was like him . . . always knew what she was doing."

Unlike Michael.

Michael suddenly had to look away for the strange prick in his eyes. When he looked up at the sky, he noticed that the sun had peaked, and he knew without a doubt that they would be missed at the midday meal. He should have been back at the palace nearly a half hour before. Still, he had one more question.

"Did you know who I was the day you rescued me?"

Slowly, Arianna nodded, her eyes wary, and Michael recalled the sailor's words. Had Arianna watched him often, as the sailor claimed? The thought was a bit unsettling at first, until Michael also remembered what Rinaldo had said about Arianna's limitations. A mermaid without the ability to dive deep or sing must have led a lonely existence indeed.

Now as they sat in the shade of the tree, Arianna leaned over the side of the boat and placed her hand in the water. The water rippled as two pretty little blue and yellow fish surfaced, nibbling the end of her finger.

What have they told you, he wondered, *to make your self-loathing so great?*

But he didn't ask that. Instead, he asked, "Want to see how fast I can row us before we tip over into the bay?"

Arianna splashed him hard, and Michael laughed.

After rowing them back to the other side of the bay, Michael held out his hand to help her up from the boat. When she was standing on the dock beside him, however, he suddenly found it very difficult to let go. Warning bells, like the ones the church tolled when a fire had begun, sounded in his head as he stared at their clasped hands.

For a moment, he had forgotten his angst. He had forgotten his country's situation and even his own problems. For a single second, there had been Arianna. Only Arianna.

Such thinking was dangerous, particularly for a prince who was barely maintaining a hold on his own kingdom. This was the worst time to be trailing after a woman. And yet, he found he wanted more than an occasional smile and nod. He wanted to keep her close. He wanted to *hear* her.

Michael was in a precarious place.

22

ACCUSATIONS

"I still cannot see why three and seven make ten," Lucy sighed as they took their seats in the dining hall. "All these figures hurt my head." Then she perked up as Rolf handed her some silverware. "Perhaps there will be date cakes tonight! That would make my head hurt less."

"We haven't had date cakes in over a year," Claire said as she took her seat beside her sister. "And it doesn't matter if the sum makes sense. Three and seven make ten. They just do. Your head just hurts because of your sniffles."

Arianna sighed a little. It would be so much easier to teach the children if she could talk. They were both quick, and she was honestly amazed that they had learned anything under her tutelage.

Renata would have known what to do.

The thought took Arianna a bit by surprise, and with it came the pang of guilt she still felt whenever her aunt's face appeared in her mind.

"Arianna. Girls." The cook nodded to each of them as he began to ladle the supper into their bowls. Arianna tried to keep a smile on her face as she saw the watery chowder splatter at the bottom of her bowl. Clams again.

But at least she had food, she rebuked herself immediately. Her face wasn't gaunt or ashen like the humans' had been in the city. And as she was feeling guilty about her dislike of chowder, more guilt poured in, as it often did when she had moments of weakness.

It had been two weeks since her last attempt at finding her aunt, the very day she'd been attacked by the old fisherman. Four times she had gone out now in total, and each trip had been cut shorter, thanks to the ever-encroaching monsters from the Deeps. That, and her fins were taking longer and longer to change in and out each time. Whatever magic had given her legs seemed to be slowly draining itself from her. Another gift of the Maker, she thought wryly.

The table quieted as Michael took his seat. He turned to the holy man and asked him to give the blessing, and while everyone else prayed, Arianna studied the tops of their heads.

As always, Bithiah and Rolf held hands. Arianna smiled wistfully as their fingers, dark on white, entwined peacefully. The queen looked as proper as ever, her fine brown-and-white peppered hair up in an elaborate twist and sprinkled with little jewels. Cook's round face was still red from the heat of the stove, and so was his daughter's, who helped him. The footman and one of the two maids held hands, too, a habit they had taken up the week before but never let anyone see after the prayer ended. Master Russo seemed to be getting the same bad cold that had kept Arianna and the girls indoors for the last week, as he continually sniffled during the prayer. And Lucas, well, he seemed to be as late as ever.

A movement to her left a few chairs down caught her eye, and Arianna found herself staring into the eyes of the eldest prince. Gently, he nodded at the holy man, who was still praying, then closed his eyes again. Embarrassed, Arianna ducked her head. Her relationship with Michael had been much easier since their boat ride. She had even been invited to the prince's study each night, and while he argued with Lucas or Russo, she sat in her little corner and checked his figures. It was a peaceful time, and while they rarely talked during such sessions, there was something nice about sitting nearby and knowing another soul was there.

She wasn't about to pledge her allegiance to a Maker who hated her, but she didn't want another bit of consternation between herself and the prince, either. Whatever truce they seemed to have struck up was already confusing enough.

As soon as the prayer was over, everyone tucked into their food, though it was with less enthusiasm than they had when Arianna had first arrived. Cook struck up a lively debate on whether or not clams should be baked or fried. Arianna knew next to nothing of cooking. Still, everyone else seemed interested, probably because there was little else to discuss. Everyone else but Prince Michael.

He stared at his food listlessly as he stirred the white watery soup continuously with his spoon. Arianna suddenly found herself missing his smile. He was generally serious, but in the last few weeks, Arianna had seen him smile less and less, until his false grins were reserved only for the girls. Now one dark brow was pulled down over his hazel eyes, and he seemed even more gone than usual.

Something was wrong.

Something was always wrong, Arianna tried to chide herself. But she couldn't escape the nagging feeling that a dark cloud was looming over their heads. If she could speak, Arianna decided, she would draw him aside and demand to know what had happened. And he would tell her. She was sure of it.

Actually, she wasn't sure. But as she stirred her own chowder, Arianna wished she were sure. There had been something in his eyes that day on the pier, something she would have paid a thousand gold pieces to see again. And every now and then, as she played with the girls in the garden or worked with them on their numbers and writing, she sometimes thought she saw it in his eyes whenever she glanced up and saw him watching them.

But she was just being silly. He was watching his nieces. Nothing else. Probably making sure they were being well cared for and keeping up with their studies. Just at that moment, however, Arianna had the sensation of being watched. When she looked up, she realized with a start that Michael was looking at her with the same undeniable intensity he'd been observing her with for weeks. Her breath caught in her throat, and for the first time it occurred to Arianna that the prince could be just as silent as she.

If no one else were there to judge or advise him, what would he say? Would she get to hear his real voice?

"Michael." Queen Drina's grating voice jarred both of them out of their shared moment.

Arianna wanted to pinch the woman. But the prince just sighed and turned to his mother, who was sitting to his immediate right, a careful smile plastered on his face.

"Yes, Mother?"

"What will you be doing tonight?"

"Going over Lucas's plans to repair our flagship. Why?"

"Won't you be examining our finances as well?"

Arianna forgot to breathe. Where was she going with this?

"I have it from a very good source," Queen Drina sniffed, "that you've been receiving help with that task."

"Yes," Michael's words were cautious. He leaned back and studied his mother with wary eyes. "What of it?"

"Is the girl helping you?"

Their entire party went silent, and Arianna had to suppress the desire to crawl under the table. The way the queen said it made her quiet evenings in the prince's study feel suddenly shameful, though she couldn't say just why.

"I thought," the queen continued, putting her spoon down and turning to glare at Arianna, "that I had made my feelings clear about her dabbling in our coffers. Also," she turned back to her son, "I thought we had taught you better than to consort with young women alone."

"Mother!" Michael's mouth fell open. "My door is open to anyone who wishes to see me in the evenings. You know this! Besides," he gestured at Arianna, which only made her blush more, "she is very good with her figures. Far better than me, actually. She's already saved us more coin than I ever did. I was getting four hours of sleep a night, and thanks to Arianna, I'm now getting five!" He stood up so fast his chair fell over. "If you had listened to me that night, you would have seen it, too!"

"Oh, I'm sure she is very good with her figure!"

"That is enough!" Michael threw down his napkin. "If you wish to have this conversation with me, you may do so in private. But do not try to tarnish her character here in front of our friends!"

The queen huffed and stuck her lip out in a ludicrous pout, but Michael wasn't finished.

"When have I ever shirked duty? When, Mother?" He righted his chair and began to stalk off.

"Wait, Michael. I am still queen here! You will respect me!"

But Michael only slammed the door. The spacious glass room was filled with a nearly stifling silence. Finally, her head held high, the queen stood, too. No one said a word as she began to walk. She stopped, however, when she got to Arianna's chair. Arianna smelled the faint scent of jasmine as Drina bent so close that their faces nearly touched.

"He may be blind to your wiles, but I know what kind of trickery you're harboring," she hissed, making Arianna's ear hurt. "I am warning you now. Stay away from my son. I forbid you from visiting his study tonight or ever again. And should you be tempted to disobey me," she touched Arianna's necklace, "do not forget that I know where you come from. I can unmake you as fast as you tried to rise to power here."

And with that, Drina straightened up, smoothed her peach silk gown, and glided to the doors, waiting for Rolf to rise and open them for her.

Arianna wrung her hands in her lap as she stared at her soup. They were all looking at her. She could feel it. And though the queen's words had been whispered, there was no way anyone could have missed hearing them.

Did she leave now before incurring the queen's wrath even more? A few months ago, the decision would have been easy. But now, the idea of leaving the girls tore at her heart. And if she was honest with herself, the thought of leaving Michael brought just as much pain. Still, surely the others would turn her out as soon as they knew her origins. Everyone had lost sons, brothers, fathers, and loved ones in the maritime war. They would escort her out of the palace themselves, no doubt.

Finally, someone clinked his or her spoon on a dish and began to slurp the chowder again. Whispers began to follow, though none of the whispers were directed to her, save that of the girls asking tearfully what their grandmother had meant.

"Come now," Bithiah stood and gently took the girls by their shoulders. "I think I may have some dry dates hidden somewhere in my wooden chest. Let us see if we can find and enjoy them before bed. Yes?"

Arianna threw her a look of thanks as the older woman ushered the girls away. With a start she realized that everyone else was still looking at her, too, but instead of the shock or even hatred she had expected to see on their faces, she saw only sympathy.

I only wanted to help! she wanted to shout. *I never tried to seduce him!*

Without speaking a word, Master Russo got up and left the room. The uncomfortable silence continued until he returned and walked up to Arianna. He was holding a single quill.

"The queen is worried about her son," he began. "She's been concerned with little else than finding him the perfect match since before he was born. I think I speak for everyone here, though, when I say that *we* need you. And more importantly, *he* needs you." He held out the quill. "I believe there's a stack of parchments sitting on his desk right now that needs you as well." A kind smile cracked his round face.

Arianna began to reach for the quill, but paused when she remembered the queen's threat.

Master Russo seemed to read her mind. "If it is the matter of your origin that concerns you," he glanced around at the table and everyone else nodded, "we have already discussed that amongst ourselves."

Arianna felt the surprise show on her face. They had been discussing her? She should have known better. Of course they would. She was nothing but odd by human standards.

"And," he continued, "we have decided it matters not. You have done nothing but good for us since arriving."

Arianna studied his shiny, red face with a frown. Surely he wouldn't mean that if he really knew the truth. But a closer look at his suddenly firm expression convinced her that he was very close to the truth, as were the others. And they had decided that it didn't matter.

With a grin, Arianna took the quill and headed to the prince's study.

~

The door to Michael's study was closed when Arianna arrived. She paused as she lifted her hand to knock. Would he want to see her? Or would he be too embarrassed after his mother's outburst and accusations?

Gathering her courage, she knocked on the thick wooden door.

If Master Russo and the others believed in her, then she, too, refused to be intimidated.

"What?" His answer was sharp.

She knocked again, and a moment later the door jerked open. His expression was fierce until he saw who stood there. She tried to give him a half smile, holding up the pen in a foolish gesture to show him what she had come for.

His face softened and he held the door open wider. "I'm sorry. I thought you were someone else." The red shade returned to his face as he jammed a wedge underneath the door to hold it wide open, then stomped back over to his desk and yanked up his quill.

Thankful his anger wasn't directed at her, Arianna quickly gathered up the papers he had left on the corner of his large desk and went to her usual place in the red chair by the window. Leaning back into the shadow of the window's dark, heavy curtain, Arianna curled her legs up against her chest then took a deep breath before she began checking the figures for mistakes.

She found it difficult to concentrate on the numbers at first. The queen's voice continued to haunt her thoughts and distract her from her work. Was Drina right? Had Arianna ever come to this study with designs other than fixing the prince's tired mistakes? She searched her memory. In the beginning, her intentions had only been to make the numbers right.

As the days had gone on, however, Arianna did have to admit that her quiet evenings with Michael were her favorite part of the day. There was a comfortable silence between them that, for once, Arianna did not wish to fill with talk. There was something warm and familiar about their evenings together. But what was it that made her yearn for more?

She couldn't put her finger on the cause until Michael shifted and put his head on the desk. Then it hit her. When she was with him, Michael simply allowed her to *be*. Not even Renata had been able to do that. There had always been something she'd been trying to fix, from Arianna's posture to her understanding of politics to her history. But Michael knew what even Renata had not. He knew of Arianna's humanity. And yet he kept her near anyway.

"I am sorry for my mother's outburst." Michael pushed his chair away from the desk and rubbed his eyes.

Arianna watched him carefully. She couldn't deny that the event had shaken her, but she didn't want to hurt or further agonize him, either. She couldn't imagine having such a mother.

"She is concerned that I marry a woman who can raise the status of our kingdom," he continued, eyes still closed.

This made Arianna's heart falter just a little. But she refused to admit why.

"Her myopic goals have made her blind to anything else that might help the kingdom in any other way that she has not personally seen in her own mind." He finally turned and looked at Arianna, his hands behind his head. "I'm glad to see that you're feeling better, by the way."

Arianna gave him a dry smile. *It is only a head cold,* Bithiah had pronounced the week before when Arianna's nose had stopped working and her throat had felt like razors were scraping its insides. Whatever a head cold was, it was possibly the most dreadful ailment Arianna had ever experienced, apart from the frill shark's bite. This had been the first night she and the girls had attended supper with everyone else. What a way to return.

"How about we do something different tomorrow?" he asked. "I know you like to take the girls to the garden after studying in the mornings. Would you be interested in learning about archery instead?"

Arianna had no idea what archery was, but Claire often went on about how she wanted to learn. Not that the event itself mattered. Spending time with Michael would be a joyful event. Eagerly, she nodded.

"Good," he leaned forward again and picked up his quill once more. "I look forward to it."

"And how is the work progressing?" Master Russo poked his head in through the open door and gave Arianna a sly smile. "I thought I might come and ensure that your *figures* were getting done properly."

Arianna blushed, and Michael tossed a wad of used parchment at the steward over his shoulder. Master Russo returned to the hall without another word, chuckling to himself all the way.

23

DUE

*A*rianna stared at the odd contraption in her hands. What was one supposed to do with a string tied to both ends of a bent stick and a bunch of long pointy sticks? She gingerly put her finger to touch the feathers near the end of one of the long pointy sticks. Then she poked the stick's sharp point, only to yank her hand back as a drop of blood beaded on it.

"Does this mean I get to go hunting with you?" Claire bounced up and down as she trailed after Michael, who was carrying three more of the strange device.

Michael chuckled. "I'm not sure what you're going to hunt, as I've never seen anything larger than a dog running through Maricanta's streets. And I don't think Bithiah would take too kindly to you hunting her greyhound. Now," he handed each of the girls their own contraption, "since everyone has a bow, let's walk to the other side of the field. We don't want to be anywhere near the palace."

"Why?" Lucy asked.

Michael bent and slung the *quiver*, as he'd called it earlier, over his shoulder. "Because if we miss, which you will on your first tries, we don't want anyone to be in the way. An arrow in the foot or arm would make an awful gift to one of our friends."

He continued to warn the girls about the dangers of playing with the bows and arrows, as they were apparently called, as their little group traipsed across the field of sand and wild grasses. It was the first time Arianna had ever ventured on the east side of the palace grounds, and the walk was warm and sunny. Smiling to herself, she only half listened to his warnings as the wind played with her gown and threatened to pull loose locks down from her hair.

What a perfect day. The sound of Michael's voice and the girls' laughter was soothing, and with the sun on her face and the sound of the ocean behind it, Arianna could really think of nowhere else she'd rather be at that moment. Of course, that thought alone made her feel a little guilty.

But, she wondered hesitantly, wouldn't her mother want her to be happy? Wouldn't Renata want her to make the best of where she was here and now? She believed it to be so. Her father, of course, would see her position with the humans quite differently, and she shied away from thinking of his response too closely. Rinaldo would have been pleased, though. She was sure of it.

When they reached the other end of the field, which was shaded by a line of squat, thick palm trees, Michael began to put together a standing rectangle with a set of circles painted inside of it, something he called the *target*. "You want to hit the middle circle with your arrow, or get as close to it as you can."

Arianna stared at the arrows on the ground before smiling to herself. This would be easier than she'd thought. Without waiting to hear the rest of his instructions, she picked up one of the arrows and walked over to the target. She turned to make sure they were watching her, then whacked the center of the target with the end of the arrow as hard as she could.

When she turned back around to gloat over her cleverness, however, the girls were rolling in the grasses, laughing so hard that tears were streaming down their faces. Even Michael, who was attempting to keep a straight face, was turning red as he bit his lip. When she frowned at him in confusion, he began laughing as hard as the girls. Arianna looked back at the target as the others continued to laugh hysterically. She'd hit the target with the arrow, she thought as she glared at it. What else could they want of her?

Still laughing, Michael walked up to Arianna and guided her back to the girls before taking the arrow from her hands. Arianna crossed her arms and glowered at him. What was so funny?

She watched with resentment as he faced the pointy end of the arrow toward the target and fitted the bow's string in a notch she'd not noticed in the back of the arrows earlier. Then he raised the bow and arrow, and to her surprise, began to stretch the string so hard that the bow began to bend. Farther, farther he drew the arrow back until his right elbow was as high as his ear. Then, in one swift movement, he let go of the arrow and it flew out of his hands before hitting a tree several yards behind the target.

"I thought you were supposed to aim for the target, Uncle." Lucy pulled on his shirt.

"I was just showing you the proper stance," he mumbled as he fitted another arrow onto the string.

Arianna saw what the girls did not, however, in the way his eyes tightened ever so slightly as he pulled the arrow back again. She put her hand over her mouth to hide her laugh while Michael missed the target again.

"All right, everyone," he said, still not looking at Arianna, "you've seen the stance. Now you try."

Still trying to stifle her silent giggles, Arianna did as she was told, and she and the girls began to let their arrows loose as well. And not one of them hit the mark. Her arrow didn't even leave the bow in the right direction, falling to the ground before she let go of the string. The girls fared little better.

As she leaned over to grab another arrow, Arianna felt the slightest tug at her own bow. Whirling around, she gasped as Lucas held a finger up to his mouth for her to be quiet. As though she had any other choice.

With a sly grin, he gently pulled the bow from her hands and lifted an arrow from the ground, right behind Michael, who was leaning over Lucy to help her adjust her stance. Then, in one fluid motion, Lucas had fixed the arrow in its proper place and let it fly, hitting the center of the target with a loud crack.

Michael jumped, and Arianna nearly fell over laughing herself as he whipped his head around to see where it had come from. When his eyes rested on his brother, he scowled. "I thought you were working at the docks today."

"And I thought you were teaching the girls archery."

"What does it look like I'm doing?" Michael snapped.

"I'm not sure, but it's not archery."

Michael continued to scowl at his brother, but Lucas sauntered over to Arianna and handed her back her bow before fetching her another arrow.

"Hold your hand up here, by your chin," he instructed her, taking her hand in his and lifting it up. "Not by your chest. Now, widen your feet." he gently kicked her worn boots with one of his own large feet.

Arianna's chest fluttered a bit as Lucas leaned in close to adjust her grip on the bow. Though she had never considered Lucas in the same light she did Michael, it was still a bit . . . shocking to have a man so close.

Why hadn't Michael tried to teach her this way, she wondered. Then she shook her head bitterly. Because he wasn't interested in her *that* way. He was supposed to marry a rich princess who would replenish all of the Maricantans' wealth and win the hearts of the people. With a huff, she tried to focus her efforts on Lucas's instructions, and not the way she suddenly resented his brother.

"Now," Lucas whispered, "let go."

To Arianna's amazement, the arrow zipped straight toward the target. And though it didn't come anywhere near the center, she did what Michael had not.

She turned immediately to see Michael's reaction, but to her disappointment, he hadn't seen her hit the target. Instead, he was quietly conversing with a stranger in yellow clothing. *A runner,* she guessed. Boys and young men, Master Russo had once explained to her, were hired to take messages from one place to another. As they spoke in hushed tones, however, she noticed that all joviality and even his annoyance had fled from Michael's face. Lucas noticed this, too, and though he handed Claire another arrow and gently angled her elbow, he studied his brother with a slight frown.

After dismissing the messenger, Michael stared down at the parchment he now held.

"Well?" Lucas took a step toward him.

"Just . . ." Michael swallowed, still staring at the parchment. His jaw tightened, and his eyes became daggers. "Keep them safe and busy," he snapped.

"But Michael—"

"Just do as I say!" Michael shouted.

Arianna and Lucas exchanged a stunned glance while Michael stomped off toward the palace. "I'll be back," he barked over his shoulder.

"What's wrong with Uncle Michael?" Lucy whimpered.

"He got a letter that he needs to respond to, and no one likes boring letters when you could be doing this." Lucas turned his attention back to the girls before Arianna could. "But don't worry," he mussed their hair in turn, "I'm better at archery anyways. You'll get a better lesson from me!"

The girls eventually returned to trying to hit the target, but Arianna couldn't bring herself to continue. Her thoughts were with the man stalking toward the palace.

"You're worrying about him."

Arianna looked over to see that Lucas's eyes were trained on the palace, too, his brow furrowed.

"You shouldn't worry, though."

Arianna frowned at him, but Lucas just shook his head.

"You can't let his poor archery skills or his gentle manners fool you," he said, giving her a hard smile. "Because my brother could be very dangerous if he chose to be."

～

Michael hadn't returned by the time the girls grew tired of the archery, nor did he appear for dinner or when she tucked Claire and Lucy into bed. Arianna's concern turned to a near panic, though, when he failed to appear in his study. Without anyone to distract her, Arianna finished the figures all too soon, and for the lack of something better to do, decided to go to sleep.

But sleep wouldn't come.

After an hour of tossing and turning, Arianna finally gave up and decided to go for a walk. She pulled on her old boots and slipped out of the palace. She managed to somehow make it out of the palace without waking anyone, to her knowledge. The guard said nothing as she tiptoed by him and out onto the walkways that sprawled all through the gardens.

It should have been a peaceful evening. Crickets chirped and the ocean lapped gently at the shore. The air had a thick, sticky feel to it. It should have been soothing to Arianna, considering it felt much like the water, but there was an undercurrent that made the hair on the nape of her neck stand on end.

As she passed the edge of the palace and began down toward the field, a light in the window of the palace chapel caught her eye. Arianna stopped and squinted. Sure enough, someone had lit a candle inside. Removing her clunky boots, Arianna snuck up to one of the chapel's color-stained front windows and tried to peer inside.

To her disappointment, it was empty. A sudden wave of frustration washed over her, and with it, a burst of anger as well. Without thinking about what she was doing, Arianna stomped into the chapel.

What are you doing to me? She stared up at the altar. *I know you can hear me.* There was no audible or visible answer, but Arianna charged ahead anyway. *Every time I have happiness within reach, you yank it away! Was that why you made me? Why I am the way I am? So that you could have a plaything when you're bored?* A treacherous tear gathered at the corner of her eye, but she shook it away angrily. *Rinaldo loved you, and you let him die! Renata took care of me, and you let her disappear! And now Michael? What horrid fate do you have planned for him?* Her breath caught in her throat as the truth rose up within her, a truth she had done her best to suppress for years. But not anymore. She was through with quieting the voices inside her.

I loved you. This time, the tears ran freely down her face, and the flickering light of the candle grew blurry. *And you turned your back on me.*

"You, too?"

Arianna whirled around. Michael was kneeling behind the second bench. Had he somehow heard her silent words?

"I couldn't sleep either," he said, and Arianna's heart was both relieved and broken at the same time. Swallowing her disappointment, she turned to go, but he reached out and caught her arm. "If it's impropriety you're concerned with, the holy man is in his study." He nodded at the corner of the room, where the outline of a door was framed by the light of a fire on the other side.

"Do you mind my asking why I never see you here?"

Arianna studied him warily, but his expression wasn't condescending or judgmental. Just curious.

"I know you go to the beach on holy days," he said, letting go of her arm. "I also know that your brother was a man of faith." He watched her for a moment longer. "What happened to you?" he whispered, "to make you stop believing?"

Michael couldn't hear her through her silence, Arianna thought. But he wanted to, it seemed. She stared down at the red rugs beneath her bare feet. The only people who had ever tried so hard to hear her were her mother and Renata. And Rinaldo. Her heart clenched up as her brother's face flashed in her mind.

"I must confess," Michael said, looking back up at the stained-glass mural behind the altar, "it's easier to remain faithful on days when life is good. And life hasn't seemed good very often as of late. There are so many nights when I feel as though my prayers are bouncing off this ceiling." He turned and met Arianna's gaze, his eyes glinting like gold in the weak light of the candle. "But I *know* there is a purpose in all this. I wish I knew what it was, to be honest, but . . . there is one. There must be."

Arianna only watched, confused.

"Our debts are due tomorrow," he said in a voice nearly too quiet to hear. "I've put it off as long as I could. And your work with treasury numbers has helped, for sure. But that missive I received this morning was from the king of Tumen. He'll be here in a week to collect his dues." Michael's neck flexed, and for a moment, fire burned in his eyes. "Or at least, what is actually due him. Not a dust mote more."

Arianna sat at the edge of his bench and hesitantly placed her hand on his arm. What wasn't he telling her?

He studied his hands. "Without the money we owe the Tumenians for our war debts, my mother and I will be replaced, and the king of Tumen will own our kingdom as well." Arianna sharply drew in a breath, and he only shook his head and gave her a sad smile. "Just another fool contract made by my beloved grandfather. We've sold most of the household goods, or as much as we could, at least, without attracting more attention than necessary. My brother has shrunk the navy so that it's as small as we can possibly function with. Most of the horses are gone. The staff is a fraction of what it was before the war." He shook his head and ran a hand through his dark, messy curls. Arianna had to resist a sudden and strong urge to run her hand through them, too.

"I've done all I know how, but there is no protocol for this." He surprised her then by taking her hand. She held her breath as he turned it over in his own. "I want to thank you for all you've done for us."

Arianna looked at the floor again, her cheeks coloring. All she had done was fix his tired mathematical mistakes.

But he wasn't done. "I suppose you are the reason we have lasted as long as we have. And I don't mean just now. If you hadn't saved me that day in the storm, my mother probably would have married the next dandy that came along. Don't ever repeat a word of this to my mother, but she probably would have picked some ignoramus with the sense of a walrus."

In spite of such a somber topic, Arianna giggled.

"Finally a smile. But in all seriousness," he squeezed her hand, "you were our gift from the Maker. Never doubt that." Then he stood. "I suppose we should get some sleep tonight. I've got some bad news to break to the household tomorrow. Might as well be rested first." He held his hand out. "Coming?"

Everything in Arianna wanted to take that outstretched hand, but she shook her head instead.

"Well, then," he said, "I will tell the guards to keep an eye out for you."

Arianna gave him the biggest smile she could muster as he turned and left. Looking back up at the altar, she tried to find words for all the maelstroms and quiet pools of peace that were mixing about inside her heart.

I don't know if that's true, she finally told the Maker. *I don't know if I can believe that you have a plan for it all. But if you really mean it . . . If you meant that as a sign of some sort, then let this work. Please let this work.*

For an idea was already forming. And it scared her to death.

24

A RISKY VENTURE

*A*rianna put her shoes in their usual place behind the rocks and then went to stand at the edge of the water. The stars above her seemed particularly bright, despite the gray that was beginning to grow on the horizon, and she was overcome with a sudden desire to simply sit on the sand and stare up at them until dawn.

Still, she knew deep down that really what she wanted to do was stall. With a sigh, she slung her borrowed bag over her shoulder and put one foot in the water, then the other, trying to ignore the warning voice in her head that wondered what would happen if she didn't change. The jellyfish that had recently taken to patrolling this section of the beach would be making his usual territorial rounds soon. If she didn't start swimming, she would never make it past the creature in time. She had seen enough of the jellyfish in her last two trips out to sea to recognize the black cloud within its clear blob of a body. The little monster, no larger than her fist, had been to the Deeps.

All right, I'm ready, she told the Maker when her feet could hardly touch the ground. As though answering her, Arianna felt the prickle begin in her toes, and she dared to smile. The transformation was no longer as painful as it had once been. Whether she was simply becoming immune to the magic or not, she did not know. Just that she was grateful.

As soon as her tail was complete, she headed for the pearl farms. They were farther away than her old tower was, so Arianna slowed to pace herself as she began to pass familiar landmarks. She purposefully ignored the broken city to her left. The last time she'd dared to look, the ocean had already reclaimed the mansion and the houses and the streets. It was almost as if her family had never been there at all.

The sight of the pearl farms brightened her dark musings considerably. Usually, her people would have harvested them back when the air and water were still cool. But the oyster beds were ripe for harvest, as no merperson had attended them in a very long time. She should get a good haul if the pirates hadn't found them already.

As a child, Arianna had begged her father on more than one occasion to let her work at the pearl farms. The framed boxes of the oyster beds were just higher than the water's surface. She could very easily work with the oysters, Arianna had argued passionately. Even during the day! But as always, her father had said no.

The irony of her gathering the shells now was not lost on Arianna as she surveyed the dozens of raised oyster beds. The long rows of shells were just high enough to stick out of the water, which meant Arianna had to push her head and shoulders above the surface to gather them. Of course, being above the surface meant she could not see what was below the surface. As Arianna hurriedly shoved the oysters into her bag, she distracted herself from the danger by imagining what their arrival might change at the palace. Perhaps the oysters themselves would give Cook something new to work with that evening, a treat the Crown wouldn't have to pay for. Perhaps the money would be enough to help pay back the Tumenian king. Perhaps they would make Michael smile.

As soon as her bag was heavy, Arianna slung it over her shoulder and started back to the palace. The sky began to turn from gray to coral pink, buoying Arianna's spirits. Why hadn't she tried this sooner?

A flash of blue floated to her right. Then it was gone.

Arianna picked up her speed, but the bag was heavy and hard to pull, and her dress was getting in her tail's way. The blue flashed again, this time below her. Arianna bolted, but it wasn't fast enough. The jellyfish had found her.

It shouldn't have been so fast! Jellyfish were slower than merpeople, Arianna thought, as if thinking the truth could make the monster change its form back to what it had been. But the jelly-fish *was* keeping up, just a few parsecs behind her. She swerved back and forth, hoping the change in direction would throw it off, but the jellyfish followed easily.

Arianna was breathing hard as she passed the city and her tower. She swerved to the left and to the right, diving deep and racing to the surface. But nothing deterred the creature. Just as she began to tire, she noticed that the water was rapidly growing shallow. *Change me!* she begged the Maker. *Change me! Please!*

But no change came, and the jellyfish was almost to her.

Arianna began to drag herself onto the beach on her elbows, curling her tail up out of the water as much as possible. Knowing exactly what kind of pain she was about to experience and most likely die from in seconds, she scrunched her eyes shut as she crawled out of the water. *So this is how I'm going to die.*

But just as the sticky tentacles should have closed around her fins, two hands grabbed her firmly by the arms and yanked so hard that she flew out of the water and landed on a body. Whoever it was let out an *Oof!*

A moment passed before Arianna was able to force her eyes open. When she did, however, she realized that she was lying right on top of Michael. For a long time, they stared at one another in shock before Arianna had the courage to look back behind her. And just where she had been lying in the water, a gray blob floated up and down. It was watching her. Arianna shuddered at the thought.

Her shudder seemed to pull her savior from his stupor. He sat up and immediately wrapped his arms around her and squeezed her against his chest, muttering prayers of thanks to the Maker. Still too stunned to even attempt to pray, Arianna huddled in his warm, strong embrace and continued to stare at the jellyfish.

"What were you doing?" he finally groaned as he pulled back to examine her. Where there had been relief in his face only moments before, now he looked, well, livid. "What in the blazes convinced you that this was a good day to die?" Then he froze.

Arianna's blue-green scales that stuck out from beneath her dress glinted in the direct sun of the morning. Out of water, they were nearly blinding. Immediately, she felt ashamed. As much as she might go about pretending to be a human woman, this was who she was. What she was. He had seen it once, of course, as a boy. But now he was a man, and men were, as Renata had assured her, very particular in their tastes. Mermen preferred the usual dark-haired, pearl-white beauties that all the other mermaids would grow to be. And Michael? Well, Arianna was sure his boyhood dreams of marriage had never involved someone with a tail.

As if in a daze, he reached out to touch, then pulled his hand back. "I'm sorry," he whispered. "I shouldn't have. It's just that . . . you're beautiful."

She was dreaming. She had to be dreaming. And yet, his words hung in the air like smoke as he continued to stare at her tail in awe.

Before he could go on with embarrassing either of them any more and saying things she knew he would later regret, she pulled the bag off her shoulder and handed it to him. Then she let herself fall onto the dry sand and soak up the reassuring rays of the sun, for each one reminded her that she was not dead.

"Arianna?" The strange tenor of Michael's voice made Arianna open her eyes and prop herself up on her arms. Only then did she notice that her legs had finally returned. But that wasn't what he was staring at. "You risked yourself for my kingdom?" His voice was incredulous as he held the bag open.

Of course she had. Arianna frowned at him, but he ignored her expression and drew her up into his arms again. *Stop,* Arianna wanted to plead. *Stop before you say something we'll both regret.* But she couldn't find it in her to pull away from his embrace. She could feel his heart beating through his soaked shirt. Had she ever felt another heart this close before?

No, she realized. And now that she had, she didn't want it to stop.

As if to make her heartache double, he kissed her hair once before whispering,

"No pearls are worth your life. You must never do anything like that again. But . . . thank you."

Her hope wanted so desperately to flutter, to take off like the little butterflies she'd seen in the garden. But instead, she pressed it down, too afraid to let it rise.

25

WHILE I HAVE YOU

The ocean looked so peaceful from above. Arianna smiled to herself as she followed the girls along the shore. The afternoon was waning, dry and hot, and she had decided as soon as she'd set foot out the door that she would pay no heed to the monsters in the water. In fact, she would pretend they weren't there at all. As long as she and the girls stayed on dry ground, they could wander wherever they pleased. Today, that meant going to look at the tide pools north of the palace, or so the girls had informed her.

"Care for some company?"

Arianna turned back to see Michael following them. He was still in the same formal clothes he usually wore, but today his trousers were rolled up to just below his knees, and the sleeves of his shirt rolled up to his elbows. Had he planned to join them? The thought sent a wave of silly nerves through Arianna's stomach, and she tried to smother them. He was just looking after his nieces. Wasn't he?

Still, Arianna felt a ridiculous grin spreading across her face as Michael caught up to her.

"So where are we off to today?" he asked.

Arianna drew a circle with her hands, then made her fingers wiggle inside the circle.

"The tide pools?"

Arianna nodded. He was getting better.

Michael stretched his arms wide and twisted his torso a few times as they walked. "Sounds perfect. I've spent all day cooped up in my study with no one but ugly men surrounding me, asking for pearls or money. I could use some pretty faces to distract me."

Arianna tried to calm her racing heart. He was talking about his nieces.

"Three pretty faces, to be exact."

Arianna gave up on trying to steady her heart and focused on keeping her eyes straight ahead. But it was hard not to notice the way the powerful muscles in his lower legs flexed as he walked, making his gait smooth and confident. So different from mermen's tails, which were exactly the same as their female counterparts' tails, except longer.

"So what's so special about that necklace?" Michael pointed at the conch shell Arianna had reached up to stroke. "I don't know if I've ever seen you without it."

Arianna paused, then removed the green fiber string from her neck. Taking his arm, she stood still and held the little conch up to his ear.

Michael's eyes looked like they might pop. "Who is *that?*" He stared down at the little conch. "I've never heard anything so beautiful."

Arianna nodded and put the necklace back on with a sigh. What she wouldn't do for a voice to tell him. She thought about trying the new skill she'd been secretly practicing, but the wind was too loud.

Then his face lit up. "I forgot!" He pulled a folded parchment, quill, and little inkbottle from his pocket. "Claire! Lucy!" he called, cupping a hand by his mouth. "Let's stop and play here for a few minutes."

"But we want to see the tide pools!" Lucy yelled back.

"We will. But I want to show something to Miss Arianna. You can play on the dunes. Just stay out of the water." Then, taking her by the hand, Michael led Arianna over to the shore near the water's edge.

Arianna held her breath as they sat down. Holding his hand now somehow felt even better than it had that first time when he'd helped her out of the boat. His skin held the same delicious warmth as the sun, and his fingers were calloused and rough, as was the top of his palm. What kind of activity calloused just part of the hand?

She didn't have long to wonder, for as soon as they were sitting he let go of her hand to open the parchment. Arianna wanted to groan as his fingers left hers, until he presented her with a completely blank piece of paper, as well as the inkbottle and quill.

"You've done so much for us," he said, holding her gaze, all laughter gone from his face. "I wish . . . I wish I could repay you in earnest, but this is the best I can do . . . for now. Your pearls have afforded me a new stack of parchment."

She looked down at the blank piece of paper in awe.

"And," he added, suddenly looking slightly sheepish, his eyes twinkling, "I might also be a selfish creature. It would be very nice to hear you speak for an afternoon."

It was a moment before Arianna could look away from his eyes long enough to focus on the paper. When she took up the quill, however, she found that her hand didn't want to stop.

My aunt gave me this necklace when I was little. I had trouble sleeping, so she told me to wear the charm around my neck. It is her voice that you hear, singing my lullaby. She infused enough of her power into the song so that it stays in the shell, and I can hear it whenever I want. It is all I have left of her since she disappeared.

Michael took the paper. Upon reading it, his mouth turned

down. "I'm sorry," he murmured, then gave her a half smile. "I would give anything to hear my father's voice in something like that." He held his right hand up and pulled the ring off his finger. When he held it up, a gold band glinted in the dying sun.

"This was my father's. It's not even worth that much, but it was his . . ." He swallowed. "My father was the youngest prince of Ashland. He and each of his siblings received one of these rings from their father." He turned the ring over, revealing a single round blue stone embedded in the gold. "I wanted to be like him. I've tried. But it's like I'm stuck in my grandfather's footprints, and my own feet won't move."

You're not like your grandfather. Not one bit. Arianna pressed so hard into the parchment that it nearly tore.

Michael placed his hand on her shoulder and squeezed, leaving Arianna momentarily short of breath once again. "Thank you," he said, staring out at the waves. But he wore no smile this time. "If there is one thing in this world that I refuse to be, it's my grandfather."

What else did he do?

"Well, aside from making deals with pirates, my grandfather was determined to fight a war that no one could win. Five years after it had begun, he took a ride on his horse one day. He left because he was annoyed that Master Russo told him that the Destinians were refusing to lend him more money. I only know this because he asked me to accompany him. I think that was the first day he realized what a hole he had dug us into. Our people had nothing to eat, our trade had vanished, and now those who had lent us money wanted it back."

This troubled Arianna. *I thought King Everard was neutral.*

"He was. He only sent money to help purchase food for the people. But when he found out that his aid to the merpeople was also stolen by my grandfather, he cut off all funds." Michael sighed. "Really, King Everard was the least of our worries. The Tumenians were the ones my grandfather really got involved with. The day after our ride, they sent word that they expected payment, and soon. My grandfather simply climbed into bed and swallowed an entire bottle of foxglove nectar."

Michael shrugged and turned his hazel eyes on Arianna. "I swore on that day that I would never let my heart lead my head. My grandfather chased pleasure and personal delight until it killed him. It was more comfortable to die of poison than to face the mess he'd created."

Is that why you don't want to marry? Arianna regretted the words as soon as she'd written them, but she could tell from the change in his expression that he had already seen. Her face burned as she hurried to scratch them out, but Michael placed his hand firmly on hers, making it impossible to hold the quill. Then he tipped her chin up to look at her eyes.

"Believe me, it's not the wife I object to," he said softly. He dropped his hand and turned to look up at the Sun Palace, its blue windows gleaming in the setting sun. "My mother insists I marry a woman with a title. And saddling a woman and her kingdom with this shipwreck wouldn't be fair. Not until I've been able to make my kingdom worth something again."

I would ask nothing of you, Arianna wanted to write, but she didn't. Instead, she kept her quill off the paper, and instead wondered when she had truly fallen in love with the prince. All of her girlish fantasies were being lived out right now. Except she still had no voice, and the prince wasn't looking for a wife. But he was suddenly looking at her with the gentlest expression she'd ever seen.

"Of course," he gave her a crooked smile, "from the way things are looking now, it will be years before that happens." He traced the bottom of her lip with his thumb, and his voice dropped to a whisper. "Do you think any woman will still have me when I'm turning gray?"

While she was still lost in his eyes, a shriek sounded from farther up the shore. Michael was on his feet in an instant, with Arianna right behind him.

The girls. Where were the girls? Every possibility of death and pain filled Arianna's imagination and threatened to drive her mad until they crested one of the sand dunes and found the girls alive and huddling together.

"Lucy! Claire!" Michael half-ran, half-slid down the dune and grabbed both girls by an arm, turning them toward him. "I told you to stay near!"

But Arianna didn't hear anything else that he said. She was too busy staring at the tide pool the girls had been looking into. Instead of the little circles of anemones, urchins, and sea stars that always inhabited the pools at low tide, the whole pool was filled with dying fish and other sea creatures. There was even a full-grown male seal. And every single one had been touched by the Sorthileige.

Arianna turned back to Michael, who was still scolding the girls, and shook his shoulder. He glanced at the water once, then turned to stare at it with wide eyes. Arianna made a few frantic motions, but Michael just shook his head as he continued staring at the creatures. They all had black eyes and black veins that bulged out from their scales and skin. Nearly beside herself, Arianna whipped the parchment out and wrote on it so fast her writing was almost illegible.

Did the girls touch? If they had, she had no idea as to what she would do.

"Did either of you touch anything?" Michael gripped the girls' arms more tightly, but this time, his face was taut and his words desperate.

Lucy and Claire just shook their heads, tears still falling down their faces. Michael drew them closer. "You're absolutely sure?"

They nodded and began to sob. Michael pulled them into his

chest and held them there as he looked up at the sky and thanked the Maker. Still clutching the girls, he finally turned to Arianna. "What does it mean?" he asked.

My people have retreated to Gemmaqua, where my grandfather lives. Without our Protectors to guard the Deeps, the creatures must be moving in and out unhindered. That's why your fishermen are stuck fishing in the bay. Only now I fear it's getting worse.

"How do we stop it?"

We don't. Not without my people.

The words weighed heavy on Arianna's heart as they left the deathly tide pool behind and began the walk back to the palace. As they did, Arianna racked her memory for some way, any way to contact her family. Surely someone would come eventually. Then they wouldn't be able to ignore her cry for help. Her grandfather couldn't be so hardhearted as to refuse peace with the new prince. Not when he saw what a different king Michael would be.

To her surprise, Arianna found that her excitement was beginning to build even as Michael accompanied the girls back to their room. Perhaps she couldn't sing. But she could write.

"I'm afraid Lucas and I will be leaving tomorrow for a few days. We have some business with the Tumenians that I'm anxious to see finished," Michael said, pulling her aside in the hall after the girls were in their room. "But don't worry. I'll be back soon. And after that," he surprised her by grabbing her hand and spinning her in a circle, "we're going to celebrate what you've done for this kingdom." He let go of her hand and bowed. "With a dance."

Arianna clapped her hands. After such a day, she should have been devastated that he was leaving her with Drina. But having seen the tide pools, she knew she couldn't leave the ocean unattended any longer. She might look like a human, but deep down, she was still a mermaid, and guarding the ocean was her duty. And now Arianna had an idea, and a few days alone was just enough time to perfect it.

STIRRINGS

"*I*f I may have your attention." Michael stood and held his goblet in the air. Everyone around the table hushed, even Lucas.

Michael wore an outfit Arianna had never seen before, a uniform identical to Lucas's, with the exception of the gold braid trim winding around the black buttons, as opposed to Lucas's silver trim. The coats were the same shade of green as the ocean on a stormy day, so dark it was nearly blue. The color brought out the green in Michael's hazel eyes, and though Arianna had seen the uniform on Lucas several times and had found it quite fetching, there was something about seeing it on Michael that made her breath leave her. But then again, she wondered, could it be the light in his eyes that was so alluring? Or that he had cut his hair closer, like many of Lucas's military men? Or perhaps the way he was smiling?

"Tonight should have been a night of mourning," Michael said, breaking her trance. "A week ago, I was contacted by the king of Tumen, who informed me that under no circumstances was he going to allow any further delay of the payment of our debts. If all had gone as it should have, I would not be wearing this uniform tonight." With that, he fixed his eyes on Arianna.

Was it possible for a mermaid to melt? Because Arianna was sure she just might.

"When our newest family member found out about our predicament, however, she did something that, had I known about it, I certainly would have forbidden her from attempting."

Arianna glanced around at the faces surrounding her, her cheeks suddenly burning.

"Many of you have asked me where the bag of pearls came from. I'm telling you now that Arianna took it upon herself to venture out into the ocean," Michael continued.

A few people gasped, and even Queen Drina's jaw dropped. She turned to peer at Arianna, who dropped her eyes to the floor, not entirely convinced the queen wouldn't burst of indignation.

"She nearly died bringing us these." Michael held up a sack, slightly smaller than the one Arianna had filled. Setting it on the table where it landed with a gentle clunk, he allowed several pearls to roll out. The others gasped again, and Cook held up his spectacles to examine the cherry-sized pearls. Arianna smiled a little in spite of herself. With no one to faithfully tend the pearl farms in five years, the oysters had grown far larger than they were ever allowed under proper circumstances.

"Due to the merpeople withdrawal, the pearls fetched a price more than ten times their usual worth. I was able to pay back the Tumenian king with less than a third of the pearls, including the interest he suddenly decided to charge us. We will be hearing no more from them."

Arianna nearly missed it, the flex of his jaw and the way his eyes tightened just slightly, despite the smile on his face. But then his eyes returned to her.

"So I give this toast in honor of you, Arianna," he said in a voice that was suddenly tender, holding his goblet in her direction. "Our kingdom will never be able to repay you for your bravery or your goodness. But we hope that somehow," his voice dropped even lower, "we can find a way to make you happy."

Their little party burst into applause and shouts as their goblets clinked. Then the room exploded into loud, cheerful conversation as Arianna tried to shake the blush and the ridiculous grin from her face as Michael left his seat and walked over to her.

"Do you like the dress?"

Arianna had to laugh. His expression was much like that of a hopeful puppy. She nodded quickly and put her goblet down to stand and spin a few times before him. No matter how many times she spun, she couldn't get over how the many layers of pink flared out when she moved. The gown itself looked a bit like a flower, with petals that draped delicately down her waist and off her hips. A thin layer of the gauzy material was draped all the way around the top of the gown, revealing just the tops of her shoulders and her collarbones. She looked back up from the exquisite gown to see Michael studying the dress as well, though his gaze took a bit longer to reach her eyes again.

"I was informed by the merchant that this is the latest style in Ashland, and that Queen Isabelle from Destin has one just like it, with jewels sewn into the back instead of buttons." He shook his head and took another sip of wine. "Not that I have any idea as to what that means, but," he cleared his throat twice, "you certainly look fine in it. I mean, it looks fine on you. Or rather—"

"I think you had better eat a little and thin that wine out, son." Queen Drina swept up to Michael's shoulder and gave him an indulgent look. "I would like to have a word with our Arianna here myself."

Arianna felt her stomach drop, and Michael fixed his mother with a suspicious frown, but Drina just shook her head. "I swear I only mean to apologize."

Arianna was convinced that Drina was the one who'd imbibed

too much wine. And by the expression on Michael's face, he seemed to be thinking the same thing. Still, when his mother gave him another contrite nod, he glanced at Arianna. Reluctantly, she nodded as well. There was little Drina could do to her in this public setting, so close to her sons.

Arianna hoped.

"Truly," Drina said as Michael walked away, "I know that I have been . . . less than fair to you since you arrived. But you must understand," the queen continued in a sudden rush, "after my husband, father, and daughter died before and during the war, I couldn't bear to look at you."

You also have two granddaughters who aren't mermaids, and they get about as much of your attention as I do, Arianna thought, but she let the woman continue.

"I know it will not make up for the way I've treated you, but," she finally met Arianna's gaze, her brown eyes glittering strangely in the light of the summer sunset as it filtered through the glass walls, "I hope that perhaps we may . . . start again."

Drina was drunk. She had to be to make an apology like that. And yet, Arianna found herself smiling shyly and curtseying to the older woman. Did she really mean it? Arianna found herself greatly wishing she did.

Supper continued in a more lively tone. As the meal went on, few actually stayed seated, but began to mingle, carrying their dishes with them. Jokes were cracked, stories of Michael and Lucas as boys were shared, and the food was more plentiful and varied than any Arianna had tasted since coming to the palace. Instead of the thin chowder and bland bread she had grown accustomed to, there were bowls of fresh fruit, brown sugar bread, dried papaya strips, two kinds of cheese, sardines, thin crackers, and date cakes, which made the girls squeal. Arianna had just heaped a thick spread of cheese atop a sardine and cracker when she found Lucas suddenly at her side.

"Sardines, huh?" He took a swig from his goblet and eyed her with a wicked gleam in his eye. "Isn't that kind of dark? I mean, aren't you half—"

Arianna elbowed him and glanced around to see that no one had heard.

He only laughed though, almost giddy like a boy as he leaned closer. "Don't worry about that. Everyone knows. I mean, not *everyone* knows, but everyone has their suspicions. And you know what? No one cares."

Arianna stared at him, not sure whether or not she should set him straight that her people were in fact, *not* related to fish in the least bit, or whether she should be shocked that the others were so close to the truth. Of course, Master Russo had hinted before that they knew she wasn't native to them. But . . . was it possible that they could know her true origins and still love her?

"In all seriousness though," Lucas's face was suddenly somber, "I truly cannot thank you enough for what you did for my brother and for all of us."

Arianna felt the blush rise to her cheeks again and shrugged as she studied her goblet.

"I mean it," Lucas continued, his brow furrowing. "It wasn't just the kingdom that you saved. Michael was going to die."

Arianna froze, but Lucas continued.

"Much to my shame, the old sailor, the one that assaulted you, wasn't silent after all. It seems that a tradesman from the south heard him going on about a mermaid before we were able to get him into the dungeon. The tradesman then took the old man's word to the Tumenian king, who immediately demanded that you be included in the kingdom's payment as well."

Arianna stared at him in horror, unable to move.

"Fool that my brother is, he agreed to hand his throne over to fulfill our grandfather's agreement. But he had fully resolved to fight the king to the death before he handed you over. He was furious. You were never part of the agreement. But the king insisted on having the mermaid."

Arianna looked down at her legs, incredulous. *But I'm not a mermaid anymore,* she wanted to protest.

Lucas dropped his voice further and leaned over to whisper in Arianna's ear. "You have no idea what a mermaid is worth in this world we live in. Even one who seems to be dormant. Just the whisper of one will send kings scrambling to their treasuries." He leaned back, but his face did not lose its solemnity. "The war took my father, my sister, and her husband. I know I complain about him and like to poke fun, but we can't lose Michael. *I* can't lose him. So . . . thank you."

In that moment, Arianna finally saw Lucas for who he really was. Past the square jaw covered in stubble, the brawny arms and ever-flirtatious smile, there was a young boy who adored his big brother. Her chest constricted as she gave him a sad smile. She knew exactly how that felt.

Even more importantly, however, she had glimpsed a glorious, weighty truth. Before she had planned to risk her life bringing him the pearls, Michael had already chosen to risk his life for her.

"Stop hogging the girl and go find your own." Without waiting for Lucas to even look up, Michael shoved his brother out of the way and grabbed Arianna by the waist. "It may not be a proper ball, but the least I can do is ask you to dance." He leaned in to breathe in her ear, "You're too pretty not to be dancing tonight."

Arianna's arms and legs suddenly felt like they were made of jellyfish. But she grinned and nodded and let him lead her out to the same balcony where she had watched him dance with the beautiful girl so many years before.

"Master Russo," he called over her shoulder, "would you do us the honor?"

Arianna looked back to see Master Russo lift a strange object to his lips and take a deep breath. The music it produced was shrill and strange, but not at all unpleasant. Michael took her hand in one of his own, and wrapped his other arm firmly around her waist. Slowly, he began to turn them in circles, whispering what she should do with her feet as they moved in time to the music. And though she wasn't at all as graceful as the young girl at the ball had been, Arianna couldn't remember a time when she had ever been so happy.

Even in the ocean.

It wasn't long before the others were dancing, too. Bithiah and Rolf, Mario and Noemi, and Lucas and Lucy twirled around them. Laughter rang in the air, and even Queen Drina smiled once before heading back inside the palace.

After a few quick, light-hearted songs, Master Russo switched to one that was slow and melancholy. Cook's daughter, Nan, joined in, plucking some kind of stringed instrument in harmony.

The song was one of mourning, and it touched Arianna in a way no mersong had ever moved her before. Its melody sang of longing, reaching out to touch something that was just an arm's length away.

And in that moment, something in the air shifted. The spinning couples that surrounded them began to fade as Michael drew her closer. Arianna trembled as he stared down into her face. And the light in his eyes confirmed what she had wondered before. Somehow, he had seen inside her soul.

Tell him, an annoying voice in her head whispered. *You have a plan to reunite your peoples. Who knows when you'll have him to yourself again?* Arianna opened her mouth, but as she did, his right hand slipped out of hers and his fingers reached up to trace the edge of her jaw. Slowly, slowly he cupped her face, his fingers making her skin tingle wherever they touched. Leaning down, he drew her face toward his own.

Arianna closed her eyes, her lips trembling as she tried to slow her breath. Her blood raced, and a hunger she'd only felt hints of before awakened somewhere deep inside her. Renata had been wrong. Arianna was worthy of being chosen. He was choosing her now.

"Michael."

The moment was broken, as if someone had thrown a bucket of cold water on it. Arianna and Michael looked up to see Queen Drina holding a parchment marked with a purple seal. She waved it a little, ignoring Arianna's look of annoyance. "I need to speak with you. Now."

Michael let out a gusty breath and met Arianna's eyes with a pained expression. "Coming, Mother."

DUTY'S CALL

"*I*s this really that urgent?" Michael asked as soon as they were back in the dining hall away from the merriment.

"Arianna may have done more for our kingdom than any of us could have imagined," Drina said coolly, holding up the folded parchment again.

"Surely you wouldn't have her go out to sea again—"

"Of course not. It is her prior sacrifice that has already done its work. It seems we are to be visited by a princess from a distant island kingdom." She held out the parchment. "This was just delivered to me by a runner. Princess . . ." She opened up the parchment and skimmed it. "Ines. Princess Ines of Espigmas Isle. The princess believes that our kingdoms have mutual interests. We might, she says, both benefit from some sort of agreement."

Michael stared at his mother for a long moment until the words sank in. "What kind of agreement is she interested in?" he growled. "It must be an interesting one, considering that until now none of us has ever heard that such a place even exists."

"She says that her kingdom rarely trades openly with others because they have always feared that someone might see them as a potential conquest. They mine gold, their ships bring in whalebone, and when the merpeople were doing their duty, they traded pearls as well. But since the pearl shortage has kept everyone lacking, they took an immediate interest when we came up with the means to produce them."

"It was a one-time replenishment, Mother. I'm not sending Arianna back down. She nearly died!"

"I'm not asking you to send her again!" Drina took both his arms in hers and looked up at him, her eyes sparkling. "I only wish that you would convince this Princess Ines to truly consider us! If they are as wealthy as this parchment suggests, then our problems could be solved! You could take the crown, and we could be free of these poverties forever!"

Michael crossed his arms and frowned down at his mother. "And you believe all of this based on a single letter without a dust mote of proof that she's telling the truth? That there even is a Princess Ines?" He scoffed. "She sounds more like a myth to me."

"Myth or not, she'll be here in three days hence. And I expect you to put on a good show." She paused and straightened his coat. "I know," she lowered her voice, "that you find Arianna pretty. And she is a very pretty girl. But you need to think of the kingdom and of your duty." She stopped. "I also know I've always been a bit . . . flighty, but you have always been my rock, as your father was before you. And the kingdom needs you to do your duty now more than ever. A union with a wealthy land could prevent us from falling into greater debt, and help restore our people's livelihoods."

Michael could only glare at his mother and choke back the roar that wanted to escape his throat. Why now? Just when his life was taking a new turn—one he had, in all honesty, not dreamed possible—this fell into his life.

"I know you're upset," Drina said.

"Upset is an understatement. When have I ever shirked my

duties?" His voice grew louder. "When have I complained about taking on yours?"

"Never. And that is why I ask this of you now!" She sighed. "I know what you're thinking. And our kingdom will be forever indebted to her. She is even technically of the right class for you. But what more can Arianna really bring us?"

"A good heart, one that sacrifices when others need it. Love and attention for the granddaughters you *choose* to neglect on a daily basis!" He rubbed his eyes. "She has been better to me than I ever deserved. To us! Particularly after all the ways you've chosen to extend your benevolence."

"Yes, she is good. And there are a thousand more good-hearted girls like her. But where is her family, Michael? They abandoned her, left her for dead! How likely are they to send a dowry of any price? What we need is money and trade. And Princess Ines has both."

WHISPERS

*A*rianna had tried to fight the feelings of disappointment when Michael didn't return to the party. She'd had something she wanted desperately to show him, and the impromptu celebration had seemed the perfect time. He didn't come to breakfast the next morning, either, until it was nearly time for Master Russo to chase him down with all sorts of business for the day. Arianna tried to catch his eye, but no matter how much she smiled at him, she couldn't get him to glance at her.

The day got only stranger. Queen Drina was having Noemi take old tapestries and decorations out of storage as Arianna and the girls gathered their things to go outside.

"It's not ideal," the queen clucked to herself, her silk-covered arms crossed as she frowned up at the faded red tapestries. "Still, it's preferable to looking completely destitute."

Arianna's time with the girls and their studies crawled that morning, and when the midday meal finally did arrive, Michael didn't appear at all. By suppertime, Arianna's stomach was in knots. She'd been sure at first that he was just busy. There were plenty more debts to settle aside from Tumen's, although that had been the greatest. No doubt he wanted to get his kingdom independent as quickly as possible. But when he spoke only to those on the left side of the table that night, Arianna decided she would have to take the matter into her own hands.

Excusing herself early, Arianna stood just around the corner to his study. He never retired for the day without setting his study to rights, refilling his ink jar and organizing his parchments for the next morning.

He'd wanted to say something the night before. She was sure of it. Otherwise, he wouldn't have touched her so tenderly. Arianna could still feel the warmth of his hand on her jaw and the way he had held her face as he'd leaned down toward her.

But, a mean voice whispered, *might he be regretting it?*

Before she could answer the mean voice, steps sounded down the hall. Arianna froze as they passed, only to realize it had been Bithiah. Another set followed soon after, however, and the quick, steady pace made Arianna's heart jump into her throat. But instead of turning the corner, where she could intercept him, the steps slowed and then stopped. And then continued even faster without turning.

Arianna kicked the wall, which only made her toe hurt, before running after him. He might have decided he wasn't going to see her anymore, but he was going to tell her to her face if that were the case. She caught up with him just as he stepped out into the garden. Not waiting for him to turn, she grabbed his arm and made him face her.

As soon as he turned, nearly all of her confidence fled her. The eyes that had been a warm gold with hints of summer green and sky blue the day before were hard now, as he leaned back slightly.

"Arianna." His voice was polite. "You've helped so much that I thought I would give you an evening to yourself."

"You're lying."

For a moment, Michael looked as though he might fall over.

Those truly hadn't been the words Arianna had planned to

speak as her first, but it was too late to take them back now.

"You . . . You spoke!"

"Just whispers. I've been practicing. And I'm not very fast yet." Indeed, speaking was almost painfully slow.

"Why didn't you speak sooner?" All the distance was gone from his voice and body now, but for some reason, that annoyed Arianna even more.

"It's rather hard to whisper underwater." She frowned at him. "And I had to practice first. I'm not used to how the air feels in my mouth."

For a moment, the warmth returned to his eyes, and Arianna's heart rose. He shook his head slowly, his mouth still open. "And you've been practicing all this time?"

"Since I stubbed my toe and let out a groan by accident. Well, a whispered groan."

Without seeming to be aware of it, Michael stepped so close she could feel the heat radiating from his arm. Standing so close he could have kissed her had he wished to, he opened his mouth, but Arianna wasn't done. Now that she could speak, she fully intended to do so.

"Why did you leave last night? And why have you been avoiding me? I thought . . ." She swallowed, but suddenly couldn't finish.

He blinked rapidly a few times before looking down and reaching into his pocket. He then pulled out a folded parchment with a purple seal, the same one Drina had held the night before. Instead of opening it, however, he only turned it over in his hands a few times. "I've dedicated my whole life to this kingdom," he finally said, nearly whispering himself. "But I never thought she would ask me to do this."

Arianna held out her hand, and to her surprise, he handed the parchment over without protest. As soon as she began to read, she felt her blood go cold. "You're going to marry her," she whispered when she got to the end.

"I haven't agreed to it!"

"But it's what your mother wants." She nodded as she handed it back.

He took her by the shoulders. "But it's not what *I* want."

"Then what *do* you want?"

He said nothing for a moment, rubbing her arms with his thumbs, though their speed made the touch feel more like nerves than affection.

"I want a friend," he said. "I want a companion who will counsel me and help me see what is right. I want a family, and peace!" He looked up at the stars. "What I wouldn't give for peace for my people and my house and me!"

Want me! she felt like shouting, but fear tied her tongue firmly to the roof of her mouth. "What will you do?" she finally asked with some difficulty.

"I don't know."

"What if . . ." Why was talking so *hard?* "What if the Maker gave you certain wants to show you what you need?" She couldn't believe she was saying those words. But after the last few days, she wasn't sure what she believed or didn't believe any more.

"But how would I know which are mine and which are his?" He crossed his arms over his chest. "My grandfather seemed to think they were always one and the same."

"You said there had to be a purpose." She paused. "Could it hurt to ask the Maker before choosing? To take a little time to think about it?"

He stared at her for a long time, so long that her legs grew sore from standing still in one place. "No," he said. "I don't suppose it would hurt to ask." He started to turn, but she grabbed his sleeve.

"One more thing. The letter says this woman is from a far-off island?" Arianna took a breath, hoping desperately that she didn't sound like a pathetic beggar.

"Yes."

"Where is it?"

Michael frowned and unfolded the letter to read it. He grimaced even harder when he finished. "I'm not sure, to be honest. My mother says it was delivered by a man who claimed it had come from over the Third Sea."

"Michael, you must be careful!" She pulled him closer without thinking. "That means she's crossing over the Deeps!" Her throat hurt from straining to shout the whisper.

"And that's a bad thing?"

"There's a reason my grandfather doesn't allow humans over the Deeps!"

"May I ask what the two of you are doing out here alone? Whispering in the night when you're not even to be betrothed is highly improper." Drina's harsh voice pierced the air. She went to stand by her son's side and took his arm. Only then did she make a face at Arianna. "Wait, you can talk now?" She glared up at her son. "That seems convenient."

Arianna shook her head. She didn't have the patience for the queen, so she continued addressing Michael. "Have you heard of Sorthileige?"

Before Michael could answer, Drina rolled her eyes. "A remnant of the Maker's enemy," she rattled off, "that is buried deep in the earth. King Everard and Queen Isabelle of Destin help expel it from other kingdoms from time to time. What of it?"

"Destin's monarchs drive it out in small quantities, yes," Arianna said. "But not like that in the Deeps. In the Deeps, it bubbles up from holes in the seafloor." She took a breath. Speaking was so much more taxing than she'd expected. "At the bottom of underwater chasms, it tries to defy the Maker in black clouds of poison. Those who are touched by the blackness are changed." She shivered at the memories.

"And you've seen such to prove it?" Drina raised one perfect eyebrow and crossed her arms.

Arianna nodded. "A mermaid lost her dolphin when I was eight years. She went into the Deeps to look for it. She spent only a few minutes inside the Deeps, but within three days, she'd grown brown scales all over her body. Even her face was scaled, and sea foam stuck to her eyes." Arianna gulped some air. She would really need to practice this more. "She writhed and screeched for days, trying to scratch her family and the healers. She even broke some furniture with her voice. She continued until the darkness was too much for her body."

Drina turned to her son. "And you expect me to believe—"

"Just listen for once! Arianna, please continue."

"If this woman is traveling from the Third Sea without a merguard escort of the Sea Crown himself or someone who has been directly blessed by him, then she has—or is being driven by—a power much greater than that which the merpeople possess."

"And it bothers you that the merpeople might not be the strongest in the sea." Drina smirked as she smoothed her silk gloves. "All the more reason to unite with them. Perhaps they'll rid us of the infestation in our waters." She raised an eyebrow at Arianna, her eyes challenging.

Arianna ignored the jab and turned to Michael. "This is dangerous," she whispered urgently to Michael. "Either this woman is dabbling in something dark, or she's taking a gamble with the lives on everyone on her ship."

Crickets chirped, and a few night birds called out their songs. Drina continued to fiddle with her gloves, and Michael stared out at the sea. Arianna just wished . . . Well, what did she wish? That he had listened to her? Well, he had. That he would leave this ridiculous notion of a strange foreign princess behind? Yes, she did wish that, fervently. But that didn't seem enough to fix the crack she could feel in her heart.

"Thank you, Arianna," he said in a quiet voice. "I will consider all you have told me."

"In the meantime," Drina sniffed, "I will escort you to bed. *Someone* around here should be concerned for propriety's sake."

Suddenly too tired to argue, Arianna let the queen lead her away. As soon as they stood outside her bedroom, however, the queen grabbed Arianna's arm and gave it a yank.

"Listen to me now, mermaid. Yes, you might have saved us a few pennies. You even found a convenient way to pay off some of our debts, though I assuredly question your means, as you didn't seem to find it necessary until the king of Tumen threatened you directly."

"I didn't even know—"

"Shut up. I need you to know now that you will *never* have my son. I did think for a short moment that you had given up on your schemes, or that, perhaps, you really did mean well for my family. But the way he looked at you last night and the way you tried to seduce him this evening told me everything I need to know."

"But I never—"

"I said shut up!" She shoved Arianna into the wall and held her there with a firm hand, her grip surprisingly strong for never someone who never lifted a finger around the palace. "This princess is coming in two days. I fully expect you to either be gone or to stay invisible while she is here. Is that understood?"

Arianna glared at her.

"I said is that understood?" Drina's shout echoed down the halls as Arianna continued to hold her gaze. When Arianna still didn't answer, Drina pressed her foot into Arianna's toes, and Arianna gasped as pain shot through her foot. Drina then jerked her from the wall to the door, banging Arianna's head against the doorframe in the process. Throwing open the door, she tossed Arianna onto the ground. Then the door slammed shut, and Arianna heard the distinct click of a lock and key.

THE KINDEST OF INTRUSIONS

*A*rianna was locked in her room for the rest of that night and into the next day as well. Somewhere deep inside, she hoped Michael might come looking for her. But he never did. This would have made Arianna angry, had it not been for the girls' absence as well. On other days when she had overslept, Claire and Lucy were banging on her door, singing at the tops of their lungs that morning was here and the last one up was a sea urchin. Only Drina came twice, to bring her water and a few slices of bread, refusing to even speak to Arianna both times. How long, exactly, did the queen plan to keep her locked up?

On the second day of her imprisonment, the sun had been up for over an hour by the time there was a soft knock at her door. Then the lock clicked, and Arianna was relieved to see Bithiah standing there with a tray of biscuits and jam.

"I am sorry it took me so long," Bithiah said as she darted in to put the tray on Arianna's table. "I do not think the queen wanted me here at all, but I knew better than to believe her." She nodded once and placed her hands on her wide hips.

Arianna threw her arms around the woman. "Thank you," she whispered.

"What is this now?" Bithiah held her back and studied her with a sly smile. "You are full of surprises, Miss Arianna."

"What did she say about me?" Arianna whispered. She was almost afraid to know.

"She announced at breakfast yesterday that you would be running an errand to a contact of hers in the city." Bithiah shook her head as she scurried around the room, taking the chamber pot and replacing it with a clean one she'd carried in along with the tray. "She said you would not be back for several days, possibly even a week or more." Bithiah stopped moving for a moment and studied Arianna.

"My child, I hope you do not take offense, but I come from a people far different than these. My country is mostly made of sand and sun, but I was born in a little village off the coast of Hedjet." She tilted her head to the side. "We had some of your kind who would trade with us from time to time."

"My kind?" Arianna stuttered. "Mistress Bithiah, I am . . ." But as she locked eyes with the older woman, Arianna could not utter the lie. Instead, she hung her head. "Am I that transparent?

"No, child. The others suspect, but I know only because my father was a merchant. I met others of your kind many times at night when he traded with them. But no more interruptions." She put the chamber pot down and took Arianna's hands. "I heard what Prince Michael was telling Master Russo about this mysterious princess. He told Master Russo of your warnings." She leaned in. "Child, I can tell you are not close to the Maker. But he has given you these understandings for a reason. If there was ever one thing I learned from my mermaid friends," a dark looked passed over her eyes, "it is never to underestimate their premonitions. Your people were put here to guard the humans from the Deeps. And if any human deserves to be guarded, it is Michael."

"But what can I do?" Arianna whimpered. "I'm locked in my room and—"

"Will a lock and key really keep you put?" The corner of Bithiah's lips twitched up. "From what I saw for years and years, not even the Sea Crown's ambassador could keep his daughter in one place for very long."

Arianna gawked at her. Not only had the old sailor seen her, but Bithiah had seen her as well.

One more soul who thought she was worthy of being looked upon.

Arianna pulled Bithiah into another tight hug, choking back tears.

Bithiah clutched her tightly. "Promise me, child, that you will save him from her. Whoever this woman is, her wiles will be poisonous. I can feel it!"

Finally, Bithiah pulled out of their embrace and left with the chamber pot, apologizing as she relocked the door.

Arianna understood, however, that it would be disastrous for all of them if Drina discovered her unfettered. So instead of trying to escape, Arianna sat on her bed and stared out at the ocean waves as they pounded the shore in their rhythmic song. She knew what she needed to do. But, as always, she was one step behind.

∽

Arianna hid her tray under her bed so that when Drina finally came with her bread, Arianna could pretend to be as cowed as ever. But aside from Drina's angry silence, Arianna's day was full of nothing but musings and annoyance. Until the girls arrived.

"Arianna!" Claire called through the keyhole. "We've come to rescue you!"

"Yes!" Lucy added with a giggle. "Grandmother thinks she fooled us, but we fooled her!"

"Lucy, move out of the way! We can tell her when we're inside and safe from Grandmother!" After several failed attempts, the lock opened and the two girls spilled into Arianna's room.

"Look what we snuck from Grandmother's evening dress!" Claire's eyes sparkled as she held up a tarnished key. "Now we just have to make you beautiful again! Where's your new dress. Put it on, quick!"

"Why?" Arianna whispered.

The girls stopped and stared.

"Well," Lucy finally piped, "isn't that something?" Then, without losing another moment, Lucy began to pull contraband from the little bag they'd brought, while Claire pulled Arianna's pink dress from the stool where Arianna had folded it nicely.

"The strange princess is arriving in less than an hour. I heard Grandmother say so. We knew she lied about you being gone, but it took us all day to get the key." Claire paused as she placed several jeweled pins in Arianna's hair, a smug little smile on her face. "And to borrow a few things."

"You have to be beautiful so he doesn't marry her!" Lucy climbed into Arianna's lap. "We don't want Uncle Michael to marry her. We want him to marry you!"

"And how do you know so much?" Arianna laughed.

Each girl fixed her with a condescending stare. "Really," Claire finally said with a huff, "you should know us better by now! We know everything."

Arianna believed that now.

"There." Claire held up a little hand mirror. "What do you think?"

Arianna turned her head from side to side. Pink jewels sparkled all over her hair. Matching jewels shaped like teardrops dangled from her ears by silver chains.

"You're masters," she whispered to the girls, who beamed.

Then Claire's eyes grew wide. "You need to be there when she arrives!" She pushed Arianna from behind. "Go!"

Resolved hardened within Arianna with each step she took toward the palace entrance. They always met guests of lesser importance in the dining hall, where Michael could greet them at the impressive hall doors. But those of great importance were met on the mother-of-pearl palace steps, flanked by the glass columns that had seashells and other ocean treasures suspended within them.

Bithiah was right, Arianna mused as she half-ran to the palace entrance. Something was not right about this woman. She was too perfect. Her timing was too perfect.

Arianna slowed only when she came to the last corner, throwing up a rare prayer of thanks to the Maker for the new pink slippers Michael had given her with the dress. At least her boots wouldn't clunk tonight.

She waited around the corner until the sun had nearly set and supper normally would have grown cold. Michael and Lucas stood conferring quietly together, both in their military attire once more. Queen Drina was caught up between fussing over the old decorations they had put up and whining about how late the princess was. But finally, just as dusk was falling, lights began to come into view from the path that wound up from the city. Arianna smoothed her dress and stepped out into the light of the torches.

"Arianna!" Michael said as he, Lucas, and Drina turned.

Drina's eyes narrowed as she surveyed Arianna's attire, but Lucas dashed forward and escorted Arianna out to their party. Michael took her hand for a moment before giving a formal bow and kissing her fingers. "You look lovely," he said.

"What took you so long?" Lucas asked.

"My apologies," she whispered, curtsying and turning to look pointedly at Drina. "I was a bit detained on my errand."

Lucas's eyes popped. "Did you just speak? But how—"

"I'm a quick learner," Arianna said, not breaking her gaze with Drina.

Drina held her eyes for a moment longer before turning stiffly back to the path, which was now filled visibly with a dozen soldiers carrying torches on the ends of their staffs. Michael straightened as the entourage reached the foot of the steps. His jaw was clenched, but his face was a perfect mask of formal politeness and kingly reserve.

All signs of stress disappeared from his face, however, as soon as their guest emerged from the shadows. Between the two lines of soldiers walked a woman with a figure so perfect Arianna had to look twice to believe it. Her eyes sparkled in the flames of the candles that lit the steps, and her blood-red lips curved into an exquisite smile as she took in the two gentlemen, whose mouths had literally fallen open.

She melted into the lowest, most balanced curtsy Arianna had ever seen. Not even Master Russo, Arianna's unofficial manners instructor, could dip that far down.

"What a warm welcome! I had hardly expected the queen and the princes to greet me themselves! Please, allow me to introduce myself. I am Princess Ines."

Arianna almost groaned. The woman's voice was painfully melodic. Listening to her speak was like listening to the Nursery Nurturers sing the little merbabies to sleep at night. And as if to pour salt on the wound, as Princess Ines moved up the steps into the light, her ebony hair flowed down her back and past her knees in ripples of shiny, loose curls. Her skin was without freckle or flaw.

It was a long second before either of the brothers could stop gaping like fish. Apparently, they had never seen a woman before. Arianna was tempted to clear her throat when Michael finally broke out of his trance and nudged his brother.

"I've brought gifts!" the perfect princess finally said, breaking the strained silence. After gesturing to a servant Arianna hadn't seen standing at the back of the group, the princess folded her hands and waited patiently as a chest large enough to hold Arianna was dragged up. "As a token of my people's hopes for a future of . . . mutual interest."

Everyone gasped as it was opened and a pile of gold pieces, pearls, and jewels began to spill out. It made Arianna's little bag of pearls look like a child's collection of rocks.

"And we are most honored to have you with us." Drina moved swiftly to the princess and took her hand, effectively blocking Arianna from the woman's view. "My sons and I were delighted to receive your letter."

"And who is this?"

The woman moved around Drina and toward Arianna. Arianna nearly smiled at the rage on Drina's face, but her amusement disappeared as the woman began to look her over. The longer the woman studied her, however, the softer and kinder her brown eyes grew.

"You, my dear, are lovely," she said in her melodic voice.

"Oh, yes," Drina hurried to Princess Ines's side once more. "This is my granddaughters' governess. She was actually just leaving to put the girls to bed." Drina turned and glared daggers at Arianna. "You would be surprised at the level of improvement she's gained since coming here. When she arrived, she had no home or way of keeping herself. But look at what she's become."

A strange look flicked across Princess Ines's face.

She looked almost . . . irritated. But Arianna couldn't be sure, for the expression was gone before Arianna was even sure it was there.

"Please," Princess Ines turned to Drina, her dark eyes wide and pleading, "let her stay with us tonight. I should love to know all of your family. Even your granddaughters if it allows this young woman to stay with us!"

It was Arianna's turn to stare now. Who was this woman, and

why for the love of kelp was she interested in Arianna? To her annoyance, Arianna was quickly finding it difficult to dislike the new princess, despite all her earlier misgivings. Anyone who ruffled Drina had to at least be a tolerable soul.

DISMISSED

*S*upper was one of the most confusing meals Arianna had ever eaten. Her desire to dislike the woman and sniff out her motivation for such a sudden proposition warred with her gratefulness for Princess Ines's kindness to her. For though Drina had consented with a very stiff smile to let Arianna and the girls eat with the select group, Drina made sure to seat them at the far end of the table, as far from the general conversation as they could get. Yet Princess Ines, to her credit, attempted to draw Arianna into the conversation whenever she could, leaning forward and trying to hear her whispers, without even batting an eye at the whispers themselves.

But every time Arianna was tempted to toss out her suspicions, Princess Ines would turn her charm on the men. Arianna had never seen such guppies as the men were that night. Lucas, of course, did not surprise Arianna. Lucas loved little more than flirting with every woman he met, but none of the lords were particularly attentive to their wives that night, either.

Michael did better than the others. She could see him trying not to gawk, his gaze sometimes resting on the table or the ceiling. But every few minutes, he would have to look at the princess for politeness's sake, and he would be enthralled all over again. Arianna was nearly ready to write him off as just as lost as Lucas, when he leaned forward and folded his hands.

"Princess Ines," he said, "perhaps you could tell us a bit about where you're from." His gaze flicked briefly to Arianna.

Good. He wasn't completely gone yet.

Princess Ines lifted her goblet and swirled its wine about. "I come from the Espigmas Isle in the Third Sea. We tend to keep to ourselves, only trading with the merpeople when they were still interacting with people. Since they paid us special heed in their dealings, they told us that it would be best if we stayed hidden. We are a small people with few ships. And gold. Lots and lots of gold."

She sighed prettily. "Alas, their disappearance has cut off our entire trade supply. When our spies relayed to us that other coastal kingdoms were also suffering, we knew that perhaps we might benefit from also dealing with others. And then," she turned her sweet smile on Michael, "we heard that your kingdom had found a way to reignite trade with some of the inland kingdoms. That's when we knew we must immediately make contact."

Arianna did the math in her head and her suspicions were raised again. "Even with an escort from the Sea Crown," she whispered as loudly as she could, "you could not have sent two messages and traveled here within one week from the Third Sea." Such a journey should have taken at least four weeks. Maybe more.

"I think it is quite rude to question our guest," Drina said, glowering at Arianna.

"Actually," Lucas lost his annoying smile for the first time that night, "Arianna is right." He turned to Princess Ines. "How did you relay your messages so quickly?"

"A fair question." The princess took a dainty sip of her wine. "I must admit that I have been on the mainland for several months, traveling about so as to learn about your people for my father. Well, you and other coastal kingdoms. I had been in your city for some weeks, posing as a visiting merchant, when news of the pearls spread. I knew immediately that along with everything else I had learned of your people, as you are mostly dependent on the sea like my own people, it was a sign from the Maker."

"I'm glad to know you've been in our city," Michael said as he put his fork down and glanced at his mother. Drina gave him the slightest shake of her head, but he turned and spoke to the princess anyway. "I will not be dishonest with you. You have seen the dismal conditions my people are surviving. We have only just escaped losing everything due to mountainous debts, and our economy is still in shambles after a five-year war that ravaged our harbors and chased away the guardians of our seas."

Arianna tensed. Would the princess's beauty cause him to forget and betray her secret? He had kept it well, but Princess Ines was not like everyone else. Even now, Lucas was back to gawking at her over his spiced tuna.

"Thanks to the brave venture of one of our citizens," Michael continued, omitting Arianna's name, much to her relief, "we are still afloat, but only just. I'm afraid I must be impertinent and ask why you believe we could benefit you. There are other coastal kingdoms farther south and a little north, but none are so dependent on the sea. Why us?"

Princess Ines leaned back in her chair and pursed her lips, giving him an appraising look. Even her thoughtful expression was breathtaking, and Arianna could see Michael's focus waver slightly as the woman stared him down.

How can intelligent men such Michael and Lucas be so incredibly stupid? Arianna thought with frustration.

"What about your part in this war that chased all our sea guardians away?" All of Princess Ines's coy playfulness was suddenly gone.

"To be blunt, my grandfather acted foolishly," Michael responded. "Both sides did, it seemed, but my grandfather would not let the war end, even on his deathbed asking me to continue it for him. My kingdom is a peninsula, and our borders end at the mainland, so to be honest, I do not know what we will do to recover if the merpeople do not return."

Arianna had been so engaged in the conversation that she didn't even notice the girls beginning to quarrel until Drina snapped her fingers and nodded at the girls to be dismissed. Arianna's face burned as she recognized that she, too, was included in the dismissal.

~

Arianna had tucked the girls in and was nearly to her own room when clacking footsteps echoed down the hall after her. She braced herself for another lecture and round of threats from Drina, so her surprise couldn't have been greater when she turned to see Princess Ines come round the corner.

"I hope I did not get you into trouble!" Princess Ines stopped several feet away and wrung her perfect hands.

Distress made her look even more beautiful, Arianna noted with disgust. And yet, she couldn't help being touched by the woman's concern. "It's not your fault," she whispered. "I'm afraid Queen Drina has never much liked me."

"I just . . ." the woman paused and bit her lip. "I hope you see how lovely you truly are, and how much worth you have. No matter how they treat you."

"Prince Michael and Prince Lucas treat me wonderfully. It is their mother, I'm afraid, who wishes I were gone for good."

"Yes," Princess Ines's voice hardened. "I see that." She looked down at her flowing green gown and sighed. "Well, don't give up hope. I like you already. You say what you mean and you have a kind heart." She beamed. "I believe we shall be quite intimate friends. And don't worry about the queen. Between you and me, we shall make sure that Prince Michael and his mother get exactly what they deserve."

"But I told you," Arianna said, frowning, "Michael has been kind to me."

"Well then," Princes Ines whirled around, her skirts flouncing, "he should have nothing to worry about."

GOOD LITTLE PRINCE

"*A*re you sure you're in the mood for this?" Lucas studied the rack of weapons, his hand on his chin. Then, without waiting to hear Michael's response, which would have been that he wasn't in the mood for *anything* at the moment, asked, "Longsword?"

"Fine."

"This is my one day away from the shipyard so don't make me miserable while I'm here."

Michael grunted in response.

"You know you miss my face when I'm gone," Lucas continued, pulling two swords down from the rack and examining them. "And *someone* around here needs to look good for the ladies." He put his nose up and sniffed the air, making a face. "You also need to get this room cleaned out. Just because it's a practice room doesn't mean it should stink."

"You've been here for the last three days. What do you mean it's your one day home?" Michael took the longsword from his brother.

"I have been quite busy working on foreign negotiations."

Michael snorted. "If that's what you want to call it. But I doubt you ever *negotiated* like this with Bras."

"If he had been as pretty as Princess Ines, I might have."

They both settled into their ready positions. Michael really didn't feel like going through their usual weapons practice as they did most weeks when Lucas was home, but the crushing weight of his upcoming decision was too heavy, and if there was anyone who would understand him, it would be his brother.

"Arianna's noticed, you know."

Lucas's words took him by such surprise that Michael nearly forgot to parry Lucas's first attack. It was a moment before he had gained back enough ground to speak.

"Noticed what?"

"That you haven't looked at her since Princess Ines arrived."

"I have, too, looked at her." Michael tried sweeping Lucas's feet, but Lucas was too quick. As Michael met his brother's next attack, however, he also was mentally battling the fact that Lucas was right.

He hadn't looked at Arianna. Not in the way he *had* been, at least. He'd seen the hurt in Arianna's expression that first night the princess had arrived, and shame had been keeping his eyes averted ever since.

"You gaped more than I did," he huffed as he blocked a thrust and leapt back. Breathing hard, both men circled.

"Ines is beautiful," Lucas said. "Startlingly so. Any man with eyes can see that."

"But it's not as if Arianna is any less." Michael frowned. Unfortunately, by the time he'd recognized his behavior for what it had been that first night, it had been too late.

"Ah, so the truth comes out." Lucas lunged again. Michael blocked it and twisted quickly, managing to knock his brother in the jaw with his elbow. He forgot to watch his knee, though, and

Lucas quickly kicked his leg out from under him. Michael rolled away just in time to avoid a nice bruise to the face.

"You think I'm proud of the way I've been acting?" He spat the words out like curses. "I did exactly what I was afraid of from the start. I raised her hopes, and mine, only to have them both dashed."

"Do they have to be?" Lucas put his sword down for a moment and fixed Michael with a hard stare that reminded Michael too much of their father. That, of course, only brought more shame.

"What do you mean?"

"I mean, are you sure that this is your only way?"

"I don't see any way around it." Michael shrugged. "We've had three days of negotiations, and I can't seem to find a single reason to refuse. Ines's people are far wealthier than we are. The secret contacts she's been building for her father would revitalize almost all of our trade posts. She's even told us about resources we didn't know we had." Michael melted back down into a ready position. "Come back on, you lout. Don't get lazy on me. You're the one who's supposed to be fighting pirates." This conversation had been a bad idea.

Lucas fell into his own position, but he kept that annoying quirked eyebrow. "So you're just going to leave Arianna to fend for herself, then."

"I never said that!"

"Oh, be real, Michael!" Lucas leapt to the side, barely escaping the particularly hard blow Michael had aimed his way. "Say you do marry Princess Ines for the sake of the kingdom *and* to escape Mother's eternal nagging. What then? Do you really suppose Mother will let Arianna remain here forever? And even if she did, would you really want that? For either of you?"

The heat that had been simmering in Michael's stomach for days boiled over, and as Lucas continued speaking, Michael lunged into a series of fast, furious attacks. He didn't realize just how hard he was fighting until his sword drew blood from Lucas's arm.

Throwing his sword to the ground, he ran his hands through his hair. "Forgive me, Lucas. I'm just—"

"I'm impressed, actually. You usually hold back." Lucas examined his arm, and to Michael's relief, showed him that the cut was rather shallow. "Bithiah will have your head, though. She just patched this up last week. Want to try knives instead?"

Michael arched an eyebrow. "Does that really seem a wise choice right now?"

Lucas grimaced. "I suppose not."

"I don't know what to do." Michael kicked the stone wall before leaning against the window that overlooked the field where he had taken Arianna and the girls less than two weeks before. For some sick reason, he felt suddenly desperate to be back in that broke, bleak moment rather than in this moment full of opportunity and promise.

"Well, let's consider both options," Lucas said, coming to stand beside him. "A wealthy, exotic princess has come to ask your hand in marriage, presumably. Your union will solve all of the kingdom's woes, and you shall bring forth many beautiful babies into the world most dreadfully lacking such."

Michael turned to glare at his brother.

"On the other hand," Lucas went on after a pause, his voice now devoid of all mirth, "you have a poor, abandoned, silent woman who risked her life for the sake of my men and your people. And you. Twice. Don't forget that. She dotes on the girls you've practically raised as your own, and her ability to do figures has somehow managed to keep the kingdom afloat on less than half of what it should have needed. Despite being royal born—"

"How do you know what she is?" Michael had been very careful to keep Arianna's secret as well as he could. Had Bithiah told Lucas?

"That man might have been drunk," Lucas said with a smirk,

"but everyone in the port knows he's the most knowledgeable old salt around. Besides, Claire told me all about your secret rescuer."

"She can't remember that. She was four!"

Lucas shrugged. "Well then, just take it on the belief that the girls know everything." His smile disappeared. "As I was saying, despite being royal born, Arianna has never raised a single objection to being clothed in the most horrendous gowns the world has ever seen, nor has she taken proper offense at Mother's ill temper or odious manners. So believe me," Lucas raised a finger when Michael opened his mouth to speak, "when I say that if *you* don't marry Arianna, I am deadly serious when I say that *I* will."

Michael leveled him a dark look, but Lucas only returned it.

"She deserves better than to nanny two children and be abused by our mother for years to come without at least a title to her name." Lucas turned and gathered their swords. "Tell me, do you want to marry Ines?"

"No."

"And you love Arianna?"

"Yes." The word was out of his mouth before he had time to consider it. Did he love Arianna? He shook his head to clear it. Even if his head wasn't sure, it seemed his mouth was. Or was it his heart?

Lucas stared at him for a minute then turned to put away his sword. "I don't know why you even bothered to ask me."

"I told you. I need to know what to do!"

"But it doesn't matter what I say. Because in the end, you are going to be a good little prince and marry the rich princess."

Michael tried to interrupt, but Lucas just held up his hand.

"You will do as duty entails. You always do."

NO REASON NOT TO

*A*rianna hopped from one foot to the other as she waited outside his study. Men's voices moved up and down inside, but she couldn't understand anything they said in their hushed tones. It didn't matter, though. She was waiting for Michael.

After nearly an hour, six or seven men emerged from the study. Arianna peeked around the corner until she spotted Michael, who was the last to exit. When he turned to lock the door, she grabbed his wrist and yanked him around the corner. Her words caught in her throat, however, when she realized he was in his military uniform again.

"Arianna." He clasped his hands behind his back and kept his eyes on the ground. "I'm afraid my time is short. What is it you need?"

"Before you go through with this . . ." Why did her voice sound so stilted, even in its whispered form? "I wanted to tell you that I have a plan that could bring my people back—"

"Arianna—"

"I could go to them. And if you're worried about me being in the water, Lucas could sail me over to where the city is—"

"Arianna. You need to—"

"I'm sure my grandfather would be open to negotiations now that you're the future king—"

"*Arianna!*"

She flinched. He had never shouted at her before.

Michael let out a huff and rubbed his eyes. "Forgive me. But now is not a good time."

"Then when will be a good time?"

He stared at her for a long moment, his brow creasing. "There won't be one, I'm afraid." And with that, he turned and marched away.

Arianna was tempted to run after him and demand an explanation, but a sinking feeling inside made her shrink back. How had the world crashed in just six days?

It was with great trepidation that Arianna forced her feet to carry her to the throne room. She had never seen the throne room before. It was never open, as they'd hosted no grand events, and Michael always said he detested its formal feel. But tonight it was packed full with all sorts of people. Arianna counted six languages spoken in the time it took her to find an empty space near the wall. Too many bright colors and frilled dresses made the room feel hot and stuffy, and suddenly Arianna only wanted to run. But her feet disobeyed and held her in place.

A trumpet blared, and Master Russo's reedy voice broke through the crowd's noise, sending everyone into a hush. "His Highness, Michelangelo Rinieri Battista Solefige, crown prince of Maricanta, has invited you to attend an announcement of great magnitude. He wishes to extend his thanks for your coming, and he hopes you find cause to celebrate."

Arianna stood on her toes to see Master Russo bow to Michael before exiting the platform. Michael and Princess Ines stepped closer to the front of the stage in unison. Her hand rested gracefully on his arm, and Arianna felt a hot, vicious stab of jealousy. In her dress of midnight blue edged with silver, Princess Ines looked like the night sky itself. And when she beamed at him, her face gave off the soft glow of the moon.

"My friends." Michael looked out on the crowd that must have numbered at least three hundred. "I am grateful, as my steward said, for your presence, particularly on such short notice. I wanted to announce, however, a turn of magnitude that will alter all of our lives for what I pray will be the better." He took a deep breath and glanced at Princess Ines, who gave him a sweet smile and a nod.

"After a week of deliberation and negotiations, Princess Ines of Espigmas Isle and I have reached an agreement. Tomorrow we will travel to her homeland, and there Princess Ines and I will be wed, thus securing our kingdoms' prosperity and goodwill. Our lands will open up trade routes across the sea as soon as possible, and our expert growers will immediately begin consultations to find new purposes for our old crops."

He continued to talk, and the crowd continued to watch the princess, looking just as spellbound as Michael and Lucas had at first, but Arianna could no longer focus. Instead, she watched the way Michael held his body. It was stiff and formal, nothing like the way he'd held her that night on the balcony as they'd danced. And yet, how long would it be before Princess Ines won him over, and his touch was more than dutiful? How many days would pass before his respect for her blossomed into something more? Until his thumb rubbed her knuckles whenever they held hands? For who could resist such perfection?

As soon as the address was over and servants were passing around some sort of wine, Arianna bolted for the door. Where she was going, she couldn't say. She only knew that she could not remain in the same room with the happy couple any longer.

Before Arianna reached the door, however, a soft voice called her name. Arianna looked up to see Princess Ines staring at her with a sad smile.

"I know this has to be hard, but before you go, please hear me."

Arianna could only stare at her.

Princess Ines folded her hands in front of her and pressed them into her dress. "I hope I am not being too bold when I ask this of you, but would you do me the honor of considering one small request? I like to think that we're something of friends now after the last week." She gave Arianna a little quirked smile, and for all of her pain, Arianna somehow found herself nodding yes when she really, really just wanted to say no.

"I'm afraid Michael was a little premature in proclaiming our engagement," she said, looking down at her hands, a few dark curls landing gracefully on her cheeks. "You see, the agreement is that Michael will marry one of the king's daughters, but I am not the only daughter. And," she gave a little laugh, "if he does choose me over one of my sisters, I'm afraid my older sister will take great offense, and I shall be short a bridesmaid." She reached out and lifted Arianna's chin so that Arianna would meet her eyes. "I've seen the way Queen Drina treats you," she said in a lower voice. "Come with us. Stay with us! If I am queen, I promise that her abuse of you will be put to an end." Her eyes darkened for a brief second. "One way or another."

It was impossible for Arianna to hide her surprise at such a threat, but the princess just shook her head and the pleasant smile reappeared. "But truly, I want to know you better. I get the feeling that we might be great friends, given the chance."

"But . . ." Arianna tried to rearrange her thoughts, "Espigmas Isle is past the Deeps."

"Oh, darling, if that's what's troubling you, have no fear." Ines gave a tinkling laugh. "I have a few friends left among the merpeople. Though they refuse to work with us officially, my friends have been willing to see my ships safely through."

Arianna wanted to argue that it didn't matter who wanted to escort her through the Deeps, that only her grandfather or his blessing had the ability to keep them safe, but a sharp longing was suddenly besting the logic in her heart. If merpeople were going to guide them through the Deeps they couldn't be passing that far from Gemmaqua. If Arianna was careful, she could go with Princess Ines and then follow the merpeople home.

She would see her parents. Even if it killed her, she would reach her own people.

Princess Ines hadn't looked away from Arianna since asking the question. "So you'll come?" She clasped her hands in front of her chest.

Arianna nodded.

A HEFTY CONTRIBUTION

*A*rianna had never been so fast, not even when riding a dolphin. Of course, the dolphins went in and out of the water, and the ship remained steadily atop the surface. She blinked through the spray at the palace as it receded in the distance. As strange as it felt to fly over the ocean, the previous day had been even stranger. She still wasn't sure she wouldn't wake up at any moment to find it all a dream. Or rather, a nightmare.

If only she could wake up. She squinted even harder up at the clear blue sky. *And I wish* you *would stop getting my hopes up.* But really, she should have known better. Her throat tightened. She had always known better. The Maker had done nothing new.

Even up until the evening before, she had retained some semblance of hope that Michael would refuse the princess's offer. Kindly, of course, as Princess Ines had been nothing but kind to Arianna. They could rebuild the kingdom without her, he would say to the princess. Then, after Ines had gone, Michael would make a peace offering to the merpeople. And who knew what kind of alliances would come from such an agreement?

But it was not to be. Arianna had boarded Princess Ines's ship early that morning after leaving gifts by Lucy and Claire's beds. She carried no belongings except what she wore. There would be no need for them under the sea.

"I will be in my quarters," Arianna heard Princess Ines call to her captain, a tall man wearing a widely brimmed hat. "Do not disturb me until I send for you!"

Arianna had twisted away from the water to examine the cabin's little round windows more closely when someone came to stand beside her. She lifted her chin and turned back to face the sea. *Someone* she didn't want to speak to in the slightest.

"I know I don't deserve it, but if you would only listen for a moment..." Michael began.

Arianna refused to look at him.

"I didn't want any of this," he continued.

Perhaps you should have thought of that before accepting a marriage invitation. A long silence ensued, filled only by the creaking of the boat and the low roar of the waves gently slapping the ship.

"They're starving, Arianna," he finally said in a low voice. "She promised to send ships full of food and supplies."

Arianna whirled around. "And the return of my people could have done nothing to help?"

"Believe me, I've spent hours thinking about that. Many, many hours." He sighed. "But after what your father said—"

"And what did he say?"

Michael frowned. "You didn't know? Your father contacted me before he left."

"I know about the truce."

"We spoke of more than just calling a truce."

"What?"

"He said he was taking your people and returning to Gemmaqua. He asked that I stop all assaults on the old city. I can only assume he was thinking of you." Michael let out a gusty breath. "He then swore to me that he was never coming back.

Neither he nor your sister after him nor any other merpeople ever again."

Arianna stared at him, openmouthed.

"Don't you see?" He leaned against the railing and let his head droop. "It wouldn't have made a difference. The Sea Crown had sent orders. No one is coming back."

For a brief moment, Arianna scanned the water, ready to throw herself into its depths then and there. She would find her father immediately, or better yet, her grandfather, and she would demand that he explain himself. *Never* was such a final word. For all those months, she'd been sure that someone would eventually come back to bring her home. And when they did, she would show her family that harmony was possible between the Sun Crown and the Sea Crown once again.

Only the memory of the jellyfish and its manic chase kept her feet on the ship. Her original plan had been to wait for the merpeople escorts. She sighed. She was still stuck.

A large, warm hand clasped hers. "Arianna?"

Arianna yanked it away. "You think you deserve an answer from me," she whispered, determined not to let her voice waver, "when your choice is loud enough for both of us."

"Arianna?"

They turned to see Princess Ines standing at the edge of her cabin steps. Michael's shoulders sagged.

"Would you join me in my cabin, please? I have some dress selections I want your opinion on."

Chin in the air, Arianna marched away from Michael and toward the princess's cabin.

"I'm sorry," she heard him say just before the princess shut the door behind them.

The princess seemed completely unaware of Arianna's somber mood as she flitted over to a luxurious pearl-white divan and threw herself down upon it. She looked up and grinned. "What do you think of my quarters? Very human, wouldn't you say?"

Arianna frowned in confusion, but looked around as she was bid. Though not large, the room was well furnished. A wooden vanity was pushed up against a wall with a little wooden chair in front of it. A bed took up a quarter of the room, and the rest of it was stuffed with trunks and chests and odd groupings of furniture. Gowns were everywhere, as were sumptuous pillows and blankets. The vanity had all sorts of perfumes and coloring powders on it, as well as many jeweled pins, earrings, and necklaces. Arianna looked back at the princess, who was still grinning.

"I suppose it is very . . . human," Arianna whispered. What an odd thing to ask. Before Arianna could comment any further, however, the princess began to hum.

A tremor moved through Arianna's bones. Listening was like swimming into an unexpectedly cold current, and she blinked several times. The room looked just the same as it had moments before, but when Arianna looked back at the princess, there was no Princess Ines to be seen. Though someone *was* lounging on the divan.

Arianna gaped. *"Aunt?"*

～

"You think I would just let you disappear?" Renata asked.

"You . . . you knew where I was this whole time?" Arianna grasped the back of a nearby chair. "And you didn't come for me? And how did you know I have legs?"

"Didn't you enjoy your time on land? It's what you've always wanted! And really, you should know by now that I know everything about you."

"Well, yes, but . . . I missed you!" And with that, Arianna threw herself into her aunt's arms, drinking in the familiar scent of brine and sweet sea grass. Her aunt hugged her back tightly, and it was all Arianna could do not to cry. "I thought you were dead," she whispered into her aunt's shoulder.

"Sweet girl," Renata whispered, rubbing Arianna's back. "Sit down and eat something before you pass out." She pushed Arianna down into the vanity's chair then turned to pour two cups of tea. She handed Arianna one of the cups and a small plate of frosted tarts.

"But . . ." Arianna tried to form a coherent sentence, "where did you get the ship? And the crew?"

Renata gave her a sly smile. "Pirates are cheap these days. With our people retreating into a few compact cloisters all over the world, the pirates have had less opportunity to do their usual damage."

They were on a pirate ship? Arianna put her tart down and stared at her aunt. Again, she fumbled for words. "Why did you look so different?"

"Oh, it's just a song, Ari."

"But that kind of song is forbidden. It's not natural . . . to us, at least."

"When you were born," Renata said, crossing her long legs and leaning back into her seat, "I immediately knew you were different. I begged your father to let me care for you. And even though your mother wasn't for it, he let me, seeing as my place as a border Protector had made me better adapted to living closer to the sun. Anyhow, as soon as I heard that you were silent, I knew that you had been given to us as a gift. And in the years since, I have only become more convinced that the Maker designed you to be special."

Arianna choked on her tea.

Renata leaned forward. "Would you believe that I've found a way to get us both what we want?"

"I'm sorry," Arianna coughed, "but I don't follow."

"I have found a way for you to marry your prince and to end the war with the humans once and for all. And you will get your voice."

Arianna dropped her teacup. It shattered at her feet, but she was too confused to do anything about it. "My voice?"

"I had wanted to wait until plans between you and Michael were a bit more decided, but your grandfather's passing, which is sure to be soon, has sped things up a bit. With the triton for the taking as soon as he dies, I will gain it and grant you your voice."

Arianna tried to stop her head from reeling so she could focus. Her grandfather was dying? "But why didn't he give it to me earlier if he had the power?" she finally managed to ask. She remembered him trying and failing several times to grant her a voice when she was a child. He'd left angry and defeated every time.

"Your grandfather never knew you the way I do. And I'm willing to take measures that he was not." Renata knelt and began to gather the broken teacup, her voice rising as she swept the pieces together. "Maricanta will have its debts paid—a loan from the Sea Crown's royal treasury, of course—and the merpeople will move back in to protect human seaports once again. I will drive the creatures back into the Deeps with the triton. Your brother-in-law will exterminate the pirates, for I have far more faith in him than I ever did his grandfather, and you will have your voice and your one true love. And our people, most importantly, will never be in danger again." Renata sat back on her knees and looked up at Arianna beatifically.

Arianna stared at her, completely unsure of what to say or think. Part of her wanted to believe that her aunt's plan could work. It seemed perfect, foolproof. And yet, something niggled in the back of her mind. Before she could ask, however, several shouts from above broke through the quiet.

"Hold on," Renata said, shaking her head. "I will be right back."

Arianna sat frozen to her spot as Renata stood up, muttering something about dimwitted pirates not being able to carry out a single order correctly. As Renata stomped toward the door,

Arianna gasped as the features of her aunt's face shifted back to those of Princess Ines. When Renata returned a few minutes later, she stopped halfway across the room, her own face returning once again. "You look distressed. What's wrong?"

"I just . . . But why the acting? Why not simply tell me what you had planned before?" As the words left her mouth they tasted sour, and Arianna was reminded of her mother's distrust of Renata, particularly after the charms had failed the humans. Arianna had always written off her mother's resentment as just that . . . resentment for not getting to raise her own daughter. But now, her mother's suspicions didn't seem so misplaced. "I mean," Arianna licked her dry lips, "if my parents really knew I loved him, why not simply let love take its course?"

Why would Renata force Michael to choose herself over me?

"That's a good question." Renata sat on her bed, and for the first time that day, looked a bit uncomfortable. "I must admit that I kept your . . . interest in Prince Michael a bit of a secret because I'm afraid his contribution to this arrangement will be a hefty one. Nothing your parents needed to concern themselves with. And completely worth it, I assure you! But it does make the situation a bit delicate."

"Delicate? In what way?"

"I needed an excuse to get you and Michael out on the ocean, and this was the best way I could think to do it. By telling the rest of his family that I would send a boat for them later, I'm saving them from unnecessary entanglement in the situation."

Why could she need Michael over the ocean? Arianna could understand being called back herself. But him?

Renata sighed. "I trust you, Arianna. I've never trusted anyone else in my life more, except possibly Angelo." She paused, then cleared her throat. "But even with your love tethering Michael into place, I'm going to need to keep a close eye on him. You see, that's how we will ensure the safety of our people. By possessing both the heart *and* the mind of the Sun Crown."

"But charms only work for a few hours or a few days at most! Unless . . . Aunt, you can't mean it! Such a feat has only been done a few times in history! And they ended badly."

Over the years, Arianna's obsession with the humans had led her to read what she could about them from the city's limited historical texts. As the waxy leaf pages had to be recopied every so many years, her father kept only a few books, but one such text had caught her eye once when she was sneaking down into her parents' home. The depth of the water was great enough that she'd nearly passed out trying to smuggle it out of the mansion without anyone seeing. Once she had hidden it up in her tower, however, the dry, ancient words had nearly put her to sleep, until she read of one particular ceremony that had disastrous results. For though the changelings usually survived the transformation from human to merperson, the pain had been described as agonizing. *Making the changelings beg for death,* the text had read.

"His mother and brother would never stand for it. They would strip him of his title," she said in a rush, trying to come up with some way to change her aunt's mind. "Then what use would he be?"

"Not if we fill their coffers and keep them happy."

"Drina, perhaps, but Lucas would fight!"

"Would his brother turn down a shipload of weapons and supplies for his troops?" Renata asked in a calm voice, her arms crossed as though she were talking to a petulant child. "Look, Ari, I know you're loyal to him. But if you hold his heart and if I hold his mind, there will be no question as to the loyalty of the Sun Crown. We will find a way to get your voice and then you and I will make sure the merpeople *and* humans are safe! What more could we want?"

"But why me? Why put so much effort into me and my love?"

She leaned forward and gestured at Arianna's legs. "I knew," she whispered, "from the moment you were born that you were the prophesied one—"

"Again, Aunt, with the prophecy—"

"And when we find your voice, you will have more power than anyone in the sea, aside from the Sea Crown. And if I am the Sea Crown when that happens, then we can have everything."

"But I still don't understand. You hate pirates. Why hire them to bring us . . . wherever we're going?"

"Why bring my own Protectors to do something dangerous when I can just pay my enemy to do it *and* die for me?"

Dangerous? Arianna frowned. Who was dangerous? Sure, Michael had brought six guards, but . . .

It was Michael, Arianna realized, Lucas's words echoing in her mind. Michael was dangerous.

In an instant, Arianna was out the door and up the cabin steps to the deck. She looked around wildly for Michael. He was still leaning against the railing looking out over the waves. She ran to him and grabbed his sleeve.

"Michael!" She panted. "We have to get off this ship!"

But just as she spoke the words, a familiar face leered at her from beneath a wide-brimmed hat. His eyes were large at first, but then his mouth curved up into a familiar, horrifying grin.

"Well," the pirate leered, "I didn't expect this job to be quite so profitable."

NO

*M*ichael turned just in time to draw his sword and block Bras's attack.

"Lieutenant!" Michael shouted. In seconds, Michael's guards surrounded them. Unfortunately, however, his guards were immediately surrounded as well.

"What did she want?" he cried out as he fought. "Why is Bras working for her?"

"She's really my Aunt Renata!" Arianna whispered as loudly as she could.

"What?"

"Ines is my aunt!"

He turned for just long enough to give her a horrified look before the fight consumed him completely.

"That one is mine!" Bras shouted, gesturing at Arianna with his sword.

Michael grunted as he thrust his sword harder and faster against the two pirates that had cornered them both. Arianna looked around in dismay as the brown-uniformed men began to break off individually. The pirates were going to pick them off one by one.

Arianna stayed behind Michael as he fought. He and his men were outnumbered three to one, and though Michael was faring well, his lean muscles showed through his sweat-soaked shirt, and Arianna wondered how much longer he could last against the brawny pirates. Particularly the one in the red coat who was charging toward them, his sword stained red.

Arianna looked around for a way to help. She glimpsed a weapon lying by itself on the far side of the deck behind her. Darting over, she grabbed it and ran back to Michael. She tried to recall what Lucas had shown her. But her fingers were clumsy, and she couldn't even get the arrow properly fitted on the bow. As she fumbled with it, one of the pirates managed to pin Michael's sword down with a short sword and small spiked weapon, while another pirate snapped the blade into two.

"The one time I forget to bring a knife," Michael muttered as he backed up, pushing Arianna behind him. Not knowing what else to do, Arianna thrust her weapon into his hands.

"Really?" he cried, glancing back at her as the men proceeded to push them toward the edge. "*This* was all you could find?"

Only then did Arianna remember Michael's true skill with the bow.

In her angst over the bow, Arianna had forgotten to check behind her, and her arm was nearly yanked out of place. As Bras was dragging her across the deck she looked back just in time to see Michael draw the bow's string back. Arianna could hear the string snap as he loosed the arrow.

And missed.

Bras laughed and jerked Arianna around to face him. "Some hero you've got there."

"That's enough."

The din stopped immediately as Renata emerged from the cabin. She glared at one of the burlier men. "I said to keep them quiet, not kill them all. Who do you suppose we'll use as leverage if they're all dead?" Then she turned to Arianna. "It doesn't have to be this way," she said quietly. "I told you, we can be happy!"

"Hold now, wench!" Bras shook his sword at Renata. "I believe we'll be taking it from here. Your services are no longer needed." His eyes moved down her form. "Although, on second thought—"

Renata closed her eyes. Then she opened her mouth.

The melody that came from Renata's throat was a familiar one, the very one, in fact, that resided in Arianna's conch. But instead of the sweet, comforting tones Arianna knew so well, this lullaby was a haunting one.

"Michael, cover your ears!" Arianna wrenched herself from Bras's grasp and threw herself against Michael. She tried to scream. Tried to sing. She wrapped her hands over his ears, but he was too strong. Just seconds into the song, he had pushed her off and stood to face her aunt. His face was almost childlike in its serenity, as was every other face on the ship.

Another few notes, and he had stepped past Arianna and stalked over to Renata. He grabbed her by the waist and drew her against him.

Arianna felt sick. "My father will never stand for this!" she whispered as loudly as she could. "They'll know you're using the siren song!"

"When I have the triton, that won't matter. I will *be* the law."

"You can't keep him this way forever!"

"Oh, but we must. Can you imagine what would happen if he awoke and realized fully what you had done to him?"

"*Me?*"

"Once you have your new voice, you will be the one to seal him to his new form."

"Never!" Arianna stood and took a step closer to where Michael stood clutching Renata tightly against him. "There has to be another way."

"I've spent twenty years trying to find an answer," Renata said. "You'll not come up with one in the next few days."

"And if I don't do as you demand?" Arianna glared at her aunt, trying not to look as brittle as she felt.

"Then I will marry him and do it myself." Her song then continued from the back of her throat, and Michael placed his lips against her temple and closed his eyes with a rough sigh. "That is not what I want, Arianna," she said. "For you or me! But our people need us. There is no other way. So, what is your answer?"

Arianna felt the tears rolling down her cheeks. "No."

Michael moved his mouth across Renata's brow, down her cheek, and finally to her lips, moaning a little as he kissed her with a passion Arianna had only dreamed him capable of.

When he was done, Renata extricated herself from his arms and walked over to Arianna. She wrapped her in a tight embrace. "When I die," she whispered in Arianna's ear, ignoring Arianna's struggles and pleas, "it will be because doing this eventually broke my heart." She looked down then and nodded.

Something metal clicked around Arianna's ankle, but before Arianna could see what the pirate had done, she was falling.

The world rose up below her as she fell headfirst into the water. Flailing her arms for something, anything to hold on to, Arianna found nothing. She only felt herself sinking deeper, dragged by the metal ball and chain that had been attached to her ankle.

Let me turn! Arianna screamed out to the Maker. *Let me turn! I can't breathe!*

But the weighted ball only continued to pull her down as the light above her disappeared.

35

FLESHLY BONDS

*M*ichael felt as though someone had rolled a boulder on top of his body, and his head throbbed. Opening his eyes was hard, and getting them to focus was even harder. The first thing he was able to make out was that he was lying on a large yellow cushion with holes in it. It wasn't particularly flat, nor was it a perfect rectangle or even circle.

Was he underwater?

Michael scrambled up to a seated position to look around him. Sure enough, the building he was in seemed to be made of several different kinds of coral—even the floor. The room itself was large and lavish in its furniture and decor, with doors leading outside to three balconies. A large vanity sat close to the foot of where he lay, and a little divan was positioned on the other side. He tried to lie back and look at the rest of the room behind him, but upside-down, all he could make out was a door. Propping himself back up on his elbows, he studied the only obvious way of escape. From what he could see of the balconies, the outside of the room looked strangely like the inside.

It sounded insane, but could he possibly be in the Sea Crown's palace?

A few little bumps to his chest got his attention. Looking down, he realized he was wearing not one, but three little shells, much like the one Arianna always wore.

How deep down was he? To go to the funeral, he had only needed one shell. Michael tried to stand to go and look through the balcony, but when he tried, he was yanked back down. Somehow, he had failed to notice the gigantic purple anemones sitting on each side of the bed, or the fact that each anemone had wrapped one of its fleshy tentacles around his wrists.

"Hello?" Michael yelled, half-expecting to choke on the water that surrounded him. His voice carried with surprising force, echoing loudly throughout the chamber. "I need . . ." He scrunched his eyes shut as he tried to remember just what had happened. What did he need? "I need to talk to Ambassador Amadeo!" he finished. "His daughter is in danger!"

No one answered his cries, however, and Michael wondered if perhaps he was wrong. Maybe this wasn't the Sea Crown's palace. As it was, he had no memory of being brought in.

Of course, he'd been wrong often as of late. His last memory was blurry at best. But he could have sworn he'd seen Arianna falling from the ship, though he couldn't remember why she was on the ship in the first place.

No. A woman had pushed her. But who was the woman? And where was Arianna now? He felt sick to his stomach as he recalled the way the jelly creature had hunted her down near the Sun Palace. How much worse would the creatures be out in the middle of the ocean?

A movement by the door caught his eye.

"Hello?" Michael called even louder.

The door, more like a circle than a rectangle, opened just a crack, and a merman with a pike stuck his head in.

"Keep it down. We have better hearing than you do, you know."

"Please!" Michael stretched out his hands toward the merman, and in doing so, realized that if he didn't move too quickly, the anemone tentacles let him stretch their arms just a bit. So he began to inch forward slowly. "I need to speak with Ambassador—"

"He's not an ambassador anymore, thanks to your people."

"It's about his daughter! She's in danger!"

"You're in no place to be raising such accusations. Your place here is to wait. Silently." The merman began to close the door again.

"Wait!" Michael searched his pockets for anything of value. The only thing he could find, however, was his father's ring. He snatched it off and held it up. "If I give you this, will you get me an audience with Amadeo?"

The merman froze, his eyes welded to the ring. He swam inside and hummed a little tune before moving over to Michael. Michael heard the sound of the lock click shut on the door behind him.

"If I bring Amadeo to you, you'll give me this ring?"

Michael nodded.

"Very well. Hand it over."

Michael pulled it back. "Not until you bring Amadeo to me personally."

"Sorry," the guard reached out and grabbed Michael's hand, trying to pry it open. "I like my way better."

Before he could get Michael's hand open, Michael struck him hard in the nose. As the merman's nose made a satisfying crack under his fist, however, a sickening sensation began to pulse through him. Michael felt his muscles seize up as he collapsed and floated slowly back down onto the bed. The pain had started in his wrists. The man hummed a little as he straightened himself, and the blood stopped flowing from his nostril. Michael couldn't move, but he watched as the man bent and pulled the ring from his hand.

"You're a fool if you think guards can get audiences with the royal family." And chuckling to himself, the guard left.

Michael began to shake, though from fear or the effects of the anemone's shock, he couldn't tell.

"Arianna!" he finally managed to cry out. With every second he lay there, screaming her name, the more real her death felt. He had no idea how long it had been since she'd fallen into the water. But he did recall his betrothed—yes, that's who she was—pushing Arianna off the ship. And as he had watched from the ship, she had sunk and her fins had not reappeared.

36

PROPHESIED

"*A*re you sure she's not just hungry? My daughter does that when she's hungry, even in her sleep."

"Look, she's trying to talk. How can you not see that?"

Arianna tried to open her eyes, but moving her eyelids was hard. Breathing was hard. Moving anything was hard. Her whole body felt as though it had been placed under a tight net that held her securely to the ground, or whatever surface she was lying upon.

Again, she tried to mouth her cries for help. But whispering under water was impossible.

"She's trying again. Mae! Mae, come quickly!"

The water around her began to churn as multiple creatures moved in and out of the area, and Arianna could feel bodies surrounding her, growing closer as they gathered. Who were these people? And why couldn't she open her eyes?

"Look, Mae! Her eyelids are fluttering! I think she's truly awake this time!"

"Yes, I see, Piero. Nereza, please hand me that charm. No, not that one. The green cockle shell. Yes, that one."

Arianna felt her head being lifted and a small weight being placed on her chest, similar to her aunt's little conch. Unbidden, her hands flew to her throat to search for her aunt's shell. Other hands, however, grabbed her wrists and held them down.

"It's working," the female voice named Mae said, "but perhaps we should take it off and speak to her first." With that, the little weight was slipped back over Arianna's head again, and the water pressed Arianna's hands to her neck where they sat.

"Our apologies," Mae said, her mouth very close to Arianna's right ear, "but if you push the charm off, you'll be immobile again. Leave it on so we can talk, please."

Arianna's breath raced in and out, a strange sensation underwater after she'd been above for so long. But she worked to calm her beating heart and do as they said. Though she wasn't convinced of the strangers' intentions, she would do no one any good stuck to the ground, or wherever she was. She could only assume that Renata's intense training in deeper water was the reason she was still alive now.

The charm was placed around her neck again, and for the first time, Arianna's eyes were able to open. As they focused, she realized why she hadn't been able to move. The sun was so far away and its light so distant in the water above that she had to be at twice the depth she'd ever reached. Even with the charm, breathing took more effort than ever before, and moving made her feel as though she'd gained twice her weight.

She blinked again, trying to focus on the blobs surrounding her, and with some effort, she began to make out faces. There was a small merwoman with unruly gray curls. Arianna could only assume she was the one named Mae. Three mermen and three other merwomen surrounded her. And they were all staring at her.

"Come, come!" Mae fussed at everyone else. "Give the poor girl some room. You wouldn't want to be gawked at after sleeping for three days."

Arianna let her head fall back again. She had been unconscious for three whole days? She glanced down at her legs, only to breathe a sigh of relief when she saw her fins back in place. But what about Michael? What had happened to Michael and Renata and the pirates? With some effort, she pushed herself up onto her elbows to study the room she was in. There was a single hole in the ceiling above her, but everything else was made of rock.

"Out, now!" Mae was still ordering everyone around. "I will call you back in if I need you. Donna, take Bo to the front of the cave and keep watch. We don't need any surprises today. And Nereza." Mae turned to a tall mermaid with the longest arms Arianna had ever seen on a female. "Stay here with me. I'd like to have you close by." Mae gave Nereza a meaningful look, and Nereza nodded once.

She's a Protector, Arianna realized. Wait, were they keeping a Protector close by because of *her*? The thought nearly made her laugh.

"Please, Mae," a young man who could have been no older than fifteen years paused and swam back into the room. He sounded like the one who had called for Mae after Arianna had awakened. "Let me stay. I won't be in the way, I promise! I just want to see her!"

Arianna looked back at Mae in confusion. He wanted to see her? She couldn't think of a less interesting specimen to watch when it came to merpeople. A silent mermaid was hardly an interesting mermaid. And yet, he continued to stare at her as though she were the sun itself, his face a mixture of fear and awe.

"Fine." Mae rolled her eyes then turned back to Arianna. "You'll have to excuse Piero. He's just excited, that's all. But now to you. You must be hungry. And wondering where you are, no doubt!" She shook her springy curls. "Piero, go get Princess Arianna some kelp and tuna."

Arianna had been examining the dark porous walls that encircled them, but as soon as she heard her name, all thoughts of her surroundings fled.

"Yes, I know who you are." Mae waved a hand and busied herself straightening the sea flower blanket that someone had draped over Arianna's lower half. "In fact, the whole kingdom knows the Sea Crown's silent granddaughter is being raised by her aunt. What few knew before this, however," she fixed her eyes on Arianna, "was that Arianna Atlantician would fulfill the prophecy."

Arianna just stared. The woman must be mad. But even as Arianna thought this, she remembered her aunt uttering nearly the same words three days earlier. Shaking her head, she motioned for something to write with.

"Piero," Mae called to the boy, who was just returning with the food. "Put that on her bed, then get her some writing tools."

Piero did as he was told, and to Arianna's surprise, Mae didn't ask any more questions until he had brought a slate, waxy leaves, and a pressing knife.

Why do you think I'm the prophesied one? Arianna wrote as fast as she could and held it up.

"I have since I heard that you were silent at birth. Others," Mae nodded at Nereza, who hadn't moved since going to hover in the corner, "have had their suspicions as well. But Renata kept you so hidden that some even considered sneaking back to see you for themselves."

Had Mae considered doing such a thing? *How many are you?* Arianna wrote. How many were that delusional?

"That believe? Dozens. Scattered about the kingdom, of course. Piero, here, works in the palace, as do Nereza, Elda, and a good deal more who are not able to be here right now."

Do you live here?

"In this cave? Goodness, no. This is just our meeting place. I live in a quiet little house on the outskirts of Gemmaqua. I sell healing charms in the city market, so I have no need to be near the palace. The others have been dropping by as often as they can to see how you're progressing." She paused. "You know, we counted it a miracle that Piero saw you fall from the boat on his way back from work."

So they weren't far from the palace. Was that where Renata had been taking them?

"How did it feel to have your legs change into fins? Or fins to legs? Or however it happens?" Piero stepped closer, his round face alight with wonder.

Arianna gave him a quick smile, then wrote again. *But why do you think I am the prophesied one?*

Mae pulled herself up to her full height, which was even less than Arianna's, and she began to sing.

Child of sun,
> *Child of sea,*
> *Destined to silence,*
> *Destined to sing.*
> *One nature to rule,*
> *One nature to fight,*
> *Only when owned can two peoples unite.*

Arianna was unimpressed. *I've heard the prophecy,* she wrote. *And I can't sing.*

"But don't you understand?" Mae knelt beside Arianna. "We've all heard how you can stay in the sunlight without feeling pain! You were destined for silence. And now," she floated up again, "you're destined to sing. Your two natures are battling against one another, Princess Arianna."

But I can't sing!

"You must find a way for your merblood to rule within you before it can rule without!" Mae's cry echoed off the cave walls.

Arianna stared at her for a long moment. Finally, she wrote, *Why is it so important that I find my voice?*

"Your Aunt Renata," Mae leaned forward and whispered, "has been a very bad girl before."

Piero cleared his throat and glanced nervously at Mae, who nodded. "And we think she's planning something even worse to take place as soon as the Sea Crown passes."

Arianna, of course, wanted to know exactly what they thought her aunt was up to, but when she asked, Mae only said that they'd talk about it later. Now, she insisted, Arianna had exerted herself enough and needed to rest. This was not at all what Arianna had in mind, but as soon as she was laid back in her sponge bed, and the flower blankets were covering her once again, she felt her eyelids begin to droop.

Instead of sweet, restful sleep, however, the last image Arianna saw again and again in her mind were Michael's lips as they traced her aunt's brow and then moved down into the kiss.

37

WHAT IT MEANS

"You're not choosing, Princess!" Mae rubbed her temples and shook her head. "You have to let go of the sun and embrace the sea, or you'll never get your voice!"

Then why have legs in the first place? Arianna wrote back, pressing into the waxy leaf a little harder than necessary.

"A sign, Princess!" Mae let out a dramatic sigh. "It was a sign to show us whom to look for. Nothing more. From now on, your concern is with sea matters, not the sun!"

If it was just a sign, then Arianna was sure it was a rather inconvenient one.

"We'll try again," Mae said.

What did she think Arianna had been doing for the past three days?

"Now, focus your heart. Think about what it is to be a mermaid."

It was probably a good thing Arianna couldn't talk sometimes. Her words would have gotten her into much trouble, she was sure.

"Think of all the reasons you love your home, and how wonderfully the Maker has created it. You must find the place in your heart that loves the water more than the sun. Then hold it tightly until your love of the ocean eclipses your past admiration for the surface."

Arianna sighed and closed her eyes as she had been instructed to countless times. She pictured the ocean in the change of seasons. She thought of the pearl farms and baby dolphins, and even the great whales who passed through their waters, filling them with exotic, foreign songs. The constant undulating of the giant kelp and the way the seal mothers cuddled their young.

But with every image of the ocean a thought of the surface crept in as well. And as much as she tried, Arianna couldn't chase away thoughts of the warm sand or the way the sun enveloped her in its complete embrace. She saw the palm trees waving in the salty breeze and Lucy and Claire as they ran shrieking with joy through the grassy fields.

"Try again, Princess."

Arianna opened her mouth and pushed. But as before, nothing came out.

"Princess Arianna, you're not trying hard enough! You have to want it!"

One would think Mae had coached silent mermaids before. Arianna squeezed her eyes shut again. As if merpersons lost and regained their voices every day! What gave Mae the authority to interpret the prophecy anyhow? She was just a charm maker, no better than anyone else. Dozens of people followed her, and for what? Because she believed in some stupid prophecy?

Just as Arianna was about to give up and put these thoughts on the waxy leaf, their practice was interrupted.

"It's happened!" someone shouted from the distance. Arianna and Mae looked up to see Piero swimming toward them at top speed. He held a waxy leaf in his hand, but it looked nearly torn to shreds by the time he got to the cave. "The Sea Crown," he panted between each word, "has died."

All Arianna's annoyance with Mae dissipated. Her grandfather was dead? She closed her eyes and sought to take control of the shuddering breaths that were threatening to overtake her. She hadn't known him well, as her grandparents had only visited a few times when she was a child, and yet . . . another piece of her world was gone. One more chunk given to the unknown.

As it was evening, enough of Mae's followers had returned from work for a chorus of gasps to go up around the cave. Some had been watching Arianna practice and others had been talking in hushed tones, but now all eyes turned to Mae, who didn't seem to notice Arianna's distress in the slightest.

"Then the contest will be in three days," an older merman named Bo said, a Nurturer from what Arianna could tell of his song. "That's not much time."

"Indeed it's not." Mae pursed her lips and tugged at one of her gray curls. Then she looked back at Arianna. "Surely you know of the contest for the crown?"

Arianna gave her a single sharp nod, still bothered by the woman's callousness. Arianna may not have been raised in the palace, but she wasn't a bumpkin. *Why do you ask?* she wrote.

"This means you have only three days to find your soulsong."

Arianna gaped at her. *You mean you want me to be in the contest?*

"Who else?" Mae gestured to the merpeople surrounding them. "We all believe in the prophecy, but none of us are royal born. Only the direct descendants can participate." Her eyes narrowed. "That leaves you. You are the direct granddaughter of the Sea Crown."

But my father will surely try. Or Lalia.

Piero shook his head. "Your sister is with child?"

Again? Arianna almost gave a silent hysterical laugh. *That was quick.*

"And your father says he doesn't feel fit to rule after what happened with the Sun Crown." Piero lowered his eyes, as though ashamed to speak the words. "That leaves only Renata and you." He sighed. "She's in the Sea Palace now, telling everyone that you got lost on the way here."

Lost was an interesting way to phrase it. Arianna frowned.

"She still has to win the triton, even if she is the only competitor," someone near the back of the throng said. "Even if there are no competitors, the triton could decide that no one is ready to win. It could simply wander the Deeps for years until it found a contestant worthy. It could even wait until Princess Lalia's children are of age."

"But this is Renata," Bo added woefully. "She'll use whatever means she must in order to win." The merpeople around them murmured in agreement.

You said she's planning something terrible, Arianna wrote. *How do you know what she's planning?* How did this all fit in with what Renata had told her?

"We don't know for sure," Mae said, glancing at Piero. "But we have reason to believe it involves the Deeps."

Before Arianna could respond, another mermaid arrived. This time it was Nereza. As usual, she talked to no one when she entered, only whispering into Mae's ear. Mae turned to Arianna.

"There is a human at the palace."

Arianna nearly forgot to breathe. He was there . . . nearby. Her heart twisted and soured at the same time.

"What do you know about him?" Mae folded her hands.

Arianna suddenly got the feeling that she was princess in title only to the woman. Mae held all the power, and she knew it. *He's the prince of Maricanta, the future Sun Crown. Why?*

"Nereza says he's screaming your name." Mae fixed her with a hard stare. "Nereza also believes that your aunt, upon winning the triton, plans to wed him."

Even if Arianna had wanted to respond, her hands were trembling too hard.

"I don't know what your connection to that young man is. But I get the feeling that you're more familiar with him than you're letting on, judging by the look on your face. So if there was ever a motivation for you to gain your voice, this should be it." Mae's voice was solemn, but a merry light danced in her eyes.

Arianna took her waxy leaf and wrote the only words she could think of. *I don't know how.*

Mae stared at her for a long time, and Arianna held her gaze miserably.

"Come on, Mae." Piero finally broke the silence as he swam between Arianna and the older woman. "Maybe she just needs some more time. She's only been here three days."

"We have resources," Mae snapped. "We have believers all over the city. We have support within the palace itself. What we do not have is time." She looked at a few of the older merpersons in the group and gave an exaggerated sigh. "We need to council. Perhaps there is a way to stall them until we know where to go from here."

Half of the group went with Mae deeper into the cave. A few others moved back to talking, and some began to drift out of the cave completely. Only Piero stayed by Arianna's side.

"Please don't worry about them," Piero said, laying a hand on Arianna's shoulder. "They just didn't expect the Sea Crown to die so soon." Then he yanked his hand back and grimaced. "And . . . I'm sorry about your grandfather." He glared at the huddled group in the corner. "They could have been nicer about that," he said in a low voice. "They're just worried. Most of them have work they're neglecting for this. The stakes are high here."

Arianna's mouth tasted metallic as she stared at the merpeople conferring together. Once again, she had been tossed out like a naughty child. Once again, she had failed someone's expectations. Her blood felt hot, and the ocean cave with its ever-present attendants was suddenly too confining. She turned toward the entrance and bolted.

"Wait!" Piero called after her. "You're not ready to go into the open ocean yet! You need another charm!"

But Arianna didn't stop. The pressure still often made her dizzy, and the speed at which she was swimming only made the dizziness worse. Still, it was better than sitting and waiting for someone else to decide her next step. Again.

The water around her became a darker, deeper shade of blue, and the weight of it nearly made Arianna's ears buzz. With the added weight, however, there also came exhilaration.

Though her parents had turned a blind eye to Arianna's surface visits, they had never, under any circumstances, allowed her to go farther into the ocean than their city mansion, which had been only two miles from the Sun Palace itself.

"I'll take you out one day," Rinaldo had promised her once when she'd protested their parents' rules.

Creatures of all colors, mammals, and plants sped by her. Schools of purple fish scattered in a tizzy as she whooshed through them. Soft, thin gray rays rippled below her, and sunfish lazily floated on their sides above. Millions of fish and plants in every color imaginable filled the seafloor, blending into a rainbow of life as she bolted over them.

If you'd let me do this earlier, Arianna thought wryly to the Maker, *I might not have sought out the sun.* But then, no, she was forced to admit. She would have sought the sun anyway.

Arianna broke off her sprint and flipped up, pushing herself to the surface so fast that for a moment, she couldn't tell which way was up and which was down. Leaping out of the water, however, was too thrilling to care. Then back down she went, even faster. This time she embraced the pain of the pressure as she dove. This is what it meant to be a mermaid.

If only she had someone to share it with.

Unbidden, Michael's face flashed in her mind, the look he had given her when they were dancing out on the terrace. If Drina had waited a moment longer to call his name, he just might have chosen her.

Arianna came to a halt. Her desire to swim melted.

The mournful call of a whale floated through the vast, lonely water around her, and its call touched Arianna's heart. Raising her head, she saw the giant body in the distance. It had no whale pup, nor did it have a mate.

I would sing with you, she wanted to call. *If I could.*

"Princess Arianna!"

Arianna turned to see Piero staring at her, a look of wonder on his young face.

Had he really followed her this whole way? She quirked an eye at him. Could she not have one second to herself before some sort of nanny caught up with her?

He swallowed hard, then gave her a shy smile. "You have a lovely voice."

PRAYING MAN

*M*ichael's head still hurt as he pried his eyes open once again. *How long have I been out this time?*

He shut them immediately, however, when he saw Princess Ines, or rather, Renata Atlantician sitting on a stool in front of the excessively large white vanity just five or six feet from his bed. He pretended to sleep until he was convinced she hadn't seen him. Then Michael peeked through his lids to see what the woman was doing.

Renata looked older than Princess Ines ever had. Michael could only guess she'd used some sort of dark power to conceal her true age. Not even Arianna had recognized her. She held a little conch shell to her lips, just like the one Arianna always wore, and was singing into it. Her voice was so low that he could hardly hear the melody at all, but she was keeping the song for later, he was sure.

A knock sounded at the door, and Michael shut his eyes again as the woman flitted over to answer it. "I'm working on it now," she whispered to whomever was at the door. "As soon as the plans are in the conch, I'll send it over with one of my girls. . . . Yes, I trust her. I wouldn't send someone I didn't." Her voice grew testier with each word. "Go back now, and don't come here again until I call for you."

Whatever Renata was planning must have been complicated, for it took her nearly another hour of singing before she laid the conch on the vanity and went over to a nearby wardrobe to stare into it. Just when Michael thought the woman would never leave, she pulled some sort of bag from the wardrobe's drawer and left the room. Not, of course, until she'd given him a long look, which Michael prayed would convince her he was still asleep.

As soon as she was gone, Michael leapt out of the bed. Unfortunately, he forgot about his anemone bindings. The shock they delivered to his wrists had him unable to move for ten minutes. He lay, half on the sponge bed and half off, as spots danced in his vision.

As soon as he was able to push himself up on his elbows again, Michael did his best to crawl in slow, smooth movements. His already sore arms screamed in protest as he leaned on one hand and stretched the other out toward the vanity's edge. His arms were barely long enough to reach. His left elbow didn't have much feeling in it, however, which caused him to slip and receive more painful jolts to his arms, enough to make a groan escape him when he most needed silence.

Just let me get it, he prayed, grinding his teeth as he tried again. *I don't know what I'll do with it, but I need to do something. If Arianna is dead . . .* he squeezed his eyes shut *. . . I know her blood will be on my head. But you are the Maker. So if you have kept her alive somehow . . . just please let me do something to help her. Please let me get this conch!*

And yet, Michael continued to fail, sometimes touching the shell only to push it even farther back on the vanity top. After being shocked over and over again, Michael came to a point where he could no longer raise his arms higher than his shoulders. His wrists felt like they were on fire from the anemone stings, and his shoulders and neck throbbed with a stabbing pain from arching his back for an hour.

In anger, Michael struck the vanity's leg. To his surprise, the leg crumbled beneath his fist, and the vanity tipped. The conch slid right into his hands.

Michael stared stupidly at the conch for a long moment before he realized just how half-baked his plan had been.

What now? he asked the Maker. *How do I get it to Arianna or someone who can help her?* Just then, he heard someone hum and the lock turning in the door. Michael dropped the conch into one of the sponge holes, praying he wouldn't forget which one it was. He had barely lain back down when Renata burst in. He could hear her stop in front of the vanity.

For a moment, she was silent. Then without turning, she asked, "Where is it?"

~

A soothing melody, much like a lullaby made of aloe, blanketed the burning in Michael's ears and skin. He blinked up at a lovely woman as she sang a quiet song, running her fingers lightly and repeatedly over his burned arms. Michael tried to place where he had seen her before, but couldn't.

"He looks rather dense in the head to me."

Only then did Michael notice a man standing beside her. The woman's face was focused and calm, but the man's face was disgruntled, at best. He also looked familiar. His gray hair was cropped close to his head, and he fingered his short gray beard in agitated flicks. And he was making his opinion of Michael no secret as he continued to glower at him.

"Hush now," the woman said in a low voice. "He has the look of a siren song to him, and you know that. You're just being petty. Look how young he is."

"What . . ." Michael tried to speak, but his throat was oddly parched. "What day is it?"

"She got you there, too," the dark-haired woman muttered, reaching up and placing her hand on his neck. She closed her eyes and tipped her head forward, a look of pinched focus on her face. After a few more moments of singing, Michael felt his throat loosen. When she finally leaned back and opened her eyes, she looked tired. "You have been here in the Sea Palace for five days."

Five days. And he only recalled waking up three times. What was the matter with him?

"I need to . . . Arianna," he finally groaned, leaning back into the bed. "I need to find Arianna."

The woman glanced at the man, her brown eyes suddenly wide in her oval face. "What do you know of our daughter?" She squeezed his hand hard. "It is of the utmost importance that we find her. Where *is* she?"

"I don't . . . I don't know. Wait." He propped himself up on his elbows. "You're Ambassador Amadeo. And Lady Giana?" He squinted at her, trying to recall her face from when he had met her years before. "I tried to speak with you, but the servant lied . . . How did you find me?"

"One would have to be deaf to miss your bellowing," Amadeo said. Then he looked down at his wife, who sat on the edge of Michael's sponge bed. "I'll go stay with her. You finish with him." He glared at Michael as he rose up into the water. "Quickly."

"Where is he going?" Michael asked when Amadeo was gone.

"He's keeping Renata busy, but we don't have much time." She scooted closer. "You have to tell us about Ari!"

Michael closed his eyes and tried to sift through the bits and pieces of memories that were drifting around in his head like clouds. "She stayed with us for . . . months, I think."

"Stayed with you?"

"Yes. After she got her legs back and was chased from the water by a sea creature. But then Renata came and lied, saying she was a foreign princess. Then she invited Arianna to come over to her new kingdom—"

"Arianna has legs?"

If Amadeo had looked at him like he was a little loose in the head earlier, it was nothing compared to the incredulous look Lady Giana gave him now. She looked so much like Arianna that it made Michael's heart ache as guilt wrenched his gut, though he couldn't exactly recall just why.

"She has legs on land and fins in the sea. They come and go depending on where she is. But when Renata pushed her into the water, her fins didn't come. Right after I . . ." Michael looked at Lady Giana in horror. "Why did I kiss Renata?"

"You're under a siren song," she said impatiently. "Now what about Arianna?"

"But what's a siren song?"

Giana pulled in a deep breath through her nose and closed her eyes. When she opened them again, she spoke slowly and deliberately. "Siren songs are forbidden to my people for a reason. They touch the parts of others' minds and souls that shouldn't be toyed with. One must harness the Sorthileige in order to successfully weave a siren song." She eyed Michael warily. "My guess is that Renata's trapped you under a partial song, since you seem to maintain control of your faculties at certain times."

"How do you know that?"

She nodded at the side of his head. "You had blood in your ears when I found you. That means you must have managed to displease her somehow, which means you aren't under her complete control all the time. Yet." She leaned forward. "Now, you said Arianna has legs?" She shivered.

Michael frowned at her. "Arianna's legs are not disgusting. They're lovely. I mean . . . she's lovely."

"Don't let her father hear that kind of talk." Then Lady Giana sighed. "If she has legs, and Renata knows about it, then . . ." She sat up straight. "Renata's been using her!"

"I was the one Renata had planned to marry."

"But don't you understand?" Lady Giana was almost shouting as she swam back and forth in short, frenetic bursts. "It was never about you! It was always about Ari and the prophecy! I told him! I told him we should never have let her keep Ari! Never!"

"Do you mean that old prophecy about the silent . . . ?" Michael searched his memories, trying to recall the old poem Bithiah had taught him when he was small. Something about two natures. And silence. And singing?

"But she still can't sing!"

"That won't matter to Renata. She'll hound Ari until she gets what she wants."

Michael pushed himself higher. "You have to take this siren song off me! I need to find Arianna before her aunt does!"

But Lady Giana was already shaking her head. "Only the one who sang the song can undo it." She paused. "Or the one who holds the triton."

"And who has that now?" Michael tried to recall just how far they'd sailed after Arianna had fallen.

"No one. My father-in-law died two days ago. That's why we were able to sneak in to see you now. Renata is busy with the funeral preparations for tonight. The triton will belong to whoever wins the contest tomorrow."

Michael swallowed. "Who's competing?"

"As of now? Only Renata." Lady Giana floated up from the ground and moved toward the door. But she paused on the threshold. "Are you a praying man, Prince Michael?"

He nodded.

"Good. Then I suggest you begin now. Pray that the Maker shows us how to rein Renata in."

"Wait!" Michael shoved his hand into his bed several times

before finding the right hole. "The Maker answered at least one of my prayers." He handed the conch to Lady Giana, then gave her a wry smile. "I don't let my ears bleed for just nothing."

Lady Giana gave him a long, strange look before rushing out the door with the conch, not even saying goodbye.

Michael lay back on his bed, and for the first time he could remember in a long time, he felt ready to rest.

39

HAUNTING MELODIES

"Wait." Arianna paused to swallow more nectar from the bulbous plant Mae held out to her. The way the thick green nectar slimed down her throat made her want to gag, but Arianna was forced to admit that it soothed her sore throat more than the salt water she was constantly drawing in and out. "What good does a voice do me when I still have no soulsong?" she asked when she was done. "This is child's play compared to what she can do. Even with a voice, I stand no chance at beating Renata without a soulsong."

"You're doing splendidly." Mae patted her arm. "Your progression is far superior to that of children, I assure you."

"Even so," Arianna paused to swallow more of the disgusting nectar, "children don't find their koroses or their soulsongs until they're fourteen years or more. I won't find mine by tomorrow!"

"You'll never know if you don't try!" Mae yanked Arianna's shoulders up and pressed her back straight again. "Now, show me your healing koros again."

With a little sigh and the desire to say something sarcastic, Arianna began singing the healing scale once more.

Never, in all of her life, had Arianna thought she would ever tire of using her voice if she got one. But now that she was singing through all hours of the day and night, or had been in the two days since she'd found her voice, Arianna was ready for a few blissful hours of silence. *You don't do anything the easy way, do you?* she thought to the Maker.

"Good. Now hold that note a little longer."

"Mae!" a familiar voice cried from a distance, and Mae rolled her eyes a bit and shook her head with an affectionate smile.

"Piero, it might do you good one day not to alert the entire ocean whenever something has happened that concerns us."

Piero stopped, panting, and looked around. "But we have no neighbors here."

"Which is precisely why I picked this cave," she said dryly. "What is the emergency now?"

"Sorry I'm late. The new height restrictions are making swimming more crowded below. But Lady Giana sought me out this morning."

Arianna felt her pulse quicken. Her mother was near. She had known, of course, that her mother would be in the capital city. But hearing that Piero had seen her? It made Arianna ache.

"She gave me this," Piero said, holding out a smooth, striped conch charm just a little smaller than Arianna's thumbnail. "She said it was of the gravest concern, and that we were to do whatever was necessary to stop Renata from winning the contest."

"My mother is a believer as well?" Arianna asked.

"If she wasn't then, she is now." Mae frowned as she took the conch. "It seems we're not as well hidden as we thought." She looked at the others. "We'll need to take precautions in the future to keep our activity quieter. But in the meantime, let's see what we can get from this." She turned and headed into the corner of the cave. When Arianna hung back with Piero, however, as was her usual position, Mae turned and waved them in as well. "You're a part of this now. You need to hear whatever is in this shell, too."

Soon they and the rest of Mae's followers were all squished around the conch charm, which had been placed on the ground. Mae instructed some of the younger members to block off the cave entrance and close the holes above them. Then she hung an algae lantern from the rock. Finally, she pulled the wax seal from the conch's opening and stood back with everyone else to listen.

A familiar voice filled the room. The song was wordless, but even without her own soulsong, Arianna knew exactly what her aunt was saying.

General Orsini, the melody hummed in a minor tone, *here are your instructions for the day after I take the crown. Memorize this message, as I will not have the opportunity or privacy to make another. My brother and his wife are suspicious already, and with my niece escaped, people will be talking. I have managed to garner enough drops of Sorthileige to infect my own family and peers first. Once they have been exposed, I will return to the Deeps and gather enough for our people to partake as well. We cannot tell them, of course. They will not understand until after they've been touched. For now, all we need to do is focus on my family and everyone that is loyal to them.*

"Oh, Renata," was all Arianna could whisper. "Why?"

But the song continued. *We will not infect the Maricantan prince. I cannot have his physical appearance too altered, as he will be returning to the Maricantan throne soon and will continue until we have an heir and it is considered a normal time for him to pass. For now, I simply need your continued willingness to dedicate your Protectors and allegiance to me and to follow my future instructions to the letter. I will take care of the rest when I have the triton.*

The song ended, but no one spoke for a long time. The light of the algae lantern made every face present look gray and drawn, but Arianna was sure they would look the same way in the direct light of the sun after having heard her aunt's message.

"If my mother gave this to you," Arianna finally turned to Piero, "surely she knows as well!"

But Piero was already shaking his head. "I'm afraid, Princess, that this kind of message can only be heard once." He looked at the ground and folded his hands behind his back. "I accidentally broke a shell once while carrying a message for the late Sea Crown's wife. I learned very quickly that not all songs can echo the way yours can." He nodded at the shell that still hung around Arianna's neck.

Arianna blushed. Did they know who still sang her to sleep every night?

Mae spoke before anyone else could comment. "What's important is that it seems your aunt plans to infect all the merpeople with Sorthileige." She fixed a critical eye on Arianna. "Would you happen to know why?"

Arianna chewed her lip as she thought. "When we were on the ship and she revealed her true identity to me, she said she believed we could free the merpeople from danger forever." Arianna frowned. Even with the proof she had just heard from the shell, it seemed wrong to betray her aunt to these people.

"But why?" Mae asked.

"Those infected with the Sorthileige are strong," Elda, another palace worker, said in her squeaky voice. "Even if their lives are shortened by the Sorthileige, their short lives make them incredibly hard to control." She shuddered. "I work near the dungeons sometimes, where I can hear them."

"That's right," someone else said. "Curiosity pushes them in, but the darkness follows them out."

Everyone looked solemn. Arianna remembered only too well the foamy eyes of the merwoman and the screeches of the merman. Each had chosen to take Sorthileige by venturing into the Deeps. But the merpeople as a whole had not. Mothers, fathers, grandparents, and children. They would all be doomed to the darkness.

"But if it shortens their lives so significantly," Arianna asked, "why would Renata wish to use it?"

"Full exposure to the Deeps leaves only a few days of life," Bo said, scratching his chin. "But if given drop by drop . . . Well, that might be dragged on for years and years."

"So if I don't win the triton," Arianna whispered, "she could use it to sentence our entire race to darkness." When no one answered her, Arianna looked up to see all eyes watching her again. Not even Mae spoke. "What did Renata do?" she asked, still whispering. "I mean, before I was born?"

"Your aunt was one of the finest Protectors we had ever seen," Bo said, glancing warily at Mae. "She guarded the seas at the southern end of our borders. You're probably aware of this, Princess, but the Sea Crown is high king of all the seas. Not just the First Sea. This is merely the capital's territory. Each territory has boundaries and its own ambassador. Your aunt worked at the far southern edge of our boundary where she fell in love with a Grower named Angelo. They were quickly engaged to be married, as unlike the humans, *our* people are allowed to marry whomever they choose, regardless of title or importance. Just before the wedding, however, they were attacked by a pirate ship."

Bo sighed. "She did all she could to keep them hidden from the pirates, but the pirates were too strong." He shook his gray head. "Angelo threw himself into their nets so she could be free."

Mae took up the story. "When she went to a nearby naval vessel to plead for help, the sailors told her they were too busy to help find one merman."

Arianna wanted to weep for her aunt.

"Instead of going to her father, however, Renata decided to take her vengeance into her own hands," Mae continued. "She flew into a rage and rushed into the Deeps. By the time she was finished with the pirate ship, not a single sailor lived. She was too late, though, and she found that Angelo had died as well. But she was spurred on by what the Sorthileige had awakened inside her so she also sought out the naval ship. She sang a siren song to the sailors and had them all dead on the rocks as they tried to swim to her during a storm she had conjured."

"But how did she live after touching the Sorthileige?" Arianna asked.

"Some say," Mae said slowly, glancing at Bo, "that the enemy of the Maker likes to make deals with those who are bent on defying the Maker."

"Then how come she was able to live with us?"

"Your father," Mae said, "took pity on her, and begged the Sea Crown to spare her life, even though she had defied the law and murdered the sailors. When she didn't turn, as others do who have touched the Sorthileige, your father was able to convince your grandfather that she must not have touched the Sorthileige at all."

"Those who saw the spectacle, however, knew better," Bo muttered.

And they wanted Arianna to go up against such power. Arianna could see all the obstacles flashing in her head. She'd only had a voice for two days. She had no real understanding of what the contest entailed. Renata knew her every fear and doubt. If things went poorly, Renata could make her pay by punishing everyone she loved.

And Arianna still had no soulsong.

What are you doing? she asked the Maker. *You've given me my voice, but what good is it without a soulsong? If I fight her, I'm sure to lose. But then again, even if I don't fight, won't it all happen anyway?*

With her prayer, a strange rock of conviction settled in her stomach. "Mae," Arianna said in a shaky voice, "take me to the arena."

40

REFUSALS

*T*he swim to the arena was longer than Arianna had expected. Piero and Nereza accompanied them. Arianna had learned through eavesdropping that the cave was closer to the shore than the palace, but she hadn't known there was nearly an hour's swim between the two.

"Keeps me on a tight schedule on days when I sell at the market," Mae chuckled as they swam over dozens of little reefs on their way.

"Why haven't you been selling lately?" Arianna asked.

"When you fell out of the sky, Princess, it all stopped. I've enough supplies to keep me for a while longer, and many of our friends are kind enough to bring meals and supplies now and then." She turned and fixed her eyes on Arianna. They burned with excitement. "We've been waiting for you, Princess."

Though Arianna knew the sentiment was meant to be comforting, she only found that it made her want to squirm even more. They were getting too close to the palace to speak, however, so she let the comment go and tried to focus on their surroundings.

When the Sea Palace came into view, Arianna gasped. *I can see why they say you gave the plans to the builders,* she thought to the Maker. Millions of coral arms were woven together to form a chaotic yet elegant rainbow of walls, towers, and balconies galore, twice as tall as the Sun Palace. Each wall was made from cylinders of coral squeezed together into a stack of majestic towers that sparkled like a multicolored gem.

Hundreds of merpeople swam in and out of the palace, forming lines that wound in and out like delicate arms dancing to a living, breathing rhythm. Some carried food or supplies while others carried only themselves. Many of the ladies wore camicetts of ornate fabrics Arianna had never seen before. Many also had jewels and shells curled into their hair. And though the men didn't wear camicetts, their brightly colored sashes were decorated just as fully as the women's. Thousands of songs floated through the streets that surrounded the palace, and hundreds more joined them from within the building. Despite their individual songs, however, each of the four koroses was audible, and they all wove together to create an intricate harmony.

It was the rhythm of life. Arianna felt her heart rise and her throat close with unexpected emotion as her body yearned to fall into a dance that felt just as natural as breathing the air ever had.

"Welcome home."

Arianna turned to see Mae giving her a kind smile.

With more conviction than she'd ever had before, Arianna took the woman's outstretched hand, and they continued their journey past the palace and north of the city. And though Arianna thought she would never be surprised again after seeing the palace, she was wrong.

Large enough to swallow the palace twice over, the arena rose up into a round bowl that surrounded a simple flat stage at the bottom of its center. Rather than coral, however, this structure was made completely of stone.

"It was all one great mountain when they began," Piero said, his voice nearly squeaking. "And it's still standing hundreds of years later!"

As soon as they had crested the edge, Arianna eagerly started down to examine the pearlescent stage at the bottom of the arena, but Nereza grabbed her by the arm and jerked her back. They all settled behind a bench on the back row.

"Ow!" Arianna rubbed her arm, but Nereza only put her finger to her lips and peeked out over the bench. Arianna followed her gaze to see what she had missed before. Dozens of merpeople dotted the stands. The arena was so large that Arianna hadn't even noticed them at first.

"Preparing for tomorrow," Piero whispered.

"Merpeople from all over the world are coming to see this spectacle," Mae added. "Some even make it from the southern kingdoms and the far east. These stands will be packed to the brim."

Arianna's stomach turned as she thought about being showcased in front of so many people. Particularly as she was likely to come out the loser. "So how exactly will this happen?" she asked.

"You'll present yourself to the court tomorrow when they announce the contestants. Once the validity of all contestants' claims to the Sea Crown has been confirmed, everyone will move out here. When you and Renata are both on that stage, the triton will be thrown into the Deeps. Your—"

"Why do we have to compete in the Deeps?" Arianna shivered. "It seems a hard enough task just to win."

"Only the Sea Crown can guide humans over the Deeps—either he or those he grants a special blessing to. If you're going to guide others through it, you should know how to survive it." Mae sniffed. "Now, as I was saying, your job will be to find the triton, using each of the four koroses at least once. If the triton goes with you, then it has decided that you are the most prepared to accept the crown, and you will return to the arena to show everyone." Mae peered at Arianna. "You *are* ready to accept the crown, aren't you?"

"Of course." Arianna squeaked. "What happens then?"

"After you return here and are proclaimed the winner, you will still need to watch your back for the three days hence. You will hold the triton, but it won't officially belong to you until you're coronated on the third day, at the coronation ceremony."

After scanning the arena again, Mae swam up and over the arena itself. The others followed. Once they were on the arena's north side, Mae pointed to a place several hundred fathoms away.

Arianna strained to make out what she was looking at. "All I can see is that murky spot."

"Those are the Deeps. Remember, they exist over underwater chasms, canyons that cut into the earth. This particular one runs from east to west, then branches out several hundred fathoms to the west. You will race for the Deeps as fast as you can. Once inside, you'll call out to the triton to try and find it, using all four koroses. Renata will try and distract you, and you her as well. There will be—"

"Wait," Arianna said. "How exactly do we distract one another?"

Piero looked uncomfortable. "Well, according to the rules, you're not supposed to injure one another, just use your koroses to create obstacles of sorts, but—"

"But there will be no one there to enforce such rules," Mae interrupted. "No one to keep you safe. You will be utterly alone with her. Utterly alone."

The ferocity on Mae's small, round face was so sharp and her voice so foreboding that Arianna nearly burst out in exhausted, hysterical laughter. *Do you hear that?* she thought to the Maker. *They say you're not allowed. I'm rather hoping this is one of their rules and not yours.*

"What's so funny?" Mae asked.

"Nothing." Arianna tried to smother her smile. "I'm simply tired and trying to find the bright side of this whole mess."

But Mae didn't smile back. "I can assure you, Princess, that there is nothing bright about this situation. You have made great strides in two days, but if you lose tomorrow, we will all suffer. Including that prince of yours up in the palace."

"I am well aware of what is at stake," Arianna snapped.

"Well then act like it!"

"What do you want me to do?" Arianna threw her hands up. "I have hardly slept, thanks to your training regimen. I have done as you've said and groveled just like all your other little followers. But I still have no soulsong, and none of your nagging is going to help me get it!"

"If you try hard enough, you will win!"

"I *am* trying!"

"No you're not!" Mae began to swim back and forth in short, agitated movements. "I had such hopes for you. You're young and bright. But your inability to commit is making me wonder now if perhaps we were all wrong. Perhaps you are just an anomaly with deathly hair and sickly eyes."

"Wait now . . ." Piero held up his hands, but Mae pushed him aside so she could move closer to Arianna.

"If you were half the woman the prophecy says you should be, you would be able to forget the sun altogether—"

"The prophecy never says that!" Arianna shouted. If she had been above the surface, angry, traitorous tears would have been rolling down her face. "You act as though you know what the prophecy means, but do you really? You're a Grower! A charm smith! Not a holy man! Not a scholar! What if you're wrong?"

Mae's cheeks burned red, and her small fists clenched and unclenched. "I have dedicated my life to this! And if you weren't so self-centered, you would see all the sacrifices we have been making for you!"

"For me? Or for yourselves?"

No one spoke for a long time. Finally, Mae said in a stiff voice, "It's time to return home. We have a big day tomorrow." She began to swim away but stopped when no one followed. "Well?"

Nereza and Piero shared a long look, but Nereza finally followed Mae. Piero, however, stayed beside Arianna.

"I'm just going to stay here for a while . . . to make sure she knows how to get back."

"I meant the princess, too." Mae's eyes narrowed. "We have training to do."

Arianna crossed her arms and began swimming back toward the palace.

"Very well. I just hope you remember this when you lose tomorrow and your aunt poisons the hearts of—"

"I thought you were leaving."

Without another word, Mae burst off, leaving a trail of bubbles in her wake. Nereza followed, though at a slightly slower pace. Then it was just Arianna and Piero. Arianna turned sharply and continued swimming until she was halfway between the palace and the arena, where she planted herself firmly on a flat rock. Piero followed and found his own rock a few feet away.

For a while, neither spoke. Arianna simply sat and listened to the distant songs of the palace and its city, straining to hear any voices that might be remotely familiar. But eventually, guilt got the better of her.

"I really am trying," she finally said as she pulled her fins up to her chest and wrapped her arms around them.

"I know."

Arianna found that she believed him, and was suddenly glad he had decided to stay. There was something calming about Piero. His expressions were as unassuming as his words. It was kind of like being around a seal pup.

Thankfully, he seemed to understand that for once, she didn't want to talk. Instead, he let her peer at the palace's hundreds of balconies and windows without interruption.

Which one belonged to Renata? Was she keeping him in her chambers? Or had she placed him in the palace dungeon? Arianna strained to see inside the rooms. As the evening light began to dim, algae lanterns were hung inside and out. The lighted rooms made it easier to see inside of them, and she studied each room to see a movement that could be attributed to a human being held captive. But they were far enough away that she had no way of knowing for sure what she saw and what tricks her eyes might be playing on her.

"Do you have a girl?" she eventually asked Piero.

Piero started a bit and then looked at the ground. "Y—well, no. She's a Nurturer in the palace nursery. She doesn't like me, though. At least . . . I mean, I don't think she sees me."

Arianna turned to study his face. "Why not?"

Piero gave a little chuckle then gestured at his torso. "I'm not exactly what you might consider a top specimen of merman. Not that Nurturers can't be. But . . ." he stared listlessly up at the palace. "It sure helps make one closer to visible."

"You'll only be invisible as long as you allow yourself to be." She shook her head. "I should know."

Piero's eyes widened. "I never thought you could be invisible, Princess. Not even when you were silent. But . . . is something wrong?"

Arianna gave a short laugh. "I'm competing against my aunt tomorrow in a competition I can't possibly win. The Maker seems to think it reasonable that I go into a fight without the most essential tool a merperson can own. And for all this, I find my mind possessed by the nagging question as to whether or not it's possible to love and hate someone as much as I do right now."

"Your . . . aunt?" Piero asked slowly.

Arianna just smiled, and Piero nodded knowingly. But inside, she was no closer to peace than she had been before.

It would be easiest just to get Michael out of her aunt's grasp and send him back to Maricanta. Without him and his ridiculous smile around every corner or awaiting Arianna at every mealtime, perhaps she could focus enough to find her soulsong and get on with her life. She could forget about every accidental brush of the hand, every moment on the boat or the beach. There would be no reminders of his arms wrapped around her protectively when the fisherman attacked her. Even the pink frills of the gown he had purchased for her fluttered in her mind whenever she saw coral or anemones of the same color. Whenever Mae had barked out new orders and instructions, she couldn't help remembering that even when she was silent, Michael had *heard* her more than anyone here seemed to, even with her voice.

I'm going into the most dangerous day of my life, she thought up at the palace's glowing balconies, *and every time I need my head clear, you refuse to leave.*

41

UNSETTLED

*M*ichael turned to his dark-haired neighbor. "Why am I here again?" he asked above the din of the colossal court. Hundreds of merpeople filled every seat, and dozens floated in the back where there were no seats to be had. The room was buzzing with anticipation. If only Michael knew for what.

"We are waiting for the triton competition's contestant to accept the challenge and begin the test," the woman answered in a strained voice before turning back to the man on her other side. Was he her husband? Michael couldn't recall, although he was sure they both looked familiar.

"But there's only one? Usually contests have more than one contestant." Michael frowned. As he did, he noticed several little shells hanging from his neck. "What's this?" He began to remove them, but the woman yanked the shells' strings from his hand and placed them firmly back on his chest.

"Do not under any circumstances attempt to remove those. You'll be dead in less than a minute." She glanced up at the domed ceiling above them. "The weight of the water alone will kill you before you run out of air."

Michael let the shells be, but he tugged on her thin, gauzy sleeve once more. "But that still doesn't tell me why *I'm* here." He glanced down at his trousers. "I'm not a merman." He also wished he knew why his ears were so sore. He reached up to rub them, but she caught his hand and firmly pulled it back down to his side, her expression darkening. "My sister-in-law has requested the presence of the future Sun Crown at the contest and ensuing coronation in order to bring peace to our peoples." Her words made sense to Michael, but for some reason, her eyes did not agree.

Before Michael could ask any more questions, however, a group of men at the center of the stage he was seated on began to hum, low reverberating tones that brought a hush to the audience. The woman beside him stiffened, and Michael began to wonder if there was any reason for him to be on his guard.

So far, everyone had been very nice to him. Just that morning, an exquisite beauty with hair the color of ebony and skin the color of porcelain had sung him a lovely song. His worries, whatever they had been, had disappeared, and all the pain in his body had gone with them. Then he'd been given a green sash to wear over his left shoulder instead of a shirt. He'd been seated on a stage chair beside the nice lady who answered all of his questions. She wore a sash as well over her strange, shiny shirt, though it was blue instead of green. But for the life of him, Michael couldn't remember just how he had gotten down to the bottom of the ocean.

More singing ensued, this time by the merwomen. Their voices were like a silken scarf rising and falling in the wind. Their song had no words, but for some reason, everyone listened intently. At any moment, Michael expected a herald to come out and announce the contest. When no one did, however, five minutes into the song, Michael leaned over to the woman beside him. "What's happening?"

She gave a little start, then a frustrated sigh. "I forgot. You can't understand them. They're saying that now we are beginning the sacred passage of receiving our new Sea Crown, a leader given by the Maker himself. The triton," she nodded to the great three-pronged spear that lay on a pedestal of its own at the center of the stage, "will only allow itself to be given to the one who is ready." At this, her lips tightened at the corners. "When the winner emerges with the triton, we will have a new Sea Crown, and together with the Sun Crown, they can rule and protect the ocean and its shores together, forever."

"It sounds like it should be a joyful event," Michael whispered.

"It should be."

"Then why are you so frightened?"

She turned to him, and for the first time, her doe-like eyes betrayed a very real fear.

The tempo and key of the song changed, and the woman looked back at the choir. "They're getting ready to call the contestants," she whispered. "Or rather, contestant. Whoever answers the choir's call and is of the direct lineage of the former Sea Crown may enter." For a brief moment, Michael thought he saw her throw a glare at the large, gray-bearded man sitting on her other side.

The choir's song continued to quicken, and soon it had moved from solemn to nearly frenzied until a voice like a harp wound itself into the melody. Michael leaned forward to see better, as the room had been allowed to fall dark. Aside from the glow of a few lamps with odd little plants inside, there was no light. Little by little, more lanterns were brought in until the woman's song rose to a crescendo, when the room was suddenly bright enough to see a mermaid's long, lean form draped all in white as she knelt on her tail before the triton.

Michael was pleased to recognize her as the woman who had awakened him that morning. Though she had done little more than give his shoulder a shake, he felt his heart swell and his breath quicken. She truly was perfect. Except for the little black circles beneath her eyes that betrayed a lack of restful sleep, there was not a flaw to be seen on her face. Even the way her full red lips moved as she sang back to the choir made him itch to rush over to her and take her in his arms.

"They're asking her who she is that she dare lay claim to the throne," the woman beside him leaned over again. "And she is answering that she is Renata Atlantician, daughter of the former Sea Crown."

"I thought only sons could inherit thrones in the western realms, outside of Destin and Cobren." Tumen had once attempted allowing a daughter to inherit the throne, Michael had heard, but that had turned out quite badly for all involved, including the princess. But where had he learned such a thing? He couldn't even recall where any of those kingdoms were, or who ruled them.

"For the kingdoms on dry ground, yes. But if you haven't noticed, we're not exactly on dry ground, are we?"

He had no answer for that, so he gave her a grin instead before turning his attention back to the voluptuous beauty still kneeling at the front of the stage. Just as she began to rise, however, a confident smile on her lips, another song echoed through the dome.

This song was different from Princess Renata's. Rather than the resonant, confident tones of a harp, this song was thin and delicate, as though the slightest sound might send it shattering to a thousand pieces. But its delicacy was elegant and its charm was exquisite. If crystal could be made into music, this song would be finer than the most expensive jewels.

With the song entered a young mermaid. Her form was not as defined as Princess Renata's, nor was her carriage as regal. She wore no flowing white, only a simple lavender shirt with a few flounces on the shoulders. Unlike anyone else Michael had seen that morning, her hair was golden, wrapped in a tight, elegant knot at the back of her head. And if his vision wasn't betraying him, he was rather sure her eyes were blue. It was the openness of her face, however, that tugged on some part of Michael's memory and suddenly annoyed him, like an itch he couldn't scratch. Gone were his feelings of perfect serenity. He couldn't be sure why, but something about the scene before him was wrong.

"Who is that?" he whispered to his neighbor.

But his neighbor didn't answer. Her eyes were the size of sand dollars, and she clutched at the hand of the gray-bearded man beside her. "It's Ari." Her words were hardly audible. "Amadeo, she has a voice!"

As the young woman swam down the aisle between the two halves of the court, her voice was the only sound in the gigantic throne room. Even the choir was silent. Finally, an older woman from the back of the stage swam forward. She had white hair and wore a green sash. "And who are you?" she asked in an unsteady voice.

"My name is Princess Arianna Fiore del Mare Atlantician, and I am granddaughter of the former Sea Crown. I come to lay claim to the triton of my grandfather. It would be my honor to compete in the contest."

The gasp from the audience was loud.

"You . . . You have a voice." The woman put her hands over her mouth.

Obviously. Michael shook his head.

But the girl looked as though she had expected such a stupid statement. "I do."

"And you want to compete?"

"I do."

Michael studied the mermaid closer, trying to discern what about her might merit such pointless questions. As he did, however, she glanced his way. Their eyes locked for one brief second.

If he had been bothered earlier, now he was unsettled to the core.

"How old are you, Princess Arianna?" the woman asked, pulling the girl's attention away from Michael.

"I turned nineteen years three weeks ago, Your Ladyship."

"You know this is a dangerous game you ask to play," the robed woman said in a soft voice. "You could die in the Deeps. Many older and more experienced than you have."

Something inside Michael revolted at the thought of the girl doing something so dangerous. Though he still desperately wanted to touch every inch of the first woman in white, another part of him, the part that she had awakened with those shimmering blue eyes, wanted desperately to protect the girl.

"I understand," the young princess said, her voice cracking at the end.

"Very well then." The robed woman nodded before returning to the back of the stage. The choir burst into a booming finale, and the two contestants were quickly ushered out. Michael turned to ask his neighbor what had just happened, but when he did, he found her eyes closed and her lips moving silently.

"What are you doing?" he asked, gently touching her shoulder.

The woman turned to him, her face whiter than bone. "Praying for my daughter."

THE SUN'S BETRAYAL

*A*rianna felt as though someone had stolen her voice once again. As they were led out of the domed throne room, she couldn't think of the first thing she might say to the beloved aunt who had tried to kill her.

I've missed you. I still use your conch necklace to sing me to sleep at night. My voice appeared without *the use of dark powers. Oh, and please refrain from trying to kill me. Again.*

"I see you've found your voice." Renata was the first one to break the silence as four Protectors escorted them into a smaller chamber behind the great throne room. "I'm proud of you."

Arianna stopped swimming and looked up at her aunt. "Proud of me? You tried to kill me!"

"I did no such thing." Renata's voice remained cool as she nodded to the guards and waved them out of the room. Before they left, one of them laid a miniature triton spear and a folded pile of clothes by the door. Once they were alone, Renata turned and began to pull off her flowing white garment. "I knew you would turn back, just like you always have. Here, turn around. Let me help you unlace that."

Instinctively, Arianna obeyed. "You knew about that?"

"I would never send you somewhere without keeping an eye on you, Ari. Now what koros did you end up with?"

"That's not really your concern." Arianna shifted uncomfortably.

"Arianna, look at me."

Arianna turned and looked at her aunt as bidden, but she could not smile.

"I never meant to kill you. I thought that perhaps a few days without your sheltering family or friends might do you some good . . . teach you to see life the way most merpeople do." She gave Arianna a half-smile and continued unfastening Arianna's camicett. "I still want you to be a part of the family after this contest is over. I even want you to marry Prince Michael! You just have to understand that life isn't as simple as you thought. Sometimes, rules must be bent." She glanced up. "You of all people should understand that."

Renata then turned and pulled two camicetts off a nearby peg, handing the smaller of the two to Arianna. Arianna turned it over in her hands. It was sealskin. At least her torso would be warm in the Deeps.

"I also know those who found you convinced you to do this." Renata paused after pulling her camicett on, and she laid a hand on Arianna's shoulder. "But you don't have to. Just let me go uncontested, and you can have all you ever wanted." She leaned forward and whispered, "Just like I promised."

"Can you, really?" Arianna asked. "Without hurting anyone?"

"Ari, you know I would never hurt you! Or anyone we love. I'm doing this for us, and our people. Why would I hurt them?"

For one short moment, Arianna believed her. Or desperately wanted to, at least. This was the woman who had raised her, after all. "So," she asked hopefully, "you won't be spreading the Sorthileige?"

Renata's smile froze on her face. "What?"

"You won't be infecting our family and people with the

Sorthileige?" Perhaps Arianna hadn't heard everything in that conch. Perhaps it had been taken out of context.

"Where did you hear that?"

"From the conch you recorded for General Orsini." Arianna's voice was suddenly very faint.

"I told you," Renata's voice was tight as she leaned in close to Arianna. "I am doing everything for the good of our people, and I am willing to make sacrifices your grandfather was not. When you're here for longer than five minutes, you'll realize just how much help our people need. Your people. The people that your prince's grandfather sent hundreds of ships after all over the world for five years. And only when you're willing to see the truth, only then will you be able to understand why I'm willing to go where I must to get that help."

"Even if you do win," Arianna tried to look taller, "I won't go along with it. I'll . . . I'll tell the others!"

"Go ahead. Who will believe you? If you've heard the contents of that conch, then the message is gone, and no one worthy of the court's consideration will be able to vouch for its song." She gave Arianna a fierce smile. "You've such a strong will, and I've always loved that about you. But as follows, you've always had to learn everything the hard way, too."

They didn't speak again until there was a knock at the door. *I'm completely at your mercy,* Arianna prayed to the Maker. *I don't know what I'm doing or why you have me here. Please make something about this situation make sense! And fast!*

Just as Renata reached the door, she turned to Arianna, a slightly softer expression on her face. "Before we go out, you should know. The reason our bloodline is the only one allowed to pursue the triton is because we are the only ones who can feel Sorthileige before it comes out of its vents in the Deeps. When you feel the heat, you need to move. Getting caught directly in one of those vents would kill an average mermaid of your size."

"What about you?" Arianna held her aunt's gaze.

Renata stared at her for a long minute. "Good luck, Arianna. I really do want you to survive."

~

By the time the Protectors escorted them to the stage, the arena was so full that merpeople were floating above its outer edges to watch. Not just the rich, either, like those who had been in the throne room, but merpeople of every class. This made locating her family difficult, but Arianna finally spotted her parents and her sister's family in the front row by the stage. Michael was nowhere to be seen, but perhaps that was for the better. The last thing Arianna needed was another distraction.

As soon as they appeared at the edge of the arena, a roar went up from the crowd, very different from the quiet, reserved group that had been seated in the domed throne room. Many chanted Renata's name, and wherever it was chanted, Renata would turn and graciously incline her head with a smile.

Arianna tried to smile, too, but it grew more difficult by the second as she realized many were glaring at her. And those who were brave enough made jeering sounds at her from the sides. So she decided that it was best to simply keep her eyes focused on the stage and to look at no one else until her mother was in plain sight.

Her mother's expression, however, was far from encouraging. Giana's face was pinched and pale, and her father's face was little better. Lalia looked terrified.

So much for their confidence, Arianna sighed to herself.

"Silence!" a large merman bellowed at the crowd. Still, the crowd was not quiet until he had sent a few more pointed glares in different directions. Only then did Arianna recognize her father's old bodyguard. "I am General Lorenzo, and today I will be Keeper of the Games." He thumped the bright blue sash where it lay across his broad chest.

"This contest," he continued, "has been handed down through generations as the Maker's way of choosing a new Sea Crown, lord over all merpersons in the northern, western, southern, and eastern seas, and even the seas beyond. The Sea Crown is responsible for wielding the triton." He held up the grand weapon for the crowd to see, and even Arianna had to gasp.

She'd never seen the weapon up close before. She vaguely recalled it being in the throne room, but she'd been too frightened to look anywhere but at the officials. Now, to see the source of power behind the legends that her mother and aunt had told her was surreal.

The triton's power had few limits in the sea, but, according to legend, its strength was so great that it took much exertion from the Sea Crown to control it, and thus could only be used in the direst of occasions. "To prevent the Sea Crown from using it for trifling matters," her mother had once explained, "such as making a finer bed to sleep in or more jewels for one's gown or sash."

And now Arianna was competing to hold that power.

A wave of dizziness washed through her as she realized the magnitude of the position she was trying to grasp. No matter how hard she imagined herself fighting, there was no scenario in which Arianna could see herself winning. And yet, if she did . . . she would be the most powerful merperson in all the seas.

I'm not ready.

"Both of these contestants have been verified as direct descendants of our last Sea Crown," General Lorenzo was saying as Arianna fought to stay conscious. "Their task is to penetrate the Deeps and find the triton, avoiding contact with the Sorthileige at all costs." General Lorenzo's voice grew stern. "As the Sea Crown is the only one with the power to touch the Deeps and escort others over them with his protection, the future Sea Crown must be able to make it through on his own." He turned and eyed Arianna and Renata with a furrowed brow. "If you make contact with the Sorthileige, you must return immediately and await the return of the new Sea Crown. Perhaps she will be able to save you if the triton comes to her quickly enough."

He turned back to the audience, which was now silent. "There are only four rules for this contest, and I will repeat them once more before we send our contestants off." He held up one finger. "First, you must venture into the Deeps." He held up another finger. "Second, you are not allowed to physically injure one another. Third, you must sing all four basic koroses before using your soul-song. And finally, you must avoid the Sorthileige at all costs." With that, he turned and swam off the stage.

Arianna was surprised to see her father coming up to take the general's place. He turned and looked at Renata and Arianna in turn, his gaze lingering on Arianna for a second longer than it had his sister. "May the Maker be with you both," he said in a dead voice. Then, taking the triton from General Lorenzo, he pulled it back above his shoulder. After a second's hesitation, he launched it into the distant dark abyss.

Arianna was so impressed by her father's strong arm that she was late in taking off after the triton. She pushed herself hard to make up for lost time, and in less than a minute had overtaken her aunt. As she passed Renata, however, Arianna couldn't help wondering how much her speed would really help. Her fins might have grown stronger, but she still had no soulsong, and from what she could guess, Renata had already been to the Deeps more than once.

If nothing else, I will at least make this difficult for her, Arianna promised herself. And with that, she burst headlong into the massive wall of gray water.

As soon as she was through, Arianna looked around, trying to get her bearings. It was only when she looked around, however, that she realized the murky water above and around was only a hint at the true Deeps. The real Deeps were down.

Below her was a gaping chasm cut into the seafloor with thick columns of black smoke rising up and sticking to the foam on the surface and giving the water above its shade of gray. Arms of rock stuck up out of the canyon like withered hands beckoning her to come, and a sweet, sickly smell filled the water. Her entire body tingled. There was no place in the world Arianna would rather be less.

As she floated above the canyon, waffling, Renata charged in behind her and was down in the chasm in a flash. Arianna's trepidation dissipated as she was reminded of her goal. Taking off after her aunt, Arianna fought to use her first koros. But what would it be?

Her question was answered as the water grew darker around her, and Arianna remembered that the Growing koros could be used to draw light from glow fish near the bottom of the sea. At first her voice was weak, and she had to slow down for fear of slamming into one of the huge rock columns. But as she continued to swim, and she could hear her aunt using her own song, Arianna's confidence grew, and with it, her song's strength. It didn't take long for the smaller fish around her, fish that would have otherwise remained hidden in the shadows, to begin lighting her way. And with the light, she could hear the nearly inaudible call of the triton.

As soon as she could see, Arianna turned and began moving further north toward the triton's sound. Just as she was beginning to feel comfortable in swimming, Renata's distant song changed, and a school of sardines encircled Arianna. Arianna's song was cut off as they pushed her up against one of the canyon walls.

To Arianna's vast relief, the fish were not the kind to have been touched by the Sorthileige so she was able to dart down and out of their school without any following her. Renata's trick had slowed her down, however, and she knew she needed to find a distraction for her aunt as well if she stood any chance at even seeing the triton.

Still using her song to provide light, Arianna tried to recall what Mae had said about focusing on the sea's elements around her and finding a song to fit them.

There. She could barely make out Renata's form approaching a kelp bed. Moving her song into a slightly softer call, Arianna used her second koros. Her Nurturing koros moved the kelp just enough to entangle her aunt as she tried to dart through them, and Arianna was just fast enough to pass her up and continue after the triton herself.

Feeling a bit buoyed by her success, Arianna tried to focus on her third koros. But as she began to use her Growing koros to slow Renata down again, it was cut short when a hollow call to her left startled her. Too late it dawned on Arianna that Renata was using call and echo to locate the triton, rather than her eyes.

Arianna felt dafter than ever. She relied too much on her human senses. Arianna paused just long enough to remember her own call and echo song, one of the Protection koroses she had learned, but too late did she realize Renata had already changed course. Arianna got a face full of squid ink just in time to realize she had fallen for her aunt's trap.

Her eyes, nose, and throat burned, and what little she had been able to see of the sun overhead disappeared as she tumbled around, crashing into rocks and coral. It wasn't until she hit the sandy bottom of the seafloor that Arianna had gotten enough of the ink from her eyes that she could see again. *Focus!* she could hear Mae shouting in her head. So Arianna shook her head and began to swim again, using her echolocation song one more time. She still had one koros to use, but she could feel the triton's power drawing closer. If only there were a way to—

The baby coral heads that were just peeking out from the sand below Arianna shot up all around her, and before Arianna could escape, she was trapped in a prison of coral. She wanted to scream as she saw the tip of Renata's tail slip into the darkness. Renata only had her Healing koros left to use before using her soulsong to finish the contest.

Arianna pushed and punched the coral bars around her, but it was of no use. The walls were too strong. Only when she stopped fighting and allowed herself to fall back into the sand, however, did she feel the rhythmic pulse of power she'd been chasing.

The triton was near. Their echolocation songs had been sending them too far! The canyons must have been playing tricks with their songs. Sure enough, with some help from nearby glow fish, Arianna spotted the barest hint of blue gold sticking out from the sand.

As her Healing koros was her only remaining required koros, Arianna decided to squeeze herself between the bars and then heal herself of whatever damage the escape caused, after taking the triton. She was nearly breathless as she imagined herself maybe actually winning. Renata was still elsewhere. Could she do this, even without a soulsong?

Pain wrenched her arm as she twisted it to pull it through the bars. Just as she was close to freeing herself, however, Arianna was overwhelmed by a warm, sickly, tingling sensation behind her. She shot back into the cage, yanking her tail out of the way as a column of black smoke and bubbles shot up from a vent behind her. Arianna curled up at the far edge of her prison as the burning mixture of sulfur and black bubbles moved through the coral bars that met at the top of her cage above her.

A large white shark happened to swim above her just then. She tried to cry out and warn it, but her cry was too late. The shark was enveloped by the dark mixture as she watched. The creature writhed and wriggled as the boiling water surrounded it. When the vent finally stopped producing its poisonous gas, however, the shark was white no more.

Its gills were enlarged, and its back was lined with spikes. Eyes that had been nearly invisible because of their gray were now black. And the hideous creature was looking right at Arianna.

Without thinking about what she was doing, Arianna found herself singing her final koros to the shark. And though the Healing koros had been slightly easier for her during practice than the other koroses, the shark showed no sign of improvement. It was as though she hadn't sung at all.

The shark rammed Arianna's coral cage so hard that it broke. Arianna threw herself in the direction of the triton, just barely grasping it in time to point it right at the shark. The triton was heavier than she had expected, but the thrill of holding it boosted her confidence enough not to falter.

Thank you! she cried out to the Maker as she and the shark stared one another down. But when she tried to access the power of the triton, nothing happened. Frowning, Arianna pointed it at the shark again. She could hear Renata's song approaching.

Let it work! she begged the Maker. *I've come so far! Just please let it work!*

The shark charged, but before it could reach Arianna, another vent between them burst forth another column of boiling gas. The shark did not make it through the vent, but Arianna knew the moment the vent stopped, she would be attacked.

She needed to focus! She was a child of the Sea. She needed to let her true form rule, for that was where she would find her strength. Closing her eyes, Arianna pictured herself as a part of the merpeople. She could see each layer of the ocean and its life and its beauty. From each grain of sand below to each golden grain under the warm sun—

Just as the triton was beginning to heat up a bit beneath her hands, the image of the sun flashed in her mind, and with it, the face of a young man. The song she had begun to sing was cut short. The triton flew out of her hands, its end catching on the current of another column of smoke and bubbles that burst up beside her. Up into the water above her it swirled, where Renata floated directly in the middle of the column of smoke. And as the blackness billowed around her, Renata smiled and retrieved the triton with what could only have been her soulsong.

Haunting and beckoning, it was Arianna's lullaby.

43

A FEAST OF DEFEAT

*T*he older princess . . . Princess Renata, Michael had been told, although for some reason, he was sure her name had been different at some point . . . stood at the head of the table and looked down at everyone around her. The other guests at the long table grew quiet and regarded her expectantly, as did those floating lazily about the large hall.

Michael gawked. But really, what living male wouldn't? She was a vision with her dark hair pulled up and pinned with jewels into large swoops all over her head. Her large brown eyes were full of compassion for those around her, and as she turned her head from side to side to look at the many occupants of her table, her long neck arched gracefully. She was wearing the flowing white gown again. Michael was surprised that she could wear such a long gown without getting her fins caught in the bottom, but that only added to her mystique. He was also sure she had looked a bit different at one time, but that didn't matter. She was only more beautiful now. She was also saying something, but it was a moment before Michael could tear his eyes away from her figure long enough to focus on her words.

" . . . as we usher in a new era for merpeople everywhere. For I am humbled and honored to find myself at the head of this table before you all now. My grandfather carried the weight of the most tumultuous reign yet known to our people. As I have promised you before, it will be my utmost goal to foster an atmosphere of mutual respect between humanity and merpeople, and at the same time ensure the safety of our people from all that might injure them, from our most respected elders to our youngest and most vulnerable." She paused to smile at the baby a woman held a few seats down.

Whom could such a little thing need protecting from? Michael wondered.

"That is why I have invited Prince Michelangelo Solefige to not only witness but partake in our ancient rites of passage while handing the triton to the newest Sea Crown." She turned and nodded at him, a cool smile on her flawless face.

Michael beamed back. A few at the table turned and glared at him, but Michael didn't care. Not when the most beautiful creature in the world was looking at him.

"I know what some of you are thinking, and I will remind you that Prince Michelangelo was not king during the major part of the war. His grandfather was. In fact, Prince Michelangelo was the one my father contacted to negotiate a truce while our people were returning to Gemmaqua."

With that, Princess Renata turned and beckoned to someone behind her. Out of the shadows swam the other princess that Michael had seen earlier. She wore white as well. This time, however, she kept her face lowered as Princess Renata gently pulled her to her side.

"For those of you who have not met my niece, this is Princess Arianna Fiore del Mare Atlantician, daughter of my brother, Amadeo. She is like a daughter to me as well, however. I raised her due to her sensitivities after a difficult birth, and if anyone treats her with a sentiment that is less than respectful or kind, you will have me to answer to. Yes, we were competitors for the crown, but all competitors are relatives, and in truth, they are family before they are opponents." She stared down each member at the table, with the exception of the girl's parents, Michael's former neighbors by the stage earlier that day. Then she looked down at the girl and gave her a kind smile. "I expect great things from Arianna, and I couldn't be prouder."

Princess Arianna did not smile back. Instead, she kept her eyes on the ground, only moving when Princess Renata told her she could go to her seat. The girl silently swam to the empty seat on Michael's right, much to his delight.

Princess Renata continued to speak, but Michael couldn't listen for he was suddenly too intrigued by his new table partner.

Michael was not an expert on general mermaid features, or at least, he couldn't remember being one. But compared to the pale, dark-haired beauties surrounding them, this young mermaid seemed noticeably tanner, as though she'd actually seen the sun once or twice in her life. Her hair, drawn into a graceful knot at the top of her head, shone like gold. Her eyes though . . . if only she would raise her eyes to his! He didn't know what he would find in them, but something inside whispered that they would be wonderful.

A holy man—or holy merman, rather—said a prayer, and it wasn't long before the chatter around them had grown merry and loud once again, punctuated with quick little songs and melodies that seemed to emanate from the merpeople constantly. The little mermaid beside him remained quiet, however, only speaking when someone asked her a direct question.

And though Michael was fairly sure he was in love with Princess Renata, there was something about this mermaid that beckoned to him. The way she tucked a stray curl behind her ears constantly poked at his mind like a splinter that wouldn't be plucked.

She's going to look at me, Michael decided as a servant placed the first course in front of him. *She's going to look at me and talk to me, and I'm going to figure out why she seems so familiar.*

Michael was going to charm her.

It shouldn't be too incredibly difficult. He tried to recall what usually impressed women. As he did, however, a goblet of yellow and brown kelp bulbs was placed in front of him. He picked one up and stared at it. Did they expect him to actually eat the bulbs? They were plump and hard. Still, it would do him no good to have the pretty girl beside him thinking he was a coward because he wouldn't try new foods. With a shrug, he popped the bulb in his mouth and bit down.

As soon as his teeth hit the bulb, it burst, and his tongue was hit by the oddest combination of salt and wine. Slowly, he began to chew the bulb, and was preparing to swallow when he heard a voice like the tinkling of small bells ordering him to stop.

He looked at the blonde mermaid in surprise. She was looking straight at him, as he'd hoped, but her expression was one of alarm rather than delight.

"You don't swallow the bulb!"

Michael froze, the bulb's remains still in his mouth. When he looked down for a napkin, however, there was none to be found.

The mermaid rolled her eyes and handed him a bowl of sand that had been placed behind the goblet of bulbs. When he stared at it blankly, she huffed and held out her hand.

"Give it to me."

Michael was more than a little surprised that the princess would be willing to touch something as personal as his food, but he couldn't deny that it made him feel a little triumphant as well. If she was this familiar with him already, how much longer could it take to charm her completely? He spit it out into his palm and handed her the chewed mess with a little bit of embarrassment, and she promptly pressed the bulb's remains into the sand.

Oh. That's what that's for.

"I must admit," he said, "I'm a little confused as to the point of this food."

She shook her head. "It's not food. Each bulb is filled with wine. You put it in your mouth and break the skin, releasing the wine. Then you spit out the skin and put it in the bowl."

"How do you get wine down at the bottom of the ocean?"

"We don't. It's made by humans. We used to supply them with the kelp, and they would puncture the bulbs with tiny holes, just large enough to fill them with wine. These are a delicacy now that the merpeople and humans aren't trading anymore." She lifted one of her own bulbs and examined it, but didn't put it in her mouth.

Her flow of words had encouraged Michael, but he could see that she was quickly slipping back into her quiet cocoon. Just as he was about to ask her another question, a young woman carrying a baby approached her and tapped her on the shoulder. This young woman had dark hair like everyone else around them, but there was something in her nose and chin that resembled Princess Arianna's. Unlike Princess Arianna, however, she wore a ring on her left hand, and though he didn't want to stare, Michael was rather sure that she was also with child. Princess Arianna turned, and as soon as she saw the young woman, she gasped. The two embraced and held one another tightly.

Michael watched, slightly annoyed at the interruption. Their voices were low, but he could hear a few words slip out, such as *sister, a long time,* and *never coming back.* Finally, Princess Arianna pulled back and cooed over the baby. That was when Michael was reminded of another trait he was rather sure impressed women.

"And who is this?" Michael peeked around the princess to look at the baby.

Princess Arianna sighed. "Lalia, this is Prince Michael. Michael, this is my sister, Princess Lalia, and her son, Johnathon."

"Michelangelo," Michael corrected her as he stood and bowed to the woman. That was what the beautiful Princess Renata had called him.

Princess Arianna gave him a funny look before shaking her head and turning back to her sister.

But Michael wasn't about to be cast off that easily. Stretching his hands out toward the woman, Michael asked, "May I see him?"

Princess Lalia gave her sister a nervous look but Princess Arianna just shrugged and nodded. That was an odd reaction, but Michael would have to think about it later. He took the boy and placed the little fellow snugly on his leg. Even with the tail, holding the baby felt as natural as walking.

"You're good with children." Princess Lalia looked surprised as he began patting the baby on the back and gently bouncing him on his knee. "Do you have any?"

Michael looked at Princess Arianna in confusion. "I don't think so." In fact, he was quite sure he didn't. But then, he wondered, how *did* he know what to do with the baby?

Very soon, Princess Lalia took her child back, and to Michael's delight, her farewell seemed actually somewhat genuine. As soon as she was gone, Michael decided to take full advantage of Princess Arianna's attention. Her blue eyes were just as intriguing as he'd imagined, and he was determined to understand the mystery behind them . . . and how she seemed to know so much about him.

"Come dance with me," he blurted, standing.

She stopped toying with the fish on her plate and looked up at him in surprise. A few of those nearby looked at him in surprise and amusement as well, although her father—he was fairly sure it was her father—was quickly turning a new shade of red. He did his best to ignore this, however, and held his hand out.

"Do you know how to dance?" she finally asked.

He was about to answer that of course he did, when she pointedly looked out at the large expanse of hall behind him. Dozens of couples were dancing, but not on the ground. Rather, they were spinning, twisting, and twirling in every direction as they moved over, under, and around one another in time to the choir's singing, and all of it took place ten feet off the ground.

"Perhaps not like that," he admitted, "but I can learn."

"Oh really." She leaned back, hand thoughtfully tucked beneath her ear, and looked at his legs. "And just why are you so determined to dance?"

"Tell me, how well do mermen see?"

She frowned. "Our eyesight is twice as good as that of humans. We see very—"

"No, I mean mer*men* specifically."

Her mouth opened for a moment before shutting again. "They see just as well as I do. Why?"

"No one else has asked you to dance," he said, holding her gaze, "and I have come to the conclusion that for this reason, mermen must be a rather blind breed."

For the first time that evening, her stare wasn't one of annoyance or condescension. For the first time, she really looked at him.

After a moment, however, she recovered herself and looked back down at her food. "You are making a fool of yourself to proclaim such a thing," she said in a low voice.

"No, I am making a fool of everyone else for not noticing."

Again, she gave him that look. And just like it had that morning, something in her eyes made him feel as though he were missing something terribly, terribly important. Her jaw trembled then clenched a bit.

This bothered Michael. If they hadn't been underwater, he would have given anything to wipe away her tears.

"If you're not up to a dance," he said as he extended his hand, "perhaps you would like to get some fresh . . . water? I'm not supposing we can get any air down here."

This time, she nearly smiled. As she started to get up from her seat, however, she cast a long look at Princess Renata at the end of the table. Princess Renata smiled and nodded once. Michael's heart jumped as he offered the young princess his arm. He was about to solve the mystery of the fair-haired mermaid.

~

Michael had been so entranced with Princess Renata and then Princess Arianna that he'd never stopped to examine the dining hall itself. From what he could see as they moved arm-in-arm to the edge of the room, the dining hall seemed to wrap around the entire base of the palace. Rather than being wide, the room was ridiculously long and tall. Of course, that made more sense when he saw the dancing merpeople spinning and twisting above the long table. Really, they were in less of a hall and what looked more like a greenhouse. Instead of glass walls and a glass ceiling, however, straight green coral bars were crisscrossed to let in light, though the light was now fast disappearing. Beneath his feet, hundreds of varieties of underwater flora lined the floor, and he briefly mourned stepping on such pretty plants.

The garden outside was no better, for as soon as he stepped out the door, the pathways were only more winding rows of plants, rather than actual stones or sand. Michael paused on the threshold. Princess Arianna turned when he didn't follow, their linked arms holding her back.

Her look of mild annoyance changed, however, when she followed his gaze to his feet. "You can walk on them. They're sturdier than they look, and you weigh less down here."

Gingerly, Michael set one foot down, then the other. If he hadn't known he was treading upon such beauty, he would have rather enjoyed the walk. It was like walking on pillows. If it could be called walking. Walking underwater was more like constantly fighting to fall in the wrong direction. Meanwhile, Arianna was floating as gracefully as a cloud through the sky.

One by one, servants floated out with lanterns and began to hang them along the winding rows of plants.

"That isn't—" Michael began, but Princess Arianna was already shaking her head.

"There's a kind of algae that grows well in our waters. We grow it directly in the lanterns." Before he could respond, however, she stopped swimming. They had come to stand behind a mound of zigzagging coral that stood just taller than Michael's head. "Tell me," she said, her azure eyes suddenly searching his eyes with a burning intensity. "What do you remember?"

Michael blinked back at her. "Of what?"

"Of anything. Where you came from. How old you are. What your name is. Anything . . ." She gripped his arms in her hands.

Michael opened his mouth to answer such inane questions, but found that he didn't have the words. Frowning, he thought before trying again. *Drat.* This was going to put a damper on his festivities. And here he'd been having such a fine evening of wooing lovely ladies and drinking wine bulbs. After much thought, he took a deep breath.

"My name is Michelangelo Solefige."

"What is your middle name?"

Again, he was caught without an answer. "Lucas?" he finally guessed.

She gave him a sad smile and shook her head, dropping her hands to her sides. Her next words were a whisper. "Do you remember me?"

Any merriment Michael had felt earlier fled him at the sound of utter loneliness in her voice. And beneath the false merriment, he found a great well of anger, though what he was angry at, he couldn't tell. "I feel as though I should," he finally said. At this, she suddenly looked so sad that Michael hastened to add, "There is something about you that makes me feel forgetful. It's like finding a dirty window and suddenly realizing you were in the dark to begin with." He caught her chin as she lowered her eyes again, and he brought her face back up to his. "Have I hurt you?" he breathed.

Her jaw clenched as she nodded then turned away.

"Then why are you here with me now?" He hurried to catch up to her. "Whatever it was, I'm sorry!" She frowned but continued swimming, so he reached out and grabbed her wrist. "Please," he said, holding it tightly. "Just tell me."

A resolute expression came over her face, and she lifted the hand that he still held. "I'm going to try something. Hold very still." And she began to sing.

It was a quiet song, but with each note, Michael could feel a hole beginning to break through the fog that filled his mind.

Arianna.

Arianna was thrown overboard, and Princess Renata did it. Michael clamped his free hand over his mouth and pulled it helplessly down his chin as he recalled the kiss. He had kissed Princess Renata. After leaving his mother, his brother, and his people, he had kissed her in front of Arianna.

"Arianna, I . . ." he stepped back, shaking his head. "I'm so . . . Wait. You have a voice! A real voice! Not just whispers?" Joy battled with horror as he stepped toward her again. "When did you get your voice?"

"So you noticed."

Michael wanted to say more, but he choked down all the inane things that wanted to bubble up. *What a fool I've been. An utterly despicable fool.* "How long?" he swallowed, "have I been like this?"

Arianna sighed. "My aunt has had you under her siren song since we were on the boat. Not that it matters."

"Whoa, now." He grabbed her hand again as she began to turn away. "Something else is wrong. I can tell. What else is it? I swear, I never would have kissed her in my right mind!" *I never wanted to hurt you.*

"It doesn't matter!"

Michael took a step back. In all his time with Arianna, he had never imagined her shouting. "But it does," he said softly.

"Very well. You really want to know?"

He nodded.

"You chose *her!*" She pointed back at the dining hall. "The kiss doesn't matter. What matters is that you chose her!" Her voice broke, and her shoulders began to shake. And though there were no tears to fall, heartbreak was written all over her face.

"I don't know what to say." He shrugged helplessly. "I . . . I am so sorry." Watching her cry was like slowly dying inside.

For a long time, neither of them spoke. He could only stand there like the horrible fool he was as she quietly wept. Voices and songs floated in on the waters from all around. Thankfully, the garden seemed to have been left alone to them, so there wasn't anyone else to witness Michael's mortification, although that did little to assuage the growing fury Michael felt for himself in the pit of his stomach.

"How long will this clarity of thought last?" he finally asked, his voice sounding not at all like it belonged to him.

Arianna sniffed. "Until she sings to you again. All I did was a simple healing song, like a break in the clouds. For you to be completely free of her, either she'll have to release you, you'll have to leave the sea forever, or the triton's wielder will have to let you go." She closed her eyes and lifted her face toward the ocean's surface. "Which will also be Renata."

"So . . . where do we go from here?"

"I don't know." She lifted her hands helplessly. "We can't leave. Renata would find us and put you back under her spell." She paused. "Unless . . ."

"Unless what?"

"Unless my niece agrees to marry you."

Michael turned to see Princess Renata floating behind him, triton in hand. It may have simply been the shadows from the algae lanterns, but there seemed to be more lines around her eyes and mouth than he recalled. They weren't displeasing, but she suddenly seemed to be more than just a few years older than Arianna, which was what he had believed when she showed up at his door as Princess Ines.

"Unless you have changed your mind?" She looked at Arianna.

Michael stared at each woman in turn. What an odd proposition. Though he was loathe to admit it, hadn't Princess Ines, or rather Princess Renata, planned to marry him just recently?

"Have you changed your mind, Arianna?" Princess Renata asked again.

Arianna stared at the ground, her shoulders slumped forward.

"Either way," Princess Renata said in a gentle voice, "the plan must commence. I would much rather it include you and your happiness."

At this, Arianna's head shot up, her eyes wide. "No, Aunt. He doesn't have to be a part of this!" She spoke so fast her words jumbled together. "We can find another way—"

Princess Renata raised the triton and aimed it at Michael. A yellow burst lit the triton for one second before moving into his legs and up to his waist.

Michael fell back with a shout of agony. Excruciating pain greater than any he had known before bit at his flesh and bones.

"You have three days to change Arianna's mind," she said to him, nudging him with the edge of her triton and sending another jolt through his body. "In three days, the spell will be complete, and you will be a merman. That is not negotiable. What is negotiable, however, is her." She pointed the triton at Arianna. "If you cannot get her to agree to marry you by the third day, I will marry you, and your forgetfulness will not be temporary. I will sing to you every morning and every night, and you and your kingdom will forever be in my grasp. Now," Princess Renata turned and began to swim back toward the dining hall, "you know your motivation to convince her."

Michael couldn't respond. The pain was too great. His vision began filling with spots as he fell over on his side. Arianna called his name over and over again, but there was no way for him to call back.

He barely managed to pry his eyes open to look down at his legs. He could see no difference through his trousers, but the pure power jarring his body was proof enough that he was beginning to change.

In the distance, Michael heard a song. Then two or three joined in. But the pain was too much even for that. Soon, he couldn't hear a thing.

44

FORMIDABLE TIDES

*M*ichael burned all night, despite the cool water around him. He hadn't felt so feverish since he'd contracted the ague as a child. But as he'd discovered earlier that night, writhing and turning as he wished to do only pained his lower half more. The sponge bed, which had been so comfortable at one time, now only hurt his legs worse. Lying perfectly still and gritting his teeth seemed the only way to withstand the pain without passing out. *Still, at least I know who I am this time,* he tried to comfort himself.

The door behind him opened, and Renata leaned over him to place a new shell around his neck and take the old one off. This only intensified the pain as it sharpened all of his senses.

Renata sat on the vanity's little stool. For a long time, she simply studied him, fingering the shell she had taken from his neck.

"I chose you for Arianna a long time ago because I knew you could make her happy," she finally said. "I love my niece—"

"Enough to push her overboard into monster-infested waters?" Michael growled through clenched teeth.

"I knew she wouldn't die." Renata shrugged. "I've known her long enough to know that. I just didn't think it would take her so long to show up at the palace. Back to what I was saying, however. I love my niece. I raised her, after all. But Arianna is strong willed, something I'm probably to blame for. I'll admit that she was rather indulged as a child. Being denied a voice will bring that sort of sympathy."

"Your point?"

Renata leaned forward on her elbows. "My niece does not know how to be happy without help."

"And you want me to convince her that your happiness is right for her."

"Convince her to marry you and to stop fighting me. Do this, and I will do two things. One, I will only use you as necessary. Two, I will not infect Arianna with the Sorthileige."

"You would do that to your own niece?"

"I will do it to all my family! To protect them from monsters like your grandfather!"

"But my grandfather is dead," Michael said. "You no longer need to worry—"

"Your grandfather turned the whole world against my people! He wasn't satisfied to merely hunt them down in your waters. No, he sent hundreds of ships around the world to find them in every sea known to man."

"But I'm not my grandfather!"

"Which is why you're not dead yet." She slammed the shell down on the vanity so hard that the shell broke. "But I will not allow my people to continue on as unprotected as they were. Soon they will all be stronger, and I will have my own bloodline wearing the Sun Crown, whether that's through Arianna's children or mine."

Michael's blood ran cold. "I will give you no children. I swear to you, woman—"

"You will have just as much opposition to it as you would have had last night."

Michael wanted to object, but he couldn't. Before Arianna's

song, if Renata had asked anything of him, he would have given it joyfully.

Michael swallowed. "Why do you think she'll listen to me? Arianna does as she pleases."

This time, Renata closed her eyes, and her voice was quiet. "Arianna has never looked at anyone the way she looks at you." She opened her eyes. "You *hear* her."

Michael laughed without humor. "Perhaps on certain occasions. But I certainly didn't hear her when I needed to." He glared at Renata. "You should try listening to her yourself."

"For Arianna's sake and the sake of my people, I don't have that luxury. But you do." She got up and swam toward the door, stopping when she was beside him. "I'm sending you and Arianna out on a tour of the city this morning. Arianna needs to see the beauty of her own people now that she can stand to live this deep. More than that, however, she needs to see why your union is so important," her eyes darkened a shade, "to both of you."

"While I would love nothing more," Michael said breathlessly as he tried to turn toward her on his bed, "I'm afraid my current condition makes me a less-than-fit riding partner."

Renata began to hum, and immediately, Michael's pain lessened. He let out a gusty breath as the stabbing subsided.

"I cannot erase it entirely. Your transformation must be yours to bear. But this will keep you until the ride is over." With that, she clapped. The door was opened, and Arianna was escorted in by a stern guard wearing a blue sash across his chest.

Despite their current troubles, Michael couldn't help noticing the graceful shape of Arianna's mermaid figure. She had on another shiny fitted shirt, similar to the one she'd been wearing when he'd found her on the beach, though this one was blue. Unlike the other one, however, this shirt had a slight skirt attached so that it looked more like a short dress. Michael wondered if all of her clothes were like that, now that everyone knew Arianna could change forms.

Though she looked at the ground again, as seemed to be her habit, her shoulders were held resolutely. Regrettably, her hair was still in that knot on top of her head. As she was escorted in, Michael found himself longing to hear her voice again, as smooth as crystal and as clear as a flute. It sounded exactly as he had imagined it might. Only more beautiful.

As Renata explained her plans for their morning to Arianna, Arianna's face remained impassive. It was a look Michael regretted knowing well.

Once Renata released them for their excursion, Arianna took his offered arm, but her fingers were stiff, and she stared straight ahead until they were seated in a sleigh behind two dolphins and a sleigh driver.

Michael tried to take stock of his situation as the sleigh began to move. *If Arianna does not marry me, I will marry Renata and father her children, carrying out her every whim until the day I die. Arianna will be touched by the Sorthileige, and Renata will use her as well. If I can convince Arianna to do Renata's bidding and marry me . . .* Michael paused. That would, of course, be his preferred option. And yet . . . *she'll be unhappy.*

Torn, Michael gripped the sleigh seat and prayed for the answer to an impossible situation.

~

Despite the lengthy tour their ride proved to be as they wound through streets and over public centers such as play areas for the children or large city gardens, there were fewer chances for them to talk than he'd hoped. Their driver also turned out to be their guide. Each monument and street was given the same level of enthusiasm as a three-day-old cake might receive.

Arianna sat the same way she had from the start. Her posture was everything a princess should have, head erect, shoulders back, hands folded nicely in her lap. Only her eyes moved.

The capital city was wide, stretching between two sets of underwater mountains. In spite of Michael's worries, he couldn't find a single attribute of the city that wasn't interesting. As with the palace, all the buildings were made of coral. Most of the coral was a pink orange, but a few buildings used other types as well. The structures were typically domed, and the larger houses looked much like a set of four or five colored bubbles mashed together. Though there were streets here, they weren't smooth or even laid down flat. Rather, the streets seemed more like guides for the lines of merpeople and their animals—dolphins and turtles and the like —that floated above them.

The city filled the underwater valley, going all the way up to the Sea Palace, which sat at the highest point, looking over the rest of the buildings as they dipped down into a bowl shape below. There were thousands of homes, and in between clumps of dwellings sat circles of what looked like markets and public places.

Michael's attention was soon drawn in particular to a group of children sitting in a circle on a bed of sea grass. A man sat in the circle with them, and was singing out a few notes at a time. The children echoed his notes. As the sleigh moved slowly by, each round of music changed by one note.

"What songs are they singing?" Michael asked.

The guide gave him a pained look over his shoulder. "They are called koroses."

Michael looked at Arianna, and for the first time, she sighed and looked back at him. "The merpeople have four koroses. Growing, Nurturing, Healing, and Protection. All children are taught the basic four koroses."

"Like the one you used on me?"

"Monument to the First Sea Crown," their guide called back in a dull voice, waving his hand vaguely at a statue twice as tall as Michael.

Arianna didn't even pretend to acknowledge the guide, and instead nodded. "When the children reach adolescence, however, they find that their voice has particular strength in one of the koroses. For example, my father is a Protector. My mother and sister are Healers."

Michael studied her face. "What is yours?"

She waited a long time to answer. So long, in fact, that Michael wondered if she might not answer him at all.

"I don't have one." The impassivity was gone from her face now as she bit her lip. "I can sing all the basic koroses, but I don't have a soulsong." Her voice dipped lower. "I think that's the reason Renata beat me so easily in the contest for the triton."

"So . . . what do merpeople do with their koroses once they have them?"

Arianna pointed to a group of merpeople hovering over and around a dwelling dome that looked half-constructed. "Those builders are made up of Growers and Nurturers. The Growers sing songs to coax the coral to begin growing. The Nurturers sing to make it flourish. By using techniques they've developed and learned over the years, they can make the coral grow in different directions. To make a home, for instance."

"What kind of work do the Healers do?"

"The Sixth Sea Monument," their guide droned from the front of the sleigh, gesturing slightly with his hand to the large pile of stones they were passing.

"They do the obvious, such as healing injuries that merpeople might suffer. Sometimes they heal coral buildings that have been damaged in some way. Many occupations can use more than one type of koros. Of course, only Protectors guard our borders for creatures that escape the Deeps. Or they watch for pirates. But most of the other koroses can be applied to many different callings."

"How do you know so much if you lived away from the city most of your life?"

A weariness crossed her face. "You learn much when all you can do is listen."

They stopped at the edge of what looked like the largest market in the city. Michael could only estimate that there were over a hundred shops in the circular clearing. Their driver left the sleigh to make a purchase. Wishing to see her truly smile again, Michael leaned over and whispered, "Is there a koros for putting people to sleep?"

Arianna followed his gaze to their guide, and the shadow of a smile breezed over her face. "He is also a Protector."

"Then why is he working inside the palace?"

"He protects the interests of my aunt." Arianna's smile hardened.

Michael turned and studied the slim merman once more as their guide settled back into the sleigh. His graying hair was pulled back into a tight tail at the back of his head. Though he'd been the most loutish guide Michael had ever heard, there had been nothing alarming about him at first. But now Michael could see why Arianna was being so selective with her words. Several shells hung from the man's waist, and Michael suddenly wondered if he was using the shells to trap their words the way Renata had trapped her song in the shell he'd stolen.

His pondering was interrupted when a little mermaid who looked to be near Lucy's age swam right into Michael. Her mother grabbed her and pulled her away, scolding her severely.

"Why is everyone swimming so low?" Michael asked as he looked around and realized just how very crowded the water around them was growing.

"The pirates are getting bolder." The guide cracked the dolphin's reins.

"They're attacking Gemmaqua?" Arianna leaned forward.

The guide gave a stiff shrug. "Just before he died, the late Sea Crown cancelled all upper-level activities. After four abductions, it was all anyone could think to do." Then, as he stopped the sleigh again, he called back in a monotone, "The new Sea Crown says you may wander the market for a bit. But stay where I can find you." He fixed his eyes on Arianna. "It wouldn't do to have the new Sea Crown's niece being lost on her first day now, would it?"

"Of course not." Arianna met his cold smile with one of her own before turning and leading Michael away.

Michael tried to keep up, but he was quickly learning that walking underwater was much slower than it had ever been on land, particularly as his legs were unusually stiff. It also irked him that Arianna had to wait for him like she often stopped for Lucy. But perhaps he could use their slow progress to his advantage.

"Your aunt told me something today before you arrived," he said as he reached for her arm, leaning on her as though he needed her assistance to walk, their faces suddenly just inches apart.

"And what would that be?" She didn't push him away, but she didn't lean very far forward either.

"If you don't marry me, she plans to use the Sorthileige on you."

Arianna stopped and her blue eyes widened infinitesimally. "She wouldn't dare." She straightened her shoulders and scowled. "She should know better than to try that."

Michael stopped behind a stall where they were at least a little hidden and pulled her back with him. "Arianna, she wants you," he said in a low voice. "I don't know what it is that she wants, but she wants you just as much as she wants me, if not more."

"How do you know that?"

"I haven't spent my life around politicians to learn nothing."

Arianna glowered at him, but said nothing. Finally, she folded her arms and glared at the ground. "What does it matter to you?"

"Arianna, I . . . How can you say that?"

At this, her face flamed and her eyes burned. But just as she opened her mouth to speak, her eyes were drawn to something above him.

Michael turned and followed her gaze up to see a large shadow floating on the distant surface. It was impossible to be sure, but he was fairly certain he was seeing colors correctly, at least. "Is that ship's underside white with a red stripe up the middle?" he asked, squinting.

"Yes. Why?"

"Lucas." He shook his head. Leave it to his foolish baby brother to try and get himself killed as well. When Michael turned to Arianna, however, her face was suddenly glowing.

"That's Lucas's ship?" Her voice went up.

"That's our flagship." He sighed. "I was afraid he would follow."

At this, Arianna began to turn away from him, but Michael grabbed her arm and pulled her back. "Where do you think you're going?"

She looked at him as though he were daft. "I'm going to speak with Lucas. She hasn't gotten to him yet."

"Hold on. If we've just now seen the ship from the most populated part of the city, don't you think Renata and her . . . Protectors saw it the moment it approached? I'll bet that they're already on the ship with their charms, telling him their version of the story."

"You're the one always saying the Maker has a purpose." She huffed. "And I believe that there is a purpose in my seeing the ship!"

Michael frowned at her. "The Maker's purposes don't give you an excuse to be a fool."

"It's a sunny day. They'd never venture up in the direct sun. I'm safe until twilight at least. Besides," she glared at his hand holding her arm. "I'm good at being invisible. I've been so all my life." With that, she tried to swim away again, but he held on.

"This time, however, you have people who will pay the price if you're not."

"Just let me go, Michael!"

Until that moment, Michael hadn't realized just how much his heart could hurt. "You're right." He let go of her arm and took a step back. "Just . . ." he struggled for words, feeling like a fool. "Just please take care."

"Goodbye, Michael." She didn't meet his eyes as she turned. "I'll see you at the palace."

45

STRIKING THE DEAL

*A*rianna tried to steady her heart as she swam away from the city and into a small forest of kelp. After glancing behind to make sure no one was following her, she swam up to the surface, using the kelp as a cover. Still, when she got to the surface and peeked out from the water, she was disappointed to see how far she would have to swim out in the open above the city to get to the ship, at least four or five fathoms.

Lucas *would* put the ship above the most visible part of the city.

"It wasn't a lie." Renata's smooth voice floated on the breeze. "I told you that he was going to marry one of the royal daughters. And he is. I never said which one."

Arianna instinctively ducked back down into the water, leaving only her ears and eyes exposed.

Drat. Michael had been right. Arianna could just see Renata's head over the ship's railing. There were several Protectors with her, men and women all wearing large charms. But how were they able to stay out in the direct sun, even with the charms?

Unable to stave off her curiosity, Arianna dipped her head back under the water and darted over to the ship's hull. *If you really do care like Michael says,* she prayed, *please don't let them see me.*

As soon as she reached the hull, she pressed herself against it and waited breathlessly for some song of alarm from Renata's Protectors. As she waited, though, she sent up another prayer, this one of thanks. Renata had at least had the decency to order camicetts for her that would work as short dresses if she changed form unexpectedly.

When there was no song of alarm from Renata's Protectors after a few minutes, Arianna peeked out slowly until she could glimpse her aunt. Upon seeing her, Arianna nearly gasped aloud. In Michael's chamber that morning, Renata's eyes had been underlined by dark circles. It hadn't looked like anything serious, just a lack of adequate sleep. But where there had been circles there were now visible veins spidering out from her eyes. The veins were black.

Arianna threw herself back against the hull. So that's how they were doing it. If she was honest with herself, it frightened her. She'd always known the Sorthileige was strong. But never had she seen anyone wield it so well. *What deals have you made to hold such a power that's not yours?* Arianna thought to her aunt. *You have the triton. Why can't that be enough?*

"I still want to see him for myself." Lucas did not sound happy.

"And you will. But we have used much of our power to prepare him for life below the surface prior to the wedding. Bringing him back up now would be too hard on his body. He needs to resurface gently. It's for his health, I assure you."

"Well, I'm staying here until he does." He fingered the cutlass at his side. "And I still don't understand the deception."

"Suit yourself. I'll send word when he's ready to ascend."

"So you not only lied, but now you're excluding my mother as well? She won't be able to see her own son wed? And our Council of Lords? You promised we would *all* be present." His voice grew sarcastic. "In case you were wondering, that's why I'm here. When no ship came to fetch us, as you promised, I knew something had gone wrong."

Renata paused. "Plans changed, unfortunately. And the deception was for our mutual benefit, to bridge the rift between our peoples that we knew you would never consider otherwise. But if you wish, we will supply you with enough resources . . . more than enough resources to have a ceremony on land afterward, if you wish. Now, as much as I have enjoyed meeting with you again, I have other pressing matters to attend to. Good day, Prince Lucas."

With a start, Arianna realized that her aunt was walking toward the ship's edge. She scrambled to swim around until she was just under the ship's bowsprit. Seven splashes sounded, and Arianna scrunched her eyes shut, praying that they wouldn't see her.

As she waited, Michael's words came back to her about the others who could suffer for her failure. Suddenly, she wished she hadn't come.

Still, she was there now. She might as well find out what she could. When a few moments had passed since Renata's group had reentered the water, Arianna swam to the opposite side of the ship. Finding a handrail, she pulled herself up high enough to where her tail was out of the water. This time, her transformation took only a few moments. As she climbed the rest of the way up, Arianna was again relieved to see that the camicett reached just below her knees. She'd almost worn one of her old short ones that morning instead.

"It's another one!" a man shouted. "She's snuck aboard!"

Before Arianna could finish righting herself, she was surrounded by a circle of sailors. Unlike the pirates, these men all wore light brown shirts and trousers. As she stared warily back at them, however, she decided that they looked just as angry as the pirates ever had.

"Arianna."

Lucas stood on an upper deck near a large wheel. He wasn't smiling, either.

"I've come to warn you," she said, eyeing the men's swords as she did. "My aunt is lying to you."

"So I gathered." He hopped down to their level. "Would you like to explain why you never told us who she was? Or," he raised his eyebrows, "why you suddenly have a *real* voice?"

"She used the Sorthileige to disguise herself. I didn't know who she was either. And my voice is . . . a long story. But," she lifted her chin defiantly, "as I saved your brother from Tumen's king, I think the least you can do now is listen."

Lucas paused for a moment then nodded at his men. Slowly, they lowered their swords. "How is my brother?" He came closer. "Is he well?"

"I'm afraid not." Arianna began to describe for him the intricate web Renata had crafted, and with each twist, Lucas's eyes grew wider. When she finished, he shook his head.

"I'm going down there to get him."

"And how are you going to do that? The palace where he's being held is far deeper than the one my family used to live in. Even if I could get you a charm, you'd never go unseen."

"Well, I'm not going to let my brother be married off to some lecherous mermaid. I never liked the idea of sending him off in the first place." He put his hands on his hips and took a breath. "Who is he marrying anyway?"

Arianna wanted to laugh and cry. "According to my aunt, me."

Lucas had turned to whisper something to one of his crew members, but at this, he stopped and stared at her. "Oh."

Arianna almost smiled. It was the first time she'd ever seen Lucas speechless. "Please," she said, taking advantage of his temporary silence. "Don't make any rash decisions. Let me see what I can do, and wait for my signal. As soon as I can, I will bring him up to you and you can get him back to land."

"I'll keep the ship here," he said, but Arianna was already shaking her head.

"You're right above the city. Everyone knows where you are." She looked over at the distant shore. "Is there some port nearby that you can take shelter in? Close enough that you can see my signal when I send one?"

Lucas folded his arms and let out a gusty breath. "That depends on your signal. There is no port, but there is a cove not far off that we can sit in for a bit."

"Good. Stay there until I send a messenger of some kind."

"I have to say, I don't like waiting around, wringing my hands and hoping my brother will survive."

"Please," Arianna said again as she walked back toward the edge of the ship. "Promise me you won't do anything rash."

"I'll wait for your signal," he said. "But if I get the chance . . . if I see an opening, I'm taking it."

Arianna nodded. That was the best she could hope for. Quietly she let herself fall back into the water and then made her way back to the kelp.

Did she have a plan? Not in the slightest. All she knew was that Michael was an essential thread to Renata's tapestry of schemes. If she could get that one thread unraveled, maybe the rest would start to fall apart as well.

But what then? a small voice asked. *What happens after you send him away? What will you do?*

She didn't need him, she argued with the voice as she swam back down through the kelp to the market. What she needed was to focus on Renata. Besides, he had made his need of Arianna perfectly clear.

∼

When she arrived in the market, their sleigh, driver, and Michael were gone, just as she'd suspected they would be.

She made her way quickly back to the palace, wondering what

kind of trouble was in store for her as soon as her aunt got wind of her disappearance.

To her relief, no one spotted her as she snuck into the palace and up to her room. Arianna's room was lavish. Surprisingly so. Renata hadn't withheld any expense when it came to the gold-edged furniture or the jewels that sparkled from every surface. According to Arianna's mother, Renata had begun decorating the room as soon as she'd arrived, though she hadn't told anyone whom it was for. From the grandeur of the room, Renata truly seemed convinced that Arianna's cooperation was sure, and that the two of them would live happily ever after.

A rolled waxy leaf stuck out from the edge of her writing desk, and Arianna hurried over to read it.

I'm not sure why you sent the letter directly to me. Do you know how much trouble I would be in if the letter had been intercepted? Don't bother contacting me again or any of our mutual acquaintances. The contest is over. You lost. Best to keep our heads down from here on and hope to escape notice.

Arianna tore the note up and threw the pieces to the floor. It had taken her the better part of an hour that morning tracking Elda down to send a note to Mae asking for advice. Now that they had lost, surely Mae could be persuaded to come up with an alternate plan. As it was, they had two more days before the coronation was permanent. But, it seemed, Arianna had assumed wrong.

As Arianna fumed over Mae's letter, her door clicked shut by itself. Arianna nearly screamed until she realized it was her father who had closed it.

"Where have you been?" he shouted in a whisper. "Renata is furious that you didn't return with Prince Michelangelo."

"I talked with his brother," Arianna said, bending to gather the pieces of the note. "We're going to get Michael out."

"Your mother and I are doing everything in our power to protect you. But you cannot keep gallivanting off! You're not a child any more!"

"I'm gallivanting off because I'm *not* a child! Someone has to do something about Renata."

He rubbed his eyes with the palms of his hands. "I haven't seen her this angry in a long time."

"What do you want me to do?"

Amadeo took a deep breath before taking Arianna's face in his hands. "You mean more to your mother and me than you will ever know. That is why I was so hard on you when you were little." He sighed. "And even after. I just don't want to see you get hurt."

"Father, she's planning on using the Sorthileige on all of us. She's using it even now on herself. In the Deeps . . . I've seen it!"

"I know."

"You do?"

"She may be the future Sea Crown, but I'm still her brother." He gave her a wry smile. "Which is precisely why I am going to help you in whatever way I can."

"Arianna!" Renata's voice echoed down the hall and sent a shiver up Arianna's spine. Before Arianna had a chance to respond, however, her aunt had thrown open her door. "You will never learn, will you?"

46

ALL YOU CAN ASK

*M*ichael could still recall who he was and why he was in the Sea Palace at least, but the pain was so bad sometimes that he really wished he couldn't. After being dragged back to the palace by their irate guide, Michael had been tossed in his room again. This time, large, thick, multilayered netting had been thrown over his balconies, and the door would not budge. After an hour of fighting to be free, demanding to talk to Arianna's parents, he'd been unable to do anything more than crawl back to the sponge bed and lie down, praying for unconsciousness to take him.

Just as he was about to fall into another state of half-sleep, the door burst open, and Renata dragged Arianna in behind her.

Michael stared as rudely as possible, but he couldn't help it. Renata's eyes were no longer ringed by the effects of a few sleepless nights. Rather, they were surrounded by inky webs of veins that were beginning to stretch down her face. Renata herself, however, paid him and his gawking no heed.

"If you didn't believe me before," she snapped at Arianna, yanking her over and pointing at his legs, "then here's your proof.

Keep making foolhardy choices like that, and I assure you that his legs will be the least of your concerns."

Arianna bit her lip, but said nothing as she stared down at Michael's legs.

Michael followed their gaze down to his feet, the only part of his legs sticking out from beneath his trousers. He had taken his shoes off earlier to relieve the pressure on his aching feet, but now he wished he hadn't. Gingerly, he pulled one foot up to examine it more closely, and his stomach lurched. Tiny blue-green scales were beginning to grow on the tops of his toes. When he tried to wriggle them, he discovered that thin layers of webbing were starting to tie them together, too.

"The wedding will be held at sunrise in two days." Renata tossed Arianna at Michael. He barely had time to hold his arms out to catch her. She shouldn't have fallen so quickly underwater, but with the speed at which she hit him, Michael realized just how very strong Renata was becoming.

"I've tried to make you happy!" she said, turning and throwing her arms up. "My goal in life from the moment I met you was to ensure that you didn't turn out like me . . . alone."

Arianna peeked out at her aunt from underneath Michael's arm.

"Do you remember when you were bitten by that poisonous eel?" Renata bent so low that she was nearly on Arianna's level. "We had to hold you down while your mother sang to get the poison out. You tried with all your might to wriggle free. We had to grip you so hard that it hurt. But we did it because we *loved* you, and we wanted you to go on thriving. We hurt you then because we knew best. And this is no different!" She paused and pressed her hands to her face.

"It is the same now," she continued in a lower tone. "You are flailing and pushing back, but if I do not hurt you now, you will never know your potential."

Arianna stared up at her but did not reply.

Renata threw her hands up, whirled around, and headed for the door. "You have one day to convince her, Michael! Really convince her! Or you are mine, and she will be alone forever."

With that, she was gone. After the door locked, Michael looked down to see Arianna still tucked under his arm, curling into him like a lost kitten. Despite the pain that was moving in waves through his legs, Michael found considerable pleasure in the sensation of being her protector. Even if he couldn't do a thing to help her.

After a long stretch of silence, he finally pulled back enough to study her face. "Are you all right?" he asked.

She blinked a few times before nodding, but her eyes flicked back to the door several times.

Now is just as good a time as ever, his conscience prodded him. *You may never get another moment alone.*

Michael almost groaned. Words he should have said long before were burning a hole in his tongue. All the ways he had failed her had been haunting him since Arianna had brought him back from the siren song.

Well, since he had agreed to marry Princess Ines, really.

"Arianna—"

But she shook her head and pushed his arm off her shoulders. "Please don't."

"No. I need to." He slowly pushed himself into a higher sitting position, making his lower back scream in agony. "I have no excuse for what I've done. I just thought . . . I was a fool to think that marrying for convenience could save my kingdom."

"Just stop." She closed her eyes.

"Nothing I say or do will ever make up for the way I have wronged you, but—"

"What do you want from me?" she cried out.

"I want you to fight!" he shouted back as loudly as he dared.

"Without taking me into consideration! I want you to pour every ounce of life into escaping her grasp and never looking back."

Arianna ran a hand over her pale hair, clutching the knot tightly at the back. "No one deserves what she has planned for you." She spoke to the ground, not meeting his eyes. "Your brother is waiting for my signal in a cove nearby. As soon as I find the chance, I'm going to send for him. My father will help me create a diversion, and we're going to get you out of the water."

"Arianna."

"The shore isn't far." She ignored him. "As far as I know, there aren't any human settlements nearby, but you'll at least be safe. The farther you get on land, the less her song will touch you. Without you, her entire plan falls apart."

"And what about you?"

Hand still in her hair, she gave him an ancient look. "My family is willing to sacrifice everything to stop my aunt. My plan is nothing less."

He crossed his arms. "Then it seems we are at an impasse."

"As if you're in much of a position to do anything about it."

Michael needed time to come up with his own plan, so he changed the subject. "What did Renata mean when she said you would live the rest of your life alone?"

She gave him a wry smile and sat down on the edge of his sponge bed. "You might not have noticed, but down here, I'm somewhat of an anomaly."

He stared at her blankly. "She meant your eyes and hair, didn't she?"

She tipped her face up toward the ceiling. "Legs aren't considered a great advantage down here, either. It's considered unnatural."

Michael vaguely remembered through the fog of Renata's victory supper that none of the young mermen had asked her to dance. Fools. With a will of its own, his hand reached out and lightly ran the back of his fingers down her arm.

She tensed slightly, but her eyes closed. "Pale eyes. Legs. And my hair is too much like—"

"The sun?"

She nodded, a look of pain on her face.

"Tell me," he whispered, touching one of her curls that had fallen loose. "Why do you always keep it up like this?"

She cleared her throat a few times before opening her eyes and staring out the netted balcony. "That story Renata just shared . . . about me being bitten by an eel?"

He nodded.

"I was only bitten because my hair got caught in a sea fan. I couldn't call for help, so I had to wait there until someone found me." She hiccupped and looked down at her hands. "When someone did find me, it was nearly too late."

Michael's heart ached as he imagined Arianna as a little girl, waiting to die alone. And yet, as she sat beside him, he did something he'd been dying to do since meeting her. Michael willed his aching body to lean forward enough to pull her hair free from its elegant perch. Golden waves cascaded down, floating back and forth like sunlight on the waves. Unable to help himself, he ran his hand through her hair.

She bit her lip and her jaw trembled.

"Maybe you needed that once," he whispered. "But you're not a child anymore." Slowly, so slowly he reached up and cradled her face in his other hand.

"Why are you making this so hard?" She opened her eyes and shoved his hand off. With one swish of her tail she was three feet away, glaring at him.

"You were right." He struggled to stand, pulling himself up using the vanity. "I should have listened to you. I should have trusted you.

I was just trying to protect my people, but . . ." He shrugged help-lessly. "What can I do to make you forgive me?"

She just shook her head.

"I mean it!" He made himself as tall as he could. "Before the Maker takes me, I need to know that you've forgiven me! And if this is about the kiss—"

"Hang the kiss, Michael! You chose *her!*" Her voice broke. "Long before you were under her spell, you had made your decision. And now it's my turn to make mine." She straightened and began swimming for the door when he called after her.

"But do you forgive me?"

She paused, her hand on the door. "I will do my best to get you safe. But you can't ask any more of me than that."

47

IMPATIENCE

"Isay that you leave him to his folly," Lalia said as she pulled the gown over Arianna's head. "I mean, I think he could be very likable under different circumstances. I just don't see why *you* must save him from his decision. Let him marry Renata and you go free."

"And how would that help?" Arianna held her arms up so her mother and sister could pull the short gown all the way down. "Renata is determined to see me infected with the Sorthileige the same as she is with all of you. Perhaps even more so. Besides," she stared at her face in the mirror, determined not to look at the dress itself, "it's not that simple."

"That's easy. You go to the shore, grow your legs, marry some dashing human who is terrified of the ocean, and never set foot in the water again." Lalia went and picked her son up out of his basket. "And you take Johnathon with you and find someone with the power to permanently change him so he can stay out of the water."

"No charm would work long enough for that," Giana said gently as she pulled Arianna's hair down to rearrange it on her head. "Besides, I think Arianna means that Prince Michael's part in all of this isn't as simple as we think."

Arianna gave her mother a grateful smile. As wonderful as it was to have her sister in the same room, talking to her and being a part of her life, Arianna and Lalia had been apart for too long. Of course, they had seen one another as children often enough, but Lalia had never quite taken the interest in keeping Arianna occupied as Rinaldo had in his spare time. Lalia had been too busy taking an interest in the young mermen who often came to admire her.

Countless times, Arianna had longed for her sister's company. As a young girl, she had imagined conversations in which Lalia told her she was lovely and they arranged one another's hair and gowns before going to a ball together. And here they were now, arranging Arianna's hair and dress the day before her wedding, complete with Arianna's voice. But even with words, Arianna now felt ill equipped to tell her sister what she really meant. On the contrary, she felt rather cross.

How could Lalia understand that Michael's people really *were* starving? Or that leaving him to her aunt's wiles would be impossible? Or how her chest hurt every time she recalled the sight of Michael's lips pressed against Renata's youthful facade?

Foolish man! If he had only listened to her, they wouldn't be in this mess. Arianna clenched her jaw to keep her anger at bay, and in the effort forgot not to look in the mirror.

The gown wasn't exactly what Arianna had imagined for her wedding day. It was far more. Delicate white material clung to her arms and hung just off the shoulders. It continued hugging her figure until it reached her hips, where it flared out until it would have reached her knees, had she been in human form. Thousands of pearls had been sewn into the bodice in swirls that resembled waves, and in the very front, a large gem the color of her eyes had been placed on the neckline.

A strangled sob escaped her lips before she could reel it in, and before she knew it, Giana had gathered Arianna into her arms.

Arianna wept into her mother's shoulder. "It shouldn't be this way," she gasped between sobs. "I don't even know why she wants me. I don't have a soulsong!"

"I know," Giana whispered into her hair as she stroked Arianna's back. "I know."

They stayed that way for a while until Arianna's sobs quieted and her chest no longer heaved. Then Giana pushed Arianna back and looked her in the eyes. "I know you probably don't want to hear it now, but I believe two truths about this situation."

Arianna just nodded, not quite ready to talk.

"First," Giana said, "Renata sees what your father and I have seen since you were born. I tried to keep you from being exposed to the sun and failed. Frankly, even those few moments of sun you experienced should have killed you on that sandbar. But from the moment I looked in your eyes, I saw a fire there, and I knew it came from your soul. You don't have your soulsong yet. But when you get it, and I say *when*, not *if*, it will be a song that makes history.

"Second," she turned Arianna back toward the mirror and began moving pieces of her hair around again, "I don't think you want to leave Prince Michael to his doom."

"Mother, I don't really—"

"He's acted foolishly, and now you're both paying for it. I won't deny you that. But let me tell you something you don't know."

Arianna pulled away and turned to frown at her mother. "What?"

"You know that shell that I sent to you before you came here? The one with Renata's plans?"

"What about it?"

"Your prince nearly killed himself stealing that for us. Your aunt dealt with him so severely after it went missing that he lost his hearing. If I had been an hour later in sneaking in to see him, he would have never gained it back. I almost couldn't heal him as it was."

Arianna felt her horror reflected on her face. She could see it in her mind, Renata singing those horrid notes of darkness. Her haunting lullaby. The power that had cowed Arianna into submission in the Deeps would have made a human's ears bleed.

Suddenly, it was hard to breathe.

A cacophony of defense songs erupted above them. The women exchanged glances, and Giana went to the door. "Stay there," she told her daughters. Just as she reached the door, however, it was thrown open by Renata.

"Arianna, come with me," Renata pushed past Giana. "See what you've done."

"Ari, no," Giana moved herself between them again, but Renata let out a short burst of song and Giana was thrown against the floor.

"Now." Renata glowered, hovering over Giana, the black veins pulsing in her cheeks.

After glancing at Lalia where she floated clutching her son, Arianna obeyed. They swam down the hall in a burst of speed, moving through a river of merpeople all trying to go just as fast. As they went, more songs echoed from above the palace. A distant explosion harmonized with the songs.

Arianna's heart sank into her stomach as she followed her aunt. Had Lucas attacked? Why hadn't he waited? Or had her father made the first move? She didn't have time to ask, however, for Renata was knocking Michael's door down, too.

"If this doesn't convince you that your actions have consequences," Renata shouted as she dragged Arianna inside, "then I don't know what will." She stopped beside Michael where he lay on his bed. His face was taut, his fists clenched so hard that his knuckles were white.

Renata pointed the triton at him and looked up at Arianna. "This is your last chance. Michael is going to fix what you and your father have meddled with. If you try to interfere or keep Michael from his work this time, then I will know that you do not love him enough to keep him from me. If you stand quietly by and watch, however, I will know where your priorities lie."

With that, a bolt of green light struck Michael. Mist and bubbles began to whirl around his legs, and Renata opened her lips to sing.

Arianna began to sing her own healing song, but without even looking at her or pausing her song, Renata raised the triton again and aimed it at Arianna. This time the green flash moved through Arianna, and a familiar sensation raced up from her fins to her throat. In a moment, the strong note she'd been holding petered out, dying as her song fell to a rasp, then nothing. Arianna tried singing, crying, and even screaming, but she made no sound, and Renata's siren song only continued to wind its way over Michael.

His tense jaw went slack, and peace moved across his face. Arianna watched in agony as Renata bent over and whispered in his ear. Whatever she said changed his expression again, and the peace disappeared. Wide, indignant eyes looked back at Renata. Renata only smile and nodded. By then, the mist had dissipated, and thin, nearly translucent fins now lay where Michael's feet should have been.

"His change is not yet complete." Renata turned back to Arianna. "His real fins won't appear until tomorrow. But these will last long enough for him to complete his task. Your voice will return as well, but only after he finishes the job." She took a deep breath and closed her eyes. "Don't doom yourself to solitude, Arianna. For the sake of your own happiness, for once, make the right choice!"

Just then, Michael darted out of the room, his tail flipping as though he'd been swimming all his life. Arianna had no choice but to follow. Down the halls they swam, deeper into the palace than Arianna had ever been. With each swish of her tail, she tried her hardest to sing, to scream his name, but to no avail.

He didn't stop until they had reached a room that was filled with all sorts of weapons. The large armory surprised Arianna, as most Protectors usually used their voices as their main defensive weapons. Michael swam back and forth until he found what he seemed to be looking for.

The knife was small and simple. Its hilt was mother-of-pearl, and its blade was only the length of her hand. He shoved it into a pouch that was attached to a strap. When he tried to pull the strap over his head, however, it kept getting caught in his shirt. Seeming to forget how the shirt worked, Michael yanked on the material until the buttons popped off and he was able to toss the torn shirt aside.

Arianna hovered by, uncertain of just how far the siren song would take him. An icy fear gripped her as Michael slung the strap over his shoulder, and Lucas's words suddenly echoed in her mind.

My brother could be very dangerous if he chose to be.

Arianna could see that only too clearly now. Without his shirt or his usual cautious demeanor, Michael looked every part a dangerous man. His muscles were lean, less defined than Lucas's, but their subtle ripple made him seem only that much more agile. That much more feral.

Once the strap was secured across his chest, he bolted for the door. Arianna blocked his way, doing her best to plead with him silently. Placing her hands on his shoulders, she tried to press him back into the room. She could see in his eyes, however, that the siren song had done its job. With a confidence he'd never exuded before, he gently but firmly took her by her own shoulders and moved her to the side.

"We'll talk later," he said. "But now is not the time."

Arianna grabbed his arm as he swam away, but she wasn't strong enough to hold him.

So this was why Renata had taken Arianna's voice. All Arianna could do was follow him and pray that Michael's beloved Maker would have a miracle.

~

They swam to the surface so fast that Arianna began to get dizzy. Though she had become used to living at such a depth, the transition between the upper and lower ocean levels was still difficult. Explosions from above and the Protectors' songs that echoed around them only made the ringing in her head worse. She pushed herself, however, to stay as close to Michael as possible.

As soon as they broke the surface, his face went from its fervent determination to a look of relief. "Lucas!"

Were Arianna's ears still ringing, or did his voice seem louder?

As confirmation of her unspoken question, Lucas peered over the side of the ship a moment later.

"We've got them both! Landon! Fuller! Help me pull them in!"

Ropes were thrown to them, and Arianna could only grab one and hold on. Their ascent was rough. The songs of her people tossed the ship back and forth, and the explosions of the ship's weapons only made it worse. As they inched up the ship's side, Arianna felt her legs return. Michael's legs returned as well, his trousers reappearing with them.

"How did you find me?" Michael called over the cacophony as they were hauled up onto the ship's front deck.

"Didn't she tell you?" Lucas nodded at Arianna. "Her father and those loyal to him helped distract the palace's Protectors. They're going to accompany us back to shore!" He turned and called to his men, "We've got them! Let's go!"

Arianna looked back and forth between Michael and Lucas in confusion. Was it possible that the siren song had lost its effect already? *Did you spare him?* she asked the Maker, her heart fluttering in her chest. Was Michael truly free? Because if he was, she wouldn't care if her voice was gone for the rest of her life. Michael would leave the water, and Renata's plans would be thwarted.

Lucas fell into his brother's arms in an embrace. As he held on, however, his face went from joy to agony. He cried out and then slumped against Michael. As the ship turned, Arianna saw the light of the sunset glinting off a bloodstained blade in Michael's right hand.

Arianna screamed silently, falling to her knees. *Why?* was all she could ask the Maker. *Why?*

As if they had been waiting, half of the Protector's songs stopped. Arianna could hear her father's men and women calling to each other, unsure of what was happening aboard the vessel, but Arianna couldn't move. Hot tears streamed down her face. Unable to even lift her hands to wipe them away, she could only stare at the red staining Lucas's shirt. Lucas's crew, likewise, watched dumbfounded as their crown prince stood over their captain.

"Take heed," Michael said as Lucas slid to the ground. "This is what happens to those who would cross the Sea Crown. For the Sea Crown will be merciful no more." Then he stepped over his brother's body and took Arianna by the hand. He tugged at her until she was forced to stand and then pulled her over the side and back down into the ocean.

As soon as the salt water had completely engulfed her, Arianna could feel her voice return. "Michael!"

He turned, smiling. "Yes?"

She stopped swimming and just shook her head. "Why?"

Michael swam back to her. "He was attacking the city. Why wouldn't I?"

"Because he's your little brother!" She tried to steady her voice so she could shout at him properly. "He was trying to save you!"

Michael just shook his head, an exasperating, patient look on his face. "She wouldn't have sent us if it hadn't been important. Now, come." His face lit up like a little boy's. "I'm getting married tomorrow! I need to be ready." He reached for her hand, but she yanked it back.

Without knowing what she was doing, Arianna began swimming away from him as fast as she could.

"Arianna!" He shouted her name over and over again, but she pushed him out. She couldn't hear herself think when his voice was wreaking havoc with her head and her heart.

Not when she knew she was going to have to give him up, one way or another.

Before she had swum for very long, however, she felt someone trailing her. Glancing back, she saw two Protectors chasing after her, and the gap was closing quickly. They sang songs to hold her back, but she sang her own songs as well. And though her soulsong would have been far more successful in speeding her escape, her simple Protector melodies propelled her forward just fast enough to keep her out of their reach.

When she began to pant, however, she knew she wouldn't last much longer at such a pace. She had been swimming for so long that everything around her had dulled into a dark blue as the night had fallen, and she hadn't paid attention to where she was going. All she had wanted to do was escape Michael and the palace. But now, as she moved into the ever-darkening water, she saw a black blur up ahead, and immediately her mind was made up.

She was going into the Deeps.

48

PLANS AND PERIL

*T*he Protector on Arianna's right let out a high, frantic note as she led them toward the murky waters, and the other echoed it with a shout for her to stop. Arianna just gritted her teeth as she plunged headfirst into the Deeps.

The dark chasm opened up below her, and Arianna dove down into its shadows. Only when she had found a little crevice in the side of one of the sea cliffs, a good distance from the nearest visible vent, did Arianna stop swimming. As she pulled herself into the crevice, she listened to their distant voices from above.

"Should we follow her?" the woman asked.

"I am not going in," the man said.

"The Sea Crown will be very disappointed if she gets away."

"Then I will stay here and watch to see if she comes out, and you go tell the Sea Crown what happened."

Their voices drifted away, still arguing, and Arianna let herself lean back into the little hole. She couldn't get too comfortable, however, as she could still hear fish and other larger creatures drifting past her hiding place. Her initial instinct was to wait for the first lull between passersby and then swim to the surface as fast as she could. She discarded the idea as soon as it was in her head, however, as she knew that was the fastest way to become infected by the Sorthileige. Without a way to see the columns of smoke, she could easily swim over a vent.

Not that she could see any better down here. With each passing moment, the thin light grew thinner, and she was quickly becoming imprisoned in a darker night than she had ever thought possible.

So this was it then. Michael would be subject to Renata's every whim. Lucas would bleed out on a ship, and Arianna would die in the Deeps. Her family and kingdom would be slowly poisoned with a darkness that ate at their souls, minds, and bodies, and Maricanta would be ruled by the king who shared a bed with the woman who hated his people. Renata's children would have his smile, the one that crinkled their eyes. Arianna felt a pang of jealousy and then one of agony. His children would have Renata's heart.

"Who wins?" she shouted, suddenly not caring who or what heard her. "Is this what you wanted?"

The Maker didn't answer her. He never did.

"I just don't understand!" she continued to shout up at the surface. "Why bring us so far? Why do you continue to dangle hope in front of our noses and then pull it just out of reach?" Invigorated by her sudden boost of courage, Arianna left her hole and began to swim aimlessly. If the Maker wanted her to swim into a column of smoke, she would have no choice in the matter anyhow.

"And why let everyone think that *I'm* going to fulfill the prophecy? I haven't been faithful to you. I've doubted. So much I've doubted." She brushed some creature that passed by in the dark, but it only kept swimming. "Michael believed, though! He trusted you! And you've given him over to the creature on this planet that will hurt him most!"

And how would you know that he trusted?

Arianna stopped swimming. The words hadn't been audible, but she had heard them in her head as clear as day. Whether it was her own mind or the Maker's, she couldn't tell. But the question was posed either way.

"He told me," she said breathlessly.

Anyone can claim something. How did you know?

"Because . . . because I saw it. For months I saw it. He loves you! And you've turned your back on him!"

Why were you there to see it?

Arianna was confused. Either her mind was moving in directions she was too tired to keep up with, or the Maker had his own agenda. "I saw it because I was . . ." she frowned, "with him."

The voice asked no more questions, but one question still remained. It was the question that had haunted her for her entire life.

What if everything had been different?

If her mother hadn't been chased to the surface by that creature of the Deeps, Arianna would have grown up like all the other children, learning the four koroses and surrounded by friends. When the time came, she would have discovered her soulsong. Eventually, she would have found another soulsong that harmonized with hers. Rinaldo would never have needed to sacrifice himself for her. He would have competed for the triton, and Renata would have lost.

Perhaps, the voice said.

Perhaps Rinaldo wouldn't have needed to sacrifice himself for her. But what if he had still been killed by the pirates? Then Arianna might still compete for the triton. But, Arianna thought to herself, she might have bested Renata in the competition because she would have had her soulsong. The following morning's coronation would be hers rather than her aunt's.

Perhaps.

Arianna nearly imagined another scenario, but it occurred to her that either way, there would never have been a reason for her to watch Michael or Lucy and Claire play out on the terrace because she would have never felt the call of the sun. She might have met Michael at a ball now and then when her family was invited above, but she never would have truly known him. Furthermore, Michael's grandfather would never have taken his own life because there would have been no war, and he would still be king, meaning the pirates would still have a contract with the Sun Crown.

Every time Arianna tried to find a new way to fix the world, more problems presented themselves. Each alternate history provided a few solutions, but offered more problems as well. Still, she was always brought to the conclusion that her connection to Michael, tenuous as it had always been, would never have existed. He would never have opened up to her. She would never have helped him save his people. She might never have been heard. And Arianna was learning now that having a voice never guaranteed that one would be heard.

A flash flashed to her left so briefly that for a moment, Arianna thought she'd imagined it. Light hardly made it through the smoky water during the day, let alone at night. But just as she turned away, she saw it again, this time more clearly. One thin ray of light had managed to pierce the dark and touch the sandy floor of the Deeps. Arianna gawked. She could only see the bottom, but from where she floated, it looked quite a bit like . . . a moonbeam?

As she drew closer, she realized that she was looking through a small hole that led from her side of the Deeps to another open area on the other side of a towering wall of rock. The hole was so small that she nearly had to scrape the seafloor with her stomach in order to get through. But when she emerged on the other side, Arianna gasped.

"This is impossible," she whispered.

Arianna found herself at the bottom of a gigantic cove teeming with life. The space was round, and large enough to nearly fit the Sea Palace's dining hall inside. Its walls rose almost to the ocean's surface, and its waters were perfectly clear, letting the distant moonlight float all the way down to the seafloor. Ocean life of all kinds thrived around her. Sea stars, blue, yellow, purple, pink, red, and green fish, sea urchins, sea cucumbers, clams, turtles, dolphins, and even sharks slipped silently past one another as though they hadn't a care in the world.

"Impossible," she whispered again. The cove was filled with creatures that shouldn't even live in the Second Sea. Many of them belonged miles away. And yet, here they were in front of her. None of their eyes were black. None of them made sudden moves to attack others. It was a paradise in the middle of the ocean's most notorious nightmare. How could such a contradiction exist?

Suddenly, unbidden, Arianna recalled the words of the prophecy.

Child of sun,
  Child of sea,
  Destined to silence,
  Destined to sing.
  One nature to rule,
  One nature to fight,
  Only when owned can two peoples unite.

The underwater cove and all of its peaceful creatures shouldn't have existed. Arianna shouldn't have been born with legs and fins. But the cove was all around her, and Arianna was a child of two natures, whether she wanted to be or not.

She closed her eyes. Michael's betrayal still hurt, and the pain of Rinaldo's death wouldn't ever be completely healed. But this . . . maybe this was the first answer to her long list of *whys.*

For a reason she couldn't explain, the cove simply existed. And it was beautiful. And for the first time in her life, Arianna realized that so was she.

Arianna had long doubted Mae's methods, but she had still tried to use them when she didn't know what else to do. Now, however, Arianna thought about her two natures. She closed her eyes and pictured the water, cool and soothing as it ebbed and flowed in its familiar rhythmic motion. Then she pictured the sun. Holding them together in her mind, Arianna sang. And when her song was done, she looked up at the moonlight and whispered to the Maker,

"I understand."

49

BITTER FATES

Michael's head pounded, hurting almost as much as his legs. Prying his eyes open, he glanced down to see that a blanket made of living sea flora had been spread over his lower half. He started to pull it off, but then thought better of it. It was night outside, so if memory served him correctly . . . his transformation would be complete tomorrow.

He had the sudden urge to be sick.

A short melody was sung just outside his door. The lock slid open, and Renata swam in to seat herself at his feet. In the light of the algae lanterns, he could see that the black veins stretched down to her chin now, and the whites of her eyes were beginning to disappear. As frightening as she was, however, her usual air of confidence was gone. Instead, her shoulders slouched, and she stared at the ground for a long time clasping and unclasping her hands.

"Plans have changed," she finally said in a low voice.

"What?" Michael croaked. Even his throat felt terrible.

"Today was a test for you and Arianna. You did your part well. Unfortunately, she chose another path, which means you and I will be wed tomorrow, at sunrise when your transformation is complete."

Michael racked his memory. What had they done earlier that day? What test had Arianna failed?

"I will give you some privacy to tell Arianna yourself." Renata left her chair and began to swim for the door.

"She's here?"

Renata nodded at the window. The netting that had covered it that morning had since been removed. "She always uses the windows." Renata smiled sadly.

Then she was gone, and Michael was left alone to try and remember what had happened earlier that day. But for the life of him, he could recall nothing.

I don't understand, he told the Maker. *Why does Renata get to have her way? You're letting her spread darkness all around the world. Why?*

But there was no reply, and Michael's pain soon had him on his back again. When he realized that he could no longer move his legs by themselves, he propped himself up on his elbows. Shaking with the effort, he pulled back the corner of the blanket.

Where his legs had lain even when he'd awakened that morning, there was now only a tail. Horrified, he poked it. The thin scales were sticky and almost the color of an unripe banana. A few spots were darker, more of a blue than the others. Disgusted, Michael threw the blanket back over his legs and lay down once again.

He floated in and out of consciousness until he heard a light thump on his wall. When he opened his eyes, Arianna was perched on the balcony, her triumphant smile lighting the room. That smile cleared his head just enough for him to smile weakly back. He tried to pull himself up, but she rushed to his side and pushed him back down.

"Michael, I found—"

"Later."

"What?"

"Tell me later." He pushed himself up into a sitting position despite her protests. "I need you to tell me what I did well."

She stared. "I don't understand."

"Renata said I did something well today. But you failed the test. What did she mean?"

She drew back slightly.

"Arianna," he reached out and took her slim hand in his, though his own hand shook as though he had aged fifty years. "I need to know what I did."

"It wasn't your fault," she mumbled.

"Arianna."

She closed her eyes and sighed. "You stabbed Lucas." Then she placed her head in her other hand and her shoulders sagged.

All of the pain disappeared along with Michael's disgust for his new body. His disgust with himself, however, was soaring up to the stars.

"That's what the siren song does," she said quietly. "It wears off now and then. You might recall a certain acquaintance or remember a little about your life before, but until it's truly broken or you're miles from the ocean, she will have you in her grasp forever. I tried to stop you, I promise."

"Is he—"

"I don't know."

"I just wish I could think!" he exploded, shooting up out of the bed. "My head has been stuffed with fog, and I can't even think enough to remember killing my own brother!" His new fins refused to keep him suspended in the water, and he floated back down as sobs wracked his body. It dawned on Michael that this would be the way he would live for the rest of his life. He would rule his people with Renata's fist. She would eventually order him to love her. He would be ordered to kill for her whenever it suited her. And if Arianna proved to be too difficult, he would eventually go after her, too.

"There must be something I can do!" He grasped Arianna's arms and searched her face desperately. "You can't shoulder the entire burden yourself. It's not fair! There must be something . . ." As the words left his lips, however, he knew immediately what it was. He stopped and looked down at the strap wrapped around his bare chest. On it hung a knife.

"She'll never let you get close enough to use it."

He looked up to see Arianna wearing a sad smile. But he just shook his head. "I won't be using it on her."

She pursed her lips for a moment, then her eyes grew wide. "No!"

"Arianna," he leaned forward, trying to ignore the burning it caused his waist. "I will take my own life before I allow her to use me against you or anyone else."

"But you said you would never be like your grandfather! You promised!"

"He took his own life to avoid living," Michael whispered. "I would give mine to make sure you live yours." Only as he said this did Michael realize what Arianna was wearing. A hunger too deep for words wrenched his soul as he took in the pearl-white gown that should have been used to make her his.

It might have, had he not been such a determined fool to begin with.

She still shook her head, though she was weeping now, too. "Give me time! I found my soulsong! I can fight her! If I can only get the triton before she's coronated, we stand a chance!"

A familiar hum sounded at the door, and before Michael could reply, Renata and a dozen Protectors filed in. Singing a low dirge, the Protectors gathered around Arianna. An unseen force pulled her hands out of his, and shackles were immediately placed around her wrists.

"Give me a chance, Michael!" she screamed at him. "Please!"

"That's enough, Arianna," Renata said over the songs and Arianna's pleas. "You've had time to say your goodbyes. Now it's time to go."

But Arianna continued to thrash against her captors. "Promise me you'll wait!"

Till sunrise, my love, he thought as they gagged her and pulled her away, still screaming his name through the cloth over her mouth. *You have until sunrise.*

WORTH THE COST

*A*rianna stared at the wall of her prison cell, determined not to look at her aunt. Everyone had gone but Renata, who had floated at the bars for an hour now, begging Arianna to look at her.

Still, ignoring her aunt only kept her from Arianna's actual eyes. In her mind's eye Arianna still saw Renata order Michael to kiss her, to hold her, to touch her. His warm hazel eyes would behold her with adoration the way they had once looked at Arianna on the Sun Palace's terrace.

Is his only other course of action death? She asked the Maker. *No.* She shook her head to herself. She had to get him before sunrise. Then she could use her soulsong where it would actually do some good. Which meant she needed to get rid of her aunt if she was ever to leave the hateful iron bars or the dark stone room behind her. Which meant she needed to lose her gag and shackles as well.

"This is for your own good," Renata was saying wistfully. "For all of us!" She smiled tentatively when Arianna finally made eye contact. "I tried to make you happy! I really did! Believe me, I don't want to go through with this nonsense tomorrow morning any more than you do."

"Yes," Arianna mumbled through her gag, "I'm sure marrying a young, handsome prince is quite difficult indeed."

Somehow her aunt understood her muffled retort. "Stealing happiness from the child I love is the most difficult thing I have ever done!" Renata snapped. Then she sighed. "But the changes are necessary. When all of our people are stronger, we will find peace." Her expression hardened. "It's only fair to warn you, however, that when someone offers you assistance, which I'm sure they will, just remember that I am the Sea Crown now." She held the triton up. "And as soon as I am crowned, anyone who seeks to thwart my measures will die. Just keep that in mind."

You're not the Sea Crown yet, Arianna wanted to shout back. But she knew better than to speak the words aloud. Renata was turning toward the door. The sooner she was gone, the better. And Renata did leave, but not without humming a few lines from her soulsong and sealing the lock to Arianna's cell and then the dungeon itself.

When Arianna was sure she was alone, she closed her eyes and imagined the sun and the sea. She could feel the song bend and sway as it fell from her throat, moving cautiously as though it hadn't moved in years. Like fingers, the song slid into the lock. Up and down she moved her voice, making it higher and lower, even using different keys as she strained to open the lock.

Eventually, however, she had to stop. She could not open the door. Not, at least, while wearing the gag. Leaning against the rock wall behind her, Arianna looked up at the ceiling. The thick carpet of barnacles suggested that the dungeons here were rarely used. Cut into the side of the rock below the palace, there were only three cells to begin with, and the cell on each side of hers had even thicker layers of growth on their walls and ceilings.

Well, here we are. Arianna sighed. *Michael says you always have a purpose. To be honest, I can't see what that might be in this, but . . .* she took a deep breath. *I trust you.*

In response, a loud click sounded from the heavy dungeon door. A single figure slid through and closed it once more behind her.

"Mother!" Arianna called through the rag as loudly as she dared.

Giana held a finger up to her lips and flitted over to Arianna's cell. She reached through the bars to remove Arianna's gag.

"But how did you get the door open?" Arianna asked as her mother began fiddling with something in the shadows of her unusually long sleeve. "Renata used her song to seal it. I can't—"

Giana held up a long, thin, metal object, just longer than Arianna's hand. "The Sea Palace and the Sun Palace were built in tandem, each using pieces of the other's world as a sign of goodwill and peace." She thrust it into the little box at the edge of Arianna's bars. When she turned it, the box clicked. "What many merpeople don't know is that one does not need the song if one has the key." Giana gave a triumphant smile. "Sometimes humans aren't so foolish after all."

Arianna rushed out of her cell and into her mother's arms. Giana squeezed her back just as hard, but after a moment, untangled herself gently. "You need to get Michael. Swim out into the Deeps. Renata will follow you in, but the Protectors won't. Prince Lucas's ship will be waiting. Get Michael out of the water and don't let him return. And I mean never." She reached up and pushed a stray lock of Arianna's hair out of her eyes. "Stay with him," she whispered, her voice suddenly hoarse. "She cannot use your voice if she cannot reach you."

"But what about you and Father and Lalia's family?"

"Your sister's family left this morning. She will find them, but . . ." Giana sighed. "At least they can face the Maker one day saying that they tried."

"And you and Father?"

Giana's brown eyes fell a little in the light of the algae lanterns. "Your father has been banished to the Deeps for assisting Prince Lucas," she said softly.

Arianna pulled back. "And . . . you mean to join him. Don't you?"

Giana shrugged and reached up to caress Arianna's face. "As soon as she's crowned, we'll be exiled. But at least we'll be in eternity together soon. And we'll know that you're safe."

"No." Arianna shook her head vigorously and pressed her mother's hand tightly against her cheek. "I won't let you. You can't give this up for me. I found my soulsong! If we stand together, we can challenge her!"

Giana just shook her head. "The best way I can help right now is by giving you the chance to get Michael as far away as you can. You have friends now to help you. I know how to handle Renata, for better or worse. Use that soulsong to get him safe. Don't waste it on me."

Arianna was about to argue further when a Protector's warning song sounded from somewhere above them.

"I'll come back for you!" Arianna whispered, embracing her mother tightly once more.

"Don't you dare," Giana said as she pressed the key into Arianna's hand. "Go and live." Her jaw trembled as she pulled her close once more, kissing Arianna on the cheek.

Another call from the Protector sounded above, but Arianna clung to her mother, physically unable to let go until Giana had, with trembling hands, pried Arianna's arms off her and shoved her at the door. Arianna turned back, but Giana heaved the door open, thrust Arianna out, and closed the dungeon door behind her.

Take care of her! Arianna pleaded with the Maker as she forced herself forward. *And if they are to meet with you tonight, don't let it be painful!*

A few wrong turns and several palace levels later, Arianna had found her bearings. She pushed herself through the empty halls toward Michael's door. The halls were eerily empty, with the exception of a few guards that darted here and there. Arianna managed to avoid them by slipping behind other open doors and large statues that dotted the halls.

It wasn't light yet. She glanced out a window at the dark blue water. But had they started preparing for the coronation already? This thought spurred her on even faster.

When she finally reached Michael's room, her fears were realized. After unlocking the door with her key, Arianna found his room empty. She stared blankly. Where did she go from here?

"They've got him in the preparation room."

Arianna turned at the familiar voice to find Piero floating in the doorway behind her.

"Piero!" She threw her arms around him. "Where have you been? I've been looking all over for you since I arrived!"

"They've kept us busy." He pulled back and gave her a guilty smile. "No offense, but your aunt is rather demanding."

"So I've noticed. But you said he's in the preparation room?"

"Yes, the one they took you to, to get dressed for the coronation."

"Is he back under her song?" She held her breath, though she didn't know why. Of course he would be. To her surprise, though, Piero shook his head.

"The holy man won't marry someone under the siren song." He shivered. "She threatened him something terrible, but he said the Maker would only bless the marriage if both parties were in their right minds. So in the end, she gave in and locked him up in the preparation room instead."

"Thank you, Piero!" Arianna pecked him on the cheek before dashing off. She stopped abruptly, however, and swam back. "Out of curiosity, why are you here? Mae said she was done with me."

"Mae might be." A deep, feminine voice said from behind her.

Arianna turned to see Nereza. She was wearing her blue guard's camicett and holding a spear, her back straight as a rod. Arianna gawked. She couldn't remember Nereza speaking to her. Or speaking aloud at all, actually.

"But many of us . . . most of us, in fact, believe you can still defeat Renata." The corner of Nereza's thin mouth tugged up. "With a little help, of course."

Arianna felt a ridiculous smile coming to her face.

"Now tell us, Princess Arianna." Piero grinned. "What do you need?"

THROUGH THE DEEPS

*A*rianna pressed herself up against the giant column as the arena above her roared to life. Steady, she told her heart as it thumped unevenly. She looked at Nereza for the thousandth time, but Nereza only shook her head. Arianna huffed. Her head told her that she should listen. Nereza was a palace Protector, after all. She of all people would know the best time to strike. Still, Arianna's heart wanted nothing more than to swoop up and over the arena now, singing her soulsong until her voice gave out. Her body itched to move.

To distract herself, Arianna peeked out at the other pillars. In each pillar's shadow was a merperson. And though she couldn't see all the pillars, thanks to the arena's slope, Nereza had assured her that there were over two hundred merpersons waiting in the shadows. Even more were sitting in the crowds above.

The crowd roared again, louder this time, and Arianna looked at Nereza once more. This time, Nereza nodded.

Keeping behind the pillar, Arianna skirted up the arena's underbelly. She paused before cresting the top. There were palace guards everywhere. "There will not be a single square footage of twenty cubits that is not watched by a Protector," Nereza had told her. Then she had smiled. "Except for one."

"Which one?" Arianna had asked.

"Mine."

Still, when she finally peeked above the arena's edge, Arianna felt like an archery target. She wore her wedding dress from the day before. It would be impossible to stay invisible in such attire. No mermaid wore dresses the way she did. And few merpeople ever wore white.

Much to her surprise, though, even the people closest to her, sitting only a few feet away, ignored her completely. Even the Protectors' eyes were drawn to the same place as the crowd's, and when Arianna glanced down at the stage below, she could see why.

Michael waited at the end of a great aisle that had been created by running a long blanket of sea flora from the top of the arena to the bottom. His tail wasn't translucent anymore, its blue-green scales almost as shiny and colorful as any merperson's might be. The traditional three sashes decorated his bare chest, though Arianna couldn't tell if there was anything hidden under the sashes. What caught her eye, however, was his posture. Michael held himself more erect than he ever had before. His shoulders were high and straight, and his chin was held high. The expression on his face was resolute.

A small part of her mourned that he had never held himself so confidently at home.

There was no time for wistfulness, however, and she was reminded of that when the giant conches were blown and the palace choir began to sing. That was their signal. Sure enough, Renata was approaching the arena from a distance. Arianna turned and looked down at Nereza. Nereza nodded once.

Just as Renata slipped into the arena's back row and began her descent, the water surrounding the arena began to change direction. Arianna smiled as the crowed started to murmur.

Renata cleared her throat loudly, and the arena went silent. Several of Renata's guards began to sing their soulsongs quietly. Their songs worked to right some of the current changes around them, but as soon as the currents began to return to their usual paths, the arena began to shake.

Hundreds of merpeople burst up over the edges of the arena, where they formed in a circle around it. Each one sang his or her soulsong with a passion that made the stone arena shake even more. Arms of blue, green, orange, and purple coral shot up into the air, their growth so fast that their cracking and groaning was audible. And above it all, songs of chaos mingled with the choir's sweet notes.

Many in the crowd shrieked and began to flee the arena. Arianna wanted to see what Renata was doing, but as soon as she saw an opening in the pandemonium, she dove through it toward Michael. *Keep everyone safe!* she begged the Maker as she pushed through the fighting. Her one requirement for her helpers had been that they hurt no one unless it was in self-defense. She only needed enough time to escape with Michael.

Her hope for a bloodless battle, however, dissolved as one of her singers was thrown to the ground by the force of a Protector's tune. She dodged the song herself, but just barely. The way she jerked, however, threw off her balance, and Arianna slammed into the stone seat a few rows from the stage. She looked up just in time to see Michael pull the knife from beneath one of his sashes.

"Michael, no!" Arianna shouted. "I'm here!"

His head jerked up and their eyes met. And for one brief, glorious moment, he smiled.

Unfortunately, her cry had drawn Renata's attention as well. As Arianna pushed herself off the stone bench, Renata's lullaby drifted toward them.

"No!" she screamed as she swam. "Michael, cover your ears!"

But it was too late. His face relaxed and he dropped the knife.

Then he turned to face Renata. He had begun to swim toward her in his trance when Arianna slammed into him with her shoulder.

He was heavier than he looked, even underwater. Arianna grunted as she wrapped her arms around his waist and began to push him upward. "Get to the Deeps. Find Lucas. Get through the Deeps. Find Lucas," Arianna chanted to herself as she moved them up and out of the arena.

But as they began to leave the arena behind, Michael seemed to regain his focus. Looking down at Arianna as she pushed him forward, he began to struggle. Their slow progress came to a complete halt as he fought to peel her arms off him and she struggled to hang on. She could hear guards charging after them with Renata leading the way.

"Princess!"

Arianna looked to her left to find Nereza swimming alongside her. Out of her peripheral vision, she could see more of her supporters swimming close by as well. "Use your song!"

Of course! Arianna had forgotten she even had a song. Self-doubt whispered that it would never work, but she had no other choice. So Arianna began to sing. As she struggled to hold him, she tried to recall the way it had felt when he'd given her the parchment and ink on the beach, and her secret joy when he'd asked her to dance at Renata's victory supper. And as she did, his resistance began to weaken. Opening her eyes, Arianna saw confusion clouding his face. She immediately pushed him forward again, but their burst of speed didn't last long as Arianna soon began to tire.

"They're getting closer!" she shouted over to Nereza, who still swam just to her left.

Nereza simply nodded. "You only have a few minutes before the sun rises. If you don't get him out of the water by sunrise, he'll remain a merman forever." She glanced back behind them. "You go on. The Deeps are close. We'll hold them off."

"No, come with me!" Arianna gasped. "I need you!"

"You need to get him out of the water. And they won't let you do that." Without waiting for an answer, Nereza spun around and let out the fiercest Protection song Arianna had ever heard. Chills ran down her spine as she heard a dozen voices echo it. *They're going to die for us. For me.* Arianna thought to the Maker as her chest tightened. *Please don't let that be in vain.*

The Deeps loomed up ahead, but as Arianna continued to press toward it, a new sorrow filled her. Suddenly, holding the confused man in her arms didn't feel like a burden. Instead, she tightened her hold on him, relishing the way his warm skin felt beneath her fingers.

This would be their last touch.

The gap between Arianna and Michael and their pursuers grew as Nereza and the others held them off. Without pause, Arianna plunged into the Deeps. She had learned in her last two ventures how to feel for the heat of the vents before they went off. Zigzagging her way around the columns of heat, Arianna moved down into the colder, darker waters. This time, however, she knew exactly where she was going. She only prayed there would be time enough. Even in the Deeps, she could tell that morning was only moments away.

Deeper and deeper she dove until the water was almost pitch black. After a few moments of panic, she found the little hole. At first, she feared he might not fit through the opening, but after pushing him in several uncomfortable positions, he scraped through. She followed easily and picked him up again, still humming her soulsong as she pulled him up toward the opening at the top of the cove. She just prayed her mother was right, and that Lucas's ship would be there.

When she broke the surface, Arianna nearly dropped Michael from the relief of seeing a white ship with a red stripe.

"There they are!" she could hear Lucas call. Lucas! Her heart leapt. Michael hadn't killed his brother. Whenever the siren song wore off enough for some of his sense to return, Michael would discover his own innocence. He would live freely.

Even if he lived without her.

Michael jerked so hard that Arianna nearly dropped him. Then he let out a cry of pain.

"Stop, please!" Arianna begged as he continued to writhe in her arms. But he didn't hear or listen as his face contorted and his muscles spasmed all over his body.

Arianna looked back at the horizon. Sunrise was imminent. Pushing her song to a shout, Arianna held onto him as tightly as she could. She could feel the head of the yellow light begin to warm her back as she reached the ship. "Get him out now!" she screamed.

STIPULATIONS

a net was cast, and she rolled Michael into its center then jumped in herself. "Now pull!"

As the net left the water, the sun's rays exploded over the ocean. Arianna felt like knives were scraping her lungs as she struggled to breathe at a steady pace. She wanted to look out over the water as they were slowly hauled over the side of the ship, but instead, she could only let her head flop back as she squeezed Michael's hand.

"We did it," she panted. "You're going to be free."

Only when they spilled out of their net did Arianna open her eyes to stare up at the golden blue of the morning sky.

To her joy, Lucas was among those who greeted them. His arm was strapped over his chest, and he looked a good shade paler than usual, but the young man was alive. As she was about to exclaim such, something dawned on her. This time, her aunt's curse wasn't temporary. Nor did it come with temporary pants. "You might want to fetch him some clothes." She turned away from Lucas as he hovered over his brother.

"Why?"

Too tired to answer, she just waited, then chuckled breathlessly when she heard the men begin to exclaim at the return of his legs, which Arianna knew would be rather bare.

Thank you, she told the Maker. *Thank you!*

As she prayed, however, shouts from the crew interrupted her. Curses were uttered, and everyone began to scramble. With a groan, Arianna rolled over on her side and pushed herself up onto her elbow.

"Pirates, Captain!" one of the men yelled down from a basket hung up on the tallest mast.

"Where are they?" Lucas called up, still standing over his brother.

"Everywhere, Sire. They're coming in from every direction. Five — No, six ships!"

Arianna's heart fell as she remembered what she had to do. "Lucas!" she called. He quickly came to kneel at her side, and she pushed herself unsteadily to her knees. "I don't have much time, so listen carefully."

He nodded.

"I don't know how you got here, but—"

"Your mother came last night. She told me what had happened to Michael. She said you would be coming, and that we needed to get Michael to shore as fast as possible."

"Good." Arianna wanted to cry as she thought of her mother.

"She also said you would be coming with us to help us break the siren song."

"I . . ." Arianna had to stop and breathe. "I'm afraid plans have changed. I will not be going with you."

"But we need you!"

Arianna shook her head. "We need to stop my aunt, and stopping her will require power from both the sun and the sea. And," she took a deep breath, "I think that's why the Maker might have made me this way. I can harness both. If I don't, she'll never stop coming."

"But Michael needs you! Your mother said—"

"If I don't do this, Michael will never be able to live in Maricanta again. It's too close to the ocean. He would be in peril for the rest of his life." She drew in a shuddering breath. "I don't know if I can win this. But perhaps I can make the fight so difficult that I have grounds to demand a trade for his release. Or perhaps with the Maker's help, I can bring her down and make way for a new Sea Crown. Either way, I am needed here." She looked up at the six ships moving in on them from all sides. "You'll never make it out alive otherwise."

"Arianna?"

Arianna looked over to see that Michael had been tended to and was propped against the side of the ship. She ran to him and kneeled beside him.

He took her hands in his and held them tightly. "I remember you singing . . ." he said, eyes full of wonder.

Arianna smiled and nodded through her tears. "Yes. I sang to you."

"You got your soulsong," he whispered.

Arianna stared at him. Even under the siren song, he had heard her. But how was that possible?

"It was beautiful. But why are you crying?" He wiped the tears from her cheeks.

"Stay the course!" Lucas yelled as he jumped up and ran to the back of the deck, leaving Arianna and Michael alone.

"I have to go." Arianna took Michael's hands. "But you must listen to me first."

"You can't go. We just got here."

"You must *never* touch the ocean again. Don't even wade in the tide pools. If you do, her curse will be completed, and you'll return to your merman form forever."

"Arianna, answer me!" He stood up and loomed over her.

She stood, too. "And if you go near the water, you'll hear her, and you'll be under her siren song again as well. As long as you stay away from the water, you're free."

"Why are you leaving!" he shouted, grabbing her arms and pulling her close. "She's going to kill you!"

"She's going to kill everyone I love, too. I can't let them die, Michael." She choked out a sob. "I can't let you die."

He searched her face for an immeasurable moment. In the fire of the rising sun, his eyes burned like amber, and for one perfect minute, Arianna knew he could see inside her soul. Finally, he began to nod slowly.

"If I'm going to listen to you, then I have one stipulation for you as well."

Arianna blinked, confused.

He pulled her hair down from its knot on her head and ran his hand through it. "Don't choose between your two natures. The Maker crafted you perfectly just the way you are."

And with that, he bent down and pressed his lips against hers.

53

ALLY OF THE SUN

*A*rianna gritted her teeth as she plunged back into the ocean. The kiss had stolen her breath and her focus, and she shook in agony as she forced her fins to propel her away from the ship. Whatever was left of her anger, any remnants of the resentment she'd nursed against him dissolved as she recalled the way his fingers had felt in her hair, on her face. How he had looked at her as his eyes glinted in the sunrise, as though he had never seen her before. What had possessed her to think she might have those arms encircle her every night for the rest of her life? She had known it was impossible. And yet . . . she had hoped.

But no one would survive this attack if she didn't stop Renata. Arianna shook her head to clear it. If Renata succeeded, it wouldn't matter in the least whether Michael had ever loved her.

Arianna narrowly missed swimming into a column of black smoke as she tried to talk sense into herself. Jerking her tail to the side, she hit a rock and found herself staring into a pair of small black eyes. She swam backward, but the eyes followed her, and as it pulled out of the shadows, she found that they belonged to a very large orca. As it followed her and passed beneath a patch of light, Arianna noticed a black festering wound in its left fin.

Perfect. Just when she was about to challenge the most powerful mermaid in the ocean, she was going to be eaten by a whale instead. It would be funny if she weren't staring the whale in the face.

Arianna backed into something hard. When she turned around, she realized she was up against the side of a cliff, one that dropped precipitously into an inky canyon below. Arianna dove down, and the whale immediately took up the chase.

She needed to sing. But as she fled into the darkness, Arianna found it difficult to focus. Sea and sun. Sea and sun. But try as she might, she couldn't think clearly enough to pull her song of two worlds to life.

Just as she began to see the glow fish below her, a sure sign that the seafloor was fast approaching, Arianna gave up trying to remember her soulsong and simply used her other koroses instead.

The Nurturing song flew from her mouth like a bird loosed from a cage. It echoed off the canyon walls, and made the orca squeal. Not waiting to see how the orca would fight as coral arms reached out to grab it, Arianna pushed herself back up toward the murky, distant light above, darting out of the way of several smoke columns as she did. As soon as she escaped the canyon, Arianna began to push through the kelp, only to find Renata waiting.

"You should have kept your hair up like I told you to," Renata said, her voice nearly inaudible. Her arms were crossed, though she held the triton in her right hand. "You might get it caught on something." She snapped her triton toward Arianna and then twirled it next to Arianna's ear. The triton caught Arianna's long golden locks and twisted them up so that her head was stuck tight against the triton itself. Renata pulled Arianna close, just inches from her face. "But then, you never learn."

She lifted the triton up, dragging Arianna along with it, and began to bring it smashing down against a boulder, but Arianna threw out a Growing song. The thin strands of sea grass that sat below the boulder shot up, and the grass caught her head before it could crack against the rock. Using the momentum, Arianna pushed off the rock with her tail, flying right back at Renata. This time, she sang a song of Healing. Her knotted, torn hair untangled itself from the triton's prongs, and she was free.

"I gave you everything!" Renata screamed. "Why can't you just be happy?"

Arianna rolled away so that she was out of the triton's reach. "It was never about you, Renata! It was about this!" She lifted her arms to gesture at the darkness around them.

"I shielded you too much from humanity's atrocities. I can see that now." Renata adjusted her grip on the triton. "You never knew the depths of their depravity."

"I watched my brother die at the hands of pirates!" Arianna twisted to the side to avoid another column of smoke. "The same pirates you're *still* using to do your dirty work!"

"Then you've chosen to forget!" Renata again aimed her triton at Arianna, and two pelican eels appeared from the shadows, their wide, sinister mouths opening and closing in tandem. They floated just at Renata's elbows, their long, thin bodies poised to spring.

"No, and I never will. But twenty-three humans died at his funeral as well. And we did nothing to help them!" Arianna felt the frustration begin to boil in her blood. "In fact, the reason they died—"

"I wasn't trying to kill them all!" Renata exploded. "I just wanted to get the old Sun Crown! The others were simply collateral."

"So it was you," Arianna whispered. "And . . . you brought the storm on, too, didn't you?" Somehow, even in the face of all Renata's crimes, Arianna had hoped to the Maker that her aunt didn't have that much blood on her hands. But it appeared now that she did. And she wasn't shedding a single tear over the men, women, or children that she had killed, either.

Before Arianna could say anything else, a bolt of green light shot right at her, then another. Arianna dodged both, but the second forced her to dive behind a large boulder. When she peeked back out, the two eels attacked. Throwing out her Protection song, Arianna covered her face as the scum on the ocean's surface above them opened enough for two beams of light to pierce through. The light hit the eels' eyes, and they wriggled back into the shadows.

"What, no soulsong?" Renata held her arms up. "I was told by a very serious young servant that you had gained your soulsong, and that you were going to use it to defeat me. Piero, I think his name was."

Arianna's heart sank, and she struggled to stay focused as she circled her aunt. Renata was trying to break her, she assured herself. And Arianna knew better than to let Renata get under her skin. But that was getting harder as Renata began to describe all the ways she was going to hurt the young servant when they were through, and how much she was going to enjoy it.

Something wrapped around Arianna's left wrist, then her right. Too late, Arianna realized that she had let her guard down. Each of the eels had curled itself around a hand.

Sun and sea. Sun and sea. What was her soulsong? Why couldn't singing be second nature to her? Oh yes. Because she was also human. Michael had picked a fine time to tell her not to choose one nature over the other.

With a good deal of annoyance, Arianna let out another Protection koros instead. The eels immediately began to loosen their grips, but Renata aimed her triton at them, and two green bolts later their grips were tighter than ever. Arianna struggled with all her might. *Sun and sea! Sun and sea!* she screamed in her head. *Maker, what is my song?* Still, try as she might, she couldn't focus enough to remember her soul's true song.

"Please, Renata!" she begged Renata, who floated just a few feet away. "Don't do this! I love you!"

And she did. Through it all, anger and love, resentment and misunderstandings, Arianna loved her aunt. Even now, she wore the conch around her neck. It had sung her to sleep the last time she had dared close her eyes.

Renata's face twisted to a grimace. "I always loved you," she said in a strained voice. "And I will hate myself forever for doing what has to be done now." She swam over to the largest vent Arianna had seen in all of the Deeps, and floated above it. Wider than Arianna's sponge bed, it reeked of spoiled eggs and hot metal.

"Renata, no! It's too much power for one—"

But before she finished speaking, a monstrous column of smoke ascended. Arianna had to cover her face with her hands to protect it from the heat. When she dared to look again, she nearly shrieked.

Renata's familiar features began to contort. Her soft face grew more angular, her bones more pointed, and her dark hair was streaked with white. Gone were the familiar, comforting eyes of Arianna's aunt. Instead, two shark's eyes looked down upon her.

"To the bottom," Renata said in a voice that wasn't her own.

Arianna was yanked back down to the seafloor even faster than she had swum to escape the orca. In just seconds, Arianna hit the ground so hard it jarred her bones. The eels didn't stop, however. Instead, they continued to push her into the sand.

They were going to bury her alive.

Just as Arianna's ears began to fill with sand, Renata floated down to watch. "I let you stay too long out in the sun. And for that, I'm sorry."

The sun. In that moment, Arianna recalled the way Michael's eyes had reflected in the light of sunrise as it moved over the ocean, like golden brown against a backdrop of perfect blue. *Sun and sea. I've found you.*

Power warmed Arianna's fingers and tail as it surged out from her heart. With her last breath, just as the sand began to cover her chin, Arianna let her song burst forth.

The eels flew backward, slamming against a nearby rock wall. Arianna launched herself out of the sand, and as she did, she was struck with an idea. She closed her eyes and imagined the texture and weight of the wet sand on a sunny day, right after being covered by a wave.

Renata pointed the triton at Arianna, but Arianna let out a low note. Then, raising her song and her hands in the air together, Arianna watched in amazement as the sand that had trapped her just seconds before now rose up and began to twist around Renata.

Renata shrieked and whirled the triton in an opposing circle around her head. She wasn't fast enough, though. The sand continued to twist up, surrounding her.

"What are you doing?" Renata screamed.

"I never wanted this," Arianna said, her hands still directing the sand. Renata screamed like a kraken as the sand closed in around her, and Arianna wept as she resumed her song. *But you've given me no choice.*

When the sand was whirling around Renata so fast that she was cut off from view, Arianna took one last deep breath and closed her eyes. "I'm so sorry." She clapped her hands together. When she opened her eyes again, there was no sign of Renata or the triton. The sand had engulfed them completely.

54

VORTEX

"We need those casum balls!" Lucas shouted from above.

"We're out!" Michael slammed the chest lid so hard the wood creaked. When he did, however, a single round clod of dirt rolled out from behind the chest. "Wait! I found one more!" Michael snatched it and sprinted up the steps onto the deck. He carefully handed the ball to his brother, who in turn gave it to one of his sailors.

"There." Lucas pointed at the pirate's ship closest to them. "Hit their quarterdeck."

The sailor pulled his arm back and heaved the casum ball forward.

"Great throw, Berardi!" Lucas crowed. Before they could celebrate, however, another explosion rocked them. Michael, Lucas, and Berardi were thrown against the deck's wall. Lucas grunted as he rolled over. Michael tried to pull him up, but Lucas shoved him away.

"Go see to the mast crew! Leave me be!"

Michael wanted to retort that his brother should not be running about a deck in the midst of battle while suffering from a stab wound, but the four remaining pirate ships attacking them didn't really leave them much choice. So he did as Lucas said and ran over to the railing. Below him, a third of the crew was trying to clean up the remains of their foremast where it hung suspended in the air, half toppled in the front of the ship.

"Need another hand?" he called down the men.

One of the old grizzled sailors shook his head. "We can't even push the rest of the mast into the sea, Sire! Not out of port! And Capii says we can't withstand another blow."

"Why not?"

"Took out our rudder! We can't even turn!"

Michael turned to tell Lucas, but from the grim set of his brother's mouth, Michael could tell that Lucas had heard. *Please,* Michael prayed, *we need a reprieve. There are just too many.*

Another set of shouts broke out from the front of the ship, calling for water.

"If Renata was underwater, how did they blasted know to find us here?" Lucas growled as he limped up behind Michael, still holding his chest.

"Renata must have told them somehow." Michael scanned the disarray of their ship. Men were everywhere trying to put out fires, struggling to free the other masts from the main one that had fallen, and searching for any remaining useful supplies. But Michael knew from his own searching that there wasn't much left.

"How?"

"A sea witch could do it." Which was exactly what Renata had become. Michael searched the waters. Still over the Deeps, since they hadn't been able to move once the pirate ships had started closing in, the waters were tumultuous, knocking the ship about even more. Dark shapes moved beneath them that sent shivers along Michael's spine. Still, as long as the waters foamed and churned, Michael knew that Arianna was still fighting. She was still alive.

"Sires!" A young man ran up to them and pointed, his eyes bright. "They're coming!"

Sure enough, dozens of ships appeared from around the distant cape. Many were still unpainted, and others obviously needed repairs that hadn't been made. But they were all in better shape than the flagship. And best of all, they would have weapons.

"How did they find us?" Michael asked Lucas.

"When I realized Princess Ines was a fraud, I sent a bird back, ordering them to come out as soon as they could." Lucas yanked Michael down. "Watch out!"

Michael fell just in time to feel the heat from a casum ball emerging from its shell several feet over his head. The ball missed them, exploding several yards past the ship's deck. Michael regained his footing just in time to look up and see an unpleasantly familiar ship coming straight at them.

"They're going to board! Gather the weapons!" Michael darted back down into the cabin and grabbed the first weapons he could find. "Jonas! Take these!" he called back to the younger shipman who had followed him down. Shouts sounded from above.

"Cut the ropes!" Lucas shouted. Dozens of footsteps thudded on the deck as Michael continued to feed Jonas the weapons and Jonas continued to run back and forth between the deck and the cabin until they froze at the sound of a familiar voice.

"Stand down! Or your prince is dead! I said, *stand down!*"

Motioning for Jonas to stay back, Michael crept to the edge of the room. Peeking through the open door, he found everyone at a standstill. Pirates and sailors stood motionless, Lucas's men with their weapons at their feet. In the center of the pirates and captive sailors was the pirate lord himself, holding a knife to Lucas's throat.

"There you are!" Bras raised his free arm as though they were old friends. "I was afraid I wouldn't get to see you before I dealt with your flagship." He turned back to his men and handed his hostage to another. "Now we'll get to see what the future Sun

Crown is really made of!" The pirates cheered, and Bras returned his gaze to Michael, still advancing as he spoke. "I've been waiting for this for a while. That sea wench merely afforded me the opportunity." He raised his sword.

Michael blocked Bras's first attack and then the series of attacks he launched after. His legs were still tingling from the transformation, and he couldn't get his footing right to make his own attacks. All he could do was defend.

"I'm going to kill you just like I killed the merprince," Bras said as he forced Michael up the deck steps. "But don't worry about your little mermaid." His red coat flared out as he took a wide swipe at Michael's arm, missing by an inch. "I've decided not to sell her. I'm going to keep her all for myself."

Possessed by a strength he hadn't known before, Michael sprang at the pirate, their swords clashing so hard that Bras stumbled back. He regained his footing only for Michael to push him back again, this time causing him to fall down the steps. Leaping down after him, Michael attacked again and again, with each attack picturing Arianna's face. The thought of Bras holding her filled him with a new wave of rage.

"You. Won't. Touch. Her." With each word Michael shoved Bras backward again. But Michael didn't see the hole one of the pirate's casum balls had left in the deck. His ankle went right through it. Bras was on him immediately, knocking the sword from his hand. Michael grabbed the pirate's knee and twisted until the pirate was down as well, losing his own sword. As the pirate scrambled, Michael finally managed to pull his ankle from the hole. Frantically, he looked around for his sword. As he looked, Bras grabbed him by the collar, and soon they were rolling on the ground, each trying to go for the other's throat.

Just when Michael's fingers were nearly numb from trying to yank the pirate around, they rolled beside a pile of weapons Jonas must have dropped on the deck as Bras's men had taken control. Bras snatched up a short sword and held it to Michael's neck.

"You should have just kept that little mermaid safe in your castle," Bras said, his black-and-white whiskers pulling up into an awful smile. "Or learned to shoot a bow and arrow. Either way, you've failed her."

"Yes, I have," Michael said as his left hand searched the wood planks beneath him for something, anything. When his hand finally touched a single weapon, however, he had to smile. *You have an interesting way of answering prayers,* he told the Maker. And with that, he brought the arrow up into the pirate's side. Shock spread over Bras's sun-weathered face, and Michael drew him near. "But I'm a fast learner." And with that, he shoved Bras's body over the side of the ship and into the water.

A loud groaning made the pirates and crew alike look up.

"The mainmast is cracking," someone yelled just before a series of loud crashes filled the air. A strangled scream came from somewhere in the center deck, and the pirates began to scramble back to their own ship. As men shouted and ran, Michael looked for the source of the scream and found a young sailor pinned beneath one of the mast's long arms. The wind was quickly wrapping the sail around the man. If the mast moved any more at all, the man would be suffocated.

"Cut the rope. Don't try to untangle him!" Lucas shouted from behind.

"I know what to do!" Michael yanked a knife from the young man's exposed boot and began to cut away carefully at the rope. Lucas had dragged Michael to the shipyard too often as children for Michael to have learned nothing.

Just as Michael cut the young man free, an unusually large wave slapped the side of the boat, sending it into a near spin. The knife flew out of his hand, and Michael grabbed the railing just in time to avoid falling into the water.

"Michael!" Lucas yanked him back so hard that they spilled back onto the deck. Lucas didn't wait for him to get up, though. Instead, he rolled over and grabbed Michael by the shirt. "You can't take risks like that!" His face was deadly serious. "You heard what Arianna said! It's not fair to our people! You cannot be king if you sacrifice your humanity!"

Michael stood up beside his brother and looked at the scene around them. All four pirate ships were turning away and heading north up the coast.

"Duarte!" Lucas shouted to his first mate. "Send word to the ships that they are to make chase!" He let out a *whoop* and turned to Michael.

But Michael couldn't rejoice. He stared down at the still waters below.

"What's wrong?" Lucas asked, looking down as well.

"If the water is still," Michael said, "that means the battle below is over as well."

Lucas's face fell, and he squeezed Michael's shoulder, but Michael felt no better.

"Renata's allies have fled," Lucas said. "Surely that means something."

Michael didn't respond. *Let her live. Please let her live.* His crown, his restored body, even his own life would mean very little without her.

"Ho, now, what's that?" Lucas pointed at a little set of ripples not far from the deck where they stood.

Michael held his breath and gripped the railing until it groaned.

He nearly collapsed with relief when Arianna's beautiful head emerged from the water. When her blue eyes met his, she gave him the most brilliant smile he had ever seen.

"Arianna!" He pulled his shirt off and started to lean forward until Lucas grabbed him again and yanked him back with a glare.

"Don't make me tether you to the deck. I swear, I will."

But Michael was too relieved to be annoyed. Arianna was alive. Renata was gone. They and their kingdoms could finally be free.

Arianna had begun to swim toward the ship when the waters around her started to churn. Arianna looked up at Michael again, but this time, there was fear in her eyes. The water continued to swirl harder and faster until a vortex had formed, its edges wider than the ship itself.

Michael turned and grabbed the closest rope he could find. But by the time he returned to the railing, Arianna was being sucked down into the vortex. He had just enough time to glimpse her tail beginning to shimmer.

55

THE RIGHT THING

*M*ichael searched frantically until he found the pile of weapons again. He snatched up an arrow and steadied himself against the edge of the ship.

"Michael?" Lucas was immediately at his side, clutching his arm. "What are you doing?"

"You were right. Our people deserve a king."

"I think that song is still in your head! Now do your duty and get off that railing!"

"A true king," Michael said softly, turning to his brother, "adheres not only to duty, but also to honor. If I can't be a man of both duty and honor for my people, then they deserve better."

"Your duty is to be king! To stay alive! What are you doing?" Lucas didn't sound like a prince or the leader of the royal navy anymore. He sounded like Michael's scared little brother.

Michael put his hand on his brother's shoulder and smiled. "The right thing." Gripping the arrow tightly, Michael dove straight into the center of the vortex.

When he hit the water, a wave of pain pulsed through him. He felt like a smelter's torch was being pressed against every inch of his waist and legs. Despite being surrounded by frigid water,

Michael forgot how to move, although the vortex was tossing him about. As the pain slid down his body, so did the scales. Michael let out a bellow as his feet fused back into fins. Compared to this, Renata's song bursting his ears had been nothing. The pain of the past few days had been nothing. This pain made him want to die.

Just as Michael's vision began to spot, it was over. Trying to catch his breath, he tumbled out of the vortex and slammed into a large rock. Once he was able to right himself, however, his tail felt as though he'd worn it all his life. Without stopping to take stock of himself, Michael turned and propelled himself back to the maelstrom's center.

When he got close to the bottom, he could see Arianna lying pressed against the seafloor. Her face was beginning to lose its color. Her fins were nearly translucent, and they were beginning to separate. She reached up, but wasn't able to lift herself off the ground. *If she has legs,* Michael realized, *she can't breathe.* He didn't have much time.

Only when he swam closer did he see Renata. Singing as she hovered just outside the vortex, Renata looked like a different creature entirely. Her once-smooth face now had three gills cut into each cheek. A sea worm poked out of one of the many holes that pierced her chin. Her black eyes shot up to meet his, and her mouth curved up into a smile that revealed three rows of needled teeth.

Even louder she pushed out her song. Arianna cried as her legs began to thicken again, and Michael was hit by ripples of peaceful confusion. He knew he was going to do something, but what was it? The woman on the ground and the woman before him both looked familiar, and both pulled parts of his heart in different directions. Looking at the older woman made him uncomfortable. And yet, her song called to him . . .

The girl on the ground had turned so pale she was nearly blue. As he began to move toward the other woman, however, the girl on the ground pierced him with her eyes, and her gaze was enough to stop him completely. She opened her mouth. At first he heard nothing, and turned his gaze back to the older woman.

A thin melody, almost like the tinkling of a broken bell, began to encircle him. The song was quieter than the older woman's song. In fact it was nearly impossible to hear. But it was beautiful. It was a song he had heard once and a song that felt as ancient as time itself. And he knew in his core that it was for him alone.

The fog began to clear from his mind, and Michael remembered what he had come to do. Charging forward with the power of his new tail, Michael readied his arm and drove the arrowhead straight into Renata's heart. Her song stopped midnote and she fell back, slamming into the coral wall behind her.

Michael swooped down and pulled Arianna up into his arms. She felt like one of Lucy's rag dolls as she lay limply against his chest. Her breaths were shallow and shuddering in a way that frightened him.

He'd begun to pull her up from the seafloor when something slammed him down. When his head stopped spinning, Michael found himself staring up at the monstrous mermaid once again. This time, however, an arrow stuck out of her chest, black oil oozing from the wound.

"You think you can best me with your weapons? Now, before you serve me, you will watch her die!" She sucked in a deep breath and let out a blast that surged through the water.

Just when he thought he couldn't stand to hear her song any longer, that other softer song joined in again. The surge slowed just enough for him to open his eyes. When he did, Arianna was looking at him. Her blue eyes were fixed on his, and she gave him a gentle smile.

Michael shook his head. *You're too weak.* The amount of power it would take to overpower Renata was far more than he was sure existed in the girl lying limply in his arms, gasping for breath. She only pressed her forehead against his chin and briefly closed her eyes. Then she took a deep, rattling breath.

Her song was a clear bell ringing in the midst of Renata's song of darkness. But this time, that bell was no longer broken. And the longer she sang, the louder her song grew. The waters around them tossed once more in tumult as hot water mixed with cool.

Renata continued to sing while raising her triton and pointing it right at them. Michael braced himself, but Arianna only kept her eyes closed. Then she let out a single high note and held it. He could feel her shake with the effort. And yet, she continued to hold the note.

The triton began to glow, but not in the way Michael had seen before. Instead of shooting out, green light sparked at both ends of the triton and began to eat its way inward. Renata looked down at her weapon in shock. As soon as she looked away from them, Michael began swimming to the surface as fast as he could, Arianna still singing and trembling in his arms. For a brief second, he considered turning around and swimming to Lucas's ship. But one glance at Arianna told him she didn't need a ship. She desperately needed land.

They reached the surface just as a boom sounded from below, followed by a tidal wave that pushed Michael and Arianna up and out. As soon as it happened, Michael felt the last remnants of confusion clear from his head. He was finally free of the siren song. Renata was really dead.

Michael was about to give a sigh of relief when he felt something flop against his chest. He looked down to see the remaining color draining from Arianna's face. Her legs lost their scales, and even though he dipped them back into the water, she did not turn.

A NEW SONG

*M*ichael's skin stung all over, and it was getting worse by the minute. The air felt strange, too, and it threatened to make his head spin. He tried his best to ignore it, however, as he gently laid Arianna on a large, flat rock in the shallow waters just off an empty beach.

"Come on," he muttered as her head flopped back.

Her breathing was shallow, and she made no move to turn or roll over or even flutter an eye.

"No, no, no, no." He gathered her up again, trying to find some way to revive her. "You brought us this far!" Michael looked up at the sky. "Don't let me lose her now! I beg you!" He brushed her cheek with the back of his fingers. "I beg you," he whispered as tears made his vision blurry.

Just when he was sure she couldn't be without air any longer, Arianna's chest heaved, and she began to cough and sputter.

Michael clutched her close and rocked her back and forth, thanking the Maker with prayers too deep for words.

She blinked up at him, and a small, tired smile spread across her face. Then her eyes grew wide. "Michael!" She tried to sit up. "You're being burned!"

He placed her back on the rock. "You're too weak to be left alone. And I've suffered worse."

"But . . . what happened?" She blinked, looking around them.

"It's over. Renata is gone."

"You mean I killed her?" Her voice trembled.

He shook his head. "She destroyed herself. We barely escaped." Then he laughed. "Why do you look so sad? We won!"

"But you . . ." she looked down at his body, and Michael felt his smile tighten.

"The sacrifice was worth it. *You* were worth it." He chuckled morosely. "Besides, Lucas will make a better king than I ever would have."

"Nonsense." A familiar spark lit her eyes as she moved closer to the edge of the rock and swung her legs over. The way the white dress hit her knees as she dangled them into the water made her look young and vulnerable. It also made him want to take her in his arms all over again and swim until they had outrun every danger that might threaten her.

She tried to press his shoulders down. "You really do need to get in the water. It took my mother days to recover from her burns when I was born."

"I'm not leaving you alone." He reached up and caressed her cheek. "Not again."

In the light of the early morning her hair began to glow as it reflected the sun. Michael tenderly ran his fingers through its wet locks. It was like touching silk. He lifted his other hand to cup her cheek. How the sun burned! But touching her was bliss, and he shivered as he moved his hand down from her cheek to her neck.

"So," she said breathlessly, "where does this leave us?"

Michael just drew her back into his arms and clutched her to his chest.

"She got what she wanted." She choked on a sob. "Even after death, she still found a way to separate us."

"No she didn't."

Arianna frowned up at him, then glared at her own legs, which were still as human as ever, but he just smiled and wiped away the tear that had rolled down her cheek. "We are free to use our minds and hearts as the Maker intended us to." He swallowed and tried to make his voice light. "I will say that I'm quite sorry to lose my legs, though. I know you liked them. I always thought they were quite nice myself."

She laughed, tears still falling.

"Do you know how utterly beautiful you are?" Without waiting for her to reply, he pushed himself farther out of the water and met her mouth with his. It tasted of sea salt and tears. Scooping her off the rock, he held her close. The way she melted against him was more addicting than any of the songs Renata had used to captivate him.

A throat cleared behind them, and Michael turned into the blinding sun to see a few dozen merpeople behind them. From what he could make out in the blinding, stinging light was that each merperson wore a thick covering over his head and shoulders. Michael was rather sure that the blurry one who had cleared his throat was Arianna's father, Amadeo. Michael considered putting Arianna down to swim by herself but then remembered that she had no fins. Not that he was in any hurry to let her go.

Amadeo wasn't looking at him, though. Instead, he was looking at Arianna. And he was holding the triton. "I believe, daughter," he held the triton out, "that this is yours."

Arianna's eyes were wide, and she turned to look up at Michael, her brow puckered. "I don't understand. I didn't win the contest."

"Renata was never officially crowned," Amadeo said. "The triton changed its mind. It abandoned her and chose you."

"But how do you know?"

"I found my sister dead and the triton several feet away. It had stopped heeding her call, it seems. It found a song more ready to take the crown. Someone more worthy." He held the triton out farther, its blue edges glinting in the sun's rays and making Michael's eyes hurt even more. But Arianna still didn't take it. Instead, her grip on Michael's arms tightened.

"Sing to it," Amadeo said softly. "Let it hear your call."

Arianna glanced at Michael with large eyes. When he nodded, she turned back to her father. "I don't know if my song will work anymore." She looked down at her legs dangling from Michael's arms into the water. "I'm not changing back."

"Just try, Arianna." His gaze flicked over to Michael, and he gave a small smile. "I would guess Prince Michael is getting a bit tired of the sun."

Arianna gasped, and immediately took the triton. Then she began to sing. At first, the triton did nothing. Her voice was small and timid. But as she continued, her voice grew in strength and began to encircle them as a rose's scent might fill a garden. Up and out it moved to touch the sea and sky alike.

As it did, the triton began to glow gold. A blinding sunbeam shot down from the sky and wrapped itself around the triton's right prong. A column of seawater likewise flew up into the air and wrapped itself around the triton's left prong.

The merpeople bowed, and Arianna turned to Michael, her eyes shimmering once again. Michael felt his voice catch in his throat as he watched her face glow.

"What is the Sea Crown's first mandate?" Amadeo asked as he rose from his bow, a grin stretching across his face.

Arianna glanced back at her family and blushed. Then she turned to Michael, a funny smile on her face. "You make a very handsome merman, but . . . I really do find your legs quite attractive." Then she aimed the triton at him, and Michael felt his body begin to pulse.

"Wait," he said.

She looked up at him with questioning eyes.

"I'll only let you change me back on one condition."

A few of the merpeople began to murmur, but Michael kept his eyes trained on Arianna. She looked utterly surprised, and possibly a bit hurt, so he willed himself not to smile.

"I'll only let you change me back if you promise to marry me."

LET ME BE THE ONE

*A*rianna's strength was slow in returning. For the first week, it was all she could do to sit up in bed. Because her fins hadn't returned either, Michael insisted that she take his room, as his chamber was considerably larger and far more luxurious, and he slept in her little room by himself. Arianna would have argued, but she found she didn't have the strength. And, if she was honest, his bed was a good deal more comfortable.

Each day, Michael would carry her down from the palace and stand in the water with her. Each day that she didn't turn, Arianna would try and hide her disappointment, leaning into his chest and squeezing her eyes shut. Still, even though it hurt to consider that her days as a mermaid might be over, she found a new kind of peace in his arms, a peace that told her healing might one day still come. If not to her body, then to her heart.

Their visits to the water weren't all sad. Often, he would take her down in the evenings, where her family could come to the surface with their charms and discuss the upcoming coronations and the weddings. That was somewhat fun, planning the most important days of her life with her parents and sister. Or rather, it was fun until the evening Drina decided to accompany them down, two and a half weeks after the battle. After listening to her future mother-in-law discuss her own plans for their wedding, Arianna developed a new, fiercer longing for her fins, which miraculously appeared the next day.

Still, even after her strength returned, Arianna wondered if her wedding day would ever arrive. There were missing merpersons to find, repairs to be made to Lucas's ships, and Michael's mother to deal with. Drina was particularly unhappy when she was told that the wedding would not be held in the Sun Palace's little chapel with their own holy man, and she had certainly made her opinion known on every detail of the ceremony. So much so that Michael gave most of the planning over to Giana, to preserve his own sanity.

But eventually, the day did arrive.

Lucy flopped down on the divan dramatically. "This wedding has taken forever to get here. I should be old by now."

Claire shook her head as she pulled her sister upright once more and dusted her dress off. "Two months is a perfectly acceptable amount of time to wait for a wedding. Weddings don't make themselves, after all." She looked up. "Isn't that right, Aunt Arianna?"

Arianna winked at her, careful not to move her head as Bithiah put the finishing touches on her hair.

"I still wish you would wear your hair up," Drina grumbled. "It would look more regal with your gown's neckline. I still don't understand why you want to wear it down."

"Michael likes my hair down. If it were up to me, I would have it up, too, but this is to honor his request."

Drina just harrumphed, as she had done to the majority of their wedding plans, but Bithiah wiped her eyes. "I think you look like a vision," she said as she tucked a few pieces of hair behind the two smaller braids that she'd pulled back to encircle the top of Arianna's head like a crown. "Now, come look."

Arianna stood in front of the mirror. It didn't matter how many times she saw the dress. It still took her breath away. Lace covered her shoulders and edged the top of her bodice. Below the lace was simple white silk with little sapphires sewn into embroidered swirls. The skirt fell gracefully over her hips and down to her toes like ocean froth in gauzy strips of white and blue.

"It looks just like the ocean!" Lucy scrambled to stand on the bed and look out the window.

Arianna laughed. "That was the idea."

"Girls, Bithiah," Drina said in a strained voice. "Could I have a moment alone with my daughter-in-law?" The girls protested, but Bithiah ushered them out. As soon as they were alone, the air suddenly seemed stuffier, despite the open windows that looked out over the beach.

"I . . . I have a gift for you." Drina motioned to a servant girl standing by the door. The girl held out a square, flat wooden box and opened it. Drina pulled something out, then she returned to Arianna and placed it on her head.

Arianna gasped and reached up to touch the circlet of delicate purple and white glass flowers.

"They're called begonias," Drina said. "I'm sorry it's not one of my more expensive pieces, but my mother wore this on her wedding day." Her jaw tightened. "So did Maura. I was saving it for Claire, but . . . I . . . I'm glad I have another daughter to wear it first."

Arianna took Drina's hands in hers and squeezed. "I am so honored."

"I must ask your forgiveness, I'm afraid. In earnest this time." Drina shook her head. "There's a reason the Maker had Michael take after his father and not me. He will be a good king."

"Yes, he will." Arianna pulled Drina into a hug.

Just then, a knock sounded at the door, and Drina left so Arianna's parents could be ushered in. Their charms rang quietly as they wordlessly drew her close. Arianna held them tightly.

"I'll only be a song away," she said as she pulled out of the embrace. For some reason, she found it suddenly difficult to talk, so she laughed. "Really, I'll see you more than I did when I lived with Renata!"

Tears flowed freely down Giana's face, but Amadeo smiled, despite the glistening in the corners of his eyes. "Are you sure you want me to be your liaison? After all that happened here?" He looked around at Michael's chambers suspiciously, as though they had been the place of war.

"Father, I trust you to be my voice when I'm not there. But really, queens do need to see their people. And I intend to be there often. I—"

Giana pulled her close again and rocked Arianna back and forth while she kissed her face. "We're proud of you, love," she whispered. "But no matter how much you accomplish, you'll always be our little girl."

"There is still one thing I don't understand," Amadeo said as Giana set to gushing over Arianna's dress. "How were you able to break Renata's hold on him in the water? She was still using her siren song, I assume?"

Arianna nodded. "I asked a holy man the same thing. He said he couldn't be sure, since the siren song is hardly ever used, but he guessed that since my song used the sea *and* the sun, it must have had the strength to severe the dark ties." She paused as Giana helped her step into her slippers. "He said that the darkness must not have been able to withstand the light."

All too soon, it was time to move to the ship. Lucas appeared at her door and escorted Arianna and her parents down to the dock.

"Lucas, it's beautiful!" Arianna exclaimed when she saw the flagship gleaming with a bright new coat of white and shiny red stripe.

Lucas beamed. "All for you. Wouldn't want you turning me into a guppy or something while I was out at sea." Arianna elbowed him before he handed her down into the ship's cabin, and Lucas laughed.

She waited in the cabin with her mother, sister, and the little girls as they moved out to sea. Through the small round windows, she watched the sun drop lower in the sky until it sat upon the horizon. She tried hard to slow her heart as it bounced around in her chest.

Just as twilight settled over the gigantic ocean sky, the hatch opened above them, and one by one they filed out. Arianna was last, and decided it was a miracle that she didn't trip and fall on her face as she climbed the steps to the deck. She hadn't even been this nervous at the triton competition.

As soon as she stepped up onto the deck, however, her fears faded at the sight of Michael standing at the prow of the ship. Wearing his uniform proudly, he stood taller than he ever had before, his shoulders straight and his chin held high. His brown curls had been trimmed into submission, and he wore a knife at his side, something he swore he would never be without again.

The ocean was filled with her own people. Thousands had returned for the ceremony, the joining of the Sun and Sea. Lucas's fleet also floated nearby, each deck holding hundreds of Maricantans where they could watch. But for once, Arianna didn't care what the humans or the merpeople saw. Because for her, there was only him. Taking his hand as she came to stand beside him, Arianna gazed at him in awe.

Lucas took his place before the assembly, giving each a big grin before opening the Holy Writ. Lucas went on to say many, many words, something about his privilege to marry them as the ship's captain, and then more words from the holy writ itself. Arianna must have said enough in return, though she couldn't recall doing so, for it wasn't long before their rings were presented and exchanged.

"Never before have the Sun and Sea Crowns been so joined,"

Lucas said with a smile. "But then again, never before has the prophecy come true." He turned and nodded to the two pages standing at the ready. Each page held a cushion. And each cushion held a crown.

"Do you, Michelangelo Rinieri Battista Solefige, vow to protect the humans of Maricanta, to protect the merpeople of the seas, and covenant your complete reliance upon the Maker who gives you this mantle until your dying breath?"

"I will run with this task until death ushers my soul up to the Maker himself." Michael bent and kissed Lucas's ring.

"And do you," Lucas turned to her, "Arianna Fiore del Mare Atlantician, vow to protect the merpeople of the sea, the humans of Maricanta, and covenant your complete reliance upon the Maker who gives you this mantle until your dying breath?"

Her voice was surprisingly clear. "I will swim with this task until death ushers my soul to the Maker himself."

Lucas beamed as he lifted each crown. "I declare from this day forth the Sun and Sea as one." With that, he placed the crowns on their heads. Arianna's breath caught when Michael stood up straight. The way the golden crown rested on his brow made her want to burst with pride. The boy prince she had fallen in love with was gone. Now he was every bit a man.

Her man.

Her awe left her unready for the part of the ceremony that she had both longed for and dreaded the most.

"Queen Arianna will now sing her soulsong," Lucas announced as he looked around at the human guests attending them. "In merperson tradition, the merman and mermaid each sing their soulsong, and the Maker combines them spontaneously to tell the story of their lives together as they will be. It is a unique miracle, a taste of what is to come, a story of where they've been and where they're going." He paused. "As my brother is not a merman, however, Queen Arianna will sing for him alone."

Arianna nearly regretted asking to keep this part of the ceremony. And yet, she wanted to give Michael this part of herself, even if her song went unmatched. He was going to have all of her, no matter what. The Maker would take care of the rest.

Closing her eyes, Arianna thought back to the first night she had seen him out on the terrace. She let her voice soar.

But it didn't soar alone for long. A deep baritone began to harmonize, nearly shocking her into silence.

Michael's voice had always been rather soft, and he had never been keen for singing. But now, as he held her gaze, his eyes reflecting the torches' light, Michael's voice was every part merman. Arianna thought she might cry.

As they sang, she forgot to see the people or the ocean or the ships around her. Instead, she saw him. She saw his face when they were children and he stared at the bush while she hid behind it. She saw the way he looked at her on the day she saved him. There was the Sun Palace, just as she remembered looking at it from below. As their story progressed, she saw the Sun Palace's terrace, the ocean's surface, the docks, the market, and the Deeps. Pain, surprise, and joy, each memory filled her with emotion as it flew by.

Then she began to see new visions. She saw the Sun and Sea Palaces, not as they were but as they could be. Two peoples and one future. When children moved into their vision, Arianna could feel herself blush, and a few people in the audience snickered. Michael caught her eye and gave her a wicked smile. The vision continued some pain and confusion, but even stronger came unity and strength. And there was love. So much love.

Before the vision had completely dissolved, Michael pulled her tightly against him and kissed her with a passion that sent heat all the way down to her toes. It was glorious.

"Friends and loved ones," Lucas said, spreading his arms, "I present to you the Sun and Sea Crowns, unified before the Maker and man." The crowds around them erupted, and Michael drew Arianna in for another kiss.

Soon after, the eating and dancing commenced. Arianna laughed as Michael spun her in circles. They had practiced several times for the dance, but having Michael ask her to dance still gave her shivers of delight.

They danced and sang and ate and danced some more until Arianna was nearly too tired to stand. Michael whispered to one of his servants, and it wasn't long before people were being ushered off, either onto other ships who came near to take passengers, or back into the ocean where they belonged. Soon, there were only Michael and Arianna, and he took her hand to gently lead her down into the ship's cabin.

As tired as she was, however, Arianna felt jumpy. The room that had seemed comfortable earlier suddenly felt so cozy that it was nearly hot. Arianna went and stood by one of the porthole windows to try and get some cool air.

"What's wrong?" Michael came up behind her and nuzzled her neck with his chin.

"Just nerves, I suppose." Arianna turned and gave him a weak smile.

"That only makes sense. Here, turn around. Let me help you with that necklace."

Arianna did as he said until she realized which necklace she still wore. "Oh no!" She covered her mouth. "I didn't mean to wear that one to the wedding! Throw it overboard. Or better yet," she picked up a heavy polished stone from the dresser, "crush it." What had she been thinking, letting Renata sing her to sleep the night before? "I . . . I meant to get rid of it this morning," she stuttered, but he only shook his head.

"Don't."

"What?"

"As misguided as your aunt was," he said, placing the necklace gently on the dresser, "she truly did love you. Don't let her last few months overshadow all the love she gave you as a child."

She stared at him, speechless. Whatever fear had played in her belly dissolved, and she pulled him down for a long kiss. His hands rubbed her shoulders until her arms felt loose and relaxed, and a deeper hunger rushed through her, stronger than she had ever felt it before. Much to her disappointment, however, he pulled away.

"I just have one request."

"What's that?" Why did she sound so ridiculously out of breath?

"Let me be the one to sing you to sleep from now on."

Arianna stared at him as it slowly dawned on her that this wonderful man was hers forever. "The Maker made a way," she whispered in wonder as his lips began exploring her temple. "Just like you said."

Michael ran his fingers through her hair, down her face, and up to her lips, which he softly kissed again. "A way," he whispered, leaning his face against hers, "that I intend to enjoy for the rest of my days."

EPILOGUE

PEARLESCENT

*A*rianna shifted again in her seat, but try as she might, she couldn't find a comfortable position for her big belly. What was Lord Hatchet pontificating on about now? She felt slightly guilty for so easily ignoring the merlord's soliloquy.

But only just. Several other lords and ladies were dozing off as well or fiddling with their sleeves or fingers or rings or charms. The merlord had been droning on for nearly a half hour, and for the life of her, she couldn't understand what he was upset about. Every time he seemed to wander about to the point, she would get a hard kick to the ribs, and he would continue droning.

"I'm confused," Michael finally interrupted, much to Arianna's relief.

At least she wasn't the only one.

"Maricanta and your people have been prosperous for four years now. Trade is better than ever, and we haven't had a pirate incident in ages. What are you dissatisfied with?"

The merlord sighed loudly, and Arianna briefly fantasized about stealing his charm, tossing it out the window, and watching him leap out after it into the water below. This thought threatened to make her smile, and she tried to sit up again and force herself to listen this time.

"There is nothing to be dissatisfied with . . . for the present. But, Maker forbid, should something happen to the Sea Crown—"

"Then I would see that your needs were met." Michael's voice was suddenly quiet and dangerous. A few of the dozing lords and ladies sat up at the sound of it.

Well, that was a rather morbid thing to be considering. Arianna frowned.

"And we have no objections to that, Your Majesty!" Lord Hatchet hastened to say. "But what happens after you die, if I am to put it bluntly? How are your progeny to know of our two peoples' needs? Who is to act as a go-between?" The pudgy merlord pointed at Michael's charm, Arianna's gift that he never removed. "You're doing well enough with the charm, yourself, but what about your children?"

Michael leaned forward, elbows on the glass table. "Just what are you suggesting?"

The merlord hesitated for a minute, his eyes flicking to Arianna several times. That didn't at all make her feel any better.

"Have your wife . . . prepare your children for life in either realm," the merlord said.

"Wait." Arianna crossed her arms. "Are you truly suggesting that I alter my children's forms in order to fit your needs?" She instinctively reached for her triton.

"You are in dangerous territory," Michael said in a low voice. "I strongly suggest you stop there. This council is dismissed until further notice."

Taking the hint, the other lords and ladies gave demure curtseys and bows until Michael and Arianna were the only ones left in the glass dining hall.

Arianna closed her eyes and leaned back, rubbing her belly methodically.

"Come."

She opened her eyes to see Michael holding his hand out. "I've had Cook whip up a surprise for you."

Soon Arianna, Michael, and their daughter of three years, Michaela, were walking down a pier. Michael carried their basket of food, and Michaela skipped ahead of them to watch the fish like she always did. Arianna smiled and shook her head. As usual, Michael had known exactly what would make her feel better. The further along she got in the pregnancy, the more Arianna longed for the cool water, where she could pretend for a little while that she was weightless.

"Michaela, please be careful. You're going to fall—" But as she said it, Arianna watched in horror as her little girl fell headfirst into the ocean. "Michael!" she screamed.

But Michael was already sprinting. Arianna followed at a helplessly slower, clumsier pace, tripping over her feet as she tried to reach the end of the pier. She stumbled twice as she neared the edge, cursing her human form as she pushed herself toward the spot where her daughter had fallen. Nauseating fear froze the blood in her veins and made every step an eternal hell.

When she finally jumped in after them, she found Michael simply floating underwater, staring out with wide eyes. Anger pulsed through her. What was wrong with him? Where was she? Why hadn't he found Michaela?

But when she tried to scream such to him, he only pointed. Turning her head, she finally spotted Michaela a little ways off. The flood of relief she felt was quickly followed by a jolt of shock. For Michaela was flitting around happily with a little pearlescent tail of her own. And like her husband, Arianna could only gape in wonder.

"Has she ever—" he began.

"No," Arianna whispered. "She hasn't."

"Well then," Michael began to smile, "I don't think our stuffy merlord will have to worry any longer."

~

Dear Reader,
Thank you for journeying with me through Silent Mermaid. *If you enjoyed this book, it would be a huge help to me if you could leave a review on your online retailer or Goodreads.com.*

If you like free stories (including more about Michael and Arianna) visit BrittanyFichterFiction.com. *By joining my email list, you'll get free access to an exclusive secret chapter from Silent Mermaid, sneak peeks at books before they're published, chances at giveaways, and much more!*

~

For more of Brittany Fichter's books, read on...

ALSO BY BRITTANY FICHTER

The Classical Kingdoms Collection
Before Beauty: A Retelling of Beauty and the Beast
Blinding Beauty: A Retelling of The Princess and the Glass Hill
Beauty Beheld: A Retelling of Hansel and Gretel
The Becoming Beauty Trilogy Boxset
Girl in the Red Hood: A Retelling of Little Red Riding Hood
Cinders, Stars, and Glass Slippers: A Retelling of Cinderella

∼

The Classical Kingdoms Collection Novellas
The Green-Eyed Prince: A Retelling of the Frog Prince

∼

Coming soon . . .
The Autumn Fairy Trilogy

ABOUT THE AUTHOR

Brittany lives with her Prince Charming, their little fairy, and their little prince in a ~~sparkling~~ (decently clean) castle in whatever kingdom the Air Force has most recently placed them. When she's not writing, Brittany can be found enjoying her family (including their spoiled black Labrador), doing chores (she would rather be writing), going to church, belting Disney songs, exercising, or decorating cakes.

Facebook: Facebook.com/BFichterFiction
Subscribe: BrittanyFichterFiction.com
Email: BrittanyFichterFiction@gmail.com
Instagram: @BrittanyFichterFiction
Twitter: @BFichterFiction

67472046R00257

Made in the USA
Middletown, DE
11 September 2019